Forever, My Love

Laura groped for the pistol lying on the counterpane. She listened intently, her senses alert to every sound. Someone was climbing the stairway. Grasping the gun in both hands, she pointed the weapon at the door. Transfixed, she watched the knob slowly turn and the door swing open.

Zach's rain-drenched figure appeared in the doorway.

"Zach!" She sobbed his name in relief.

He was beside her at once—kneeling and pulling her into his arms. "You're okay, love, you're safe now, love," he murmured, raining kisses on her tear-streaked cheeks and eyes. Tenderly, he cupped her face in his hands, and his mouth found hers . . .

Forever, My Love

Ana Leigh

AVON BOOKS ▲ NEW YORK

FOREVER, MY LOVE is an original publication of Avon Books. This work has never before appeared in book form. This work is a novel. Any similarity to actual persons or events is purely coincidental.

AVON BOOKS
A division of
The Hearst Corporation
1350 Avenue of the Americas
New York, New York 10019

Copyright © 1995 by Ana Leigh
Published by arrangement with the author
Library of Congress Catalog Card Number: 94-96260
ISBN: 0-380-77351-1

First Avon Books Printing: February 1995

AVON TRADEMARK REG. U.S. PAT. OFF. AND IN OTHER COUNTRIES, MARCA REGISTRADA, HECHO EN U.S.A.

Printed in the U.S.A.

RA   10   9   8   7   6   5   4   3   2   1

PART I

LAURA

Chapter 1

Texas, February 8, 1874

Today's my birthday, Laura Randolph suddenly remembered.

She continued to gaze sorrowfully out of the coach window. She closed her eyes. For a brief moment she dozed. And in those scant seconds, the ghastly events of the horrendous night only thirty days earlier flashed through her mind in nightmarish clarity: being jarred from her sleep to the sound of her mother's scream, gunfire, thundering hooves, black smoke, and hot, consuming flames—then the horror of running out of the burning house to find her father . . . her mother . . . both dead.

She opened her eyes, but the images remained. Even knowing that former Texas Rangers, friends of her father, had trailed and killed the outlaws who had murdered her parents brought no consolation. Retribution could not bring back her mother and father. Her father's grin . . . her mother's gentle touch . . . *Oh, if only I hadn't wakened, I could have died too*, she thought remorsefully.

"Gawdammit!" The loud curse coming from outside the coach jolted Laura out of her sorrowful reflection.

"Gawdammit to hell!" the driver of the stage repeated. Yanking on the bulky set of harnesses, he reined up the galloping team and pulled on the brake. With a shrill screech, the heavy wooden block ground against

3

the back wheel, and the coach came to an abrupt halt,
sending passengers and baggage lurching from side to
side.

Laura grabbed the edge of the window to keep from
being unseated, then hastily covered her nose and mouth
with a handkerchief as a swirling cloud of suffocating
dust drifted through the open window.

When the grime settled, she looked out to see what
had caused the delay this time. Several cattle had strayed
onto the road, and she saw a cowboy astride a sorrel stallion herding them off the trail.

With mild curiosity, she swung her gaze to the rider,
a young man in his late teens. He sat his saddle with
a relaxed slouch that disguised, but could not hide, his
unrestrained vitality. With light flicks of the reins and
gentle prodding of his long, muscular legs, the cowboy moved the huge sorrel among the mewling, lumbering cattle, and, with casual effort, he eased them off
the road.

When he halted just outside her window, Laura was
able to observe him at closer range. Fascinated, she
watched him remove a battered Stetson and, despite the
red bandanna circling his neck, wipe his brow with his
sleeve. Perspiration had flattened his dark, shaggy hair to
his head and nape. Stretched tautly across his wide shoulders, a blue cotton shirt that clung in wet patches to his
chest and back outlined his sweat-slickened muscles.

The sharp crack of the driver's bullwhip suddenly rent
the air like a rifle shot. Spooked, the sorrel shrieked
a high-pitched whinny and reared up on its hind legs.
Laura brought a gloved hand to her mouth to stifle her
alarmed gasp as the frightened animal's front legs flailed
the air in panic.

The rider brought the horse under control. Leaning
forward in the saddle, he calmed the sorrel with several
reassuring pats and soothing whispers.

Suddenly, the cowboy turned his head and Laura
sucked in a quick breath at the rugged handsomeness

of the rider's face. A light dusting of whiskers failed to disguise his youthfulness, and yet the lines creeping from the corners of his eyes suggested a quality of maturity. Dark and somber, his eyes were fixed on her face in an open stare. Embarrassed, Laura blushed and quickly turned away. She looked rigidly ahead as the stagecoach jolted forward.

Slyly, she looked back for a final glance and discovered the rider had not moved. His deep-blue eyes, hooded with thick dark lashes, were fixed on her. For a brief moment her sad, brown-eyed gaze locked with his brooding stare. The corners of Laura's mouth curled up in a shy, maidenly smile before he disappeared from her view. She was tempted to lean out the window again for a final look, but modesty prevented her from doing so, and she settled back in her seat.

The coach resumed its former speed and Laura brushed the dust off the skirt of her gown. The hot air whirling through the window offered little comfort to the two passengers in the coach. She was sweltering. Buttoned to the neck, the blue merino jacket she wore had fitted sleeves with lacy cuffs and a round narrow collar of matching lace. The suit had been donated by neighbors when everything she owned had been lost in the fire, set by the outlaws, that had destroyed her home.

She yearned to remove the jacket, but the cotton blouse underneath fit too snugly across her full breasts; she kept the jacket closed to conceal the ill-fitting bodice.

Laura unpinned the cheap straw bonnet perched on her head. Even the artificial flowers adorning the hat were coated with dust.

She had just begun to wipe them off with her handkerchief when the creaking stage jolted to a stop once more, much to the disgruntlement of the obnoxious dry-goods drummer sitting in the opposite seat, who had added to her discomfort by smoking a smelly cigar during the entire trip.

Laura leaned her head out the window to see what was responsible for this new delay. She saw the driver and shotgun rider talking in low tones to a grizzled stranger sitting on the seat of a buckboard. After a brief conversation, the driver of the stage climbed down from his high perch and opened the door.

"What is it now, driver?" the loudmouthed salesman grumbled. "I could get to Galveston a lot faster by walking."

"Then I reckon next time you do just that, mister." He nodded to Laura. "Miss Randolph, there's a driver out here from the Lazy R. Your aunt sent him to fetch you from the coach rather than have him go all the way to Bay Town. I'll get your luggage." The shotgun rider tossed down a worn tapestry bag from the top of the stage.

Shoving back the long, straight hair that hung past her shoulders, Laura offered an apologetic smile to the scowling drummer and pinned her hat back on top of her head.

As she climbed out of the carriage, she could feel her trepidation mounting, knowing she would soon be meeting her Aunt Lavitia. She knew so little about her.

Whenever he spoke of his family to Laura, her father, Joseph, had always kept any references to her grandfather and aunt succinct and guarded, admitting only that he was a disappointment to both of them. However, Laura recalled, her father made no secret of his dislike for ranching, which is why in 1854, at the age of twenty, he left the Lazy R and moved across the state to Laredo, where he fell in love, got married, and joined the Texas Rangers. When Laura's grandfather died four years later and bequeathed the Lazy R Ranch to Lavitia, Laura's father felt no bitterness at being disinherited, despite the fact that he earned just enough to support his wife and daughter.

Laura smiled, remembering the many times he would hug her and her mother and remind them that a man's wealth could not be measured by money or land.

With tears glistening in her eyes, Laura recalled her and her mother's anxiety when he, like so many other Texans, had gone east to fight for the Confederacy. When the war ended, he returned to Laredo and rejoined the Texas Rangers. Then in 1871, after the Rangers were disbanded due to lack of funds, her father had become sheriff of Laredo. And then—Laura choked back her tears—three years later both her parents were ruthlessly murdered. . .

"Miss, can I help you?" The question wrenched her out of her painful reverie. The stagecoach driver waited with an extended hand to assist her off the stage. She put her hand in his and stepped down. He doffed his hat. "Good-bye, Miss Randolph."

As he climbed up onto his seat, he turned back to her and offered a kindly smile. "And good luck, miss."

Once again the lumbering stagecoach lurched forward, this time leaving a slim figure standing alone in a cloud of dust.

For several moments, Laura watched the coach shrink from view until only a billow of dust floated back to her in a plaintive farewell. Turning, she looked around her with a despondent sigh. As far as the eye could see there was nothing but miles of scrub grass and an occasional clump of sycamore. She felt as lonely and barren as the land around her.

The desolate scene struck her with the full magnitude of her grief and despair. Tears began to trickle down her cheeks.

"We best get going, missy," the buckboard driver called out.

Jolted back to an awareness of the old man, Laura discovered he had climbed down from the buckboard and was waiting patiently. She ducked her head, hastily brushed aside her tears, and walked over to the wagon. The old man nodded, and after helping her climb up on the wagon seat, he clambered up and sat beside her.

The driver had a gray bushy beard and light blue eyes that sparkled with warmth as he smiled at her. "Howdy, missy. I'm Whiskers Merten. I knowed your pa when he was just a boy."

Laura felt a glimmer of reassurance to discover that someone here had a link to her father's past—someone other than her Aunt Lavitia.

"I'm very pleased to meet you, Mr. Merten."

"Shucks, missy, just call me Whiskers, same as everybody else." The man flicked the reins and the wagon began to roll.

A movement on a distant rise caught her attention. The cowboy she had seen earlier sat watching them. She could not see his face, but she recognized the blue of his shirt. Somehow, she knew his eyes were on her.

After they had traveled a short distance, Laura turned to look back once again. She was too far away to distinguish anything except the patch of blue. The horseman had not moved.

As the wagon creaked along, Laura's anxiety continued to build. "You said you knew my father, Mr. Merten," she managed to murmur.

"Yep. Sure felt bad to hear about him dy—"

"How long have you worked on this ranch?" she asked hurriedly in an attempt to ward off her rising panic.

"Shucks, gal, longer than I should admit. Hired out in '36 right after Texas won its independence from Mexico. Your grandpa, Will Randolph, had left his farm in Wisconsin and come here totin' your aunt and pa."

"I never knew my father was born in Wisconsin," she said, surprised.

"Reckon so." He scratched his whiskers. "Let's see . . . Miz Lavitia was 'bout fifteen then. Thatta make Joey . . ."

"He would have to have been two years old," Laura quickly calculated, "because my father was born in 1834."

"Will Randolph was a good man. Darn shame him and Joey couldn't make a go of it. Through no fault of theirs," he added. "Will started the Lazy R on just fifty acres south of Houston. Course the city was new then . . . just established. Ten years later, the ranch had grown to 150,000 acres, stretching between the Brazos on the west and Galveston Bay to the east."

"What did you mean that the trouble between my father and grandfather was not their fault?" Laura asked.

"Well, you might say Miz Lavitia and your pa didn't get along." The old man glanced askance at her. "Course you've got to give the devil her due. Joey never had his heart in ranchin', but Lavitia took to it like a bear to a honeycomb. Since her pa died, Lavitia added another fifty thousand acres to the Lazy R."

Laura was about to ask him about the trouble between her father and aunt when she caught her first glimpse of the ranch house. She stared, speechless.

Like a massive monolith shimmering in the sunlight, the white, two-story ranch house, with its gabled roof and mullioned windows, suddenly rose up from the flat valley plain. Surrounded by an assortment of outbuildings and fenced corrals, the house sat near the south end of the sprawling Lazy R Ranch.

When the wagon pulled up in front of the house, a young man halted his whitewashing of the building to open the door for her.

"Thank you," Laura said.

The man's mouth curled into an insinuating smirk as his offensive stare swept her from head to toe. "Pleasure's all mine."

"Don't pay him no mind, missy," Whiskers said, attempting to brush past the brazen young man.

"Ain't you gonna introduce me to the lady, Whiskers?" the younger man asked. His insolent glance returned to her face.

"This here's Whitey Wright, Miz Randolph."

"How do, Miz Randolph." When the cowboy shoved his hat to the back of his head, several strands of hair, so blond that they appeared white, tumbled to his forehead.

Laura nodded. "Mr. Wright." She judged him to be in his mid-twenties. Although some women might consider his blond handsomeness appealing, his cold green eyes reminded her of a serpent.

Whiskers followed her into the house and dropped her tapestry bag on the floor. He pointed to a nearby open door. "Go right in there, missy. Miz Randolph is most likely waitin' for you." The old man doffed his hat to reveal a pate sparsely covered with gray hair. "You need anythin' else, you just let me know. Your pa and I wuz good friends."

Laura smiled gratefully. "Thank you, Mr. Merten."

"Whiskers," he reminded her. "I'll tote this bag up to your room."

"That won't be necessary," said an imperious female voice from the nearby room. "You have other work to do, Whiskers. I suggest you get to it."

"Yes, ma'am." Winking, Whiskers squeezed Laura's arm and hurried out the door.

"Come in here, Laura." The command was issued in the same cold tone with which she'd spoken to Whiskers—the tone of a woman used to giving commands and having them immediately obeyed.

Laura stepped into the room. A tiny woman sat behind a huge oak desk. Lavitia Randolph offered neither hello nor hug. Not bothering even to glance up, she continued scribbling in a ledger book sprawled open on the desk before her. As Laura waited uncomfortably for her aunt to finish the entries, she had further time to study her.

Seated in a large chair that must have been her father's, Lavitia Randolph appeared almost diminutive. She had a head of pure white hair, that curled and arranged in a feminine fashion, could have been attractive; however, the fifty-three-year-old spinster wore it straight and cut off just below her ears.

Whiskers's words regarding Lavitia came to Laura's mind; it was clear she was a working rancher. Her plain and practical attire consisted of a checkered muslin blouse, black skirt, and leather boots. Neither fluff nor frill softened her severe appearance. The braid from a low-crown Stetson hanging between her shoulders was lightly looped around her neck.

As Laura's solemn gaze continued her inspection, she saw little family resemblance between her handsome father and his unattractive sister. Lacking the wide hazel eyes of Joseph Randolph, Lavitia had pale blue eyes, set close together above a long nose. Bitterness had deepened the lines at the corners of her mouth, and years in the hot sun had dried and baked her skin to the appearance of leather.

Lavitia finally put aside the pen, closed the ledger book, and leaned back in the chair. Laura felt awkward in her ill-fitting clothing as her aunt scrutinized every detail about her.

Even a melancholy expression could not mar the flawless beauty of her niece's young face with its small, straight nose, generous mouth, and delicate, rounded chin that flowed pleasingly into high cheekbones. Raven black hair, sloe eyes, and a faint tawniness of complexion reflected the Spanish heritage of Laura's mother: the resolute set to her jaw and proud lift of her head were reminders of her Texan father.

As if to mock her last observation, Lavitia declared, "You don't look much like a Randolph. More like your Mex mother, I'm thinking."

"My Mother was Spanish, Aunt Lavitia," Laura corrected politely.

"Spanish . . . Mex . . . they're all the same to me."

Taking a deep breath, Laura attempted to express her gratitude. "It's very kind of you to take me in this way."

"I'm your only remaining relative. After the church notified me of my brother's demise, I didn't have much choice. I understand everything you owned was lost in the fire," Lavitia said. Laura nodded. "What about a bank account?"

"Daddy only made enough to get by on. He never had any bank account."

"That's unfortunate."

Laura saw no compassion or sympathy in her aunt's eyes. "I hope I won't be a burden to you."

"I hope so too," Lavitia declared. "Course if you're anything like your father, you better start to change your ways right now. You can see what that got him."

Laura adored her father and the pain of his loss was still too vivid to allow such defamation of his beloved character. "I hope that I *am* like him, Aunt Lavitia," she lashed out, not realizing her jaw had settled into the same purposeful angle as the man she defended.

The lines around Lavitia's nose and mouth pinched in disapproval. "Hmmm . . . 'pears to me like you are."

As the older woman rose to her feet, Laura realized how tiny she was. The woman couldn't have been more than five feet tall even in the leather boots she was wearing. "Your room's to the right of the stairs. Last door at the end of the hallway. Dinner's at seven o'clock sharp. We don't wait for stragglers at the Lazy R."

With that parting message, Lavitia Randolph pulled on her Stetson and strode from the room, leaving her niece standing alone, desperately yearning for a comforting embrace from her only remaining family member.

Chapter 2

$\sim\!\!\circ\!\!\circ\!\!\circ\!\!\sim$

The worn tapestry bag, which someone had carried upstairs and dropped on the center of the floor, looked as bleak as the spartan room. If the room had ever had an identity, it had been stripped away years before. Only a bed, a nightstand, an oil lamp, a battered armoire, and a commode bearing a basin and ewer remained. The window was devoid of drapery, the walls of adornment, the bed of sheets or quilt.

Despite its drabness, the room was spotless. Laura walked over to the commode. The ewer had been filled recently because the water was still cool. Gratefully, she poured some of the liquid into the basin and dipped in her handkerchief. The cool cloth was a welcome relief to her warm brow as she rinsed the grime off her face and hands. Using the hem of her skirt, since there were no towels, she dabbed a few drops from her eyes and left the rest for the air to dry.

In the hope of catching a breeze, Laura made several attempts to open the window. As she struggled without success, she turned her head at the sound of a light tap on the door. A young Mexican girl entered carrying bedding and towels.

"I am Teresa. I have come to make up the bed."

"Let me help you," Laura said.

"No, it is my duty." The girl could not have been more than twelve or thirteen. She began to spread the sheets on the bed. Laura felt awkward and useless as she watched

13

the girl labor, so she returned to the task of trying to open the window.

"Is there anything else you wish?" Teresa asked after finishing the bedding.

Laura shook her head. "*Graciás*, Teresa." She gave the window another tug. "*¿Podemos abrir esta ventana?*" she added, hoping the two of them together would have better luck with the window.

Teresa hastened over to help her. Together, they were able to force it up. "*Graciás*, Teresa."

"Miss Randolph say we must speak English if we wish to work in ranch house."

"Oh," Laura said, surprised. "Well, you speak it very well, Teresa."

The girl smiled shyly. "Thank you, Miss . . ."

"My name is Laura."

Teresa nodded. "Welcome to Lazy R Ranch, Miss Laura." She hurried from the room.

"Welcome, indeed!" Laura said desolately. She crossed her arms over her chest and leaned back against the window frame. She didn't feel very welcomed. If only there was somewhere else she could live, some other relative she could turn to. Maybe she could secure a position as a tutor . . . or even a teacher. If not, at least she would be eighteen in another year. *My birthday! Oh, Mama . . . Daddy*, she thought desolately, *I miss you both so much*.

Brushing her tears aside, she swept her gaze over the sprawling ranch yard below. She had had no idea that the ranch her father had been raised on was so large. Viewing the well-kept yard, she saw a bunkhouse, barn, cookhouse, blacksmith shop, smokehouse, henhouse, and several other buildings she could not identify. None of the buildings were ramshackle or dilapidated, but appeared sturdily built, all sporting fresh coats of whitewash.

She watched her aunt mount a piebald mare and ride off accompanied by several ranch hands. Whiskers disappeared into the large barn.

The neigh of a mare calling to its colt drew her attention to a herd of at least fifty horses grazing in a pasture. A stream meandered through the field of grama grass and past a nearby fenced corral. Everything looked serene and orderly.

For a brief moment, Laura wondered what her duties would be on the large spread. Knowing she could ride as well as any cowhand, she hoped whatever would be expected of her would keep her a far distance from her Aunt Lavitia. Sighing, Laura turned away to unpack her few pieces of underclothes.

Promptly at seven, Teresa knocked on the bedroom door and informed Laura that dinner was ready. Laura hurried down the stairway to the dining room where Lavitia sat at the head of a large table. Lavitia nodded toward an empty chair on her right and Laura sat down.

As the two women ate in silence, Laura could not help but compare the shared pleasure of dinners at her parents' table with this silent and uncomfortable meal. Finally, after Teresa had placed plates of cherry cobbler before them, Lavitia suddenly spoke.

"Do you ride, Laura?"

"Yes, Aunt Lavitia."

"Can you handle a pistol?" At Laura's nod, Lavitia asked, "A rifle?"

"Yes, ma'am. My father taught me. He was an excellent shot."

"Yes, Joseph could shoot the eye out of a gnat," she added gruffly.

Falsely deceived by the words of praise, Laura relaxed her guard and said proudly, "He was the best shot in the Texas Rangers."

"'Bout the only thing he *was* good at." The pinched lines appeared again around Lavitia's nose. "And what did it ever get him but an early grave?" To avoid responding, Laura shifted her gaze back to her plate.

As if sensing her withdrawal, Lavitia said, "I noticed

you're growing out of those clothes you're wearing."

Blushing from the tactless remark, Laura lifted her head. "I'm sorry. I haven't anything else. All my clothes were destroyed in the fire."

"You mean you don't have anything except the clothes on your back?"

"I have a change of bodice . . . and underclothing," Laura replied. "I'm a good seamstress, Aunt Lavitia. Perhaps I can earn enough to buy a bolt of cotton."

"Well, first thing in the morning, we'll go to town and get you something different to wear. The way you're bulging out of that bodice is liable to stir up the hot blood of a couple of these ranch hands." Mortified, Laura kept her eyes on her plate as she finished her meal. Then, after excusing herself, she hurried back to her room.

A short while later, Teresa knocked and entered carrying a ewer of water. "Fresh water, Miss Laura. Do you wish for anything else?"

"No, thank you." As the girl prepared to leave, Laura asked, "Teresa, do you live in the ranch house?"

"Yes. Ever since my mama die last year."

"And what about your father?"

"He is gone." The girl's black eyes were round and luminous.

"Oh, I'm sorry to hear that, Teresa. I just lost my parents, so I know how you must feel."

"After my mama die, Miss Lavitia say I can stay on ranch."

"That was very kind of her," Laura said. But her impression of the older woman did not change. And after Teresa's departure, as Laura lay in the strange bed staring at the ceiling, she wondered again if it would have been more merciful for her never to have awakened the night of the fire.

Bright and early the following morning Whiskers harnessed the buckboard and drove Lavitia and Laura into Bay Town. The small town, erected for the convenience of the local ranchers, lay on the coastline of Galveston Bay. As Whiskers pulled up in front of the mercantile, Laura saw that the town was not much more than a string of houses and stores clustered along a dirt road.

Upon observing Laura's look of disappointment, Lavitia said primly, "Despite its size, Laura, the village prevents the neighboring ranchers from having to make the two-mile ferry trip to Galveston." She swept ahead of her and Laura followed her into the store.

The shopkeeper's glance swung to Laura and her aunt as the bell tinkled above the door. "Mornin', Miz Randolph," he said when they entered, then he returned his attention to the young male customer standing at the counter.

Laura recognized the young man at once by his blue shirt; he was the cowboy she had seen on the trail the previous day. Without so much as a sideways glance, Lavitia marched past them to a table holding bolts of material.

"How's your pa doing, Zach?" the shopkeeper asked his customer.

"Not so good, Mr. Stevens. Seems like he's taken a turn for the worse." Laura could not help but overhear them. Having just lost her own father, she felt instant empathy for the young man.

"Mr. Stevens, I'd like some service please," Lavitia declared impatiently. Embarrassed by her aunt's rudeness, Laura pretended to be interested in a bolt of gingham.

"Comin', Miz Randolph." The shopkeeper hurried over to the table. "What can I do for you today, Lavitia?" he asked cheerfully.

As soon as her aunt began to speak, Laura could tell she would have no say in the selection of clothing or material. She wandered off to look around the store. Unexpectedly, she found herself in the same aisle as the departing young cowboy. Once again their gazes met. At this close range, she saw that he had the bluest eyes she had ever seen. The thick dark lashes that capped his sapphire-colored eyes made them appear even darker. She nodded and half-smiled. "Hello."

"Ma'am," he acknowledged.

"I . . . uh . . . remember seeing you yesterday when I arrived on the stage. You were driving cattle . . . on the trail."

"Yes, ma'am. I remember."

"I . . . uh . . . couldn't help overhearing you mention that your father's ill. I know how you must feel. I just lost my father."

"Sorry to hear that, ma'am."

Laura feared she sounded as if she were looking for sympathy, or worse, using the excuse just to talk to him. Flustered, she started to stutter. "I didn't mean . . . that is . . . I only wanted to . . ."

"I appreciate it, ma'am." Laura was relieved when he changed the subject. "Are you here visiting?" he asked.

"No, I've come to live with my aunt. My name's Laura Randolph."

"Laura Randolph." For a moment she saw a flickering of recognition in his eyes. "And your father was a Texas Ranger by the name of Joseph Randolph?"

"Yes. Did you know him?"

"No, but my dad did. Your father and mine were good friends. My name's Zachary Houston." He suddenly grinned, the smile transforming his face to boyishness. "And before you ask, I'm not related to Sam Houston." His grin broadened at the sound of her infectious giggle. "You sure have changed a lot from your picture."

"My picture? What picture?" she asked, surprised.

"When you were about three years old, your father sent a picture of you to my dad."

"Oh, my!" Laura exclaimed. Her mouth curved into a smile. "I didn't know that, but my father often spoke of a Wes Houston."

"That's my father. He always said Joe Randolph was the best friend he ever had."

Her eyes sparked with increased interest. "I hope I can meet him."

"Laura, come here at once!" Lavitia Randolph's command snapped the air like a whip.

Zach tipped his hat. "Pleasure meeting you, Miss Randolph."

"Thank you. I hope your father recovers soon, Mr. Houston." She hurried over to the older woman who waited with a frown of displeasure.

"Laura, I do not want to see you ever again talking to that young man."

"I don't understand, Aunt Lavitia. Mr. Houston's father and mine were best friends."

"I do not intend to discuss it further. You know my wishes; I expect you to honor them." Lavitia picked up a bolt of material and added it to those in the shopkeeper's arms. "This will do, Mr. Stevens."

Laura resented the obdurate command. Certainly, her parents had disciplined her whenever the situation required, but neither had ever given her an order without a reasonable explanation. Seeing that the conversation had caught the ear of the shopkeeper, Laura did not wish to make more of a public scene than had already transpired. She bit her tongue and followed her aunt.

Laura tried to broach the subject of Zachary Houston on the ride back to the Lazy R, but once again her aunt cut off any discussion. So despite her aunt's objections, Laura reached her own decision: until her aunt offered her a feasible explanation, she intended to follow her own counsel.

The days passed swiftly for Laura as she adjusted to the routine of her new home and learned about the hard work that went into running a ranch the size of the Lazy R. Lavitia started her out with feeding the livestock and mucking out the horse stalls, but as the weeks progressed, Laura's skilled horsemanship soon advanced her to herding cattle and grooming horses. And with Teresa's help, she spent most of her free time cutting and sewing clothes for herself.

Unlike the western border of Texas, this eastern area was safe from marauding Indians, so whenever possible, Laura saddled the mustang that had been provided for her and explored the ranch, alone or accompanied by Whiskers Merten.

Despite the new diversions in her life, her thoughts frequently turned to the Houstons. Her desire to talk to Wes Houston was foremost in her mind—a desire intensified by the lingering memory of Zachary Houston's blue-eyed gaze.

A month after her brief encounter with him, she rode deliberately toward the Houston ranch. On the day of her arrival, Whiskers had pointed out a stream that formed the boundary between the two ranches, for despite the size of the Randolph spread, less than five miles separated the two ranch houses.

Reaching the narrow river, she stopped and dismounted in order to water her horse. The mare lowered its head and began to drink. At the sound of a nearby nicker, the horse lifted its head. Apparently satisfied that the low whinny posed no threat, the mare returned to nibbling on the grass that grew along the river.

Laura was not so easily appeased. Her gaze swept the terrain. She saw nothing. Curious about the location of the other animal, she tethered her mare and moved cautiously through the bushes.

After rounding the bend of the stream, she spied a riderless sorrel on the opposite bank. She drew up sharply at the sound of splashing, and her glance swung to midstream. Laura gasped in surprise when she recognized Zachary Houston.

Seemingly unaware of her presence, he stood up, exposing his sleek nakedness to her view, and shook his head. Water sprayed in all directions, and he raised his hands to brush the dripping hair from his forehead. Rivulets of water rolled off his broad shoulders, slid past bulging biceps, and dropped from his bent elbows.

Her gaze remained riveted on his hard, muscular body. She marveled at the lean and sinewy male physique with the slender hips and long, muscular legs of an equestrian.

Her stomach began to churn with excitement generated from the strange and unsettling desires aroused by his nakedness. Through a haze clouded with the virginal blush of newly discovered cravings, her gaze shifted to the manly shaft cloistered in a nest of dark hair. A tremor rippled along her spine as her feminine sensuality responded to the sight of this provocative male appendage.

Unimpeded by the water's swift current, he moved with easy strides to the riverbank. Her characteristic modesty dueled with sheer fascination; she could not turn away from the naked beauty of his body.

Transfixed, she watched him toss the bar of soap into his saddlebags, then towel himself dry with his shirt. He pulled on his drawers, pants, socks, and boots. Shirtless, he strapped on his gunbelt. He picked up his hat, slapped it several times against his leg to shake off the dust, then, after lacing his fingers through his wet hair a few times, he plopped the hat low on his forehead, hiding the mesmerizing eyes she recalled so well.

Finally, he hooked the damp shirt on the pommel of his saddle and, with lithe grace, he swung onto the horse. Turning the sorrel, he disappeared up a worn path.

For several moments after his departure, Laura remained motionless, her heart pounding in her breast. She had never spied on anyone before, yet she felt no guilt. *He's so beautiful*, she thought with awe. *Surely, there can be no shame in gazing at perfection!*

She returned to her mare and rode back to the ranch house as fast as the horse could carry her.

*   *   *

The following Sunday, Laura feigned a headache and retired to her room. As soon as Lavitia left the house to attend a Sunday afternoon quilting bee, Laura saddled up her mare and headed for the Houston ranch. This time she did not stop at the boundary, but splashed across the narrow stream and followed the well-worn trail that led to the small ranch house, which was really more like a cabin. For the first time since leaving the Lazy R, she wondered if she would even find Zach at the house.

Her heartbeat quickened when his tall figure appeared in the doorway as she approached. Once again she felt a tingling in the pit of her stomach. Nodding, he said politely, "You lost, Miss Randolph? You're on the Double H."

"I know. I hope you don't mind my coming uninvited," she said. "I wanted to pay my respects to your father and mother."

"My mother died when I was born," he said.

Laura wished the ground would open up and swallow her. How could she have forgotten her father mentioning that fact? "Oh, . . . I'd forgotten. I'm so sorry." She dismounted and tied her mare to the hitching post. "How is your father?"

Zach shook his head. "Not too good."

Her smile disappeared at the sight of his solemn gaze. "Perhaps I shouldn't disturb him."

"No. Come in. Dad'll enjoy the company. He doesn't get to talk to anyone but me."

The cabin consisted of a large room, a bedroom, and a loft. Zach went to the open door of the bedroom. As she waited in the main doorway, Laura took the opportunity to glance around the room. Although sparsely furnished, the cabin appeared to be well-kept.

"Dad, Miss Randolph's come to visit you."

"Lavitia Randolph?" Surprise sounded in the man's voice.

"No, Dad, her niece. Laura Randolph. Remember, I told you about her. She's Joseph Randolph's daughter."

"Joey's girl! Bring her in, son." Zachary turned to Laura and motioned for her to come forward.

Emaciated from consumption, the frail figure lying in the bed was a travesty of what once must have been the muscular body of Wesley Houston. In sharp contrast to his pale face, ravaged from the effects of the prolonged illness, his dark hair lay thick and wavy against the pillow.

His welcoming smile was suddenly wrenched from his face as a violent spasm of coughing overcame him. He brought a handkerchief to his mouth as he feebly clutched at his chest to ease the pain.

"Gotta tell you, you're sure better looking than your father," he said when the seizure subsided.

Recalling the lingering glances her handsome father had drawn from women, Laura smiled in response to the teasing remark. "Thank you, Mr. Houston."

"You must have gotten your good looks from your mother. Was she as lovely as your father boasted in his letters?"

Laura conjured up the image of her mother's flashing dark eyes and delicately curved jaw. "She was very beautiful. I'm sure he did not exaggerate."

Wesley's eyes closed as his thin frame was again gripped with another spasm of wracking coughs. Laura cast a sympathetic glance at Zachary, who stood solemnly near the wall. He had not said a word since they had entered the room.

"What happened to 'em, Laura?" Immediately, her eyes clouded with grief. Seeing the change in her expression, Wes quickly added, "I shouldn't have asked. Can see it's painful for you to talk about."

"No . . . I mean, yes . . . it's still painful, but it is kind of you to ask, Mr. Houston. Not even my aunt has done so. It seems as if nobody really cared."

Wes reached out and squeezed her hand. "Maybe

they've just all got more sense than I have, honey. I shouldn't have opened my mouth. It only dredges up bad memories for you."

Laura knew she would be haunted by the terrifying memories whether she talked about them or not. And maybe talking about that night would help. She drew a deep breath to garner the fortitude to relate the painful details.

"As the sheriff of Laredo, Daddy had tracked down an outlaw who had killed a rancher and his wife." She stopped momentarily. The atrocities that the murderer had inflicted on the poor woman before he killed her were too brutal to be discussed. "The man was tried and sentenced to hang. His brother swore vengeance if Daddy carried out the sentence." She paused as she remembered her mother's scream. "The night after his brother was hanged, he and his gang came to the house. They . . . they hanged my father . . . and . . . and . . . shot my mother when she tried to stop them. Then they set our house on fire. I was asleep in the loft. I guess they didn't know about me . . . or they probably would have killed me too." Laura's voice had wandered off to almost a whisper.

"Hard to think of Joey being dead." Wes shook his head sadly. "We sure had some good times when we were younger." Laura had to wipe her eyes, and Wes stared past her.

After an awkward silence, Wes came out of his reverie. "Ain't much consolation, but I reckon it's better to die quick like that . . . than to take years hacking your lungs out." He covered his mouth, gripped by another, more severe paroxysm of coughing.

Alarmed, Laura swung her glance to Zachary. His silent anguish showed on his troubled face as he stood by helplessly and watched his father expectorate phlegm and blood into the soiled cloth. Shocked, she felt her heart wrench as she realized that Wesley Houston was not simply ill—he was dying.

She felt overwhelmed with sadness. Knowing she would soon lose this link to her father's past was almost like losing her father all over again.

"Your aunt know you came here?" Wes asked. She shook her head. "Didn't think so. She's not going to like it when she finds out."

"I know." Now aware of the severity of his condition, Laura was convinced she had made the right decision in defying her aunt. She asked him eagerly, "Mr. Houston, will you tell me about my father? What was he like when the two of you were young?" She smiled in reminiscence. "Daddy often would tell Mother and me about some of your boyhood pranks."

Wes raised his brows. "Hope he didn't tell you everything. Some of it might bring a blush to those pretty cheeks of yours. We sure raised holy hell sometimes."

For the next hour, Wesley delighted her with tales of the deeds and misdeeds of the two boys growing into manhood. Listening to him relate the many incidents, Laura regretted she could not have known this man when he was healthy and strong.

When he tired, she rose to leave. "May I come back next week?"

Wesley grinned and squeezed her hand. "I'd like that, honey. It's kind of like . . . well, having something of Joey again."

"That's how I feel about you, Mr. Houston. It makes me feel Daddy's close by." Shyly, she bent down and kissed his cheek.

Zach walked her to the door. "Thank you for coming, Miss Randolph. I could tell Dad enjoyed it."

"Please call me Laura," she said.

He grinned, his teeth flashing against his tanned face. "Everybody calls me Zach."

She was caught off guard by the warmth and appeal of his smile, and she found herself responding again to his virile magnetism. Swallowing, she managed a feeble response. "Well . . . ah . . . I'll see you next week, Zach."

"Yeah," he said.

Zachary stood in the doorway and watched her ride away. Each time he saw her, he felt more drawn to her. There was a tangible and magnetic bond between them.

Although there was no sign of Zach the following week when she rode over to visit, Laura spent another enjoyable hour with Wesley Houston. When she noticed he was tiring, she departed with the promise to return the following week.

As her horse splashed across the stream, a smile settled on her lips at the recollection of her visit with Wesley. But about a mile from the ranch house, a rider blocked her trail.

"Well, howdy Miz Laura," Whitey Wright drawled. "You out for a Sunday ride?"

"Yes, please let me by."

Laura disliked the cowboy intensely. From the time of her arrival, he had made a habit of annoying her. Frequently he approached her when she was alone, and his remarks were always suggestive, his long, insolent looks insulting.

"Looks like you've been riding that mare hard. Why don't you rest her for a while? You and me could settle down under that sycamore over there."

"The mare is not winded, Mr. Wright." When she started to move off the trail to pass him, he grabbed her horse's reins. "Ah, come on, darlin'. You and I could have us a good old time."

"Mr. Wright, if you don't stop annoying me, I'll be forced to tell my aunt."

"You wouldn't want to do that, darlin'." He released the reins. "Then I'd have to tell her you've been sneakin' over to the Randolph spread. Don't think she'd like that too much." His teeth flashed in a wide grin as he doffed his hat. "Enjoy your ride, darlin'."

With a look of loathing, Laura goaded her horse to a gallop and returned to the Lazy R.

*   *   *

Eager for her weekly visit to the Double H, Laura found that the week passed slowly. Upon leaving church the following Sunday, she received a shock when they stopped to say good-bye to the pastor. "Miss Randolph, did you hear that Wes Houston passed away?" he asked Lavitia.

Laura's gasp of shock went unnoticed by the other two. For a moment, she thought she saw a flicker of remorse in her aunt's eyes, then Lavitia's expression settled into impassiveness. "I hadn't heard. When did it happen?"

"Zach and I buried him two days ago." Laura felt numb. She wanted to cry.

"Come along, Laura," Lavitia said, and moved on. Deeply saddened, Laura forced back the tears and silently followed her aunt.

Fortunately, Lavitia was quiet on the ride back to the ranch. Laura meditated on the frail man whom she would never see again. Several times on the return trip, she was tempted to ask her aunt about the trouble with the Houstons, then changed her mind. Laura felt too grief-stricken to tolerate any of Lavitia's vindictiveness. Had she really seen remorse on Lavitia's face, or had she imagined it?

Claiming a headache, Laura retired to her bedroom upon arrival. She wasted little time changing into her riding clothes, then slipped out of the house, hurriedly saddled her mare, and rode south toward the Houston spread.

Grief etched Zach's face as he stepped out of the cabin to greet her. "I hope you don't mind my coming by. I just heard about your father today. I'm so sorry, Zach."

"Well, I reckon it was for the best. He'd been sick for a pretty long time."

"I'm glad I got to know him before . . ." She could not speak the dreadful words.

"So am I. He liked you very much, Laura."

An awkwardness developed between them and, not knowing what more to say, she thought it best to leave. "Well, I guess I better go. I just wanted to pay my respects."

"Would you like to come in and have a cup of coffee?"

Dismounting, she shook her head. "Not coffee, but a glass of water would be fine."

Once inside, he pulled out a chair at the table. "Sit down here and I'll get you the water."

Laura sat solemnly watching him as he went to the sink to pump water into a pitcher. After filling her glass, he sat down opposite her. Once again, she found herself at a loss for words. Smiling, she picked up the glass and began to sip from it. His gaze remained fixed on her.

"I don't imagine your aunt's too happy about your coming over here."

Laura put down the glass and lifted her chin. "That wouldn't stop me from coming, Zach."

For the first time since she had arrived, he grinned. "Nope, I don't much imagine it would. Dad said he could tell you had your father's spunk."

Laura's chin quivered as she tried to hold back a smile. Glancing up sheepishly, she said, "Aunt Lavitia calls it mulishness." They both laughed, and the tension between them dissipated.

"Well, it sure was nice of you to come and visit. And it meant a lot to him." He went over to the hutch and began to root through the drawers. "I've got something to show you." Finally, Zach looked up and smiled as he pulled out a battered photograph album. He flipped over the pages, then hunched down beside her chair and pointed to one of the pictures.

Laura tried to ignore his nearness, but she felt a fluttering in her chest. To check her mounting awareness of him, she hurriedly glanced down at the album. Instantly, tears began to roll unchecked down her cheeks when she looked at the yellowed daguerreotype of a handsome young man standing stiffly with his hand on the shoulder of a lovely, dark-haired woman, seated and holding a child.

"Why, it's my parents!" Her voice quivered with a mixture of awe and poignancy.

"I told you, you've changed since then."

She dragged her scrutiny away from the couple to look at the dark-haired youngster the woman held on her lap.

"Is that really me?"

"Says so on the back."

Zach turned over the picture. Scratched across the back in her father's handwriting was the message, "Linda, me, and our Laura, born February 8, 1857." Overcome by nostalgia, she lightly traced the disorderly scrawl with her fingertips. "I couldn't have been more than three or four."

When she started to hand the photograph back to him, Zach shook his head. "No, you keep it, Laura."

"Do you mean it?" she said ecstatically. "I haven't any picture of them. Everything we owned was destroyed in the fire."

"Then I know Dad would want you to have it."

He turned over another page of the album. "Here's a picture of my mother."

"Oh, Zach, she was very beautiful," Laura said sincerely as she admired the blonde woman.

"Her name was Carissa, but Dad always called her Carrie."

He continued to flip through the album. "Here's another one with her, my dad, and your father. Must have been taken before your father left here. Looks like they were joshing around." Laura smiled through her tears at the picture of her father holding Carrie Houston arched backward in his arms in a feigned romantic embrace with Wesley Houston reaching to draw his pistol.

Joy fused with her sorrow as she raised the family portrait to her cheek. "Thank you, Zach. This is the most precious gift anyone could give me."

Only inches separated them. For a long moment they stared eye to eye: her brown eyes luminous with tears, his deep sapphire gaze seeming to probe her soul. The intensity of his stare caused a shiver to race the length of her spine. And the familiar nervous twittering in her breast resumed in response to his nearness.

Zach quickly bolted upright. His senses felt inundated by the scent of her, and the disturbing and exciting awareness of her. Closing the album, he returned the collection of treasured photographs to the hutch.

As she tucked her picture into her bodice pocket, Laura was surprised at the firm feel of her breast, the peak hard and distended. She had felt this same change to her body when she had come upon him bathing. Blushing, she hurried to the door. "Well, I guess I better be getting back."

"I'll ride as far as the stream with you, Laura." Neither thought of how comfortably each had begun to use the other's first name.

"What are you going to do now, Zach?" she asked as they guided their horses down the worn path.

He shrugged. "Try to keep the ranch going, I guess. That's what my dad would want."

"Do you have anyone to help you?" She thought of the more than one dozen ranch hands who worked the Lazy R.

Zach shook his head. "Nope."

Laura didn't voice her opinion of how gruelling she knew the task would be for one person alone. They rode silently until they reached the stream.

Zach reined up his sorrel. "Gotta leave you here. This is the boundary between the two spreads. Your aunt doesn't allow me on the Lazy R."

"Why not, Zach? I wish someone would tell me."

"My father said it was because she wants our spread, to add to the Lazy R."

Laura didn't doubt Zach's sincerity, but she sensed the real reason went much deeper than just a desire to acquire more land. "Thanks again for the picture, Zach."

For a long moment, they gazed silently into each other's eyes. "Thank you for coming, Laura."

"I'm so grateful I got to meet your father. And I'm so sorry . . ." Before she could finish, he nodded in understanding. "Well . . . I'll . . . ah . . . see you around some time."

"Yeah, see ya," he said.

She goaded her horse across the stream, then turned back and waved. Zach watched her until she disappeared from sight.

Chapter 3

"**L**aura, come here at once." The sharp command sounded as soon as she entered the door. Sensing an unpleasant scene, Laura heaved a deep sigh and walked into the library.

Looking Lilliputian in the chair behind the mammoth desk, Lavitia Randolph sat with crossed arms, her stern frown never wavering as Laura approached.

"Where have you been, Laura?"

"I went out for a ride, Aunt Lavitia."

"A ride. To where, Laura?"

"To—"

"To the Houston ranch," Lavitia interrupted with a sharp snort. Her face squeezed into grim lines of disapproval." You deliberately lied to me so you could sneak over there, didn't you? What do you have to say for yourself, young lady?"

Nothing would be gained by hedging the truth, so Laura gave a direct answer. "Yes, I did ride over to the Houston ranch, Aunt Lavitia. I regret having lied to you, but I felt I should pay my respects. Wesley Houston was my father's best friend."

The older woman's pale blue eyes flared in anger. "And I specifically ordered you to stay away from the Houstons."

Prepared to face the consequences for her actions, Laura rallied her courage. "Aunt Lavitia, I try to honor your

32

wishes, but I won't obey any unreasonable order. Unless you're willing to offer an explanation, I must follow my own conscience."

"Conscience? More like stubbornness, I'd say." Lavitia's face pinched in a frown. "You're just as headstrong as your father always was."

Laura's delicate chin thrust up defiantly. "Thank you for the compliment."

Bolting to her feet, Lavitia slammed her balled fist on the desk top. With lips compressed to a narrow slit, she leaned across the desk. "I will not tolerate your sass, young lady."

"I don't mean to be disrespectful, Aunt Lavitia. I appreciate your offering me a home . . . and I'm sorry if I appear ungrateful. But . . . I will not listen to any more of your abusive references to my father." As long as she had come this far, Laura figured she had nothing more to lose. "Furthermore, I feel I'm old enough to select my own friends."

Just making the declaration made Laura feel as if a weight had been lifted off her shoulders; it was not in her nature to sneak around behind another person's back. "If you wish, I'll return to Laredo."

Laura's attitude seemed to take Lavitia by surprise. Apparently she was not accustomed to being challenged. Sitting down, the older woman softened her tone. "Laredo? I never said you must leave."

Laura felt a rush of relief. Despite a brave show of independence, she knew she was destitute and had no place to go. "If you'll please excuse me, Aunt Lavitia, I'd like to retire to my room since I *do* have a headache." She hurried away before any more could be said.

After Laura departed, Lavitia Randolph remained at the desk. Annoyance gleamed in her cold eyes. No one appreciated her efforts. Throughout her life, she had been subjected to ingrates . . . repaid for her labor with ridicule and betrayal. Were it not for her, there would not be a Lazy R today; only the sweat of her brow had prevented the ranch from being sold when her father died.

Deep in thought, she leaned back in the chair, nervously drumming the fingers of her right hand on the desk top. She had begun to form an affection for Laura. Her pale blue eyes narrowed with bitterness. Now it appeared the girl intended to abuse her trust just like the others who had betrayed her—her father, her brother . . . and Wesley Houston.

She raised her hands and, to her astonishment, discovered they were trembling. Disgusted, she jumped to her feet and began to pace the floor as anger hardened her face to a glowering mask of mounting rage.

Anger and disillusion rippled across the twisted plain of her countenance. Laura, too, would pay the price for her betrayal and ingratitude.

"Well, young lady, we'll see who has the final word," she mumbled ominously.

Forlorn, Laura plopped down in the middle of her bed. The situation with her aunt was becoming more uncomfortable by the day.

"Come in," she said in response to a light tap on the door. She hoped her aunt hadn't followed her. Still feeling depressed over the death of Wesley Houston, Laura did not want to argue further with the woman.

Teresa entered carrying a pitcher. "Miss Laura, I brought you some fresh water from the well. It is cool and should refresh you on such a warm day."

"Thank you, Teresa." Laura sighed dejectedly.

The girl cast a sorrowful glance at her. "I'm sorry to hear Mister Houston die."

"Did you know him, Teresa?"

"No, but my mother always say Wesley Houston was a nice man."

For a few seconds, Laura debated the wisdom of involving Teresa in her family squabble. Then, beset with curiosity, she asked, "Teresa, do you know why my aunt hates the Houstons so much?"

Teresa shook her head. "Whiskers, he know," she said.

"I've already asked him," Laura said. "He told me to ask my aunt because he doesn't want to carry tales. I don't understand why I can't get an honest answer from anyone." She buried her chin in her hands.

Shaking her head in commiseration, Teresa put the pitcher on the table and hastened from the room.

As a result of the quarrel, the atmosphere remained strained between Laura and her aunt when they ate their evening meal—which was perfectly fine with Laura. She had no intention of apologizing for her outburst, although she was certain Lavitia expected her to.

The situation between them hadn't changed much by the following morning. After breakfast, Lavitia gave Laura a list of needed supplies. Accompanied by Whiskers, Laura left for Bay Town.

After the shopping had been completed and the buckboard loaded, Whiskers cast an anxious glance toward the saloon. "Ah . . . missy, you got somethin' to do for ten minutes or so?"

Knowing full well the old man hoped she would agree, Laura concealed her smile. "Well, come to think of it, there is one thing I forgot to buy, Whiskers."

"Well, you just take your time, missy." While he headed for the saloon, Laura returned to the general store.

"Forget something, Miss Laura?" the shopkeeper asked.

"Mr. Stevens, do you have any frames for photographs?"

Shoving his spectacles up to his brow, he scratched his head. "Think we might have a couple in the stock room. Haven't had too much of a call for them in the last couple years. Let me take a look."

After a few minutes, he returned blowing dust off a small pewter frame ideally suited for her parents' picture. Even though she knew she should save her meager funds for a more practical use, Laura bowed to sentiment. Using the last remaining dollar the church had given her, she purchased the metal frame.

With parcel in hand, she left the store, eager now to return to the ranch so she could frame the cherished picture. She stopped on the steps of the boardwalk when she noticed Whiskers had not yet made it to the saloon. He was talking to Zachary Houston.

Laura's first impulse was to rush over to speak to Zachary, then she decided it would be wiser to wait until the two men finished their conversation. She did not intentionally mean to eavesdrop, but the sound of their voices carried to her ears.

"Sorry about your pa, Zach. First Joey, now Wes. Hard to think of 'em both gone." Sorrowfully, the old cowpoke hung his head. "Ain't right for a man to be outlivin' the two young scalawags he helped to raise."

Zachary put a hand on Whiskers's shoulder, and, ironically, the roles of the two men became reversed as Zachary comforted the older man.

As Laura watched, she became aware that her overall impression of Zachary had been misleading. Whiskers had told her Zach was only two years older than she was. She had not thought of him as an adult male, any more than she considered herself a woman. But now as he spoke with Whiskers, she had a chance to study Zach more objectively and saw there was nothing boyish about Zachary Houston. He was all man. Standing beside the older cowpoke, Zachary's long, lean body radiated strength, power, and a raw sexuality that evoked a surge of excitement to her feminine breast.

His dusty Levis hugged his long, muscular legs, and his worn blue shirt stretched tautly across his broad shoulders. Even the set of his hat enhanced his manliness. Worn low and square on his forehead, the brim of the hat shrouded his dark blue eyes in mystery and highlighted the firm, sculptured line of his jaw.

Her gaze traced a path down the corded column of his

neck to where several open buttons of his shirt exposed a patch of dark hair. Recalling the sight of that rugged body unclothed, she felt the pleasant and exciting hardening in her nipples again. Swept with a heated flush, she recognized a shocking truth—her femininity was responding to his masculinity. Sometime in the past weeks, she had advanced beyond girlhood.

With awe, she fixed her brown-eyed gaze on the man responsible for this new and electrifying realization. Despite a growing urgency to be near him, Laura stepped back out of sight so she could watch and listen, unobserved.

"You gonna try and keep your spread going, Zach?" Whiskers asked.

Zachary shrugged. "That's why I came to town. I have to talk to Mr. Davis at the bank. The note's due on the Double H. I don't have the money to pay it, but I thought if Davis was willing, I could sell part of the herd to pay just the interest. By next spring, I can round up some mustangs, break 'em, and get enough to make the rest of the payment."

"Well, I've got a few dollars saved up in my poke, Zach. Ain't much, but you're welcome to it."

"That's good of you, Whiskers, but I don't want your money."

"Well, if you change your mind . . . it's yours for the askin'." Whiskers's glance shifted to the door of the saloon. "I'm fixin' to get me a drink of rotgut before Miss Laura finishes up her shoppin'. Come along and I'll buy ya a drink."

Zachary shook his head. "Next time, Whiskers."

"Well then, you take care now, son. You hear?" He slapped Zach on the shoulder and hurried away.

After Whiskers had departed, Laura stepped out of the shadows. "Hello, Zach."

Nodding, he appeared pleased to see her. "Hi, Laura. Heard you were in town."

She held up the parcel wrapped in brown paper. "I

bought a frame for my parents' picture. Now I can't wait to get back to the ranch to frame it."

"Think you might have a wait on your hands. Whiskers just headed for the saloon." The sight of his crooked grin warmed her heart. She wished he would smile more often.

"Well, I thought I'd walk down by the dock anyway. I haven't had a chance to see it yet."

"Can't say there's too much to see," Zach replied. To Laura's delight, he remained at her side as she strolled down to a ferry barge bobbing on the water. For a moment, she watched the ripples lap at the rotting timbers of an aged pier.

A dozen mewling cattle shifted restlessly in a pen on the deck of the vessel that was preparing to make the daily run to Galveston Island.

"This certainly isn't much of a wharf, is it?" she commented.

"We're not on the ship channel. This is just a ferry dock for Bay Town. The ferry's about the only ship you'll see here. Everything else docks at Galveston or farther inland at Houston."

Laura glanced out to sea. "Is Galveston as busy a city as they say?"

"Sure was the times I've seen it," Zach remarked. "Farther north, there's a train trestle that links the island to the coast, but most folks around here still use the ferry for the two-mile run to Galveston."

"Hard to believe two miles can make such a difference," she said, casting a desultory glance at the ramshackle town behind them.

"Well, who knows what Bay Town'll be like a few years from now. Look at Galveston Island. It used to be the lair of Jean Lafitte."

"You mean the notorious pirate?" she asked, glancing seaward toward the island's hazy outline off the Texas coast.

Zach nodded in reply. "But with the Gulf of Mexico on its windward side and Galveston Bay on the leeward, the island just naturally developed into a bustling seaport. Now it's the leading commercial center in the state."

"That is quite a change," Laura agreed, brushing back several strands of long hair whipping at her face.

Zach watched the willowy movement of her hand. Everything she did appeared graceful to him. She was the most beautiful woman he had ever seen. He never tired of looking at her.

"I reckon time can change just about anything. 'Pears so, just like it changed you."

"Me?" she asked, surprised. "Don't tell me you're referring to that picture again? After all, Zach, I was only two or three years old then."

Zach shook his head. "I'm talking about the change in your appearance just lately. When you first came here, you were dressed in a Sunday gown with a hat of posies on your head. Now look at you."

Laura glanced down at her clothing. Her bodice was a simple white cotton blouse and a divided skirt of biscuit-colored serge flared over a pair of calf-high leather boots. Her hair was plaited in a thick braid that hung down to the center of her back, and a low-crowned felt Stetson kept the sun out of her eyes.

Giggling, she shook her head. "Zach, I haven't changed. Those clothes you described were all donated to me. I lost all my clothing in the fire. But this is the way I always dressed in Laredo." She shook her head in amusement as they walked back to the buckboard. "You talk like I'm some eastern gal who just climbed off a stage."

"Gotta admit you sure look like a Texan now," he said. The husky tremor in his voice revealed the passion behind the remark. His gaze traveled across her face and probed the warmth of her eyes. Then he added hastily, "Well, I reckon I better get going. See you around." And in a smooth, long-legged stride, he headed toward the bank.

"Bye, Zach," she murmured in a soft voice that faded to a whisper.

*   *   *

In the weeks following their argument, Lavitia made a concentrated effort to assign Laura duties that kept her in or near the ranch house. Upon her arrival at the Lazy R, Laura had been occupied sewing her own clothes. With Teresa's aid, she had made several outfits from the various bolts of material Lavitia had purchased. When Laura completed that significant task, Lavitia then turned over the ranch's bookkeeping to the young girl as well as the responsibility for ordering all of the supplies needed for the household. However, Lavitia still kept a firm hand on ordering whatever was needed to run the business end of the ranch.

Lavitia even began to forego her Sunday afternoon quilting bees in order to keep Laura busy with some kind of contrived job—anything to keep her niece from having the spare time to ride over to the Double H.

Laura found her aunt's constant supervision oppressive. It wasn't until an afternoon in the beginning of June that Laura received a welcome break from her jailer; she rode out with Whiskers to deliver a wagonload of supplies to one of the line shacks.

Laura rejoiced in this rare opportunity to ride her mare over the open range without anyone looking over her shoulder. Anyone, that is, except Whiskers, whom she considered a friend.

After unloading the supplies, their return route led them near the Double H. Glimpsing a familiar blue shirt through the trees, Laura waved Whiskers on. "I'll catch up with you in a little while."

"You listen to me, missy. Your aunt's gonna be proper mad if she finds out you rode over to the Double H," the old ranch hand warned.

"She won't find out unless you tell her," Laura called back gaily as she galloped away.

When Laura rode up to Zachary, he was standing in the shade of a high bluff. "How have you been, Zach?" she asked, dismounting.

"Okay," he replied succinctly. His face appeared more solemn than ever, his eyes more sorrowful.

He removed his hat long enough to wipe his brow on the sleeve of his shirt, then he plopped the hat low on his forehead. "What are you doing way out here?"

"Whiskers and I just took some supplies to one of the line shacks. You've got the right idea; feels good to get out of the sun."

Laura glanced up toward the top of the granite wall above them. Erosion had shirred off the face of the mountain to form a straight drop of at least a hundred feet. "This is kind of a weird-looking place, isn't it?"

"It's called Blind Man's Bluff."

Laura grimaced. "I hate to ask why."

"More than one cow's ended up down here after straying over the top at night or during a storm. The drop is so abrupt up above, if you come upon it too fast, you can stumble over the top real easy."

"Have you ever been up there?"

"Oh sure. But I try to stay away from it, if I can. That's where your father almost got killed."

"Almost killed!" she said, astounded. "Good heavens! What happened?"

"Your father and mine were just boys when it happened. They were up there and my dad said Joey tripped. Dad grabbed your father's hand, but he wasn't strong enough to pull Joey back up. So your father dangled in the air with my dad holding him by the hand."

"Oh, my goodness!" she exclaimed.

"After awhile, Dad said his arm felt numb, but he wouldn't let go of Joey's hand."

"Well, how did he ever get my father back up?"

"Whiskers Merten finally came along and helped rescue your father."

"How old were they when this happened?" Laura asked, totally absorbed in the story.

"I guess the two of them were only about eight years old."

"My father could have died if it weren't for your father," she said with reverence. Laura glanced up at the high, sinister-looking face of the cliff. "I don't like this place."

Zach reached for the reins of his sorrel. "Well, I'm out looking for strays. Thought I'd check out the ravine over by that stand of oak up ahead." She followed his gaze to a string of tall trees in the distance.

"I'll help you." Her eyes lit with mischief. "And I bet I can beat you to those trees."

For a brief moment, she saw a flicker of enthusiasm in his eyes. "Your mare doesn't have a chance against my sorrel," he scoffed.

"We'll just see about that." She hopped into the saddle and galloped off in a cloud of dust. Zachary hesitated for a few seconds, then he swung onto his stallion and followed in hot pursuit.

Splashing across a narrow creek and leaping over whatever obstacles lay in their path, the two horses raced across the countryside toward the distant trees. Lying low across the neck of her mare, Laura led for about a quarter of a mile, but the strength and size of Zachary's sorrel made the outcome a foregone conclusion.

Laughing, they dismounted and plopped down on a hillside carpeted with wild daisies. "Where'd you learn to ride like that?" Zach asked.

Still breathless from the strenuous run, Laura stretched out on her back among the sweet-smelling flowers. "My father taught me."

Zach stretched out beside her. He broke off two stalks of dried grass, handed her one, and began to chew on the other.

They lay in contented companionship, chewing on stalks of grass and gazing up at white clouds floating across the blue sky.

"See that little cloud up there in the middle? Don't you think it looks like a camel?" Laura asked. She leaned on her elbow and propped her head in her hand. Mesmerized, she studied the line of Zach's rugged profile as he concentrated on the cloud overhead.

After a long moment of intense deliberation, he finally said, "I think it looks like a bent-over old woman carrying a heavy poke on her back."

Skeptical, she dragged her eyes away from him to glance skyward. "Old woman? Why not an old man?"

"Because the head is covered with a scarf or hood of some kind. A man would be wearing a hat."

"Well, maybe he's a monk," she said, giggling. They both broke into laughter. When he turned on his side to look at her, their faces were suddenly only inches apart. Their laughter died. Laura held her breath as, for one exquisite moment, the eyes of one unmasked the soul of the other. Then Zach turned away and sat up.

"I guess I better get to checking out those strays."

"Yeah, I better get riding to catch up with Whiskers."

"I'm glad you stopped today, Laura. I've been feeling kind of . . ." His voice trailed away.

Her heart swelled with compassion. "I know what you're going through, Zach."

"Yeah, I guess you do. Losing both parents at the same time, the way you did." He raised his head and she saw the raw pain in his eyes. "I sure miss him, Laura." His voice seemed near to breaking. "It's always been just the two of us. And we used to do so much talking together when I got back at night."

She felt she had to touch him—to absorb some of his pain, to let him feel her compassion. She picked up his hand. His long fingers closed around hers as if clutching at a lifeline. "I wish I could tell you it gets easier, Zach. The priest told me I would get used to the pain after a while. But I haven't yet. I guess it's still too soon."

He stood up and pulled her to her feet. "Well, I didn't mean to tell you my troubles, Laura. I reckon you've got enough of your own." Zach was a proud man, and Laura could see how ashamed he felt for exposing his emotions to her.

They walked over to her mare and Zachary gave her a lift into the saddle. "I'm your friend, Zach. Anytime you want to talk, I'm willing to listen. Maybe we can help each other."

She goaded her horse to a trot and rode away before any more could be said. After a short distance, she turned to look back. He was still standing there watching her.

Laura caught up with Whiskers about three miles down the trail. He had pulled the wagon under the shade of a tree to wait for her. Without a word, the old man flicked the reins and they returned to the ranch house.

Lavitia continued to keep Laura so busy that often, too exhausted to do anything else, she collapsed into bed at night. But in the quiet darkness, Zachary Houston invaded her thoughts. Aware of the mysterious changes that had come over her, she would shift restlessly as she wrestled with disturbing, but pleasant, erotic fantasies. The vision of the bronzed perfection of Zach's long, muscular nakedness dominated her waking dreams.

Time sped by swiftly for Laura, and before she realized it, another month had passed. The long, hot days of July descended on the Texas range.

The Fourth of July was a sacrosanct holiday to all cowboys from the Mississippi to the Pacific Ocean. Certainly Bay Town, Texas, was no exception.

So on the Fourth, everyone for miles around packed picnic baskets, climbed on their horses or into their buckboards, and headed to Bay Town to commemorate the nation's day of independence. A few of the more adventuresome took the ferry to Galveston, but the majority of the local ranchers preferred the more intimate and familiar atmosphere of the small town.

American flags and the Texas Lone Star flew from every building. Toting baskets containing pies and cakes, potato salad and beans, the celebrants began arriving by early morning. A calf had been roasting on a spit since dawn. And, of course, the highlight of the celebration would be the pyrotechnic display from Galveston later that evening.

Following an afternoon ceremony that eulogized the fight for Texas independence, as much as for the nation's, one end of the street was cordoned off for dancing. At the other end, tables covered with red and white checkered cloths had been set up and lavishly spread with the contents of the picnic baskets.

Clearly, Lavitia Randolph reigned supreme. Making good use of the occasion, she formally introduced Laura to all the local citizens, particularly the few eligible males.

But a group of single girls had their eyes on the marriageable young men too; and although Laura did not want for dancing partners throughout the day, after dancing with her, each young man was immediately reclaimed by a determined young woman who was not about to allow her intended, or "future intended," to fall under the charms of the newest arrival to the territory.

As much as Laura enjoyed the music and dancing, she was more relieved by than resentful of each girl's possessiveness toward her particular local bachelor, for none caught Laura's eye. There was only one man she sought. After every dance, she eagerly scanned the crowd, hoping to see the tall figure of Zachary Houston.

However, he did not appear. By nightfall her anticipation had turned to anguish—then outright fear that something terrible had happened to him. With every passing hour, her anxiety increased; she could no longer follow the rhythm of the music or the steps of her partners.

As the darkness continued to deepen, the crowd dispersed into assorted groups: the young couples slipped away to sit on scattered blankets and await the fireworks, the married and older women sat in a circle exchanging the local gossip while trying to keep a watchful eye on the young couples, the male spouses circled around the beer keg to enjoy a smoke and discuss the price of beef. Ranch hands who had not taken the ferry to Galveston congregated in the saloon, and youngsters eagerly huddled around the ice cream churns to sample and savor the mouth-watering delicacy.

Wishing for a quick end to the evening, Laura strolled down to the dock. Gazing sadly across the black water, she stood in the dim glow of the dock light as a soft breeze tugged at her long hair and swirled the ruffled skirt of her yellow and white dimity gown around her ankles.

Deep in thought, she believed she was alone until a voice spoke suddenly to her from the shadows. "Hi, Laura."

Startled, she turned to discover Zachary Houston. Her hand fluttered nervously to her breast. "Zach, I didn't see you over there."

Zachary, who had been sitting under a giant oak, stood up when she walked over to him. The pent-up anxiety she had suffered because of him throughout the day now exploded in an angry outburst. "Zachary Houston, where have you been? I've been half out of my mind worrying about you." At his stunned look, she stopped her shrewish tirade and asked sheepishly, "Are you enjoying the celebration?"

"I reckon so," he said, clearly perplexed by her shifting moods. "What about you?"

"Oh, yes. I can't remember when I've danced so much."

"Yeah, I saw you dancing. You sure looked like you were having a good time."

"I didn't see *you* dancing," she said, trying to keep from sounding too reproachful. *How could I have missed him? And why didn't he ask me to dance?*

"Oh . . . I'm not good at dancing. Never being around women, I never really had the chance to learn how." His grin flashed in the darkness. "My dad tried to teach me a time or two."

"Well, I can't believe one of the girls around here wouldn't have been more than willing to teach you,"

she said. Her earlier distress now appeased, she was
excited just having him near. Her eyes sparkled with
sauciness. "I'll be more than glad to teach you myself."

Horrified, she suddenly realized she was flirting with
him. She began to stutter. "That is if . . . if you . . . want
me to." *Good God, I've shifted from shrew to coquette!* she
agonized, relieved it was too dark for him to see her flam-
ing blush.

"Maybe some time," he said. "Sure was a good day
for the celebration," Zach added, casually changing the
subject.

"Yes, the weather has been perfect."

Grateful for his tactfulness, Laura leaned back against
the tree trunk and listened to the deep cadence of
his voice. "Good thing, too," he said, moving closer.
"Around these parts, the Fourth of July and Texas Independence Day are about the two most important holidays
of the year."

"Did you go to college, Zach?" Laura asked all of a
sudden. She had often noticed his manner of speaking
seemed much more literate than other ranch hands.

"College?" he scoffed. "I never had the time, much
less the money, to go off to college. My dad educated
me from the books my ma had. Originally, she came
to Texas to be a schoolteacher." He moved closer to
Laura until their bodies almost touched. "But I could
ask the same about you, Laura. Where'd you get your
education?"

"From the priests . . . and my mother," she added hastily. "My maternal grandparents were landed Spaniards
and she was very . . . well cultured." Laura knew she
sounded stuffy. "They died during the Mexican War."

"With your father being a Texan and all, I'd guess that
with that kind of mixed sentiment, you must have had
a revolution right under your own roof."

The breeze whipped at her hair and carried off the
lilt of her soft laughter. "Oh, no," she exclaimed. Her
voice grew husky at the thought of her beloved parents.

"My father and mother worshipped each other. I hope some day, I'll be lucky enough to know such a love." Brushing the hair off her cheeks, she glanced up into his dark eyes. "Have you ever thought about falling in love, Zach?"

"Never gave it much thought."

"Haven't you ever courted one of the girls around here? You're old enough to wed. You understand, of course, that I'm just curious because I'm your friend."

"I never had much time for girls, Laura. Besides . . ." his steady gaze rested on her upturned face, ". . . I really don't have much to offer a wife." Before she could say more, he turned away, clearly uncomfortable with the conversation. "Wonder when those fireworks are going to start."

Laura wanted to bite her tongue. Why had she pushed the conversation so far? She had practically thrown herself at him.

Suddenly, the boom of cannon carried to their ears from a distant shore. The sky lit up in a brilliant phosphorescent glow as a fusillade of Roman candles rocketed heavenward from Galveston Island. In a dazzling aerial display, shimmering, luminous streamers streaked across the sky and burst into incandescent colors against the black firmament.

"Oh, have you ever seen anything so lovely?" Laura whispered with breathless awe when the fireworks ended a quarter of an hour later.

"Never," he said solemnly.

Smiling, she turned to find his intense stare riveted on her face. Self-consciously, she offered him a nervous smile. "How have things been going for you, Zach?" she asked, unable to prevent broaching the subject that had tormented her since their last meeting.

"I'm okay, Laura."

He looked at her with longing. Throughout the bleak weeks of his grieving, she had been his emotional lifeline, offering the purity of her compassion. Alone in his cabin at night, he had felt her caring love across the distance that separated them.

But soon a more powerful feeling overpowered his senses—a feeling driven by a physical need that threatened to betray her trust. It seemed to intensify with every thought of her and with each encounter; he had the overwhelming desire to take her in his arms and feel her flesh against his own. He felt a stirring in his loins.

"I guess I better get going," he said, and departed hastily.

"Good-bye, Zach," she murmured softly—once again for her ears alone.

Chapter 4

Sunday morning had dawned hazy and humid and, despite the fact that she had just bathed, Laura felt clammy. As she brushed her hair, she walked over and sat down on the windowsill. Not a leaf stirred outside. Throughout the long month of August, a stretch of miserably hot weather had dried the grass to hay and much of the land had been baked to hard clay. From her bedroom window, she noticed that the earth was cracked, like the severed pieces of a jigsaw puzzle.

Teresa tapped on the door. She had come to braid Laura's hair, and, in turn, Laura braided Teresa's. While the style kept the long hair off her neck, it was of little comfort when Laura put on the binding corset and long white hose to wear to church.

By the time church ended, the heat was sweltering. The heavy air seemed to squeeze her chest in a vise, and adding to her discomfort, dust clung in moist patches to the perspiration that coated her body.

Seemingly undaunted by the heat, Lavitia insisted Whiskers drive her to Houston to attend a bull auction. They were not expected to return until Tuesday. Much to Laura's immense relief, Lavitia did not ask her to accompany them.

With most of the ranch hands enjoying their day off in Galveston or Bay Town, only a few remained at the ranch, lounging in the bunkhouse trying to stay cool or struggling to write letters to loved ones.

The vision of Zachary Houston's solemn face and long, lithe body filled Laura's head as she curried her mare in the barn. She had had no contact with Zach since the Fourth of July. Absorbed in thoughts of him, she was unaware of the man who stealthily approached from behind her.

"Gotcha," Whitey Wright exclaimed, grabbing her around the waist. Squealing in shock, Laura dropped the curry comb and spun on her heel to face her nemesis.

"Take your hands off me, Whitey Wright, and leave me alone." She stepped out of his clutches. The cowboy's persistence in trying to force his unwanted attentions on her had become more frequent despite Lavitia Randolph's stringent orders against fraternization between the ranch hands and the household. All of the men except Whitey were courteous to Laura but maintained a polite distance.

"Ah, you know you love it, darlin'," Whitey declared smugly.

Since she had made her dislike for him quite clear in the past, Laura didn't bother to deny his boast. Instead, she turned her back to him and bent down to pick up the fallen comb.

Whitey seized the opportunity and shoved her onto a nearby pile of hay. She tried to roll away, but he threw himself on top of her. Pinning her arms above her head, he covered her mouth with his own to stifle her scream.

Her struggles to free her mouth only caused him to increase the pressure. He opened his mouth wider, drove his tongue past her teeth, and began licking and stroking the inside of her mouth. The wet kiss revolted her. Combined with the heat and weight of his body, she couldn't breathe and began to feel nauseated. Feeling the rise of bile in her throat, she ceased her struggles to avoid regurgitating.

Accepting her action as a sign of capitulation, Whitey raised his head, and his mouth curved in a confident smirk. "Knew it was just an act you was puttin' on."

He released her arms and sat up, straddling her hips. The new position relieved the pressure from her chest and she began to suck welcome breaths into her lungs. Whitey opened her bodice and shoved up her camisole. For a long moment his lascivious gaze fixed on the dusky puckered tips of her breasts. His tongue snaked out to wet his lips as he reached out both hands to cup the rounded mounds. Wide-eyed, Laura lay still in an effort to settle her upset stomach. She felt mortified and humiliated by his debasement.

"Yeah, darlin', nice. Real nice. Round and hard as fresh-picked melons," Whitey mewed, pawing at her breasts. "I figured ya couldn't hold out too much longer." The smirk on his face widened. "You ain't fooled me. You've been lettin' Houston stick ya, ain'tcha, darlin'?"

Clicking his tongue, he shook his head in mockery. "But I ain't seen ya hot tailin' it over to the Double H for a few weeks now. Whatsa matter, darlin', the two of you have a fallin' out?" Whitey snickered as he continued his one-sided conversation.

His roughened fingertips rasped painfully at her nipples until the sensitive nubs hardened into peaks. As he mistook her shudder of revulsion for a tremor of arousal, his eyes gleamed with lust. "Yeah, you like that, don't ya, darlin'? Hot little gal like you must be real-l-l hungry for it by now."

Grinning salaciously, he stood up and started to unbutton his pants. "Well, Ole Whitey'll take care of ya, darlin'. Just wait 'til I stick mine into ya. You're gonna find out what you've been missin'. Didn't your mama ever tell ya not to send a boy to do a man's job?" He lowered his trousers to his knees. "This time you'll know you've been—" The breath whooshed out of him as she raised her foot and kicked him in the groin.

Whitey doubled over in pain, and Laura scrambled to her feet. Grabbing a nearby pitchfork, she threatened him with the sharpened prongs. "If you ever touch me again, I swear on my parents' grave I'll kill you." She motioned toward the door with the pitchfork. "Now get out of here."

Cursing vehemently, Whitey pulled up his pants. "You teasin' little cu—"

"Get out," she cried, waving the pitchfork. He stumbled out the door.

Laura fumed in anger as she restored her disheveled hair and clothing. At the sound of hoofbeats, she walked to the barn door in time to see Whitey gallop off toward town. Too agitated to return to the house, she began to saddle her mare.

Just as Laura prepared to leave, the cook, Juanita Morales, entered the barn. "Miss Lavitia say you no leave the ranch, Miss Laura."

"I don't care what my aunt says, Juanita. I am not a prisoner here."

Whiskers Merten and Teresa were her only friends at the ranch. Juanita was amicable, but only to the degree of not jeopardizing her position as a household servant. "You ride to Double H," she accused.

"Yes, I am, Juanita. I'm worried about Zachary Houston."

The cook's black eyes flashed slyly. "Your Mr. Zachary is one handsome *gringo*."

"He's not *my* Mr. Zachary," Laura quickly denied. Then her face broke in a devilish smile. "I just wish he were." The two women giggled in understanding.

"Miss Lavitia be angry if she hear I no try to stop you."

Laura grasped the cook's hand and squeezed it. "This will be our secret, Juanita. Everyone's gone, so nobody will even know."

"I no want to know when you go. When you return." The woman threw her hands up in the air and walked away. "Is best to see nothing . . . know nothing."

"Bless you, Juanita," Laura called out to her.

* * *

Heading south, Laura followed the familiar trail to the Double H. Since the Fourth of July, she had twice managed to slip from under her aunt's watchful eye and ride over to the ranch, only to discover that Zach was gone. She had not even glimpsed him from afar during her trips with Whiskers around the Lazy R.

"Maybe he's trying to avoid me, Sunshine," she commented to her mare, when she once again found no sign of Zach at his house. "I guess I couldn't blame him if he were . . . considering the way I threw myself at him the last time we met." Nevertheless, she rode on to continue her search for him.

The warm air on her face felt like a furnace blast. After riding for about thirty minutes, she regretted her hasty act and decided to return to the ranch. Reining up, she sat down in a clump of sycamore and cypress pine to allow her thirsty mare a much-needed drink and rest. The effect of the devastating heat caught up with her. Her eyelids drooped.

When Laura opened her eyes, she had no idea how long she had slept. She started to rise, then drew back abruptly, startled by a figure sitting on the ground opposite her. The outcry died in her throat when she recognized Zachary Houston.

"Hi, Laura. Didn't mean to scare you," Zach said. He grinned sheepishly. "I just finished rounding up some strays and thought I'd go for a swim. Didn't think I should leave until you woke up."

Laura glanced over and saw a half-dozen cattle grazing nearby. She couldn't believe she had slept through their approach. Embarrassed at being discovered in such a vulnerable position, she thought of how Whitey Wright would have taken advantage of her under the same circumstances. "I guess I must have dozed off."

"It's this heat." Zach took off his hat and wiped the inside with his red and white bandanna.

Her brown eyes warmed as she slipped off her own hat and slid a hand to her nape to lift her heavy thick braid of dark hair. "A swim would feel good, wouldn't it?"

"Well, you're welcome to come along."

"Where?" she asked, surprised. If he intended to return to the stream between the two ranches, it had dried up to nothing more than a creek. Certainly it was too shallow to swim.

"Just follow me," Zach said. Laura quickly plopped her hat back on her head, mounted her horse, and followed him.

After a short distance, Zach turned onto a narrow, well-worn trail. Tall wiry stalks of sunflowers thrust up from a field of rye grass. Cresting a small rise, she reined up and stared with mouth agape at the expanse of blue water stretching to the horizon. Below, gentle waves lapped a small, sandy beach hidden in the center of a horseshoe-shaped string of sand dunes.

"My own private beach," Zach said in response to her surprised look. "Trouble is, I don't have much time to enjoy it."

"I didn't know your ranch bordered the Gulf!" she exclaimed.

"Only this small section does. But the Gulf of Mexico runs all the way down the coast. If a person had a mind to, he could sail to Galveston from here . . . or even the Atlantic Ocean with a big enough ship."

She raised her hand to shade her eyes against the glare of sunlight on the water. "Have you ever sailed before, Zach?"

"Yeah, on the Bay Town ferry to Galveston." He grinned crookedly. "If you want to call that sailing." His dark gaze scanned the distant surf. "Maybe someday I'll be able to buy a boat big enough to sail to Galveston," he said wistfully.

They rode over to a clump of cottonwood and dismounted. "We'll leave the horses up here," Zach said.

After tying the reins to a shrub of catclaw, he pulled a towel and blanket out of his saddlebags.

Laura followed his example when he sat down and removed his boots and socks. With warm sand slithering between their toes, they walked barefoot down a steep, reddish-golden dune speckled with sea swallows and plovers pecking on leafy green sprouts of marsh elder.

Zach spread out the blanket, shed his shirt and hat, then unbuckled his gunbelt and tossed it down. He started to unbutton his pants, then suddenly hesitated. "Oh, oh!"

At the same moment, realization dawned on Laura. Her hands stalled on the buttons of her bodice.

"What do you want to do now?" he asked.

Her gaze shifted to the foamy surf, to Zach, then back again to the inviting water. *Modesty be damned*, she decided. Smiling impishly, she declared, "I want to go swimming."

Grinning, Zach dropped his trousers. Dressed only in his drawers, he raced toward the water and dove into the surf. Less bold than her words, Laura hesitated for a fraction of a minute, then she pulled off her bodice and riding skirt. Dressed only in her camisole and calf-length underdrawers, she was in the water before his head broke the surface.

For the next half hour, they frolicked like children. Laughing, they ran back to the blanket. They were circumspect in their effort to avoid looking at each other. Grabbing her clothing, Laura dashed behind the rocks, wiggled out of her underclothes, and hastened into her bodice and skirt. In her absence, Zach quickly removed his wet drawers and pulled on his trousers. After laying out their wet clothing to dry in the sun, they sat down on the blanket.

Zach lay back on the blanket and plopped his Stetson over his face. Laura released her hair and began to towel it dry. She didn't know if he wanted to sleep, so she remained quiet, content just to sit beside him.

Lowering the towel, she watched a nearby sandpiper hop along the beach and then stop to dig its long bill into the sand, rooting for crustaceans. Overhead, calling to each other in their raucous squawk that sounded like laughter to her, several gulls circled in graceful swirls, then lowered their dark, red legs and glided onto the surf.

"Zach, what is that plant over there?" she asked. He lifted his hat off his face to glance at several green stalks thrusting out of the sand near the water's edge.

"Sea oats," he mumbled, lying back.

"Sea oats! I didn't know oats grew in the sea."

"Well, what else would . . ." He began to chuckle, and soon his body trembled with laughter.

"What?" she asked, perplexed yet delighted by the outburst, which was so out of character for him. Instantly, the sound of his husky laughter became infectious and she began to laugh too. "What's so funny?"

"Well, what else *would* sea horses eat?" he finally managed to blurt out between guffaws.

She lay back laughing. The unrestrained gaiety became an emotional release for them after they'd held their grief in check for so long. Clutching at each other, they rolled around with mirthful tears streaking their cheeks.

When the laughter faded, they found themselves in one another's arms. For a long moment, each looked deeply into the eyes of the other. The hilarity was all gone now, and that familiar, but forbidden longing began to emerge.

Awkwardly, he lowered his head to hers. His mouth was firm, yet tentative—hers, unresisting and guileless. Their mouths found a fit and his lips settled on hers.

Although they were inexperienced, each responded instinctively to the overwhelming power of awakening sensuality.

His lips hardened; his mouth moved more aggressively. Savoring the tantalizing contact, she slipped her arms around his neck, and his hands clutched at her back to draw her tighter against his long, muscular length.

Abruptly, he pulled away and sat up, his eyes clouded with guilt. "I'm sorry, Laura. I didn't mean to take advantage of you."

Flushed with excitement, she smiled up at him. "That's okay, Zach. It was just a kiss."

Just a kiss—which happened to be the most exciting thing that had ever happened to her. The kiss she had yearned for, had fantasized about. She wanted to admit as much to him, but the words seemed too bold to confess.

For a long moment they stared at each other. She thought he was going to say something, but then he stood up. "Guess we better get going. Looks like we're finally in for some rain."

Glancing skyward, she saw dark clouds rolling swiftly in from the east. As a further sign of the approaching storm, hundreds of gulls were circling overhead seeking shelter on shore.

She rose to her feet and began to brush the sand off her skirt. Once again she dashed behind the rocks and put on her underclothes while he redressed on the beach.

When all their clothing had been restored, Zach took her hand and they scampered up the dune to their horses. Just before they mounted, he paused and glanced over at her.

"Laura."

When he hesitated, she waited, her eyes inquisitive. He appeared to be waging an inner struggle and she held her breath, fear running rampant. She was afraid he would suggest they shouldn't see each other again because of what had just transpired between them.

Finally he turned, and his steadfast stare fixed on her gaze, now rife with apprehension. "Laura, will you be my girl?"

The anxiety in her eyes changed to boundless joy. "Oh yes, Zach," she replied breathlessly.

He grinned, his teeth flashing against the deep tan of his face. Then he lithely swung up into the saddle.

Chapter 5

⟪ ∽◯◯◯∽ ⟫

The boom of thunder and distant flashes in the sky heralded the quickly approaching storm. "You better get back home before this storm hits," Zach warned when they reached the spot where his cattle were grazing.

"What about your cattle?" she asked.

"I'll come back for them as soon as the storm's over. I'm more worried about the rest of the herd. They're on low ground in a dry streambed."

On the ride over, Laura had seen the cattle grazing in the floor of a ravine. "I'll be glad to help you move them now, if you want me to."

"No, they'll be okay unless this storm really kicks up. I'll move them out of there first thing in the morning."

"Well then, I'll get going."

"Be careful on your way home, Laura."

"I will, and I'll come back tomorrow," she called out and began to ride hard back to the Lazy R. But she could not outrun the storm. Large raindrops began to splatter the ground, turning the area into a steam bath. By the time she reached the house, Laura was soaked to the skin.

She put Sunshine in the barn and quickly rubbed her down with hay. Then, thoroughly drenched, she ran into the house.

Shaking her head in displeasure, Juanita met Laura at

the door. "Is not good, Miss Laura. You get sick and Miss Lavitia blame me."

"Stop your fretting because I'm not going to get sick, Juanita. I never catch a cold."

"Well, you go to bed. Teresa bring you soup."

"That's not necessary, Juanita. I'm going to get out of these wet clothes. Then I'll get something to eat. After that, I intend to go to bed and curl up with a good book."

The woman rolled her black eyes. "I go now to bed too." Nudging Laura with an elbow, she added, "But I no curl up with book."

Laura's eyes widened with shock and her cheeks deepened to crimson. "Juanita! You must delight in shocking people! Who . . ." Too embarrassed to finish the question, Laura turned away. Although curious, she did not have the nerve to continue the conversation.

The Mexican girl arched a brow, and then her eyes flashed with devilishness. "He is one of my people." Smiling, she added, "And he no smell of horse and cows like *gringo* cowboy. Teresa bring you soup first."

Laura nodded and hurried to her room. After shedding her wet clothes, she squeezed the water out of them and hung the garments up to dry. By the time she finished, Teresa tapped on the door and entered carrying a tray holding a steaming bowl of hot chili and a pot of tea.

Laura had just climbed into bed when the storm hit with full force. The windows rattled from the driving wind, and rain pelted the roof. At the continuous roll of thunder, Laura got out of bed and hurried to the window, peering out at the black night. Lightning flashes disclosed that the baked clay was not absorbing the rain quickly enough; water had begun to run in small rivulets.

Laura knew the heavy rain would be of grave concern to Zach. Flooding in the lower ground could put his herd in jeopardy, and she wondered what he would do. Would he be crazy enough to try to move his herd in the storm? She knew he would be desperate enough to try. And he couldn't do it alone.

For a moment she considered asking some of the Lazy R crew to help, but she knew she would only be wasting time. Whiskers was the only Lazy R hand who would even consider helping, and he was in Houston with Lavitia. There was no one but her to help Zach. They might not save all the cattle, but at least they could save some.

Dressing quickly, she stole out of the darkened house and ran across the yard. Entering the barn, she found Sunshine very restless; the little mare shifted nervously as thunder reverberated and lightning streaked the sky. After saddling the horse, Laura slipped into a waterproof slicker she found hanging in the barn, and rode south.

When she reached the Double H, Zachary was just preparing to ride out. "Laura, what are you doing here?" She could tell her presence distressed him.

"I thought you might need some help to move your cattle to higher ground," she shouted, trying to be heard above the roar of the wind.

"I sure can use the help, but it's getting treacherous underfoot. I'm afraid you might get hurt."

Rain was dripping off the brim of her hat and running down her face. "Don't worry about me, Zach. I can take care of myself. And I won't take no for an answer."

"Well, I haven't time to argue with you, so let's get moving." He wheeled his horse and took off.

The fury of the storm increased as they galloped toward the coulee where most of the herd had been grazing. Wind-driven rain pelted the earth with near-hurricane force. Luminous spears of lightning, followed by the deafening clamor of thunder, streaked from the sky and pierced the blackness of the trail ahead of them. Visibility was reduced to a few feet, their voices impossible to hear.

When Zach and Laura reached the cattle, water rolling down the sides of the granite walls had begun to flood the once-dry streambed. Cattle milled restlessly, seeking shelter as the mewling calves tried to remain with their mothers.

Laura and Zach began trying to drive the frightened herd to higher ground. Mercifully, the thunder and lightning abated, which helped to calm the nervous cattle, but the relentless rain increased the danger of flash flooding. Time and time again, either Laura or Zach had to double back to round up a stray animal.

Several times Sunshine stumbled on patches of slippery shale, and only Laura's quick tightening of the reins prevented horse and rider from tumbling.

Finally, after several gruelling hours, they succeeded in driving the herd to the higher and safer ground near the ranch.

"We've done all we can for now," Zach shouted, suddenly looming beside her. "Let's get back to the house." She nodded and followed him.

Weary and sodden, they returned to the cabin. "Get inside. I'll take care of the horses," Zach said.

Relieved to be out of the force of the wind and pelting rain, Laura wanted to sink to her knees inside the cabin. Instead, she hung up her slicker and hurried over to the fireplace. Her hands were shaking so much, she could barely strike a match to start a fire.

The door opened and the blast of wind almost extinguished the small blaze from the hearth. Slamming the door, Zach slid the bar in place to keep it firmly closed.

"Seems like the storm's letting up a bit," he said. "But I'm sure glad we're out of it." He shook off his poncho and hat and hung them on pegs on the wall.

"Do you think you lost any of your herd?" she asked worriedly as he hung his gunbelt beside the dripping clothing.

"I'll know in the morning. Good thing I already sold most of the herd."

Coming over to her, he hunched down before the fire and rubbed his hands in an effort to get warm. Then rising, he went to the hutch and came back carrying a towel. "Here, use this to dry off."

Zachary added several logs to the fire and within minutes the hearth radiated restoring warmth. She released her hair from the thick plait that hung down her back, then vigorously began to towel the sodden strands while Zachary set a pot of coffee to perk.

The quick shiver that shook her spine did not go unheeded by Zach. "If you want, you can put on one of my shirts."

"It's just my skirt that's wet."

Zach went to the bedroom and emerged carrying a worn pair of Levis. "Here, put these on and we'll hang up your skirt to dry out. I'm gonna change too." He left her and returned to the bedroom, this time closing the door behind him.

Laura quickly pulled off her boots. Her stockings were wet, so she removed them as well. She felt slightly wicked when she pulled Zachary's Levis over her own slim hips. Even though she stood midway between five and six feet tall, the legs of the pants bunched over the tops of her bare feet. Realizing she must look more comical than sinful, she grinned and sat down on the floor to turn up the legs of the trousers.

With her skirt and stockings now strung out to dry, Laura had become comfortably entrenched before the fire when Zach opened the bedroom door. He too had shed his boots. Dressed in dry clothes, he had taken the time to brush back his damp hair.

"Sure feels good to get out of those wet things. We'll feel even better when we get some hot coffee down us," he said.

"Zach, do you have a brush I can use?" she asked. "I have to get rid of these snarls."

He returned to his bedroom, reappearing carrying a silver-handled brush. "Here, use this. It was my ma's."

"Your mother's? Oh, Zach, I don't want to use this. You've been saving it."

"I want you to, Laura."

She finally relented, and he settled down beside her. "Sure was nice of you to come and help me. I'd still be out there if you hadn't." Grinning, he added, "You're a real good wrangler, Laura."

She laughed shyly. "I've had a chance to practice on the Lazy R herd." She began to run the brush through her long hair.

After pouring a mug of coffee for each of them, Zach handed her a cup. "Hope you like it black."

She did not like coffee, but she wasn't going to say so. As soon as the brew cooled a bit, she drank it just to get something hot down her.

Occasionally sipping from the cup at his side, Zach leaned back on an elbow and watched her brush her hair. "You sure have pretty hair, Laura. It's as black as a raven." He reached out and fingered a few strands. His voice deepened to a ragged huskiness. "And it feels like silk."

Impaled by his sapphire stare, she lowered the hairbrush. He laced his fingers through the thick hair, and shifted his gaze to her mouth. Mesmerized, she watched the slow descent of his head—her long, spiky lashes fluttered shut when his mouth closed over hers. The warm, sweet kiss set her pulse to pounding.

When he lifted his head, she smiled shyly. His responding grin tugged at her heart strings. "Did you mean it when you said you would be my girl?" he asked.

"Of course, Zach."

His gaze shifted to find the truth from deep within her brown eyes. "I've never had a girl before, Laura."

"And I never had a beau," she said, knowing that her eyes shimmered with love and trust.

"I figured you must have had a dozen marriage proposals by now."

"I just never gave much thought to men before, Zach."

"That doesn't mean they didn't give thought to you."

"Well, no man ever caught my eye until now."

Firelight warmed her flesh and cast her face in a rosy glow. He cupped her cheek in his palm. "You're the prettiest girl I've ever seen." His hand slid down her slender neck to where her quickened pulse throbbed against his touch.

Again he claimed her lips, this time more aggressively. She parted her lips and opened them to his. Guided by the undeniable force of inherent sensuality, she deepened the kiss.

She slipped her arms around his neck as his weight pressed her to the floor. At first, his tongue was tentative, then, finding no resistance, he grew bolder with exploring sweeps of the chamber of her mouth. Once again, she felt that exciting titillation draw at her breasts. Swelling, the sensation coursed through her body and settled into an exquisite tugging at the junction of her legs. Restlessly seeking closer contact, she shifted against him. His virile, male body responded instantly with a hardened bulge that pressed against her own demanding urgency. Instinctively, she parted her legs. Their clothing became the only barrier between the heated pressure of his throbbing arousal and her sensual core.

Zach raised his head and probed her eyes; her own gaze was confused. "We better stop, Laura."

"I know," she said.

Reluctantly adhering to an older code of morality that restrained the passions gripping their young bodies, they sat up.

Zach got up and walked over to the window. Glancing out, he said languidly, "Storm's over."

Her body still trembled with the turbulence raging inside of her . . . that storm had not subsided.

When she began to gather her damp clothing, he brought her a pair of his socks. "Wear these."

"I'll bring them back tomorrow," she said, offering him a grateful smile.

The water from their slickers had formed a pool on the floor. "I'm gonna ride back with you," he said, strapping on his gunbelt.

"You don't have to, Zach. It's late," she protested when he pulled the damp poncho over his head.

He set his wet Stetson on his forehead. "I'm not going to let you ride back alone in the dark." After helping her with her slicker, he grabbed his rifle. She wanted to ease his mind about what had just happened between them, but before she could think of what to say, he headed for the barn.

They rode slowly back to the Lazy R. The rain had added a silvery moisture to the parched earth so that it glowed in the moonlight like glass.

The red and gray glow of dawn had begun to haze the horizon by the time they reached the corral of the Lazy R. Before departing, he leaned across his saddle and lightly kissed her.

"I'll ride over tomorrow," she said.

"You mean today." He grinned. "Bye, Laura."

She watched him gallop away. "Bye, Zach," she murmured.

After unsaddling Sunshine, she slipped into the house. Wearily, she climbed into bed.

Laura slept until almost noon. By the time she had risen and dressed, the Lazy R crew had already returned to their normal routine. Only Teresa and the cook remained at the ranch.

Laura sat down at the table, and Juanita set a plate of ham and potatoes before her. "Good morning, Juanita. What a storm last night. Have you ever seen so much lightning?"

Juanita rolled her eyes. "Is true. Oh, that Benito!"

The woman's ecstatic sigh brought a quick smile to Laura's mouth. Then, recalling the titillating sensations she had felt in Zach's arms, her brow creased in a perplexed frown. Obviously Juanita had the answers to some of her nagging questions.

In a bold move, Laura pulled out a chair. "Juanita, sit down." Surprised, the maid seated herself in the proffered chair. Leaning toward her in confidence, Laura asked, "Juanita, what is it like to be . . . ah . . . you know . . . to be with Benito?"

"Oh, that Benito. *Ese es un hombre muy macho.*" She sighed rapturously.

Laura took a deep breath. "Well . . . ah . . . how do you feel, for instance, when he . . . ah . . . kisses you?"

Juanita clutched at her heart. "*¡Qué hombre!* My heart pound like drum. And when he kiss me . . ." She clutched her hands together. ". . . I am on fire!"

Feeling awkward and embarrassed, Laura pressed on. "And do you get a strong tugging . . . at your breasts . . . so that you want . . . Benito to touch them?"

"And kiss them . . . and suckle at them like a *niño*," Juanita added.

Laura's hand flew to her mouth. "Really! Oh, my," she gasped, her eyes widening with shock.

Caught up in excited reverie, Juanita continued to ramble. "And then I think I will die when his hands and his mouth make the love on my body until . . . until . . ."

"Yes, until what, Juanita?" Laura asked breathlessly.

The woman closed her eyes in sublime reflection. "Until he drives his *pico más tremendo* into me and . . . then—"

"And then what happens?" Laura beseeched, lifted to the limit of expectation.

Juanita's eyes suddenly popped open. "Is not for you to know. You are too young. Miss Lavitia would be angry with me if she hears that I tell you of this."

Laura turned crimson. "Oh, Juanita," Laura lamented. "She won't find out. You must tell me everything. I have to know."

"No. Is not proper. Benito will soon take me as his wife. When Mr. Zachary say he marry you, then you will learn for yourself." Clucking in sympathy, Juanita pushed herself away from the table and walked away.

Laura sat picking at her food and wondering if Zachary would ask her to marry him some day. Often she had lain at night envisioning Zach and herself as man and wife, laughing and joking together just as she had heard her parents do so many times. But most of her fantasies had been dominated with thoughts of being in his arms and feeling his muscular strength pressed to her own curves. Now that she had felt the excitement of his hands and mouth on her, she easily anticipated the realization of her dreams.

Just thinking about Zach started her pulse pounding. She shoved her plate aside and hurried to the barn to saddle Sunshine. Within minutes, she was headed for the Double H.

After a hard ride, she reined in Sunshine when she encountered three Lazy R riders stringing a wire fence along the bank of the stream that separated the two ranches.

"What are you doing?" she asked, appalled.

"Well . . . howdy, Miz Laura," Whitey Wright greeted with a simper. "Just followin' Miz Randolph's orders. She wants us to run a fence of this fancy new kind of wire she's tryin' out."

A string of posts had been driven into the river bank and rolls of wire placed about every twenty feet along the ground. Sharp barbs cut from sheet metal were fitted between the twisted strands of wire.

"That wire looks like it could rip the cattle or horses if they came near it," Laura said.

"Meant to," Whitey said. "It's called barbed wire. Suppose to keep what you want *in* . . . and what you don't want *out*," he taunted, glancing over at the Double H. "Heard tell that last year some farmer in Illinois got the idea for it. Seems funny that it took some sodbuster up in Illinois to think of it, 'stead of a good ol' Texas boy."

Their attention suddenly turned to a loud mewling from around the bend of the stream. A young calf had strayed across the shallow stream and had become bogged down in a mud hole. The frightened animal was bawling to its mother on the opposite bank.

The noise had attracted Zach as well. Seeing the young animal in trouble, he rode across the stream and roped the calf. After wrapping the loose end of the rope several times around the pommel of his saddle, he began to pull the calf out of the mud.

"Get off the Lazy R, Houston," Whitey ordered.

Zach glanced at Laura among the riders, then turned his back to them. "I will as soon as I free my calf."

Whitey walked over to him and took a quick look at the wallowing calf. "I don't see any brand on it."

"Haven't had time. But that's my calf. It just wandered over here." Zach pointed to the cow on the opposite shore. "You can see the Double H brand on its mother."

"That ain't no proof. 'Pears to me like you're rustling cows, Houston. Ain't that right, boys?" Whitey smirked. Having been often encouraged by Lavitia Randolph to harass the Houstons for any reason, the other two men nodded in agreement.

"Don't be ridiculous, Whitey. You know that's a Double H calf," Laura declared.

Zach succeeded in freeing the trapped animal. Climbing off his horse, he released the lariat. The calf splashed across the stream to its mother.

"Will you look at that?" Whitey snorted, feigning surprise. "Right before our very own eyes. Don't even wait 'til dark to do his thievin'." His mouth curled into a malevolent expression. "I think we oughta teach this rustler a lesson he won't forget, boys."

Zach turned just as Whitey rushed him. He managed to get off a punch that landed square on the jaw of the charging cowboy. Whitey reeled backwards.

The principle of fair play was never a consideration; the two other cowboys immediately jumped Zach and pinned his arms to his sides. Whitey drove his fist into Zach's stomach, knocking the wind out of him. Zach slumped over, but was yanked back up by the men holding his arms, and Whitey began to pummel Zach's face.

"Stop it!" Laura screamed, trying to pull Whitey away. Snarling, he shoved her aside, and she landed on her backside in the mud. She frantically glanced around for a weapon.

Blood streamed from Zach's nose and a cut on his

cheek. When Whitey paused to catch his breath, the two men released Zach's arms and, nearly unconscious, he slumped to the ground. Whitey's malevolent glance fell on a roll of the wire.

"Let's wrap him up all tidy-like, boys," he growled.

They dragged Zach to the bale. After stringing out some wire, they began to roll him in it. As the wire curled around Zach, the sharp barbs ripped at his clothing and cut into his flesh.

Laura pulled the rifle from the scabbard on Zach's horse. She fired a shot that kicked up the dust at their heels. Visibly startled, they turned to find her pointing the weapon at them.

"Cut him free this instant!" she ordered.

Squaring his shoulders, Whitey snickered in his insolent drawl, "You ain't gonna shoot us, Miz Laura, or you would have done it when you had the chance."

She responded instantly by putting a shot between his feet. "Cut him free right now, or my next shot's gonna be higher." Her eyes were as stony as marble. "Right in that area that you're so proud of, Whitey."

Suspecting now that she meant it, the cowboy paled. "Get the clippers, Sam."

Laura kept the rifle trained on Whitey as Sam retrieved the wire clippers and knelt down at Zach's side. "If I were you, Sam, I'd be very careful when you use those clippers," she warned.

"Yes, ma'am," the cowboy said.

"Give him a hand, Charlie," she snapped at the other cowboy. "You were quick enough about it before," she accused.

"Yes, Miz Laura," Charlie replied. "Didn't mean no harm by it. We was only joshin' around."

"Well, I don't see any humor in it, Charlie," she declared. This barbed-wire treatment on Zach was typical of the cruel sense of humor some cowboys perpetrated against animals and one another. She had witnessed these tragic escapades before. They had always sickened her as a child.

Gritting her teeth, she concentrated on keeping the rifle pointed at Whitey and tried not to think about Zach's pain as the cowboys nipped at the wire.

"That's the best we can do with clippers, Miz Laura," Charlie said.

"All right, the three of you get out of here. *Now*. And take that wire with you," she ordered.

They didn't have to be told twice. They hurriedly tossed the bales into the wagon.

"Your aunt's not gonna like you drivin' us off like this," Whitey threatened with a backward glance.

"Get moving," she ordered.

As soon as they pulled out, Laura fell to her knees beside Zach. He was bleeding from dozens of wounds all over his body. Pieces of wire were still embedded in his flesh. "Oh God, Zach," she sobbed.

He started to rise to his feet. Her hand trembled as she reached out to help him. "Don't. Don't touch me, Laura. Please," he cried out.

"Zach, we've got to get you to a doctor."

"No doctor. Let's just get back to the house."

"But you can't ride, Zach. There's still pieces of wire in you."

"I'll walk back," he said.

Carefully putting one foot before the other, he crossed the stream. His long-legged, relaxed stride had been reduced to a stiff hobble. She knew that every step, every movement was sending shock waves throughout his body. Biting her bottom lip to keep from sobbing, she trailed behind him, leading Sunshine and Zach's sorrel.

Once inside the cabin, he braced himself against the wall with his hands as she removed his boots and stockings. After setting several kettles of water on the stove to boil, she fortified herself for the task ahead. "Where are your scissors?" she asked.

"In the top drawer of the hutch." She found a sewing kit containing thread, needles, and a tiny pair of scissors.

Laura checked his rear and the back of his thighs. A small piece of wire still clung to his right thigh, but the thickness of his Levis and drawers had kept the barb from becoming deeply embedded. Gritting her teeth, she carefully worked the jagged piece of metal out of his flesh. He didn't utter a sound.

When she finished, she looked at him squarely. "Zach, to properly treat all your wounds, I'm afraid I'll have to cut your shirt and pants off you."

He nodded. Perspiration dotted his brow, blood oozed from his wounds, and he was becoming too weak to remain on his feet. She slit the shirt up the back and pulled it forward. Snagged by wire, the shirt clung to his arms and chest in several places. She cut away the material and tossed aside the shirt.

Next she lowered his trousers. The pants proved easier than the shirt because she had removed the wire from them. "Now let's get you into bed. I think it will be less difficult if you lie down." Stripped to his drawers, he moved to the bed and gingerly lowered himself onto his back. She began to remove more of the barbs.

"I'm sorry to be so much trouble, Laura." His eyes were glazed from pain.

"I'm the one who's sorry, Zach. Those were Lazy R riders who did this to you."

"It's not your fault. Besides, it's not the first time."

She halted her ministrations long enough to glance at his face. "You mean they did this to you before?"

"Oh, not with wire. But they've roped and dragged me a couple times. Shot my pet dog when I was ten. Couple of them even took a bullwhip to me once when I was about fourteen."

"Then it isn't just Whitey Wright. I thought he was to blame. He's so ornery and mean."

"No. Your aunt's the one behind it all. The trouble started after her father died. My dad always said Will Randolph was a fair man, but after he died, your aunt has always been able to find someone to do her dirty work."

"Haven't you reported it to the sheriff?" she asked, aghast.

"Maybe you haven't noticed that Lavitia Randolph's the queen bee around these parts. Everybody buzzes around to please her."

Laura had observed as much at the Fourth of July celebration, when it was evident that Lavitia's power extended far beyond the gates of the Lazy R.

"Why does my aunt hate you so much?" Laura asked, picking out scraps of shirt from one of his wounds.

"Dad told me she wants our land. But I think it's more than that."

"Maybe Aunt Lavitia wants her own private beach," she said, trying to sound lighter than she felt. She wanted to keep their minds off the unpleasant task at hand. She knew how much pain he was suffering, yet he never uttered a single complaint throughout the ordeal.

Laura had yet to attend to the most serious wound, a deep laceration on his left shoulder with a barb firmly embedded deep in the flesh. She saw she would not be able to work it free; she would have to dig out the barb with the tips of the scissors.

She paused momentarily from laboring over him. "Zach, I think this wound on your shoulder is the last one. But the barb is embedded deeper than the others."

He forced a grin. "Saved the best for last, huh?"

His battered face had paled, his voice had weakened, and with each breath, his strength appeared to be waning.

Drawing a deep breath, she steadied her trembling hand and began to probe the wound with the scissors. In a paradoxical twist of nature, the pain finally became too severe for Zach to bear—and then it mercifully released him. He passed out.

Chapter 6

O nce certain Zach was breathing normally, Laura felt relieved that he had passed out. She wished he had done so sooner to lessen his suffering. By the time she finished digging out all the wire, the water had come to a boil. After cleaning the wound, she threaded a needle. For a long moment she stood poised over the figure on the bed. She had never actually sewn flesh before, but she had seen her mother do it often enough to her father. Drawing a deep breath, she began to ply neat little cross stitches to the deep gash. She sighed with relief when the unpleasant task was accomplished.

Now she was faced with a very difficult decision for a chaste young woman to make. In order to properly cleanse the rest of Zach's wounds, she would have to remove his drawers. Laura realized she had no other option. *Thank God he's not conscious*, she thought with a maidenly blush.

Before she might lose her courage, she lowered his drawers past his hips and pulled them off his legs. With some darning in a spot or two, the drawers could be salvaged, she reasoned.

Laura sponged Zach's wounds with hot, soapy water. When she finished, none of the facial bruises Whitey had rendered on his helpless victim appeared serious; the shoulder wound was the only injury that required a bandage.

Laura continued with the warm, soapy sponge bath, rinsing the blood and mud off his long, muscular body. With acute concern for his welfare now behind her, she couldn't help but admire his naked form. Having been around horses and cattle most of her life, the differences between male and female organs were not a mystery to her. But for the first time, she had the opportunity to closely study a naked male physique—and more thrilling, the physique was Zach's. He had a long, superbly proportioned body of hardened muscle and bronzed skin with provocative patches of crisp dark hair that drew her attention and touch.

His body was more beautifully molded than she remembered; the flaccid mound at the junction of his legs more fascinating than she had fantasized.

No mother's touch on her infant child, no woman's caress on her lover's body could have been more tender than that of Laura's as she washed away the blood and grime from the heinous wounds inflicted upon him.

Laura sat at his bedside throughout the night making sure he remained covered as he tossed restlessly with a low fever.

By the following morning, she had washed and dried his bloodstained clothing, darned his drawers, and prepared breakfast. The fragrant aroma of baking biscuits and perking coffee filled the cabin.

"How are you feeling, Zach?" Laura asked when he awoke. Her warm brown eyes were fraught with concern.

"Okay, I guess." When he tried to sit up, she put a hand on his chest and gently pushed him back.

"Don't try to move around. You'll make those wounds bleed. Please lie still. I have to check your shoulder anyway."

Just the slight movement had made him ache, so he willingly obeyed. Laura sat down on the bedside and removed the bandage. Lying still, he fixed his blue-eyed gaze on her face as she examined the wound. She glanced at him, then smiled. He liked her smile—the way the dimples appeared to dance in her cheeks. And he liked waking up and finding her in his kitchen . . . and he liked the faint scent of lavender when she was near . . . and he liked . . .

"This should heal faster since it's stitched," she commented. "At least that's what my mother always said after she stitched up one of my father's wounds." She packed the wound with a clean towel.

"I feel like I've been trampled by a herd of mustangs. Hope I don't look as bad as I feel," he said lightly.

"Well . . . I have to say, Zach, you look pretty bad," she said gravely. Then she smiled. "But I think you'll live. Only you're going to have to move a little slower for a while. Your shoulder's the only serious wound. You're going to have to keep a bandage on it until it heals."

"You mean I'm not busted up inside?"

"Not that I can tell. Of course, I'm no doctor." Her brow creased with a worried frown. "I still think you should let me take you into town to be examined."

"I'll do just fine right here," he declared.

"In the meantime, would you like something to eat? I'm baking . . ." She suddenly stopped. "My biscuits!" She dashed from the room.

Smiling, Zach closed his eyes and returned to sleep.

A short time later, Laura returned carrying a bowl of oatmeal and several freshly baked biscuits. Gently, she put her hand on his cheek and he opened one eye.

"Just coffee," Zach decided.

"I think you should try and eat something, Zach. You've lost a lot of blood and food will help to strengthen you. I've put on a kettle of rabbit stew for your dinner."

"Rabbit stew? Where did you get rabbit?"

"I shot it," she said matter-of-factly. "Right outside the door. I'm surprised the shot didn't wake you."

When she helped him sit up in bed, Zach soon discovered he was naked. Mortified, he quickly pulled the blanket up to his chin and gave her an astonished, quizzical look.

She nodded and tried to appear nonchalant. "I had to . . . to treat your wounds."

Zachary appeared to struggle with her response for a lengthy moment, then he said, "Will you please get me a pair of drawers out of that chest?"

"After you eat. This oatmeal will be more palatable if you eat it while it's hot."

He silently ate the hot cereal and biscuits, washing the meal down with a cup of coffee, but she could tell that his thoughts continued to dwell on the issue of his nudity. When he finished eating, Zach handed her the bowl.

"I reckon you did what you had to do, Laura. Just don't get any ideas about bringing me the slop pot. I'll crawl to it, if I have to."

Laura forced back a smile. "Whatever you say, Zach." She rose to leave.

"Laura."

She turned at the door and looked back. "What is it, Zach?"

"Thanks for all you've done. I'd have been in a heckuva mess without you."

"I'm just thankful that your injuries aren't as bad as they might have been." She turned away.

"Laura." Once again, she turned back, her eyes questioning.

For a long moment he stared at her, waging an inner struggle. Finally he managed the words. "I . . . I love you, Laura Randolph."

Her heart leaped to her throat and tears threatened to cascade down her cheeks. She tried to keep her voice steady and her tone lighthearted. "No need to go overboard, Zach. I've heard it's not uncommon for a patient to fall in love with his nurse."

His face broke with his rarely used grin that always left her devastated. "Figured there had to be a good explanation for it," he said. She grinned back at him.

After washing the dishes, as much as she wanted to remain with him, she knew the time had come for her to leave. After setting the kettle on the hearth to stew, she saddled Sunshine for the ride back to the Lazy R.

Zach felt well enough to get out of bed and test his legs. He was unsteady on his feet, but she had the assurance he could fend for himself now.

"I'll try to come by as soon as I can get away," she told him outside as she prepared to mount her horse. "Don't try to ride for a couple days, Zach. You'll run the risk of opening your wounds."

"Yes, Nurse Randolph." Hesitantly, he reached out and cupped her cheek.

She didn't know if he drew her closer, or willed her closer, but only inches separated them. His steady, sapphire gaze looked into the warmth of her brown eyes. "You're the first woman who ever took care of me, Laura. Makes sense why men fall in love with their nurses, especially if they look like you."

He lowered his head and kissed her—a deep kiss. Hungry. Exciting.

When breathlessness forced them apart, she glanced up at him. Shaken by the passion in the kiss, Laura tried to toss it off lightly. "I guess you're stronger than I thought."

Then in a rash moment of uninhibited affection, she threw her arms around his neck and kissed him quickly. "I love you too, Zach." Too embarrassed to look him in the eye, she flung herself onto Sunshine's back and goaded the mare to a gallop.

Later that day, when Lavitia Randolph returned from Houston, Laura immediately complained to her aunt about the incident between Zach and the Lazy R hands. She described it in full detail.

By the time Laura finished, Lavitia's face had pinched up into the expression of disapproval Laura had learned to recognize. "It distresses me, Laura, that you raised a rifle to hands riding for the Lazy R."

Laura widened her eyes in shock. "They almost killed Zachary, Aunt Lavitia!"

"Rustling is a serious crime in this area, Laura."

"Rustling! Zach Houston is no more a rustler than I am," Laura declared indignantly. "That calf belonged to him. They all knew it as well as I did."

"Before I make any judgement on this matter, I'd like to hear their side of the story. I'll speak to them myself," Lavitia informed her. "But from what you've told me, it would appear Mr. Houston got exactly what he deserved."

Exasperated, Lavitia sat down at her desk. "I fail to understand why you choose to burden me with such petty grievances when there are more important matters to consider. My trip to Houston was unsuccessful; I didn't find a bull." She harrumphed in derision. "Since the war ended, every Yankee east of the Mississippi who thinks he can ride a horse has been coming to Texas and starting to run cattle. They're snatching up all the decent stock. Now I'll have to wait and go all the way to New Orleans for the spring auction. That means we'll be going all fall and winter with only Old Jethro for a bull."

Lavitia's mouth narrowed grimly, bitterness spilling over into her voice. "Do you know what a serious effect that'll have on the future size of the herd?" Her pale blue eyes appeared icy cold. "As a Randolph, that should be your major concern at this time. But you're just like your father, Laura. You worry more about those damn Houstons than you do your own family."

"What has Zachary Houston ever done to you, Aunt Lavitia? Why do you hate him so much?" Laura asked, appalled.

Lavitia's pale eyes narrowed. "I'm not accountable to you for my actions, young lady, any more than you feel obligated to justify your illicit conduct with this young man to me," she said, in a voice as hard as stone.

"Illicit conduct? How can you make such an accusation? Zach and I have done nothing to be ashamed about."

"You consider spending the night alone with him in his cabin 'nothing to be ashamed about'?" Lavitia challenged vindictively.

"He was wounded. I nursed him. That was all that happened."

Lavitia responded with a mocking smile. Frustrated, Laura spun on her heel and strode from the room.

Teresa was in the hallway and had overheard the conversation. She followed Laura up the stairway into the bedroom. With round, wide eyes, she glanced sadly at Laura. "*Señor* Zach is hurt?"

"He's going to be okay, Teresa. No thanks to Whitey Wright and his stooges."

"I am glad," Teresa said.

"Aunt Lavitia is being unreasonable as usual," Laura bemoaned. "I know she has the responsibility of running this big ranch, but she's so uncompromising."

Teresa nodded sympathetically, then she turned her head when a shout sounded from below. "Teresa, come here," Lavitia called out.

"You better go," Laura said with a sigh.

"Teresa!" This time the shout sounded more impatient.

Rising to her feet, Teresa offered one of her rare smiles. "But it is good Mr. Zachary will be okay."

As Teresa hurried from the room, Laura couldn't help but notice how pretty Teresa was when she smiled.

Fall slipped into a mild winter. An occasional norther sweeping across Galveston Island scattered snow flurries along the coast that soon melted the following day when the sun appeared. The Christmas holidays came and went. Laura gave Zach a new shirt she had sewn for him, and he presented her with a deerskin vest he had cut out and hand-stitched himself.

Throughout the winter, Zach spent most of his time rounding up and breaking wild mustangs to sell in the spring. And whenever Laura and Zach had the opportunity, they met on the beach. Holding hands, they sat bundled in their coats to stay warm and talked of their childhoods as they watched sea gulls whirling overhead or fog drifting in from the Gulf. Between shared kisses, they spoke of their plan to wed in the future.

They were in love and the few stolen hours they spent together were very precious.

Before Laura realized it, a year had passed since her arrival at the Lazy R.

Since the incident with the barbed wire, the relationship between Laura and her aunt had remained polite, but reserved. Therefore, Laura could not understand why Lavitia insisted upon having a party on the afternoon of Laura's eighteenth birthday. An open invitation had gone out to the local residents—and an invitation to the Lazy R from Lavitia Randolph was not to be ignored.

As a gift, Lavitia had ordered a fancy gown for Laura. The dress of pale green taffeta had capped sleeves and a long-waisted cuirasse bodice, the popular style made to mold the figure to perfection. A small bustle of green and white stripes of the same fabric flattered the slender sweep of Laura's spine. Several flounces of the same pattern flared around her ankles.

Teresa had spent an hour brushing and pinning Laura's thick dark hair on top of her head, and after an artful application of the curling iron, two long, thick sausage curls hung past her shoulder.

As the younger celebrants waltzed to the music from the small orchestra hired from Galveston for the occasion, the older folks sat on chairs lining the walls of the room and chatted as they watched the dancers.

At the far end of the long room, several large crystal bowls of tasty fruit punch were set on a long table holding trays of savory finger sandwiches and small decorative sponge cakes, also ferried in from a French restaurant in Galveston.

Juanita and Teresa carried in a tiered cake ablaze with candles. With the guests singing the traditional birthday song to Laura, she paused to make a wish, then blew out the candles to the clapping of the assembled guests.

As Laura sliced the cake, the room quieted to hushed whispers. She turned to see what had caused the silence, but her vision was blocked by the people clustered around her.

Across the crowded room, Lavitia Randolph had risen to her feet. Gradually the musicians stopped playing and lowered their instruments.

"How dare you enter this house. Get out at once." Aunt Lavitia's harsh command laced with scorn was directed to the young man who stood in the entrance.

"I only came to wish Laura a happy birthday, Miss Randolph," Zachary Houston replied politely.

Laura gasped at the sound of Zach's voice. She dropped the carving knife and began to shove her way through the crowd to reach him.

"You are not welcome on the Lazy R. Leave now, or I shall have the ranch hands drag you away," Lavitia declared. Without waiting for his reply, she turned to the maid. "Juanita, go to the bunkhouse and get some of the hands."

"That's not necessary, Miss Randolph. I'll leave. I should never have come. I don't want to spoil Laura's birthday party."

"Zach, wait!" Laura cried out, but he was gone by the time she wormed her way out of the crowd.

"Don't you dare chase after him," Lavitia commanded when her niece sped past her.

Laura yanked open the front door, but was too late to stop him. Zach was already galloping away. She leaned her head against the door and fought back her tears.

The room was buzzing again with noise and music when Laura returned despondently to the party. Awaiting her at the entrance to the room, Lavitia held her gray head rigidly, and a suggestion of a smile appeared on her narrowed lips. With a triumphant gleam, the woman's pale blue eyes met Laura's. Then, wordlessly, Lavitia turned away and rejoined the guests.

Dejected, Laura felt no joy during the remaining hours until the last guest departed. Then she quickly changed into her riding clothes. Before departing, she carefully wrapped a piece of cake in a napkin.

With her head held regally like a queen reviewing the colors, Lavitia stood at the foot of the stairway. Laura passed in review, but did not offer her even a side glance.

Darkness had descended by the time Laura galloped up to the Double H. Zach heard her approach and opened the door. Barefoot, he stood in the dim light gleaming from behind him and waited as she dismounted. Wordlessly, she ran into his arms. They kissed and he drew her inside, closing the door against the night's chill.

"Why didn't you wait today? I tried to reach you," she said, hurriedly shedding her coat and hat. Zach hung them on a peg on the wall.

"I never should have come in the first place, Laura. Should have had enough sense to know Lavitia would make a scene." He resumed his seat on the floor before the fireplace where he had been reading.

She plopped down on her knees beside him. "Well, I brought you a piece of my birthday cake just the same."

Grinning, he opened the napkin and took a bite of the confection. "Tastes as sweet as you do." With a pleased smile, she watched him as he finished the cake. "That was real good, sweetheart."

"And guess what? I blew out all my candles, so my wish will come true."

"Wish?" he asked, puzzled.

"You know, the wish you make when you blow out the candles on the cake."

"Oh." He glanced away.

Her smile slowly dissolved. Hooking her fingers under his chin, she turned his face to hers. "You really don't know, do you?" she asked, her astonishment mixed with shock.

"Guess I don't, Laura. I never had a birthday cake with candles."

"You mean you never had candles on your birthday cake?"

He raised his eyes to her. "I never had a birthday cake."

She stared, appalled. "Of course you did. Every child has a birthday cake at some time, Zach."

"Well, I suppose you're right," he relented. "But there was only Dad and me, and neither of us could bake a cake."

Her heart began to ache. How much more of childhood had been denied to him? He never knew a mother's love. Or touch. Simple luxuries she had taken for granted. Not even a birthday cake. He had grown up in a spartan existence, yet he never complained.

In a lighter vein, Zach added with a grin, "Dad did give me Buckwheat for my fifth birthday."

"Buckwheat? Was that a horse?" she asked, forcing a smile.

"No, my dog. Had him for five years before he died."

"You mean before someone from the Lazy R ranch shot him," she added sadly, remembering his telling her about the wanton killing of his beloved companion.

"Yeah . . . well, sometimes having someone to love for a short time is better than having no one at all, Laura." He stood up and went to the hutch. "I wanted to give this to you for your birthday." He handed her a small package.

Her eyes filled with excitement as her fingers pulled at the string. Glancing up at him, she smiled. He grinned back at her.

"You better let me open that," he said when the string knotted.

Zach patiently slipped off the tie, and handed the package back to her. Eagerly she unwrapped it, then gasped in surprise at the plain gold band looped on a chain.

"The ring was my father's. I know it's too big for your finger, but I thought you could wear it around your neck until I can afford to buy you one."

With trembling fingers she lifted the ring from the package. "Oh, Zach," she could only murmur.

He took it from her and held the ring up in the air. "The Double H brand's engraved on the inside. Do you see it?" She put her head close to his, and nodded. "My mother gave this to him on the day they were wed." He slipped the chain over her head. "The chain was my mother's. It's not real gold, but it belonged to her, so Dad always kept it."

Tears glistened in her eyes as she pressed the ring to her breast. "I'll always cherish them, Zach."

He reached out and touched her face, grazing her cheek with his fingertips. "You'll always be my girl, won't you, Laura?"

"Forever, my love," she whispered.

He lowered his head, his mouth claiming hers, his tongue examining the honeyed chamber that opened to him.

This was a game they had often played. His tongue circled her parted lips and, quite naturally, his teeth began to gently nip and tug at the tempting pink flesh of her lips. The sensation tantalized. Her own mouth sought to capture his, seeking more solid contact. She reached up and grasped his face between her hands.

Responding ardently, he pressed his lips to hers, tasting the sweetness over and over again until they were both intoxicated by the divine nectar of their aroused passion.

His hand slipped down to fondle her breast. But the contact did not satisfy Laura, for she had known the touch of his naked flesh, and she wanted him to know the touch of hers.

When she stepped out of his arms, his initial disappointment turned to confusion when she removed her boots and stockings. Then she pulled her bodice over her head. Her skirt followed. Only her camisole and drawers remained. Boldly, she raised her head and met his gaze; the eyes meeting hers were inflamed with passion. The next move would be up to him.

In a quick movement, he shed his shirt. Her glance shifted to the patch of dark hair on his chest which tapered in a narrow trail down his stomach and disappeared beneath the pants that hung loosely on his hips.

Transfixed, she watched his fingers fumble with the buttons of his Levis, then the pants slipped down his long legs and he stepped free of them. He was not wearing drawers.

For a brief moment she felt rising panic at the sight of the extended phallus projecting from the nest of black hair. Then it became too late for doubts because he reached out and pulled the camisole over her head.

Now, for the first time, her firm, round breasts fell under the perusal of his hungry gaze. His dark sapphire eyes devoured the sight of the milky-white mounds with their dusky puckered tips hardened to pointed peaks. The chain holding his father's ring nestled between them.

His loins flooded with hot blood. Restraint no longer remained possible to Zachary, in the throes of sexual awakening.

Powerless to stop, he claimed her mouth with hot sweeps of his tongue. She welcomed this invasion, hungrily wanting more. Divine sensation swelled her breasts and streaked out to coil around the sensitive hub between her legs.

Lust carried him beyond reason as his palm closed over one breast. It filled his hand. In a compulsive search for assuagement, he lowered her to the floor. Cupping the underside of one of the quivering mounds, he brought it to his mouth.

Like a nursing babe, he suckled the firm globe. She

arched her back reflexively, and he shifted his mouth to the other upthrust breast. Low, blissful moans escaped her lips as he suckled, licked, nipped, tugged—then suckled again.

She began to thrash beneath him, her breath coming in ragged gasps. His palm flattened against her to steady her squirming body and encountered her cotton drawers. He slid his hand under the waistband, his roughened fingertips against her bare flesh creating an excitement that crept ever nearer to the throbbing core of her passion.

He buried his mouth in the cushioned cleavage of her breasts, then his tongue toyed with the sensitive peaks as he shoved the drawers past her hips. He tossed them aside and his hand slid up the bare slender limb to the junction of her legs. He parted her thighs and palmed the heated center.

As if he were unaware of his own movements, his fingers massaged her with the same voracious fervor with which his mouth and tongue feasted on her breasts. She writhed mindlessly, her body convulsing with spasmodic tremors. Then, through her delirium, she felt him drive into her, stretching her virginal chamber until she thought it would burst. Pain replaced rapture. She began to struggle to free herself, but he had gone beyond halting. She sobbed when he pierced the thin membrane and sunk deeper into her, his seed flooding her womb.

He collapsed on her, cushioning his head once again against the swell of her breasts. Only the sound of their raspy breathing carried to her ears.

She opened her eyes when he rolled off her. He was staring down at her, his eyes suffused with guilt. "I hurt you, didn't I?"

"A little," she lied.

"God, Laura, I'm sorry." He lay back, covering his eyes with a bent arm.

"It doesn't matter, Zach. Truly it doesn't." She lowered his arm away from his face and leaned across him.

"I love you, Zach." She pressed a kiss to his lips.

His hands clutched at her back, drawing her closer against him. "I never wanted to hurt you, Laura."

"I know," she said. She laid her cheek against his chest and thought of her conversation with Juanita. In her description of making love, she had never mentioned the pain. Laura raised her head again and gazed into his tormented eyes. "Did you . . . enjoy it, Zach?"

His arms tightened. "Oh, God, yes, sweetheart! It was . . . ah . . ." He shook his head helplessly. "I don't know the words to describe it."

Her smile carried to her eyes. "Then I'm glad." She caressed his muscled chest, then slid her hand up to his shoulder. Her stroking fingers encountered a scar on his shoulder—a reminder of that nefarious incident with the barbed wire.

But more, the disfiguring mark was a symbol to her of the pain and suffering he had born so stoically throughout his life. She lowered her head and pressed a kiss to the puckered flesh.

"When we get married, things will be different for you. I'll make you so happy, Zach," she said fervently, her heart bursting with love for him. "You'll see."

Zach rolled over and cupped her face in his hands. His eyes gazed solemnly into hers. "You already have, Laura. The past is over. Your love makes up for anything I've ever missed. Nothing matters anymore to me but you." His eyes deepened with anxiety. "I could never bear to lose you, Laura."

Her eyes glowed with love for him; her heart felt near to bursting. "You never will, Zach. I'm your girl forever. Remember?"

His adoring gaze swept every facet of her face. "It's as if you're a part of me now . . . as if our souls are joined."

"They are, Zach. Our souls and our hearts . . . and now our bodies."

He kissed her, then he lay back and drew her to his side.

She cuddled contentedly against him, her cheek pressed to his chest. When he toyed lightly with her breasts, much to her amazement she felt her body responding again to his exciting touch. He lowered his head to kiss her, and she willingly opened her mouth under his urgent prodding. The tender kiss soon deepened with aroused passion.

"I love you, sweetheart," he murmured in a provocative whisper at her ear. The hard bulge of his organ pressed against her side. His body stiffened and he tried to pull away, but somehow found her tighter in his arms. "Oh, God, Laura, I need you. But I don't want to hurt you anymore."

Her arms curled around his neck, drawing him to her. "Make love to me, Zach. I want you too."

Their bodies melded together as he entered her again. This time she felt no pain. He sucked in his breath when she tightened around him, and in perfect rhythm, the sensual waltz of lovers began. Their rapture escalated in an ever-swelling tempo until, at last, the dance of ecstasy ended in a triumphant crescendo that wrenched a cry of jubilation from them both.

Chapter 7

Throughout the night, Lavitia had waited for Laura to return. Stripes of red had begun to marble the sky by the time Laura and Zach finally rode up to the Lazy R. Lavitia snorted in disgust at the sight of Laura nestled in the circle of Zach's arms. Her mare trailed behind them.

As they lingered over their good-bye kiss, Lavitia knew the young lovers were unaware of her watching them from the darkened shadows behind her bedroom curtains. When Zach finally rode off, Lavitia Randolph stepped away from the window in silent fury. Her pale, calculating eyes narrowed to slits, and her lips compressed into a line of grim determination. She had purposely given Laura the birthday party in the hope that one of the young men would distract her away from her obsession with Zachary Houston. Instead, the ungrateful little chit had run right back into his arms.

"Well . . . happy birthday, my dear niece," she murmured ominously. "We'll just see about that."

The next morning Lavitia did not make any reference to the previous day's squabble, and the two women returned to their normal weekly routines in a mutually undeclared truce.

During the weeks that followed, Zach branded the calves in preparation for selling the remainder of his herd. He had also corralled more than a dozen mustangs, and with only a few remaining to be broken, he planned to finish the task once he disposed of the cattle herd.

Laura's and Lavitia's tenuous truce became threatened on a Sunday morning in April when Laura appeared at the breakfast table in riding clothes. She had agreed to help Zach drive the cattle to Bay Town that day.

"You are not properly dressed for church, Laura," Lavitia said, glancing askance at her niece.

"You'll have to excuse me today, Aunt Lavitia. I've promised Zach I would help him drive his cattle herd to Bay Town."

"Sunday is the Lord's day of rest, Laura," Lavitia reminded her, managing to stay outwardly calm.

"Perhaps so, Aunt Lavitia, but Zach has no day of rest. There's too much for him to do alone. When we get married, I'll be able to give him more help."

"You intend to marry this young man, Laura?" Lavitia's extreme displeasure was reflected in her tone of voice.

"Of course, Aunt Lavitia. Zach and I love each other. As soon as he pays off the bank note, he'll be able to afford to marry me."

"First things first," Lavitia remarked. Her face remained impassive, but as she lowered her head, a wily gleam glowed in her eyes. The glint remained as she watched Laura ride away.

A foreboding of bad news struck Laura when she reached the Double H and saw that the corral which had contained the mustangs was empty. "Where are the horses?" she asked, aghast.

"Gone. Somebody scattered them last night." Zach's young face was drawn with frustration. "It'll take weeks to round them up again. Damn it, Laura, all that work for nothing."

"Oh, Zach." Laura wanted to cry, but she held back her tears, trying to show as much strength of character as he. "I suppose it was some of the Lazy R hands," she said desolately.

"Who else would it be?" he snapped, and angrily stormed away.

Laura hurried after him. She grabbed his arm and faced him. "But, Zach, it's not my fault."

"I didn't say it was. But the horse you're riding is wearing the Lazy R brand, isn't it," he said angrily.

He might as well have slapped her face. Unable to believe what she had heard, she stared at him—her sorrowful brown eyes wide and fearful. Zach drew in a shuddering breath, then shoved back his hat and pulled her into his arms.

"I'm sorry, honey . . . I didn't mean it. That was stupid. Please forgive me."

Forcing back her tears, she nestled her cheek against him, but her heart lay heavy in her chest. Had her aunt succeeded in driving the first wedge between Zach and her?

The same thought must have crossed his mind, for his next words calmed her dread. "We won't let anyone or anything come between us." Stepping back, he looked steadily into her stricken face. "Nothing is as important as our love, Laura. All that matters is that we still have each other." Grinning crookedly, he slipped a finger under her chin and tipped her face up to meet his hypnotic gaze. "You'll always be my girl?"

When she nodded, he lowered his mouth to hers. At the first touch of his warm lips, Laura's lingering fears were forgotten. Her lips opened under the demand of his as he drew her closer against his hard body.

They drove the small cattle herd into Bay Town. However, as Zach had anticipated, the proceeds from the sale did not come near to meeting the payment due on the note. Hand in hand they left the cattle pens and headed for their mounts. "What are you going to do now?" Laura asked worriedly.

"I'll ride into town tomorrow morning and talk to Mr. Davis at the bank. Maybe he'll give me another extension on the note. If he does, I'll try rounding up those mustangs again." He slipped an arm around her shoulders in a reassuring hug. "Don't worry, honey. I'll work it out somehow."

"Will you look at the lovebirds, boys. Ain't they purty?" The mocking voice had come from Whitey Wright, who lounged against a nearby building along with Sam Benson and Charlie Johnson. Laura and Zach stopped and looked at the speaker.

Stepping forward, Whitey twisted his mouth into a smirk. "You're lookin' a lot better than the last time I saw you, Houston. By the way, I ain't seen no pay for that barbed wire you walked away in." He laughed at his own joke.

"Been hoping to run into you, Whitey," Zach said. "Have to settle up that little score with you."

"No time like the present, Houston. Right boys?" Whitey said, nudging an elbow into the side of his closest cohort.

"You've done enough damage for a while, Whitey Wright," Laura declared. "Don't you boys start with your bullying again."

Zach gently shoved her aside. "Honey, you go to the horses and wait." He unfastened his gunbelt and handed it to her. "Take this with you."

With Zach now weaponless, Whitey grew bolder. "Yeah, honey, you go fetch the horses. You'll need one to tote your boyfriend's carcass out of here when we get through with him. Let's get him, boys." With clenched fists, the three men prepared to converge on Zachary.

"Not so fast." The telltale click of a rifle cock brought them to an immediate standstill. Turning, they discovered Whiskers Merten. "Let's keep it a fair fight, boys." He motioned with his rifle. Sam and Charlie lowered their arms and stepped back. With Whiskers's attention focused on his two confederates, Whitey started to inch a hand toward the pistol on his hip.

Laura snatched Zach's Colt from the holster. "Don't try it, Whitey. Get rid of your gunbelt."

"Laura, you stay out of this," Zach said. "This is my fight."

She stood her ground, her eyes never wavering from the bully. "And real slow, Whitey, if you please," she warned. "You're not beyond shooting down an unarmed man."

Glaring at her, Whitey unbuckled the belt. Laura kicked it aside and then holstered Zach's gun.

"Kind of looks like the odds have evened up, doesn't it, Whitey?" Zach said.

Zach's first blow sent the cowboy stumbling backwards. Whitey regained his footing and charged back. Both men were equal in height and weight, both muscular and powerful from years of hard work. Now, driven by hatred and vengeance, they pummeled each other mercilessly. Laura turned away cringing each time one of Whitey's blows fell on Zach.

The scene attracted the townsfolk and soon a crowd had gathered to watch: the women silent and disapproving, the men cheering and hooting whenever a well-aimed blow found its mark.

Zach dealt a blow to Whitey's chin that knocked him off his feet. The crafty coward gathered a fistful of dust and jumped to his feet, tossing the dirt into Zach's face and eyes. Momentarily blinded, Zach lowered his guard to brush the dust out of his eyes. Whitey charged and drove his head into Zach's stomach.

Winded, Zach doubled over, but he managed to grab Whitey's shirt and pulled the bully to the ground. They grappled in the dust, each man trying to deliver a damaging blow to the other.

The crowd scrambled in all directions as the thrashing bodies rolled toward them. Whitey broke free and stumbled to his feet. Blood streamed from his nostrils and it was clear that he had begun to buckle under Zach's incessant blows. He tried to bolt away, but Zach tackled him. Drawing back, Zach threw a punch that flattened Whitey.

Whitey lay on the ground, too dizzy to rise. Zach got to his feet, and stood over him with clenched fists, but Whitey had had enough. With a final look of contempt at the coward, Zach turned his back and walked away.

Whitey used that opportunity to crawl over and snatch the pistol from his discarded gunbelt lying in the dust. But a warning from the crowd alerted Zach, and he turned in time to see Whitey take aim. Zach threw himself against Laura to knock her out of the line of fire, and the shot went wild, fortunately harming no one.

"Don't try it again, Whitey." The obdurate command came from Sheriff Barkin, who stood nearby with a drawn pistol in hand. "We don't go for backshooting in Bay Town." Seeing the odds against him, Whitey threw down his pistol.

The sheriff looked at Lavitia Randolph, who had also just arrived on the scene after leaving church. "You hirin' backshooters at the Lazy R now, Miz Randolph?"

The attention of the clustered spectators turned to Lavitia. Because of the woman's position in the community, the local townsfolk had willingly closed their eyes to her actions against the Houstons as long as no loss of life had been involved. But this attempt to shoot Zach Houston in the back by one of her ranch hands could not go unchallenged.

The tiny woman lifted her head, and her pale-eyed glare bored into the man on the ground. "Whitey, that fool act of yours could have killed my niece. I want you to pack up and get out. Be sure you are gone from the Lazy R by the time I return there today." She made no reference to Zach Houston.

"And if you're still in this county by sundown, Wright, I'm lockin' you up," the sheriff declared. "Now get movin'."

Whitey scrambled to his feet and wiped his bloody face on his shirtsleeve. He glanced at Lavitia Randolph. Her stern countenance remained inflexible. Sam and Charlie both lowered their eyes when his gaze shifted to them.

"What the hell!" he said with contempt. "I've seen enough of this territory anyway. There's plenty of other towns . . . plenty of other ranches. Been thinkin' about ridin' on for some time now."

Picking up his gunbelt, he started to leave. Hesitating for a moment, he looked back at Zach. "Heard those mustangs you've been bustin' your butt over ran off on you last night." He shook his head, his tongue clicking against his teeth. "Too bad, Houston. Maybe Miz Randolph there might have a guess just where they wuz headed." With a cocky saunter, he moved away.

A hushed gasp followed the bold accusation. Everyone stared at Lavitia Randolph. With an arrogant lift of her head, the tiny woman's steadfast gaze never faltered. "Mr. Stevens, I have some purchases I would like to make." Squaring her shoulders, she turned and entered the general store. The shopkeeper followed.

The crowd quietly dispersed. Despite their disapproval of Whitey's actions, no one came to offer moral support to Zach. Not with Lavitia Randolph in town.

The distressed look in Laura's eyes conveyed her feelings as she handed Zach his gunbelt. He strapped on the belt, then picked up his Stetson, shook off the dust, and plopped it on his head.

Laura's eyes glistened with moisture and her chin quivered as she took her handkerchief and wiped away the blood that trickled from the corner of his mouth.

"I'm okay, honey," Zach said. He slipped an arm around her shoulder. "I just need a cup of coffee. Let's go to the diner."

He used two of the dollars from the cattle sale to buy lunch for him and Laura. After eating, the couple rode slowly back to the Double H. The day was unusually warm, and they halted at a copse of spreading oaks to water their horses.

"Well, after today, I'm sure the whole town will know how we feel about each other," Laura said.

"Good. Now we don't have to keep our feelings a

secret any longer," Zach said. He walked over to one of the trees.

Laura sat down and propped her chin on her knees as Zach traced the outline of a heart with his knife on the trunk of the tree. He carved their initials in the center of the heart. When he finished, he turned around, grinning. "What do you think?"

"Zachary Houston, you have missed your calling," she enthused. "You should have been an artist." But she couldn't help teasing. "'Z H Loves L R,'" she read, straight-faced. "Who are they?"

"Who are they?" Sitting down behind her, he stretched out his legs alongside hers. His arm hooked around her waist and he drew her to him. Sighing, she settled back against the firm wall of his chest.

He pressed his cheek against hers, his warm breath fluttering the hair at her ear. "Us. That's our brand. Yours and mine. For God and the whole world to see." His lips slid to the sensitive hollow behind her ear. "Zachary Houston loves Laura Randolph," he whispered.

She nestled even closer against him, and his embrace tightened in response. When his hand cupped her breast, she felt its warmth through her bodice. His fingers worked the buttons until he could easily slip his hand into the opening. Then she felt him lift her camisole and fill his palm with her breast.

She closed her eyes and savored the sensation. His thumb gently rasped the nipple, sending erotic waves to her loins. She was unaware he had freed her bodice until she felt his other hand begin to massage her other breast. Coos of bliss emanated from her throat.

Her breath quickened as his hand slid under the band of her skirt, into her drawers and past the soft dark curls until it reached the throbbing center of her need.

"Oh, Zach," she groaned when his fingers covered, caressed, then probed. His name became an incessant purr from her lips as her body shuddered under wave upon wave of rapturous sensation.

He shifted, turning to lay her on the ground. His mouth found hers. Hungry. Waiting. Moving beneath his. Returning his demand with her own aching desire.

When he finally wrenched his mouth from hers, she was breathless. Shoving up her camisole, he feasted his gaze on the beauty of her breasts. Then he succumbed to temptation and lowered his head to draw a turgid peak into his mouth.

Her hands reached into his dark hair and pressed him tighter to her breasts as his tongue sent exquisite shock waves through her. When he raised his head, she opened her eyes. He sat up and began to pull off her boots and stockings.

Her slumberous eyes were leaden with arousal. Unresisting, she waited as he released her skirt and pulled off her drawers.

Now that she lay naked before him, he gazed on the curve of her slender neck and shoulders, her upthrust breasts, the silken length of her waist and hips, and the dark patch above her long, slender legs.

Hard and aching, he tugged at his clothing until he was free of it and then he stood above her, the throbbing need of his virile, male body in bold erection.

With each encounter, the two lovers had discovered new paths of intimacy with which to delight each other—ways of touching, stroking, moving, kissing, tasting. Ways of pleasing . . . and of being pleased.

Their complete commitment transcended any barriers of modesty or morality, and the mutual cravings of their passions were made virtuous by the purity of their love.

Smiling, she opened her arms to him and he lowered his body to hers.

Later as Zach basked in the afterglow of their lovemaking, he stretched out on his side with his head cradled in his hand. His eyes caressed Laura as he lightly ran his fingers across her dusky nipples.

"I never knew the human body could be so beautiful," he said in a low murmur.

Love swirled in her eyes as she reached up and cupped his cheek. "I didn't either until I saw yours."

He slowly walked his fingers down to the indention on her stomach, then idly drew circles around the navel with his forefinger.

"Zach, what are you doing?" She giggled. Then she sighed when he dipped his head and pressed a kiss to the navel. She threaded her fingers through his hair. "Oh God, I love you, Zach," she whispered.

He raised his head and saw desire in her eyes. Shifting, he leaned over and kissed her, sending the passion he had ignited spiraling through her. When he rolled to his back she followed. Straddling his hips, she sat up.

"Why, Miz Laura, you plannin' on goin' ridin'?" he joshed.

"Guess that depends if the bangtail I've mounted still has some run in him." The devilment in her eyes caused him to grin broadly.

Accepting the bold challenge, he raised his dark brows in amusement. "Oh-h-h . . . is that right, lady. Well, I've heard tell there's a lot more to riding than just sitting on a horse with your legs dangling."

She arched her own delicate brow. "Well, my daddy always claimed that the whole trick to good riding is to keep one leg on each side of the horse and your mind in the middle."

With a slow sensuous glide, he slid his hands up her legs and rested them against the outside of her thighs. "'Pears like you got the leg part right, ma'am. Now . . . hope you listened to your daddy . . ." he grasped her hand and directed it to his male member, ". . . about minding the middle?"

"Oh, my mind's on the middle all right," she said throatily and began to caress his swollen phallus. The corded muscles of his arm stretched tautly as he tightened his grasp on her thighs. Groaning, he closed his eyes. She lifted her hips and brought him into her.

As the tempo of his thrusts escalated, she closed her eyes, threw back her head, and rode mindlessly out of control until she cried out in an ecstatic release and his shuddering climax filled her with the seed of his love. Then, breathless, she collapsed onto his chest and he gathered her into his arms.

The following afternoon, Laura waited on tetherhooks, wondering how Zach was doing with the banker. As soon as she finished her bookkeeping, she decided to ride over to the Double H and surprise him by making a meal for him.

By the time Zach returned, the sun had set. He stopped in the doorway to survey Laura's handiwork. Two plates, napkins, knives, and forks were arranged on a red and white checkered tablecloth she had spread on the floor before the fireplace. Flanked by a pair of candlesticks, a small bouquet of bluebonnets in a water glass graced the center of the setting. The candles and the glow from the fireplace offered the only light in the cabin. Holding her breath, she waited for his reaction.

"Gosh, Laura, this is really nice."

Relieved by his comment, she smiled enthusiastically. "I used your mother's plates. Her tablecloth and napkins, too. I hope you don't mind."

"No . . . no, that's great." He took off his hat and hung it up. "I've never used them before."

"Well, sit down while I put the meal on. Everything's ready."

He came over and sat down on the floor, crossing his long legs. "It sure smells good."

"I roasted a chicken." She went to the stove and opened the oven. After lifting out a pan of chicken, she removed two baked potatoes.

"Chicken? Where'd you get a chicken?"

She glanced over her shoulder. Her eyes sparkled with devilment. "From my aunt's henhouse."

His heart seemed to leap to his throat at the sight of her dimpled grin. "Hey, if you're not careful, you're liable to get strung up for chicken rustling," he joked.

Holding a bowl of dandelion greens, she sat opposite him and crossed her legs. "Now tell me what the banker said."

His face sobered and he toyed with the food on his plate. "What did he say, Zach?" she repeated.

"I have two weeks to get off the Double H." The emotionless declaration caught her off guard.

"What?" She put down her fork. "Why wouldn't Mr. Davis extend your note?"

"Because the bank didn't really own it. "

"I don't understand. If the bank didn't own it, who did?"

"Laura," he said with a deep sigh, "who do you think owns it? Your aunt, of course. I guess your grandfather put up the money for the loan years ago. The bank's just the fiduciary for William Randolph. After he died, as long as we were paying the note, Lavitia couldn't do anything about it, as much as she would have liked to."

Laura jumped to her feet. "Well, what are you going to do about it? This is your home. You've lived on this ranch your whole life. Are you just going to let her take it away from you?"

Zach shoved aside his plate. "Laura, she already has. She owns the Double H. I don't have the money to fight her. If I did, I never would have lost the ranch to begin with."

"It's not fair . . . it's just not fair," she whimpered, pacing the floor. "You've lived on this ranch your whole life," she repeated sadly. No longer able to control herself, she went over and gazed out the window, hiding her tears.

Zach got up and went over to console her, drawing her back against him. "Honey, please don't cry. Maybe it's for the best. My dad worked this ranch for twenty years and couldn't make a go of it. I've still got the money from selling my cattle. I heard there's some homesteading near Brownsville. Thought maybe I'd go down and see if I can stake a small spread."

She turned in his arms, her eyes round with alarm. "You're going away?"

"Not for long. Soon as I find a place, I'll come back and get you. Then we'll get married just as we planned. It'll be a fresh start, honey. You lost everything and had to start over, and you made it."

She cupped his cheek in her hand. "Only because of you, Zach. Your love is what got me through . . . drove away the nightmares."

"And your love will get me through this . . . like it got me through the loss of my dad."

Her eyes glistened with tears as she smiled at him. "I'm the one who's supposed to be trying to cheer you up. Not the other way around."

His arms circled her waist, drawing her nearer. "You do cheer me, sweetheart. Just knowing you're close cheers me," he murmured right before he kissed her.

He took her hand and drew her back to the fireplace. "Come on, honey. I want to see if your cooking tastes as good as you do."

Chapter 8

Laura returned to the Lazy R, and immediately sought out her aunt. As usual, Lavitia was sitting behind her desk. "Aunt Lavitia, why did you buy the note on the Double H?" she demanded.

Lavitia put down her pen and leaned back in the chair. "I have run the Lazy R for years, Laura—*and I alone*, thanks to your father shirking his responsibilities by running away," she said acridly. "In that time, I have expanded the ranch whenever the opportunity presented itself. I see no reason why this latest acquisition should be any different."

"Because you did it just to destroy Zachary Houston," Laura declared.

"You may think what you choose, Laura." Lavitia picked up a pen and resumed writing. "I should also tell you that I have dismissed Teresa."

"Teresa? But why?" Laura asked, shocked.

"I'm sure you know why as well as I. Since *I* run this ranch, *I* set the rules. Teresa has grown so attached to you that her loyalties have become misguided. A pity that you dragged the young girl into your intrigues."

"Teresa was never disloyal to you. She's just been very kind to me, that's all. Her parents are dead, Aunt Lavitia. She has no place to go."

"I'm aware of that, Laura, which is more reason why she shouldn't have betrayed me," Lavitia retorted without the least sympathy.

"Betray you!" Laura exclaimed. "In what way? By showing me some kindness?" Laura cried out in frustration. "Where is she now?"

"I understand Juanita has taken the girl in."

"That's no place for her. Juanita's getting married soon. She won't want Teresa around. Please, Aunt Lavitia, I beg you to reconsider."

"I have made my decision," Lavitia announced in a rancorous voice. "Teresa has lost the privilege of working in the house."

"You're just a bitter and spiteful old woman, Aunt Lavitia. I understand why my father left here."

Lavitia's hand paused in writing, but she did not glance up. "I am sorry you feel that way, Laura, considering all I have done for you. Perhaps I should not be surprised that you are as stubborn and self-centered as your father."

Once again she put aside the pen. She stood up, her shoulders rigid and head held high. Moving to the door, she glanced neither right nor left. "I will be sailing for New Orleans on Wednesday to attend the bull auction. I had intended to allow you to accompany me, since I thought visiting the city would be an exciting experience for you. However, your behavior leaves me little choice. You shall remain behind. Perhaps you can put the time to good use by reflecting on how to improve your attitude." She walked out of the room without a backward glance.

Laura gave little thought to Lavitia's admonition in the days that followed. She was too upset about poor Teresa and Zach's leaving the Double H to lament over a missed trip to a big city. However, on the day of Lavitia's departure, Laura did go with her aunt as far as Galveston. Out of respect, she placed a good-bye kiss on Lavitia's cheek.

As the ship sailed from the harbor, Laura turned away, glad to be rid of the unpleasant woman whom she held directly responsible for Zach's loss of the Double H.

She drew up abruptly when she saw the very focus of her thoughts perched on one of the many crates piled on the wharf. Grinning, Zach stood up, and with a squeal of pleasure, Laura rushed into his open arms.

"What are you doing here?"

"I came to Galveston to see if I could get a good price for my sorrel. Thought I'd have a better chance here than in Bay Town."

"Oh, Zach," she said sadly, thinking of how much he had depended upon the stallion. She slipped her hand into his.

Together they explored the sights of Galveston. Laura had never seen such a grand city. When they reached the Strand, the famous financial and commercial heart of the city, she stared with mouth agape at the tall buildings with their cast-iron fronts. They passed before a seemingly endless variety of establishments: banks, cotton exchanges, shipping companies, restaurants, a telegraph office, a grand hotel, and even a Chinese laundry.

They rode the streetcar, walked the sidewalks, and crossed paved streets lined with gaslights. Standing on the train trestle that spanned the Gulf to the Texas coast, they watched a train carrying freight bound for Houston. They stopped to admire an elegant opera house at Tremont and Market, and gawked like children at the stately Victorian mansions lining Broadway and Market Streets.

Zach slipped his arm around her waist and drew her to his side. "Someday, we'll have a house just like this," he promised when they paused to admire a gracious three-story brick villa set amidst sprawling lawns and towering palms.

"I'll be happy with just a one-room cabin as long as we're together," she assured him.

Toward evening, they sat on a park bench surrounded by fragrant dark red and salmon-colored oleander. Soon, a roving Mexican band stopped to serenade the smiling, and so obviously in love, young couple.

"We had better think about getting back," Zach reminded her as the band strolled away. "The next ferry will be leaving soon for Bay Town."

Laura sighed deeply. "This has been a wonderful day, Zach."

He reached out a hand and pulled Laura to her feet. "I'll check on my sorrel to see if I've got a buyer, then we'll leave."

They walked down Market and turned onto Postoffice Street. Too late, they realized they were in the vice district of the city. Laura was appalled by the sights and sounds. Tinny piano chords and raucous laughter came from several saloons. She gaped openly at the colorful, suggestive posters tacked to many buildings. The billboards seemed to promise delights that far exceeded conventional vaudeville theater. Her eyes widened with shock as scantily-clad prostitutes called out from the balconies of bawdy houses to the passing gentlemen and groups of sailors on the street below.

Laura clutched Zach's hand tighter when a brazen young woman linked her arm through Zach's and tried to pull him into the open door of a saloon.

"You're the best-lookin' thing I've seen on this street since I got here, sweetie." The curly-headed blonde fluttered long, dark lashes at him. "Come on inside, good lookin', and I'll show you the real sights of Galveston," she said, flashing a wicked smile.

"No thanks, ma'am. Not at this time," Zach said good-naturedly, extricating her arm from his.

"The nerve of the woman!" Laura stammered as they moved on.

"Ah . . . she was just joshing," Zach said.

Laura stopped and stood with arms akimbo. "And what did you mean by *not at this time*?"

"Just being polite. Besides," he said with a crooked grin, "she can't hold a candle to you. You're the best-lookin' thing I've seen on this street since I got here, sweetie."

Laura looked at him askance, then firmly slipped her arm into his.

They were strolling along the street when Zach stopped suddenly at a shout for help. Glancing down a narrow alley, he saw an older man being menaced by two knife-wielding ruffians. "Try to get help," Zach shouted to Laura as he ran to the man's aid.

The scoundrels had knocked their victim to the ground, and, yanking him by the hair, one of the blackguards was about to slit the throat of the hapless man. At the sound of Zach's approach, the two spun around in surprise. Zach's blow slammed one of the villians into the wall. The other managed to inflict a light cut to Zach's arm before he lashed out with a booted foot and kicked the legs out from under the rogue. Both men scrambled away as Laura came rushing down the alley followed by two uniformed policemen, who ran after the fleeing criminals.

"Are you all right, sir?" Zach asked, helping the older man to his feet.

"Thanks to you, son," the man said gratefully. As the well-dressed gentleman brushed himself off, Laura could see he was still visibly shaken. She picked up a silver-handled cane and handed it to him. "Would you like us to see you to your home, sir?"

"Actually, I'm staying at the Tremont Hotel," the man informed them. "Senator James Long, of Louisiana, sir. I had been enjoying your fair city until this regrettable occasion." Using his elbow, he wiped off the crown of a black beaver hat. His hand trembled when he set the top hat on his head. "Those scoundrels intended to kill me."

"Zachary Houston, sir. And this is Miss Randolph," Zach said. The two men shook hands.

The senator doffed his hat and offered Laura a broad smile. "My pleasure, Miss Randolph. Would you and Mr. Houston join me at my hotel so I can properly express my gratitude?"

Zach began to decline the offer. "Well, sir, we were just on our way back to catch the ferry to the mainland."

"I shall not take no for an answer, Mr. Houston. Surely, there will be another ferry."

Zach cast a questioning glance at Laura. She nodded her acceptance. "Good," Long said. "Let's get a carriage and return to my hotel."

By the time they reached the Tremont Hotel, the senator had regained his composure. Immensely grateful to Zach, Senator Long insisted the young couple join him for dinner.

As they waited for their meal, Laura glanced in awe at the lavish dining room. The hotel had been recently rebuilt after the old one had burned down following the Civil War.

"Are you a resident of Galveston, Miss Randolph?" Long asked, interrupting her silent inspection of the room.

"No, Senator. Actually, I was raised in Laredo. I moved to this area a little over a year ago."

"And you, Zachary?"

"I've lived near Bay Town on the coast my whole life, Senator."

The senator's eyes sparked with interest. "And I guess the two of you are—"

"Intending to wed, sir," Zach added proudly. "That is, as soon as I get settled again."

"Settled again?" Long asked.

"I lost my ranch. I only came here to Galveston to sell my stallion."

"Indeed! That's a coincidence, Zachary. You see, I came to Galveston to purchase some stock. I'd be interested in looking at that horse of yours after dinner."

"Well, sir, I'd be glad to show him to you."

As soon as they finished eating, Senator Long accompanied Zach and Laura to the livestock exchange. "He's a handsome animal, Zachary," the senator said, pleased. "I think we can do business."

"He's a good cow pony, too, sir," Zach assured him.

Senator Long grew more serious. "Are you experienced with cattle, son?"

Zach grinned. "I've been punching cows since I was old enough to sit a saddle."

"And you say you are at loose ends at the present time?"

"Only until I find a small spread. Then Laura and I are getting married."

"Well, I'm in need of a good . . . what do you call it . . . ah . . . wrangler, to get my horses and cattle back to my plantation in Louisiana."

"You mean drive them back, sir?" Zach asked.

"No, I'm shipping them. But I need an experienced cowboy to handle them on the ship. Would you be interested? I'm scheduled to sail on *The Windsong* the day after tomorrow."

"Well, I gotta say, I sure could use the wages." Zach glanced hesitantly at Laura. "What do you think, honey?"

At the thought of the distance, Laura had reservations. "How long would it take?"

"Two or three weeks at the most," Long said. "You think you could get along without this Texas boy for a couple of weeks?"

Laura sighed and smiled at Zach. "I won't like it, but I guess I'll have to."

He squeezed her hand and turned to Long. "You just hired yourself a seafarin' cowpoke, Senator."

"You take the stallion with you, son, and be back here day after tomorrow." After completing a few more plans, the men shook hands and said good night. Senator Long doffed his hat, then hailed a carriage to return to his hotel.

Laura and Zach caught the last ferry back to the mainland. With their remaining time together quickly dwindling, they didn't want to separate, so Laura returned to the Double H with Zach.

The difficult and emotional task of packing awaited them in the morning. With loving care, Zach put the photograph album along with the few dishes and linens that belonged to his mother into the trunk. "I'll keep it in my room until you get back," Laura said sadly. She couldn't meet his eyes. "What about the rest of the furniture?"

"Just have to leave it, I guess." Seeing her despondency, he added cheerfully, "We'll get a fresh start with everything, honey. As Senator Long said, I shouldn't be gone more than two or three weeks." He drew her into his arms. "And when I get back, I'll have enough money to start a little spread, Laura. We can get married right away." He tipped up her chin to force her gaze to meet his. "Another month at the most, then we'll be man and wife. We'll never have to be separated again," he murmured just before he kissed her.

Later they rode to the beach. After swimming, they made love, and Zach built a fire on the beach. Sighing in contentment, Laura sat cuddled in his arms as they roasted a rabbit on long sticks.

"Tell me again about our wedding, Zach."

He laced his fingers through hers, then lifted her hand and pressed a kiss to the palm. "As soon as I get back, we'll go to Bay Town and have Father Jacoby marry us."

Smiling, Laura closed her eyes and visualized herself and Zach standing together as the town priest pronounced them man and wife. "Then we'll go to Brownsville—"

"Oh no," he interrupted. "First thing we'll do is take the ferry to Galveston and spend our wedding night in one of those fancy rooms in the Tremont Hotel where I'll make love to my *wife* for the first time."

"The first of many times, I hope," she said.

The sound of Zach's chuckle warmed her heart. She snuggled closer against his chest and he tightened his arm around her. "And then we'll never be separated again," she continued, repeating his reassuring words.

"Hey, who's telling this story?" he said lightly.

"We'll be together forever," she said.

He turned her in his arms and cupped her cheeks between his hands. For a long moment, he gazed into her eyes.

"Forever, my love," he whispered, claiming her lips.

After eating, they made love again, then fell asleep and slept in each other's arms until sunrise. Waking, they swam and loved again until it was time for Zach to leave.

Laura went to Galveston with him. After a final farewell, she waved good-bye to him as *The Windsong* sailed out of the harbor. When the tall ship was no longer visible, she sadly turned away.

Chapter 9

Laura resolved to keep herself so occupied, she would not have time to pine over Zach's absence. As soon as she returned to the Lazy R, she sought out Teresa in Juanita's house. Tearfully, the two young girls embraced.

"I have some exciting news," Laura said. "Come back to the house and stay there with me while my aunt's away."

"That would be unwise, Laura. Your aunt will punish you when she finds out."

"I don't care. She can't hurt me anymore," Laura declared. With more coaxing, she finally convinced Teresa to come with her.

That afternoon, threatening purple clouds rolled in from the sea. Everyone at the Lazy R scurried about getting the animals under cover.

By nightfall, the barometer dropped quickly and soon the coast was hit by a raging storm. The evening tide sweeping the Texas shore rose over thirteen feet higher than normal. From the force of the ferocious wind, part of the corral fence flattened and the roof of the smokehouse was picked up like a piece of firewood.

Juanita had hurried back to her small dwelling to be with Benito. Huddled before the fireplace, Laura and Teresa sat alone in the big house and tried not to be frightened.

"Do you have a boyfriend, Teresa?" Laura asked.

She shook her head. "Benito's brother wants to court me, but I do not wish for it."

"Benito's brother? Do you mean Carlos?" Visualizing one of the Lazy R riders, Laura rolled her eyes in approval. "Oh, he's very handsome, Teresa."

"Is true," Teresa agreed. "But I do not know about love."

"Then ask me, Teresa, because I certainly do," Laura said ecstatically. "I'm in love with Zachary Houston. I just have to talk about it with someone." She lowered her head toward her friend. "Will you keep a secret?"

"I swear on the Holy Virgin," Teresa said solemnly.

"Zach and I have been intimate." When the young girl's eyes widened, Laura added hastily, "Please don't be shocked, Teresa. Zach and I love each other so much."

"But what will your aunt say when she finds out?"

"I don't care what she says. Zach and I are getting married as soon as he gets back."

Tears glistened in Teresa's eyes. "I am so happy for you, Laura. He is a good man."

The two girls hugged. "And we're going to Brownsville after we're married and start our own spread. You're welcome to come with us, Teresa. I know Zach wouldn't mind."

Teresa hesitated, then smiled shyly. "I have been thinking about going to the convent to become a novice."

Laura clutched her hands. "Oh, Teresa, that is wonderful, if you are certain that is the life you want. But are you certain? It is such an important decision to make. I know I would never want to spend my life any way except married to Zach."

Teresa smiled in understanding. "It will be a marriage for me too, Laura. I have thought about it often. I do not believe I will ever fall in love."

"A few years ago, I didn't think I would either. In fact, I didn't even think about falling in love. My father was the only man who mattered to me. Now, I can't imagine life without Zach."

"You have much love for him," Teresa said kindly.

"Oh yes, Teresa. And I always feel so safe and content with him."

She slipped into thoughts of Zach and the memory of the night when the two of them had rounded up his cattle. Funny, that night she had not been afraid of the storm at all. Being with him had made all the difference.

With the warm memory of sitting beside him in his cabin, Laura lay back and fell asleep.

Waking the next morning, she felt ill and rushed to the chamber pot. She attributed the illness to the way she was pining over Zach's absence. Determined to get a grip on herself, she buckled down and worked twice as hard. There were strays to be rounded up and fences to be repaired. She kept her mind and body occupied by helping the men repair the damage caused from the storm.

The following morning as soon as Laura awoke and raised her head, she felt nauseated again and rushed to the chamber pot. By mid-morning the illness passed.

In the days that followed, the morning sickness continued, and Laura realized the time for her monthly menses had come and gone. With a woman's instinct, which until now, she had disregarded because of her despondency over Zach's absence, Laura knew she was in a family way.

The thought of Zach's child within her brought Laura instant joy, although she knew that having a baby would make it more difficult to give Zach the help he would need on a new spread. She told Teresa about the baby, and Teresa promised to remain with them as long as Laura needed her help.

All the same, Laura thought, now her aunt could not stop her from marrying Zach. Every day she waited anxiously for his return.

Two weeks after his departure, Laura received a wire. Eagerly, she tore it open, only to discover a message from Lavitia informing Laura of the date of her return.

On the day Lavitia was due to arrive, Laura rode to town with Whiskers to meet her aunt. While the cowhand visited the saloon, Laura wandered into the general store. Inadvertently, her glance was drawn to a carved cradle on the floor next to the counter. Surreptitiously, Laura glanced around to make sure she wasn't being observed. Upon seeing Mr. Stevens occupied with another customer, she went over to examine the cradle. Her mouth curved into a poignant smile as she visualized hers and Zach's baby sleeping contentedly in the tiny bed. She reached out and traced her fingertips along the tiny crib carved out of pine. Mesmerized, she watched the cradle rock back and forth on its curved runners.

Suddenly, the sound of approaching voices caused her to jerk out of her reverie. Guiltily, she reached out and picked up a copy of the *Galveston Daily News* from the stack on the counter.

Barely aware of what she was reading, she scanned the paper. Her perusal stopped at a boxed caption at the bottom of the page, "NO SURVIVORS FROM *THE WINDSONG* DISASTER."

Horrified, she read the article recapping the details of the destruction of the New Orleans–bound ship during the hurricane that had ravaged the Gulf of Mexico two weeks earlier.

Later, Laura was told that she fled from the store . . . that Mr. Stevens called out to her . . . that she ran toward the dock. She had no memory of regurgitating under the very tree where she and Zach had stood and watched the fireworks on the Fourth of July. No memory of slumping to the ground to vent her tears of despair.

Awareness of her surroundings returned only when the shrill blast of the ferry rent the air. She raised her head and forced her mind back to reality. The passengers were disembarking. Through the trees, she saw a man who appeared to be European assist her aunt off the ferry. Woodenly, she rose to her feet. In a dazed state, Laura went through the motions of greeting her aunt.

"My dear, this is Luis Esposito. My niece, Laura Randolph," Lavitia said.

The handsome, dark-haired Spaniard took her hand and raised it to his lips. "My pleasure, Miss Randolph," he said warmly.

"I met Mr. Esposito on the ship," Lavitia gushed. "Luis has a plantation in Florida."

"Unfortunately, I have experienced some crop failures in the last several years. I have journeyed to Galveston to seek some much-needed financing," he added. Throughout the explanation, the man's dark eyes remained fixed on Laura.

"Well, good luck in your endeavor," Laura said impassively. Whiskers's timely arrival gave her the opportunity to turn away from Luis Esposito's unwavering gaze. "It was a pleasure meeting you, Mr. Esposito."

"Oh, but I've invited Luis to be our houseguest, Laura," Lavitia declared.

Laura just wanted to get away from them. The man's unrelenting stare unnerved her. "If you'll excuse me, I'll meet you at the carriage." She hurried back to the shay and hunched down in a seat.

If Lavitia discerned the anxiety in Laura's behavior, she withheld her curiosity behind a disapproving frown.

While Whiskers loaded the luggage, Luis gallantly assisted Lavitia into the carriage. The older woman preened under the man's attention. In despair, Laura turned away.

During the return to the ranch, Luis made several attempts at conversation, but Laura ignored him. When they arrived, she immediately excused herself and went to her room.

After seeing to her guest's comforts, Lavitia entered Laura's room without knocking and discovered her niece stretched out on the bed, weeping.

"Laura, what is Teresa Moreno doing in this house? I dismissed her. I will not tolerate having my orders disobeyed. And further, your conduct toward Luis has been unpardonable. I suppose you intend to offer more weak excuses for your continual mulish behavior?"

With tears streaking her cheeks, Laura raised her head. "I . . . I . . . think Zach . . . is . . . is dead," she sobbed.

"Zach . . . you mean Zachary Houston?" Lavitia asked.

"Zach sailed for New Orleans on *The Windsong* a . . . a couple days after you *went away*," Laura managed to stammer.

Lavitia recognized the name of the ship at once. "Oh yes, that ship destroyed during the hurricane. The disaster was the main topic on everyone's lips in New Orleans. Seems there was a Louisiana senator on board, and the wreckage was discovered with no survivors."

Having slid back into a black abyss of grief, Laura did not reply.

"So, you say that Houston boy was on the ship?" There wasn't a vestige of pity in Lavitia's voice.

Zachary Houston dead! Lavitia felt triumphant. She saw this twist of fate as a sure means to make Laura come to her senses and acknowledge the errors of her ways. She, Lavitia, was the one person who had Laura's best interests at heart. Now the girl would no longer dare turn her back on her. And to show my good intentions, Lavitia reflected, she would even extend an olive branch to Laura by permitting Teresa to stay.

Lavitia went to the bed and picked up Laura's hand. "It is God's will, my dear."

Appalled, Laura stared at her. She saw no sign of compassion on her aunt's face. The hand holding her own felt cold and stiff. "I loved Zach, Aunt Lavitia. I can't bear to think of life without him."

"Nonsense, you barely knew him," Lavitia said impassively. "You're just being emotional. Time heals all wounds," she reminded Laura. "But until you are feeling better, Teresa has my permission to remain."

"Oh, God," Laura sobbed. "You really have no idea how I feel," she said in disbelief. "I loved him. Don't you understand? *I loved him.* I'm carrying his child."

The cold fingers pulled away and Laura's hand dropped limply to the bed. Lavitia stood up. Her blue eyes had hardened to ice. "You're *what*?" The voice was as cutting as a slap across the cheek.

"I'm carrying Zach's child."

"Are you certain?" she asked with a tight-lipped grimace.

Dazed, Laura looked up at the woman. "My monthly flow is several weeks late . . . and I've been sick each morning."

"How could you do this to me, Laura?" Lavitia crossed her arms across her breast and began to pace the floor.

Immersed in grief, Laura did not have the fight left to challenge the selfish remark. "I'll leave the Lazy R, Aunt Lavitia. I do not intend to embarrass you. Now, if you'll excuse me, I'd like to be alone."

Lavitia walked to the door. She glanced back at the pathetic picture of Laura huddled on the bed. "I will decide how we will handle this situation. I expect your cooperation." She raised her head haughtily. "And I shall extend your apologies to our guest."

After Lavitia departed, Teresa came into the room. Laura lay on the bed crying. The young girl sat down on the bed and put a hand on Laura's shoulder.

Laura raised her head and saw the commiseration in Teresa's eyes. "Oh, Teresa, I don't want to live without him." Sobbing, she flung herself in her friend's arms. Teresa rocked her as she would a baby.

Laura cried throughout the night, reliving every moment she had spent with Zach. All their plans . . . their hopes. She denied the belief that he was dead. Soon Zach would come back to her.

The next morning, as she prepared to ride over to the Double H, Luis Esposito joined her in the barn. "Miss Randolph, your aunt told me of your loss. May I extend my sympathy," he said kindly.

"Thank you, Mr. Esposito," Laura said.

"Perhaps you would not object if I join you."

Laura shook her head. "Please do not be offended, sir, but I prefer to be alone."

Esposito nodded. "As you wish. I understand."

Luis Esposito walked to the entrance of the barn and watched her ride away. His dark eyes remained enigmatic.

She rode to a copse of trees and dismounted. Her fingers traced the initials Zach had carved in the tree, and she tenderly pressed her cheek against the heart. "Oh, Zach," she sobbed, "I'll always love you. I'm your girl forever, my love."

Dusk had started to descend when Whiskers Merten found her there, curled up in the spot where she had cried herself to sleep. The saddened old man rode back with her to the ranch.

Lavitia met her at the door. "Laura, where have you been all day? I have been worried sick about you. We've even held dinner for you. And you know my strict rule about punctuality."

"I'm not hungry, Aunt Lavitia. Please excuse me." Laura rushed up the stairway to her room, leaving behind her exasperated aunt and a reflective Luis Esposito.

At dawn the following day, Laura saddled up Sunshine and rode to the Double H. She entered the deserted cabin and walked aimlessly into the bedroom. Sinking down on the bed, she buried her face in the bare mattress. Tears streaked her cheeks. Lying back, she wrapped her arms around herself. She lay there for hours.

Finally, toward midday, she rose to her feet. Despite the warmth of the day, a shiver raced down her spine. With a feeling of hopelessness, she sped from the house.

With every passing day, Laura struggled to hold on to the hope that she would receive a message from Zach telling her that he was alive and would soon return. But the days passed into weeks without any word.

Despite the fear of Lavitia's disapproval, Teresa could no longer hold back her feelings. She grieved along with Laura, sharing her heartache.

Throughout that time, Luis Esposito also tried to cheer her up. Laura appreciated his kindness, but just being with people seemed unbearable. She cut herself off from the outside world—not speaking to anyone. All she wanted was solitude.

Finally, after a month had passed, Lavitia called Laura into the study. Entrenched in the chair behind her desk, Lavitia regarded her niece through cold, emotionless eyes. Smoking a cheroot, Luis Esposito sat in a cordovan leather chair in the corner.

"Laura, I have been discussing your situation with Luis."

"My situation, Aunt Lavitia? I don't understand," Laura said, confused.

"Your delicate condition, Laura," Lavitia said with an impatient shrug of her slim shoulders. "Let us not mince words."

"You had no right to discuss my private business with a stranger," Laura struck out indignantly.

"I have told him nothing more than your condition and financial situation. Despite this, Luis has graciously suggested marriage. He has not even asked the name of the father of the child because he is willing to give it his name."

"When my baby's father returns, he will give our child a name," Laura declared.

"Oh, for Heaven's sake, Laura, the man is not going to return. Luis's offer is most generous."

Laura swung an angry glance at the silent man blowing smoke rings in the corner. "Generous? How much are you paying him to take me off your hands, Aunt Lavitia?"

Lavitia bolted to her feet, her eyes flashing with scorn. "You are not in a position to cast stones, Laura. The reality is that you are carrying a bastard. Luis and I have a business arrangement. You should be grateful that there are people who are concerned enough about you to try and resolve this predicament you've created for yourself."

"I told you, I will leave the Lazy R. I do not intend to cause you any embarrassment, Aunt Lavitia."

"And where will you go? You are pregnant. You have no money. How do you expect to support yourself, or the baby when it is born?"

"You could lend me the money until after I have my baby. Then I can find a job and repay you."

"That is out of the question, Laura."

"I don't understand why you are willing to give Mr. Esposito money, but not me."

"Because Luis will make an honest woman of you."

"Honest? What is honest about marrying a man I do not love? Who does not love me?" Hysterically, Laura raced from the room.

By rote she saddled Sunshine, then without direction, she rode wildly across the countryside. When she finally reined up, she found herself near the beach where she and Zach had spent their final private hours together. She climbed down the dunes, and sank into the warm sand in the very spot where she had lain in his arms.

Beckoning whitecaps washed the shore then rolled back out to the sea. Somewhere out there Zach lay at the bottom of those watery depths, she thought over and over again.

For hours she stared transfixed at the endless expanse of blue water. Her fingers toyed with the chain around her neck that held the ring Zach had given her. Then with dawning clarity, she realized there was a way she could be with him.

Rising to her feet, she walked to the water's edge. The surf lapped at her boots. "Yes, Zach, I can be with you," she murmured. Her eyes glistened with tears from a resurgence of hope. "Why didn't I think of it sooner? We can be together forever. Just the way we planned." She walked into the surf. "I'm coming, Zach. I'm coming to be with you."

The water curled around her knees, then her hips. Knowing that soon they would be together, she closed her eyes and smiled.

But then, as if obeying a spoken command, she suddenly stopped and opened her eyes. With the weight of her sodden clothes tugging at her, trying to draw her deeper, she slipped her hand to her stomach where her baby lay nestled in her womb. Zach's child. The fruit of their love. As long as his child existed, a part of Zach would remain too. She, alone, carried the legacy for Zach's immortality.

A week later, Laura sailed away from Galveston as the wife of Luis Esposito. As a consideration, Luis allowed Teresa Moreno to accompany them.

PART II

ZACHARY

Chapter 10

Florida, October 13, 1882

Father Joseph Montevideo laboriously climbed the stone stairs. His steps were stiff and painful. Aged joints, swollen with rheumatoid arthritis, protested the morning ritual, a ritual he had been celebrating for the fifty years he had lived in the Florida Everglades.

The stairs led to a narrow galleria, more rampart than balcony, on the inside of the upper story. He paused at the top of the stairway to catch his breath before shuffling along the balcony to the rear wall. He sat down on a backless wooden bench overlooking the sea just as the sun was beginning to appear over the horizon.

Now at daybreak, the rising sun cast a carmine and golden glow across the deep, blue waters of the Gulf of Mexico. It always seemed an awesome sight to Father Montevideo and at these moments he felt closest to God. The unique location of the mission, built on a rise that jutted into the sea and thus faced both east and west, enabled the priest to repeat this rite at sunset when the scene was most spectacular to behold.

As he opened his prayer book to begin his morning breviary, he thought with a contented smile, *God has made another beautiful day.*

As the sun appeared above the horizon, two boys hurried along a crude trail toward a tall mangrove tree, its top branches recently broken and burned by lightning. Little light filtered through the thick canopy of the twisted thicket, and the younger lad's legs trembled as his round brown eyes repeatedly swept the dense foliage lining the trampled path. The forest was full of shadows that frightened the six-year-old Peter Esposito, but he had promised Ramon he would come with him.

Ramon had vowed to kill Old Slither, the crocodile who inhabited the hammock. The sight of the huge croc sunning himself at the base of the tree always struck a chord of terror in Peter's chest. But the thought of Ramon attempting to kill the reptile frightened Peter even more because Ramon was only ten years old and Peter feared for his half-brother's safety.

Peter knew he should have told Pilar of her son's intention, but then Ramon would have been angry with him. And Peter did not want Ramon's anger. Ramon was his only friend.

Peter peered cautiously about him as they neared the tree. What if Old Slither was on the ground right now? Peter reached into his pocket and fondled a tiny silver box. The miniature chest contained his treasured keepsakes and the feel of the hard metal bolstered his courage. He never went anywhere without it.

"I wish the lightning had killed Old Slither when it struck the tree," Peter complained.

Ramon beat his chest with his free hand. "That could not be, because *I*, Ramon, am destined to kill him," the older boy boasted.

"I bet Old Slither's a thousand years old," Peter said.

Ramon snorted. "Crocodiles don't live that long."

"Well then, I bet he's at least ten hundred years old," Peter reasoned. "I bet he's the oldest crock in the whole Everglades."

They paused a safe distance from the tree and peered cautiously at the ground. "He is not here," Ramon grumbled.

Peter sighed with relief. Maybe Ramon would put

aside the idea of killing Old Slither, at least this day.

The younger boy glanced with adoration at his companion. Ramon was the bastard son of Peter's father and native mistress. But the two boys bore little resemblance. Ramon was small in stature; despite the four-year difference in their ages, he was only slightly taller than Peter. However, his arms and chest were unusually muscular due to his daily practice of wielding the heavy machete that was now clenched in his hand.

Ramon had a flat nose, broad cheekbones, and straight black hair that hung to his shoulders, while Peter had the straight nose of his American mother and the dark hair of his father.

Ramon hated their father and vowed, much to Peter's distress, that soon he would leave the plantation and join his Seminole uncle, Gregorio, in the swamp. He often taunted Peter with this threat in order to gain the younger boy's subservience.

"We're too early," Ramon complained, his black eyes flashing with disappointment. "Old Slither isn't here."

Suddenly Ramon perked up his head and raised a hand to his mouth, cautioning Peter to remain silent. He listened for a few seconds, then pulled Peter into the bushes just as rapidly moving figures appeared on the path.

The two boys remained concealed in the foliage and watched as about fifty natives passed. They all carried machetes or long knives tucked into their waistbands. A few held bows and arrows. Peter's eyes were wide with alarm. He had never seen any of these men before. There was something sinister about their presence that frightened him.

"Who are they?" he asked when the band had disappeared.

Ramon could not conceal his pride. "They are Seminoles."

Peter was trembling. "I know. But there's so many of them. What are they doing here?"

"I don't know. I did not see my uncle among them."

"I'm scared, Ramon. I'm going to tell Papa."

"You can't tell him. He'll whip me for bringing you out here," Ramon snapped with undisguised bitterness.

"All right, but let's tell my mother or Teresa. You know they won't whip you."

Ramon nodded in agreement and the two boys began to race along the path back to the house.

Juan DeVarga had overslept. Hurriedly he began to dress. The sun was rising and he still hadn't completed his morning toilet. *Those shiftless natives are probably lolling around instead of working,* he thought with a disgusted frown. The laborers could never be depended upon to give an honest day's toil unless he was there to prod them.

DeVarga sat down on the edge of his bed. At the sight of the bloodstains on the sheet, a thin smile broke the flat plane of his face. The young Indian girl could not have been more than ten or eleven years old.

With a broadening smile, he remembered how she had trembled with fright when he removed her clothing. Her black eyes had widened with fear and he could still see the sharp little peaks of her tiny breasts. His tongue snaked out to moisten his lips, and he felt himself swelling as he recalled her scream of pain as he thrust into her.

The sound of smashing glass forced aside his lustful reminiscence and DeVarga grimaced in irritation. "What has that clumsy woman broken this time?"

His face contorted with contempt at the thought of the plump, uneducated peasant woman who was his wife. He leaned over, peered into the mirror, and began to carefully clip his goatee.

Juan DeVarga was a vain man. He prided himself on his suave appearance, particularly his goatee, which came to a neat point slightly below his chin and did not contain a single gray hair. Every morning he spent a quarter of an hour trimming the whiskers.

He took a backward step and turned his dark head. With a side glance, he studied his image in the mirror, admiring his profile. He thought himself every bit as handsome as the old don, Carlos del Rey y Castilla.

For years DeVarga had secretly envied the *patrón*, and he tried to emulate the imposing old man who had been the village leader. Then, a year ago, the don had returned to Spain and DeVarga could not have been more relieved; not only had he been able to purchase the *patrón's* plantation, but now with the don gone, no one in the village could boast such a distinguished beard.

He picked up a tarnished, silver-handled brush and applied a few additional strokes to his hair. Laying aside the brush, he smiled with satisfaction at his image just as the chamber door burst open.

Startled, he spun around. His eyes bulged with terror, and then his open mouth froze forever as one powerful swing of a raised machete decapitated him.

Chapter 11

Florida, October 16, 1882

The trip along the Florida coastline had been long and hot. Having started from Miami on the east coast, they were now nearing their destination of Dario on the west coast. They had been on the open boat all night. He preferred a horse on hard ground.

Lord how he hated boats.

Boats! The very thought disgusted him. He was a cavalryman, but he felt he had spent more time on damned boats and tramping through stinking swamps than he had on horses.

His somber gaze shifted to the ragged coastline capped by thick foliage. The wide brim of his campaign hat, set low on his forehead, exposed only his chiseled profile—a handsome profile, seasoned by sun and wind, with a straight nose and a resolute chin. A thick black moustache drooped around the corners of his firm, sensual mouth.

He removed his hat and wiped his brow with his shirt sleeve. His dark hair, clipped short and damp with perspiration, lay in matted curls.

He got to his feet and stretched his cramped legs. Standing two inches over six feet, he had a lean, muscular build. His blue cavalry pants were tucked into knee-high boots, and a holstered Colt revolver hung from his hip. The blue flannel uniform shirt he wore clung to him in wet patches.

His deep sapphire eyes clouded with irritation. He was hot and sweaty. The white suspenders crisscrossing his broad back felt like a vise in the hot sun. *Christ! Why couldn't the army issue them something other than flannel in this heat? Idiotic!*

Of course, since leaving West Point, he had discovered a great deal about the army that was idiotic. With a wide-open frontier to patrol, why in hell had the army shipped cavalrymen to the goddamned Everglades anyway? A horse in the swamps was useless. The government didn't need a cavalry in these accursed Everglades—all it needed was the goddamned navy and infantry. Why didn't President Arthur just steam up in one of the goddamned new steel warships he was so goddamned proud of and blow apart the goddamn swamps?

Lord, how he hated these swamps.

And now this problem with the Seminoles. The government claimed a problem didn't even exist ... After all, the Seminole Wars had ended almost thirty years ago! He snorted in derision. As long as there was breath in some of these Seminoles, they would keep on fighting.

Why the hell didn't the government let the Seminoles have the goddamned swamp? he reasoned. They were the only ones who knew how to exist there anyway! Except the goddamned snakes and the goddamned alligators.

"And the goddamned mosquitos," he grumbled aloud.

He knew what he was doing to himself: getting angry was the only way he could handle going into combat.

Despite his irritation, Lieutenant Zachary Houston grinned.

They were standing together in waist-high water, the sun glistening on Laura's wet breasts. Her beautiful, firm breasts.

A tall whitecap engulfed her and she emerged laughing, looking up at him, the water dripping off her hair and face.

Her mouth bowed into an enticing smile that tied a knot in his groin. Opening her arms, she reached out to him.

Her breasts filled his hands. He dipped his head and began to tease the hardened peaks with his tongue. They tasted of salt. But more intoxicating, they tasted of Laura.

She groaned and slid her arms around his neck, flattening her body against his. Her skin felt warm and as soft as silk. "Oh, God, I love you so much. I can't bear the thought of your leaving."

He raised his head and gazed down into her warm brown eyes, now misted with tears. "It will only be for a short time, honey. I'll be back for you soon." His dark eyes deepened with an anxiety bordering on panic. "You'll wait for me, Laura?"

She drew his head down to hers. "I'll wait for you forever. I swear, I'll wait for you forever." Her lips clung to his.

He was ready for her again—engorged and throbbing. He slid his hands down to cup her firm buttocks and lifted her. Her legs parted and encircled his hips. He entered her.

"I love you, Laura. I love you," he whispered hoarsely, covering her face with frenzied kisses.

"I love you, too. I'll always love you," she sobbed before his mouth cut off her cries.

They stood with the surf breaking against their locked bodies.

A wave slapped against the boat, splashing Zach as he stared transfixed into the water. Startled, he was pulled from his reverie and sat up. He had been thinking of Laura again. He hastily glanced around at the seven men stretched out on the deck. They were all still asleep. At the wheel, the boatswain and his mate spoke in low whispers.

Despite the undulating movement of the boat, Zach's step remained steady and his back ramrod straight as he crossed the deck.

He paused at the feet of a sleeping soldier and nudged the man's foot with the toe of his boot.

"We're almost there, Sergeant."

Returning to the bow of the ship, he sat down to reflect

on the mission ahead. Colonel Scott had received word through a native informer that Gregorio and his renegade band of Seminoles intended to attack the small village of Dario. Headquarters had immediately dispatched Zach's squad to the area. He had been told that most of the villagers were Spanish, with the exception of a few Seminoles who had converted to Christianity. A Catholic priest and several nuns operated a mission hospital there, and five sugar-cane plantations bordered the village.

What did he know about the Seminole leader, Gregorio? For years the guerilla's band had been terrorizing Americans and Europeans living in or on the outskirts of the Everglades: stealing livestock, destroying crops, and driving the settlers from their homes. Until three days ago, no one had been killed or seriously wounded, but now weary survivors staggered into Miami reporting stories of death and carnage.

Deep in reflection, Zach swung a troubled gaze to the coastline. Why had Gregorio suddenly changed his tactics and become murderous? If this was the outbreak of an Indian war, then Gregorio would be a cunning enemy for the army to track down. Always successful in eluding his pursuers, the wily renegade seemed to know every foot of the tide-swept maze of islands, saw grass marshes, mangrove hammocks, sand bars, and mud shallows that made up the two and a half million acres of the Florida Everglades.

As O'Hara began rousing the men, Zachary's attention was drawn to the sergeant. Michael Patrick O'Hara, a short, barrel-chested man with red hair and the broad grin of an Irishman, had fled Ireland during the riots in the late seventies—mainly because he had been in the center of many of them. Zach liked the Irishman. O'Hara had been with him since '80 and could be trusted in combat.

Within minutes the sergeant had the men on their feet waiting to disembark. They all wore uniforms similar to

Zachary's, and carried the same basic gear—a canteen, machete, and a long-bladed knife worn at the waist. Slung across their shoulders and crossing their chests were haversacks containing survival rations of cracked corn, dried venison, and coffee beans. Each man also wore a bandoleer to carry extra ammunition for his Winchester repeating rifle.

The boatswain brought the boat to a stop and pointed to a map in front of him. "Dario is about five miles down the coast from here, but this is as close as we can get you to the village, Lieutenant. The rest of the shoreline is too rocky. I can't risk running aground."

At least the sailor had enough conscience to look apologetic. *Damn! A five-mile hike through hostile territory . . . and we're loaded down with packs and rifles*, Zach thought grimly.

His orders to the two sailors were sharp and succinct. "It will be dark soon. Stay a safe distance off shore. We'll fire two shots as a signal, but if we're not back by midnight tomorrow, get the hell back to HQ and bring reinforcements."

The boatswain and the other sailor saluted. "Good luck, sir."

Zachary returned a quick salute. His gut feeling was that they would need a damn sight more than luck.

"Crack your rifles and move your asses, laddies," O'Hara called out. "And, Ryan, be sure and keep this dry." He gave an affectionate pat to a dynamite gun one of the soldiers was toting.

Frank Ryan threw the sergeant a disgruntled glance. Fearless to the point of recklessness in battle, the tough kid from New York's Hell's Kitchen had joined the army to avoid an arrest. "This damn thing is heavy, Sarge. The charge alone weighs five pounds. Besides, this goddamned weapon don't fire worth a damn. It ain't never been accurate that I seen."

"What in hell are we gonna do with dynamite in the middle of this swamp anyway?" Stan Zanowski asked.

The ex-brewery worker from Milwaukee was Ryan's ammunition carrier, and the two men were inseparable.

Flint Bryce, the squad's corporal, smirked. "What we're gonna do, Zanowski, is have you stick it up Gregorio's ass and pull the trigger."

"Maybe you'd like to carry the dynamite for a change, Bryce?" Ryan quickly retorted, coming to his buddy's defense.

Bryce's smirk broadened. "I wouldn't wantta break up the two of you. You make such a good-lookin' couple." Ryan made an obscene gesture at him, and the wiry corporal grinned. "Thanks for the invitation, Frankie, but you ain't my type. Your armpits are too hairy."

"Yeah, well, how come I'm always the one carryin' this stinkin' dynamite?" Zanowski interjected. "If I get hit, I'll go up like fireworks on the Fourth of July."

"If you do, Ski, we'll all stand up and sing 'The Star Spangled Banner,'" O'Hara gibed, slapping him on the back.

Zachary saw the appalled look on the face of Fred Hoffman, the new replacement. The young man, fresh off an Iowa corn farm, was shocked by the obscenities and banter among the men. He did not yet realize that the talk hid their fear and that the tight-knit squad held one another in deepest respect.

"Johnson, you and Malloy take the point and head due north," Zach told the two men who were just sliding into the water.

"Sure, Lieutenant." Norman Johnson smiled agreeably. "But which way is north?"

Zachary tried not to grin. Johnson's flippant remark was meant to cover up the soldier's tension. The new recruit appeared to be the only one of the men naive enough not to know what might be waiting for them on shore. He motioned to Bryce and the corporal came over to him.

"Flint, if things get hot, keep an eye on the new kid if you can."

"Sure, Lieutenant."

Holding their Winchesters above their heads, they began to slide one by one over the side of the boat into the water. Zach followed. The water felt refreshing as they waded to shore.

O'Hara moved up beside him. "Well, at least we're not going in under fire. Do you suppose any of those bastards are in them trees watchin', Lieutenant?"

"You better hope not, Sergeant." Zachary's gaze shifted to the dense foliage that reached to the ocean. Not a leaf stirred.

Michael O'Hara flashed a wide Irish grin. "Maybe headquarters was wrong, Lieutenant. Maybe there ain't no attack. Maybe this is just gonna be a bloomin' picnic."

"Yeah . . . maybe you're right, Sergeant."

Once on shore, the squad proceeded no more than half a mile when Private Johnson came running back to them. "There's a house about four hundred yards ahead, sir."

One look at Johnson's flushed face told Zachary the man's agitation was not the result of exertion. "What did you find, Johnson?"

"I think you better see for yourself, sir," he said grimly.

Hurriedly, the squad followed Johnson to a huge iron gate that opened into the courtyard of a large stucco house built in the Spanish manner. They found Malloy digging a hole in the yard.

Zachary stopped at Malloy's side as the others continued into the house. "Report, Malloy."

David Malloy, a tall, slim young man with blond hair and cornflower-blue eyes, was well-liked and held in high esteem by the other men because he had a spiritual serenity about him. However, unlike O'Hara, Malloy never tried to preach or lecture. He had joined the army to experience a part of life before attempting to follow in the footsteps of his father, a Presbyterian minister from

Pennsylvania. Reserved by nature, David did not ordinarily express displeasure toward anything or anyone—a rare trait among army men who usually followed the rule, "If you can't say something nasty about someone, don't say anything at all."

Malloy was an enigma to Zachary. He understood this soldier less well than the others. For, despite the man's considerate ways, in battle Malloy was one of the most ferocious fighters in the squad.

The soldier never raised his eyes from his task. "Two bodies, sir: a dead woman in the kitchen with her throat cut, and a decapitated man in an upstairs bedroom. Both victims appear to be Spanish."

Zachary's expression remained inscrutable. "Any others?"

Malloy raised his head and Zachary saw the pain in the young man's eyes. "Not that I know of, sir."

"What about servants? Field hands? A house this large must have had some."

"I didn't see another soul around, sir . . . dead or alive." Malloy returned to his digging.

"What are you doing, Malloy?" Zach asked gently. Obviously, the soldier was digging a grave, but Zachary felt the effort was a waste of precious time.

"I thought I would bury them, Lieutenant."

The screen door slammed loudly as O'Hara came out of the house. "I'm no sawbones, Lieutenant, but from the smell and condition of the bodies, I figure they've been dead a couple of days. Everything in the house is broken or hacked apart. Nothing looks salvageable. Funny they didn't just burn the place down."

"Maybe they didn't want to alert the countryside. A fire might eliminate the advantage of a surprise raid. We better get to that mission. Round up the men, Sergeant, and let's move out."

Malloy looked up in surprise. "You mean we can't bury them, sir?"

"We don't have time, Malloy. Not if we hope to find anyone alive anywhere else."

*   *   *

When they reached the next house, darkness had closed in with the suddenness of a tropical night. The lower floor was dark, but a light shone from an upstairs window.

The squad remained concealed in the brush while Zachary examined the courtyard through binoculars. "What do you think, Sergeant?"

He handed the glasses to O'Hara, who raised them to his eyes and trained them on the house. "I can't see nothin' movin', but there's a lamp burnin'."

Zach was leery. "I know. It almost looks like we're being invited to walk right up and knock on the door."

The sergeant grinned. "I've got an awful itch to oblige them. I think we should go in."

"I think so, too, Sergeant. If it's a trap, then they know we're here, so we won't be fooling anyone. Let's move in. Tell the men to advance in pairs and proceed with caution."

Crouching and darting from tree to tree, the squad warily approached the house. By the time they entered the courtyard, they still had not met any resistance.

Corporal Bryce and Private Hoffman were moving in from the right when Bryce stumbled over an obstacle on the ground. "What the hell?" he cursed, and glanced down at a hill of swarming ants. "Holy Christ!" he mumbled.

Hoffman stopped to look back at what had attracted Bryce's attention. Instantly repulsed, he turned away and began to vomit; under the swarm of ants lay the partial remains of a human head.

Apparently, the victim had been buried alive with his head protruding above ground, and then syrup had been poured over him. Now, thousands of insects swarmed over what remained of the head.

Unaware of Bryce and Hoffman's discovery, Johnson and Malloy had reached the house. They stole along the wall of the porch until they came to the front door. Johnson raised his carbine and nodded to Malloy. The soldier turned the knob and shoved the door open. With pointed rifles, the two men sprang into the room.

The cloying smell of blood alerted them to the ghastly scene they immediately encountered: several bodies, hacked to pieces, lay scattered on the floor and religious symbols, drawn in blood, plastered the walls. Johnson lowered his carbine and walked outside to wave an all clear to the other men.

Malloy continued up the stairway to the bedroom where a lamp was still burning. He found a bedridden old woman, dead. Her body had not been mutilated. A single swipe of a knife had severed an artery and she had bled to death.

But the other victims had suffered a different fate. Pieces of their bodies were scattered all over the downstairs. Even parts of the family dog were strewn among the carnage.

"Why hack up bodies like this?" Hoffman asked, stunned.

Bryce, stepping carefully among the remains, shrugged his shoulders. "Don't much matter what happens to a man after he's dead."

Wide-eyed, Hoffman asked, "But why did they do it?"

"Can't get to heaven unless you're in one piece," Bryce said.

"Hey, Bryce, remember that time in the Arizona territory when the Apaches took Lieutenant Rettiger's patrol prisoners," Ryan said. He shifted his attention to the new recruit. "By the time we got there, they was all hacked to pieces." Ryan shook his head. "Never made no sense to me."

"That's what I've been trying to say," Hoffman said, hanging on to every word.

"Yep," Ryan said, "no sense at all. Apaches usually roasted their prisoners alive."

"Squelch that kind of talk, Ryan," Zachary ordered and went outside.

"Did you ask them why they did it?" Hoffman

inquired. Still pale from the gruesome sight, he was struggling not to be sick again.

"Hell no! We killed every one of the goddamned bastards and burned down the village," Ryan said.

"You heard the lieutenant, Ryan," Bryce said curtly. "Drop the subject."

Flint Bryce, the oldest in the squad, was a seasoned veteran of thirty years and an ex-Indian scout who had volunteered for the regular army when there seemed to be no further use for him out West. Lanky and rawboned, Bryce had an uncanny instinct for survival, which had often saved the squad from walking into an ambush.

He put his arm around Hoffman's shoulders. "Come on, kid, let's go outside. The smell of this place is making me sick."

Outside Zachary was formulating his next move. *Still three plantations to go. What in hell are we going to find at that mission?* He had to keep the men moving. "Johnson, Malloy, take the point," he ordered sharply.

The patrol moved on. It was now pitch dark, and they all realized how susceptible they were to ambush—none more so than Zachary. But he had orders to get to the mission, which he figured had to be close by.

Walking beside Zachary, O'Hara started muttering to himself. Finally, Zachary could no longer ignore him. "What are you mumbling about, Sergeant?"

"No man deserves to die like that poor soul back there in the courtyard," O'Hara declared.

"That's an old Indian torture. Ask Corporal Bryce; he'll agree. The Apaches used it often."

O'Hara's craggy face grimaced. "If any of those heathen bastards have hurt those holy sisters, I'm gonna kill each and every last one of them," he vowed. His eyes glowed fervently.

"Let's hope we're in time, Sergeant. Maybe they won't harm them because they're clergy," Zachary said, with a reassurance he did not feel.

"When I finish this hitch, I'm going back to Ireland.

I've had enough of this bloody fightin'. What about you, sir? You've never told me where your home is, Lieutenant."

The mention of home raised memories Zachary had tried to forget. "I don't really have a home, Sergeant. I lived in Texas before I went to West Point, but I don't have any desire to go back there. *Nothing for me there*, Zachary thought bitterly.

"You mean you ain't got no family you want to get back to?" O'Hara asked, astounded.

"No. No family."

Trying to lift Zachary's spirits, O'Hara pressed on. "Must be at least one little gal waitin' for you. I can see why an ugly mug like me ain't got no gal watchin' for my return, but you're a fine handsome figure of a man, Lieutenant."

Zachary's face had turned to granite. "I said there is no one, Sergeant. No one, at least, who thought I was worth waiting for." *Damn you, Laura. Damn you to Hell*, he cursed silently.

The terse, negative response returned the thoughts of both men to the present. They continued their march in silence until Malloy and Johnson came running back to them.

"The village is ahead, sir," Johnson reported. "We heard sporadic gunfire."

Zachary nodded grimly, relieved to know that at least they were approaching their objective. "All right, we'll go in slow. Let's try to remain undetected until we get the layout. Don't fire your weapon unless you're forced to."

They moved to the edge of the village and hid in the bushes while they assessed the situation. Dario spread out from a large mission standing on a high rise overlooking the ocean. Several torches blazing in stationery posts revealed over fifty natives congregated near a dozen grass huts at the opposite end of the village. The other huts had been burned down.

Occasional gunfire flashed from the mission walls as the defenders attempted to drive back natives who ventured too close.

"Well, at least *somebody* must have made it to the mission," Zach said. "I'm sure the priest and nuns aren't the ones firing those weapons."

O'Hara was the first to speak. "Shall a couple of us try to make it to the wall? I'm volunteerin', sir."

"Like hell you are, O'Hara. If something happens to me, you have to take over the squad."

"I'll try to get in, sir," Corporal Bryce offered.

"Damn it! I haven't asked for volunteers, yet," Zachary snapped. "I'm trying to figure out if we should try to get behind the walls and fortify their defense, or attack the Indians in the open. We do have the element of surprise."

"Which ain't worth a tinker's damn once they make it into the trees," O'Hara declared. "We'll be sittin' ducks when we try to get back to the boat."

Zachary cursed himself for not formulating a plan sooner. "I think our wisest move is to get into the mission and hold out until reinforcements arrive. From what I can see of that mission from here, it looks like the back wall overhangs a cliff, so we will have only three walls to defend. When we don't show up by tomorrow night, the boatswain should have enough sense to take off to get help."

His mind was working rapidly. "I figure a day to get back to Miami, then another day to get back here, which means we have to hold them off for three days." He frowned. "I doubt we'll have enough ammunition if they launch a major attack. God, I wish I knew how many people are in that mission . . . and how much ammunition they have."

"Why don't we send a man back to the boat to save time?" O'Hara asked.

"Because it won't buy us much time, Sergeant. One man could easily get picked off alone. We have to use every available man and every bit of ammunition. Those sailors have their orders. They know what to do when we don't show."

"I hate trusting my fate to a swabbie," Bryce grumbled.

"I'm trusting my fate to that Winchester in your hands, Corporal," Zach said grimly. "Right now, we need a diversion to get into the mission. Ryan, lob a blast from the dynamite gun into one of those huts down the road. I'm hoping the explosion will draw their attention."

"Yeah, and let's hope the hut will be full of those bastards," O'Hara muttered.

"As soon as Ryan fires, we'll make a run for the mission. I just hope someone inside sees us coming and opens the gates."

Ryan checked the chamber of his weapon. "I have to get closer if this gun is going to be effective. Ski and I will work our way a little farther toward the end of the village."

"We can't spread ourselves out too thin," Zachary cautioned.

Ryan nodded. "Don't worry, Lieutenant. I ain't planning on being no hero."

Zachary turned to Zanowski. "How do *you* feel about it? I'm not ordering you to do it."

"Where Frankie goes, I go," Zanowski said, grinning.

"All right," Zach said. "Malloy and I will stay here to cover your retreat. O'Hara, move the rest of the squad up the hill as close to the mission as you can get. When you hear the explosion, rush for the gate."

Ryan and Zanowski moved away and the other four men began to work their way toward the hill. The minutes seemed to pass as slowly as hours for Zachary and Malloy.

"Aren't they in position yet?" Malloy finally whispered.

Zachary had kept his eyes trained on the backs of the two men. He shook his head in frustration. "Damn it, where did they go? They've disappeared."

Suddenly a flurry of activity erupted at the far end of the village as natives began running. Zachary's stomach knotted. "Oh, Christ! They've been discovered."

Ryan and Zanowski had gotten into position to fire the dynamite gun when a dozen Seminoles had come out of the trees a few yards away. Stepping forward to launch the charge, Ryan exposed his position. One of the Indians carrying a torch spotted him immediately and yelled to the others.

Ryan pulled the trigger, but nothing happened. "Damn it, this goddamned thing won't fire," he shouted to Zanowski. He threw down the rifle and swung his Winchester off his shoulder.

The two men began firing until they emptied their rifles into the crowd. Before Ryan could reload, he fell to the ground under the swinging machetes of a hoard of Seminoles.

With no time to put another cartridge magazine into his rifle, Zanowski pulled out his machete. Grabbing the torch bearer, he used the man as a shield and began backing away with the knife pressed against the man's throat. The native dropped the torch and it fell to the ground, casting an eerie glow on the unfolding scene.

Smelling blood, the Indians swarmed like a school of sharks in a killing frenzy. With raised machetes, they advanced on Zanowski, their eyes glittering with fanatical lust.

Several got behind him and were able to inflict numerous wounds. He began bleeding profusely and realized his situation was hopeless. The big brewery worker picked up his hostage as if he were a keg of beer and tossed the man into the advancing mob. Then he dove for the fallen torch.

"I'll see you bastards in hell," Zanowski shouted, and thrust the lighted torch into the charge of dynamite strapped to his chest.

Chapter 12

❧❧

At the sound of the explosion, the Seminoles near the mission raced down the hill. Another blast immediately followed when the second charge of dynamite exploded. O'Hara and the men encountered only minor resistance in their dash for the gate, which was opened by a priest.

"Get up on the wall and give them cover fire," O'Hara ordered. Hoffman, Bryce, and Johnson scampered up the stairway and took positions above.

"Here comes the lieutenant," Bryce called out as Zachary and Malloy came racing toward the gate. Having no time to stay under cover, Zachary and David Malloy were running in the open with ten Seminoles in pursuit. The three men on the wall began picking off the pursuers with rifle shots.

Within a hundred yards of the gate, Malloy stepped into a hole, twisting his ankle. He stumbled and fell. Zachary turned back to help him, but one of the Indians, his machete raised, jumped on the downed soldier. Too close to aim and fire before the native's arm would descend with the lethal blow, Zachary swung his carbine and knocked the man off Malloy.

O'Hara rushed out of the gate and knelt on one knee. "I'll cover you, Lieutenant," he shouted to Zachary, who was helping Malloy to his feet. Zach slung the soldier over his shoulder as O'Hara took aim at an advancing

145

Seminole. The bullet sent the man spinning backwards.

With a bombardment of rapid fire, the three soldiers in the mission drove back the remaining pursuers as the soldiers entered the gate.

Bryce came leaping down the stairway followed by Johnson and Hoffman. "Where's Frankie and Ski?" he asked.

"They're not coming," Zachary said.

The corporal's face hardened. "Son of a bitch!" He turned away.

The soldiers were immediately surrounded by a priest, several nuns, a man, a woman, and a young boy. In the excitement, all tried to talk at once.

Finally, to clarify the situation for the soldiers, one of the men silenced the others and stepped forward to speak to Zachary.

"I am Luis Esposito, Lieutenant," the handsome Spaniard said in a fine Castellan accent. "We certainly are glad to see you soldiers."

Zachary acknowledged his greeting with a brief nod. "Are you in charge here?"

"I am Sister Francesca. I am in charge of the hospital," announced a nun, who stepped forward. She, too, spoke with a Spanish accent, and, although not as precise as Luis Esposito's, her English was understandable.

"I mean, who is in charge of your defenses?" Zachary asked.

"Our Beloved Lord, young man," the nun replied with haughty dignity.

Zachary tried to control his rising temper. "Madam—"

"Sister," she corrected sternly.

His patience snapped. Ryan and Zanowski had just been blown to oblivion and this woman was arguing goddamned protocol. "Sister, two of my men have just died in our efforts to get in here. I want some answers. Now!"

"Perhaps I can be of service, Lieutenant. I am Father Montevideo," a priest said quietly, stepping forward.

"Sister Francesca operates the hospital, but I am in charge of the mission."

The priest's composure had a calming effect on Zachary. "Thank you, Father. I'm Lieutenant Houston. Can you tell me how many people are here?"

"There are six survivors from the Esposito plantation, as well as two wounded Christian natives, four nuns, and myself," Father Montevideo replied.

Zachary calculated quickly and glanced at O'Hara. "I make it thirteen civilians." O'Hara nodded. "And how much ammunition?"

Luis Esposito spoke up at once. "I have a rifle with about thirty bullets remaining." This announcement caused an exchange of woeful glances among the soldiers.

"Are you an advance patrol, Lieutenant?" the priest asked. The smile on his face indicated that he probably expected the whole United States Cavalry to come charging up the hill at any moment.

"You might say that, Padre," O'Hara interjected.

Bryce snorted. "Yeah, about four days' advance." The corporal turned wearily away and climbed the stairs. One by one, the rest of the squad followed him. Without being ordered to do so, the squad stationed themselves at the corners of the galleria. O'Hara positioned himself on the wall that arched above the front gate.

"Father, how secure are these walls?" Zach asked.

"Why, Our Mother of Perpetual Hope has stood for over a hundred years, my son."

As Zach listened, his gaze swept the courtyard. Stairways, barely wide enough for one person, flanked either end of the inner front wall and led to the galleria above. "Any holes in the walls large enough to penetrate?"

"No, Lieutenant," the priest said proudly. "The walls weren't part of the original construction. The mission was built as a church, then later divided into a hospital and chapel."

"And what's behind those doors near the foot of each

stairway?" Zach asked as he continued to scan the complex.

"The door on the right opens into my quarters, Lieutenant. The four doors on the opposite wall are the quarters of the Dominican nuns who operate the hospital. At the present time, two of the rooms are being used by the refugees."

"Are the rooms windowless?"

Father Montevideo nodded. "The windows were sealed shut in the thirties at the time of the First Seminole War."

Greater consideration had been given to the protection of the inhabitants than to their comfort, Zach thought. The high walls obstructed most of the breeze and there were no windows in the rooms for ventilation. It would make the job of defending the mission easier than he had thought.

"How long have you been here, Father?"

"For fifty years," Father Montevideo declared. "Our Mother Of Perpetual Hope and I survived the Seminole Wars."

"Let's hope your luck continues to hold, Father," Zach said drolly. "I'm going to check above, then I'd like to see the rest of the mission."

"Of course, Lieutenant. I'll wait for you down here." He smiled at Zach apologetically. "The stairs . . . my legs."

"I understand. I'll be right back."

Zach climbed the stairway for a quick inspection. The mission stood like a sentinel on a high rise overlooking the sea. Fortified by stone walls two stories high, the arched front wall was secured by a heavy wrought iron gate. As he had suspected, there were only three walls. They formed an enclosed and shaded patio, so that the mission had become a large rectangular complex.

He hurried to the rear of the galleria. The back of the building extended to the edge of an unscalable fifty-foot cliff that plummeted into jagged boulders protruding from the sea below.

In essence, the mission was a citadel, Zachary thought.

He quickly returned to the priest. Now alone, Father Montevideo took him into the infirmary. Zach nodded politely to the nuns and two women, one whom he remembered seeing earlier.

The front of the building was divided into two rooms and opened into a long dormitory that ran across the rear. Patients occupied two of the eight cots that lined the walls.

"Who are they?" he asked, glancing at the two patients.

"They are Christian Indians who were wounded in the attack," the priest informed him.

The room felt hot and airless. Heavy shutters on the side windows had been firmly latched. Zach removed his hat to wipe his brow.

"The back of the building is impregnable, Father. Why not have windows on the back wall, at least?"

Father Montevideo smiled at him. "Nature can often offer a greater threat than marauding Indians, Lieutenant. They have been eliminated because we are pelted frequently by wind and water from the sea, often with hurricane ferocity." Putting a hand on Zach's arm, the priest directed him toward the door. "Come, Lieutenant, let me show you our church."

"Thank you, Sister," Zach said, nodding politely to Sister Francesca as he left.

Laura Esposito had just drifted off to sleep in one of the nun's rooms when an explosion jarred her awake. Her head jerked up, and her eyes popped open in alarm. The blast awoke her son Peter, who cried out for her.

Leaning over, she pressed a reassuring kiss to his forehead just as the second explosion rocked the night. "What's that noise, Mama?" Peter sobbed. His little body trembled with fright, so she gathered him into her arms and hugged him.

"It's okay, honey, go back to sleep," she soothed. *Dear God, what is happening?* The noise had been so loud it sounded as if it were right outside the gate.

Her heart pounded fiercely. *Is this the end? Have the Seminoles blown the gate open?* Laura knew it was only a matter of time before the natives succeeded in breaking through. There were just too many of them.

Her eyes brimmed with tears as she cradled Peter's head against her breast. *Dear God, please don't let him suffer,* she prayed when the sound of gunfire became deafening. Waiting for the inevitable, she began to rock Peter in her arms.

Suddenly the door burst open. Laura screamed, her every nerve taut with tension. At the sight of Ramon, she spread her arms to include him in her embrace. "Come over here with us, Ramon." The poor boy didn't deserve to die alone, she thought with sympathy. *Oh God, if I could only stop my trembling,* she beseeched in a fleeting petition.

"What's happening, Ramon?" she asked when the boy remained standing in the doorway.

His eyes were wide with excitement. *"Americanos, señora."*

Confused, Laura asked, "Americans?"

"Sí, señora. Soldados."

Laura still couldn't believe what he had said. "American soldiers? Are you saying American soldiers have rescued us?"

"Sí, señora." The young boy ran off before she could ask any more questions.

Peter sat up in the cot and wiped away his tears with a balled fist. "What's happening, Mama? What does Ramon mean?"

"We've been rescued, Peter. The American army has come to save us."

"Where is Papa? We must tell him," the young boy said with the spontaneity and innocence of youth.

"I'm sure he already knows, honey. Why don't you try to go back to sleep?"

The boy would not consider such a thought. "I want to see the American soldiers, too, Mama."

Now that relief was replacing her numb terror, Laura laughed and hugged her son, so tightly that Peter squirmed in her embrace. "Well then, young man, I suggest you quickly put on your shoes and we'll go out and see them."

She waited as Peter sat down on the floor to pull on his boots. Her eyes, which only moments before had been filled with fear, now sparkled with motherly pride as she watched her young son. When he finished the task, she took his hand and they stepped outside.

Laura paused momentarily as a young blond soldier hobbled down the stairway. He nodded politely as he limped past her. "Could you direct me to the infirmary?" he asked. Laura pointed to the proper door.

"Just my ankle, ma'am," he said at the sight of her compassionate smile. His bright blue eyes reminded her of the bluebonnets back home, and to Laura his grin seemed as American as the flag on the Fourth of July.

"Thank you, ma'am." He nodded and limped away.

A soft smile graced Laura's mouth as her gaze followed his progress until he entered the building. It felt good to see an American face again. Despite the fact that most of the Spanish population had left the state forty years earlier when Florida had been admitted into the union, Dario had remained a Spanish community.

She had forced the passing of time from her mind, and she hadn't realized how long it had been. After seven years of seeing only dark eyes and raven hair, the sight of the American soldier's golden hair and light eyes brought a sharp pain of homesickness tugging at her heart.

Spying Ramon, Peter dashed away, leaving Laura alone. She remained in the shadows near the stairway. As she scanned the courtyard, she saw Father Montevideo talking to an American officer. The American stood over a head taller than the priest, and suddenly, Laura sensed a familiarity about the width of his shoulders and the set of his head—a startling familiarity that stirred her very soul.

In a daze she watched the officer remove his hat to rub the back of his neck. She saw the shape of his dark head and the characteristic movement of his hand. She became completely unnerved.

How was it possible? Her eyes must be playing tricks on her.

Her heart began to bludgeon her chest and, unbeknownst to her, her breath was coming in quick, short gasps.

As he talked to the priest, who had remained to discuss the available food and supplies, Zachary felt a tingling at the back of his neck—the feeling of someone watching him. His grip automatically tightened on his rifle while he struggled to concentrate on what the priest was saying.

Every second that Zachary delayed turning around, the sensation grew stronger until he was unable to ignore the feeling any longer.

With rifle raised, Zach spun around. He saw no one behind him, but he still felt eyes boring into him. Then, peering across the dimly lit courtyard, he spied the lone figure of a woman standing in the shadows near the stairway. Her figure and face were obscured, but he knew she was the one who had been staring at him. Relieved, he lowered his weapon.

Driven by an inexplicable curiosity, he slowly crossed the courtyard. His body throbbed with sensory anticipation. In surprise, he felt the increased tempo of his heartbeat. He stopped at the stairway, but the woman remained in the shadows. By now, every nerve in his body seemed strangely attuned to this obscure figure. Then she stepped into the light. He felt as if he had just taken a slug in his gut as he found himself looking into the brown eyes that had tormented him for the past seven years.

Unable to believe her eyes, Laura had stood in a state of shock as she watched Zachary Houston approach. Zach had died seven years ago.

She stepped out of the shadows and her eyes met the intensity of his deep sapphire stare. Time and place slipped away as their locked gazes triggered the awakening of cherished memories.

Joy replaced her shock. "Zach." Her lips formed his name in a soft, reverent whisper.

"My wife, Lieutenant." The voice of Luis Esposito suddenly intruded on their intimate moment. He stepped to Laura's side. "Lieutenant Houston commands the American soldiers who have just arrived, my dear."

Still stunned, Zach wrenched his gaze from her face and focused on the man's possessive hold on Laura's arm. A young boy's sudden arrival covered up the awkward moment. He came dashing up to them. "Mama. Papa," he shouted excitedly. "We can go home now that the soldiers are here."

"Mind your manners, Peter," Esposito scolded. "Your mama and papa are talking to the lieutenant."

Laura lifted the child into her arms. "He's just excited, Luis."

Slipping an arm around Laura's shoulders, Esposito curved his mouth into a smile. "And this is our son, Peter," he said to Zachary.

As Zachary stared at the family scene, his words remained lodged in his throat. Pain and bitterness hardened his gaze. "Mrs. Esposito." He nodded to acknowledge the introduction, then turned and walked away.

Laura shrugged free of Luis's arm. "Well, my dear," he said, "I can see that the American lieutenant does not waste his time with social graces." She could tell by the gleam in his eye that his remark was not as casual as it had sounded.

"I am sure he has a lot more on his mind than social graces, Luis."

Teresa hurried out of the hospital doorway and over to them. "The American lieutenant, isn't that—"

"Yes, American," Laura said hastily. "Isn't it wonderful?"

Still visibly shaken, Laura had enough presence of mind to remember that Luis did not know the name of the man who had fathered her child. Teresa saw Laura's stricken expression and fell silent.

"Teresa, let's get the boys to bed," Laura quickly murmured.

Luis's dark eyes narrowed. "Have you ever met the lieutenant before?" he asked suspiciously.

Having just seen the bitterness in Zach's sapphire eyes which, until a moment ago, had always looked on her with warmth and adoration, Laura replied without hesitation. "No, I have never met *that* man before." Glimpsing a woman watching them, Laura quickly changed the subject. "I believe your mistress is trying to attract your attention."

Luis casually glanced at the beautiful native woman holding Ramon's hand. He curled his narrow mouth into a smirk. "You will excuse me, my dear." With an air of indifference, he sauntered away.

His callousness was wasted on Laura; she had already shifted her gaze back to the tall figure in the American uniform.

"Is that Zachary Houston?" Teresa asked. She had been unable to believe her eyes when he had walked into the hospital.

Laura nodded. "But Luis must never know . . . the real truth, Teresa."

Seeing the fright in Laura's eyes, Teresa squeezed Laura's hand. "I understand," she said sympathetically. She loved Laura with all her heart and wished there was something she could do to bring her the happiness she deserved. She glanced at Luis Esposito walking away with his mistress. The very sight of him caused a feeling of loathing in her.

Across the courtyard, Zachary was waging his own internal struggle. He had received extensive instruction at West Point on how to react to the unexpected, but nothing could have prepared him for the shock of seeing Laura. His hands trembled and his body felt tied in knots. He drew on every tactical lesson he could remember in an effort to forget his personal problems and concentrate on the emergency at hand.

After checking out the ammunition and supplies, he joined O'Hara on the galleria. "How does it look, Sergeant?"

"All quiet, Lieutenant. From what I can tell, the hostiles have gone back down the hill and it's pretty quiet in that village. I think Frankie and Ski must have done a lot of damage and those bloody heathens are all lickin' their wounds or buryin' their dead."

"Well, I'll relieve you now. Put the squad on two-hour watches. How is Malloy's ankle?"

"He's okay. One of the sisters wrapped it up for him."

"Well, keep Bryce and Hoffman at their posts. You, Johnson, and Malloy get some sleep. There are empty cots in the hospital."

"Should I assign duty to the civilians, Lieutenant?"

"Not at this time. I'm prone to agree with you; those Seminoles can't have much fight left in them right now. The squad can handle the duty through the night. With ammunition as scarce as it is, I don't want any civilian wasting it by shooting at anything that moves in the dark."

When O'Hara left, Zachary took his post. The courtyard below was deserted, silent except for the muffled voices of the men in his squad heading for the hospital. Only the diffused glow from a single lamp offered any light. When they entered the building, a shaft of amber light pierced the darkness, only to be snuffed out when they closed the door. Once again, the mission became cloaked under the mantle of the moonless night.

It's too dark. Much too dark, Zachary thought. First thing tomorrow we get some torches in that courtyard and around the perimeter. *You can't put up a defense against something you can't see.*

The tall trees that surrounded the village shrouded the mission in shadow. At the far end of the village, red and orange sparks from the campfire fluttered in the air like fireflies. He made out several sleeping forms around the campfire. *Or are they bodies?* he wondered.

Zachary sensed Laura's presence before the faint fragrance of mimosa teased his nostrils. His fingers tightened around the rifle clutched in his hands. *You used to smell like lavender, Laura.*

He turned just as the moon slipped from behind the clouds. He saw her long black hair enhanced in the silvery rays. Then a wave of heat rushed to his loins at the sight of her exquisite face silhouetted in dim light. Then moving clouds drifted across the moon and Laura's image disappeared from sight. Her scent remained.

"Sneaking around in the dark could get you shot, *Mrs. Esposito.*" He turned away.

"I wanted to talk to you, Zach," Laura said, moving to his side.

"I'm on duty right now."

"I know, but I wanted to speak to you privately."

"Privately! What would your husband have to say to that, *Mrs. Esposito?*"

His mocking tone was painful to bear. She bit down on her lower lip to keep from sobbing. "I wanted to tell you how happy I am that you survived the shipwreck. When I . . . when I thought you were dead, I—"

"Was so grief-stricken, you immediately rushed out and married a rich man," he interjected scornfully.

She gasped with shock at the unjust accusation. "That's not true. That's not the way it happened at all," she cried. "I refused to believe you were dead. I waited as long as I . . ." She stopped, realizing that if she said more, she might reveal the truth about Peter.

"As long as what? A whole month? 'Til a good offer came along, *Mrs. Esposito?*"

"Stop calling me that!" she lashed out in hurt and frustration.

"That is your name, isn't it?"

Her heart felt near to bursting at his rancor. Fate had played the cruelest of tricks on them, but it was too late now. The past could not be changed. She had made a decision, and she must live by it.

Lifting her head, she met the contempt in his dark eyes. "Yes, that is my name. I just wanted to tell you that I am relieved to know you are still alive." Unable to bear another moment of the hateful scene, Laura fled down the stairway.

"Well, that makes one of us, Mrs. Esposito," Zach said softly. All the mockery had left his face and voice. Only naked pain remained.

Disoriented, Laura paused at the foot of the stairway. In the past few hours, her emotions had run the full gamut: terror, relief, exhilaration at discovering Zach alive, despair at knowing their love was forbidden. *Zach, her kindred soul mate . . . the man she would love forever.* But now the bitterness and loathing he felt toward her seemed too painful to bear. Her heart ached so much, she feared it would burst.

She could feel the strength that had sustained her thus far now draining from her. Unable to return to the stifling, small cubicle, she slumped down on a bench in the courtyard.

From the darkened doorway of his own sleeping quarters, Father Montevideo watched the dejected woman. Laura Esposito held a tender spot in his heart. Since her arrival in Dario, he had watched her bear the abuse and humiliation of her marriage with dignity, courage, and faith.

And through her own confessions, he had come to know that only deeply rooted religious conviction kept her bound to the husband who dishonored her.

Now, sensing her distress, he walked over and sat down beside her. "At such a late hour, you should be in bed, my child."

"I can't sleep, Father. I don't know what to do."

"I understand, Laura. This is a distressing time for all of us. You must not allow your courage to falter now."

"It has nothing to do with the attack, Father. This concerns something in my past."

"Would you like me to hear your confession?"

"No," she cried out in desperation, her control dangling by a tenuous thread. "I'm not talking about penance. I've done my share of penance these past seven years by living with a man I loathe." Her voice faltered and she drew a deep breath to calm herself. He squeezed her hand to give her strength. "I need advice, Father."

"Then perhaps I can be of help." His eyes warmed with humor as he tried to lighten her mood. "With Sister Francesca in charge, I have almost no opportunities to offer advice, and unfortunately, fewer ears to listen to it."

Laura hesitated only momentarily. "Father, as you know, Luis is not the father of my son."

"Yes, you have confessed as much."

"Well, not even Luis knows the name of Peter's real father. Now, I don't know what to do because . . . because my son's father is here now."

Prepared to listen to admissions he had heard before, Father Montevideo had settled into a relaxed, drowsy state, but on hearing her statement, his eyes widened in surprise. "Here? You mean in the mission?"

"Yes, Father. Zachary Houston is Peter's father."

"Zachary Hous—? You mean Lieutenant Houston!"

"I don't know what to do," she said helplessly. "I thought he was dead. But now that I've seen him again . . . I just don't know what to do. I love him so much, Father."

"But that love is forbidden, Laura. You are a married woman."

"I know, Father. But doesn't Zach deserve to hear the truth about Peter? He never knew I was carrying his child. He hates me because he thinks I didn't wait for him. He believes I married Luis for money. It isn't true, Father. Maybe if I tell him the truth he will understand."

"If you feel so strongly about it, why are you hesitating?"

"Because of Peter. If we survive this attack, how will the truth affect him? He believes that Luis is his father. Dare I disrupt his young life by revealing the truth to him now? Especially at this time?"

"You must examine your motives, Laura. Do you wish to best serve Peter's interests, or are you acting out of your personal need to regain the love of Lieutenant Houston?"

"That is unfair, Father," she lashed out. "I have never put my personal needs above Peter's."

"Then the choice is a simple one, isn't it? Remember, Laura, as difficult as it may be to honor, you made an oath before God to be the wife of Luis Esposito."

"And I took an earlier oath to love Zach forever," she said.

He patted her hand, then stood to leave. "And you have remained true to both of those pledges, my dear."

Befuddled, she watched him move slowly across the courtyard and enter the church. Laura rose and returned to her sleeping quarters. Lounging in the open doorway, Luis watched her approach.

"Tell me, dear wife, what did you confess to the good father this time?" he said mockingly.

"It wasn't a confession, Luis," she said, weary of his constant snide remarks. "We were merely talking. Where is Pilar?" she asked, seeing Ramon sleeping in the corner cot with Peter.

"She is helping the nuns nurse the two wounded Indians in the hospital. I am most anxious for her return."

"Well, I'm going there now, so the good sisters can get some rest."

"I am sure you will get your reward in Heaven, my dear."

"I hope so, Luis. Because, married to you, I've certainly had enough of Hell."

Chapter 13

❦ ～◌◠◌～ ❦

Concealed in the shadows of oleander bushes behind the stairway, Luis and Pilar clung together in the throes of lust. He slammed her back against the mission's stone wall, his tongue ravaging her mouth. Glorifying in the sensation, she welcomed the assault and threw back her head to give him freer access to her neck. He licked a trail down the slender column, shoving her bodice aside to bare her breasts. He bit down on one of the hardened nipples.

Her groan brought a salacious smile to his lips. Swooping the firm globes into his hands, he spoke obscenities as he voraciously licked and suckled. Pilar clenched her lower lip between her teeth to keep from crying out.

"I've missed my little *chica*," Luis whispered against her mouth. Licking the curve of her lips, he drove his tongue again into her mouth until she whimpered for release. He lowered his head to suckle at her breast and she squirmed wildly against him, arousing him more, until he lifted his head and looked into her dark eyes, laden with passion. Raising her skirt to above the knees, he slipped his hands between her legs. "Have you missed me, *chica*?"

"Oh, *si, querido. Si*," she moaned as he probed her heated, moist chamber.

He narrowed his mouth into a teasing grin. "I don't think so, little *puta*. How have you shown me?"

Pilar smiled seductively, then she reached for him. Opening his pants, she released his engorged phallus,

161

then slumped to her knees and ran her tongue lightly across the tip of the organ. She took him into her mouth and the sweet sensation intensified. He felt himself swell under the artful manipulation of her mouth and tongue. Hissing with pleasure, he reached out and his long fingers clutched the top of her dark head, pressing her closer, driving himself deeper. The rhythm of her action accelerated.

Perspiration dotted his brow and his breath came in short gasps. The veins at his temple bulged tautly as the blood rushed to his head and a throbbing pulse pounded in his ears. He grasped her under the arms and lifted her. Pilar wrapped her legs around his hips and Luis drove into her, pressing her harder against the wall. She curled her arms around his neck and her sharp, little teeth nipped at his earlobe, drawing blood.

Luis only laughed. His hips began to rotate, and his mouth reclaimed her breast. He bit, then suckled, eliciting a whimper from her that bordered between pain and ecstasy.

"*Eso buen, querido*! It is so good!" Pilar cried out in a tangled mixture of Spanish and English. "*Otra vez. Otra vez.* Again! Harder! *Mas fuerte! Mas fuerte!*"

He pumped harder, more furiously.

As she grasped and clawed at him, her nails left bloody streaks on his sweat-slickened back. "*Si, querido! Si!*"

Their bodies convulsed in an intense, shuddering climax. For a moment they clung together, her head slumped on his shoulder, as they struggled to regain their breath.

Luis finally lowered her to the ground. "You're such an insatiable little *puta*. Is it no wonder I love you?"

She leaned her head against his chest. "Do you, Luis?" she asked breathlessly. She raised her head and her slumberous gaze worshipped him. "Do you really love me, *querido?*"

"Of course," he said. "Of course, I love my little *chica*." Pilar was the most responsive and uninhibited lover he had ever known. At times, she created erotic delights almost beyond his endurance. For over a decade, this sensuous native girl had been his undisputed mistress; no other woman came near to rivaling her in his bed. But Luis lied when he said he loved her. He loved no one but himself.

He pulled her into his arms, slipping his hand down to fondle her breast. "Who else can set my blood to boiling?" he growled, nipping at her neck.

She giggled and leaned into him, rubbing her heated pelvis against him. He felt himself swell.

She slid her hand between his legs and rubbed his erection. "Ah, you are hard for Pilar again," she murmured as she licked the curve of his ear, then curled and tantalized the interior with darting probes.

"Yes, you make me hard," he groaned softly. "As only you can do."

"Mister, if you've got that much energy, we could use you on watch."

The sound of Flint Bryce's drawl carried to Zach's ears as he came down the stairs. "What's going on here, Corporal?" Zach asked, seeing the two men who had just come off duty standing at the foot of the stairway leaning on their rifles.

"We heard some noise, Lieutenant, so we stopped to check it out. Thought maybe a couple of those hostiles might have slipped into the compound."

Luis Esposito quickly arranged his clothing. He stepped out of the shadows. "Gentlemen, my apologies. I just came out for a cigar. A late-night smoke."

"Yeah, smokin' enough to set the place on fire," Bryce said with a snicker.

"What the hell are you talking about, Corporal?" Zach snapped.

"The *señor* ain't quite alone, Lieutenant. There's a lady with him. And from what we've been listenin' to, I sure could use a *smoke* myself," Bryce remarked. "Sounded to me like the little lady had a few to spare."

At the thought of Laura in Esposito's arms, Zach curled his hands into fists. Bryce's barrack-room humor added to his torment. He wanted to smash Bryce in the face for the obscene remark, but he wanted even more to smash Esposito. "That's enough, Corporal, you're out of line," Zach snapped. "You and Hoffman go inside and get some sleep."

"Yes, sir," Bryce said.

When the two men departed, Luis said sarcastically, "I thought your men were soldiers, Lieutenant, not voyeurs."

"Mr. Esposito, it is late, and this mission is under siege. I advise you and your wife to remain inside at night or . . ."

The words died in his throat when Pilar stepped out of the shadows. Startled, he swung his glance to Esposito, then back to the beautiful native girl.

"My . . . ah . . . housekeeper, Lieutenant." The smirk on Esposito's face told Zach much more.

Zach's dark eyes filled with contempt. "I repeat, sir. I advise you to remain inside at night *with your family* or you could easily get yourself killed." He turned away and headed for the hospital. The sound of Luis's mocking laughter followed him.

Laura glanced up when the door opened. Seeing Zach in the hospital doorway, she felt her heartbeat quicken. He entered and plopped down on a bench at a table where Bryce and Hoffman were just finishing cups of coffee.

How could he be moving freely about in her life again: resurrecting memories, longings, passions . . . guilt? He hated her now. He had told her as much just a short time ago. The past must be put behind them. He had done so; now she must too. Lives were at risk . . . Peter's life. She had to treat Zach with as much composure as she did any of the other soldiers. Walking over to the table, she set a cup of coffee in front of him.

"Thank you," Zach said, glancing up. When he saw it was Laura, he tried to conceal his surprise with a casual remark. "Thought you'd be in bed, Mrs. Esposito."

At his mention of her name, Zach saw Bryce and Hoffman exchange confused stares. Apparently, they had thought that the woman outside with Esposito was his wife.

Bryce winked at Hoffman and stood up. "Reckon we'll get some shut-eye, sir. Let's go, Hoffman." The private quickly followed the corporal to a tiny room set apart for the soldiers.

With the departure of the men, an awkward silence fell between them. "What are you doing up so late?" Zach asked when Laura sat down at the table. The obscure glow from a candle offered the only light as they spoke in quiet tones.

"The sisters have been working tirelessly since the attack," she said. "Teresa and I told them we would take over here tonight so they could get some rest. You remember, Teresa, don't you, Zach?"

"Teresa?" He glanced across the room at the young woman rolling bandages. "Don't tell me she's the girl from the Lazy R."

Laura smiled. "Teresa's nineteen now."

"I guess we're all getting older. Is your son here with you?"

"No, Peter's with Luis in one of the nun's rooms."

Like hell he is! Your husband's outside in the bushes with your housekeeper. Anger and frustration swirled in his head. *Why would the sonofabitch cheat on a wife like Laura?*

Zach wrapped his fingers around the cup and tightly grasped the mug. "I think it would be wiser for you to keep your son with you while you are here. In fact, tomorrow I'm moving all the civilians into the hospital."

"Into here? But why?" she asked.

"We're too spread out. Best thing is to get everybody under the same roof in case we're infiltrated."

She put a hand over her mouth to stifle a yawn. "Yes, I see what you mean." His gaze lingered on her dark head when she propped her elbow on the table and rested her head in her hand.

His guarded stare noted the lines of weariness on her face. "When was the last time you got a night's sleep?"

She half-smiled and shook her head. "I don't remember. A couple of nights ago, I guess." Sighing, she closed her eyes. "Everything seems so unreal. First the attack. Then you showing up here. Just knowing you're here makes me feel safe for the first time in days." In her somnolence, she began to ramble. "Are you really alive, Zach? I suspect I'll wake up and find . . . it's all been . . . just . . . another . . . cruel . . . night . . . mare." Her voice trailed off as she lay her head on the table and weariness overcame her. She slipped into slumber.

For a long moment, Zach sat staring at her. He wanted to reach out and touch that dark silken hair just inches from his hand. A muscle twitched in his rugged jaw as he fought to control his emotions. He gulped the coffee, then he slowly got up and walked around the table.

Slipping an arm under Laura's knees and another behind her shoulders, he lifted her into his arms. He waited as she stirred slightly in her sleep, settled familiarly into his embrace, and nestled her head against his chest.

He carried her into the dimly lit room. He saw that six cots were occupied, two by the wounded men and four by sleeping nuns. He gently laid Laura on an empty cot and covered her with a blanket from the foot of the bed.

For a long moment, he stood silently gazing down at her sleeping figure. He realized nothing had changed. He still loved her. Despite her marriage . . . seven years of telling himself he hated her . . . that she had never existed—he would go to his grave still loving her. He set his jaw in a grim line, spun on his heel, and walked away.

As soon as he returned to the other room, Teresa asked, "Would you like another cup of coffee, Lieutenant Houston?"

"I'll get it." He glanced askance at her. The scrawny little girl he remembered from years ago had developed into a dainty, very feminine young lady with dark hair and brown eyes. Just like Laura's, he thought. But not the same; he could never look at Laura's dark hair and eyes without wanting to take her in his arms. "You've grown into a lovely young woman since I saw you last, Teresa."

"Thank you, Lieutenant," she said. She returned to the table in the corner and resumed rolling bandages.

Zach poured himself a cup of coffee and sat down at the table. His nerves were too raw to sleep. At least two hours until daylight. He hated this time of the night . . . his thoughts played havoc when he couldn't sleep.

Zach laid his head on his arms. He closed his eyes, thinking about Laura and wondering how they would get out of the mission alive.

Still tuned to the sounds around him, he dozed. But at a loud creaking coming from the next room, he raised his head. He hesitated momentarily, then rose to investigate.

A shot rang out from outside just as the first scream sounded from the next room. "Laura!" Zachary dashed to the room.

Jolted to wakefulness, the startled nuns shrieked in terror as half-naked savages, brandishing machetes, leaped through a trap door on the infirmary ceiling.

Cots overturned and trays of medical supplies crashed to the floor as the hysterical nuns scrambled to flee from the invaders.

Pursued by one of the savages, Sister Francesca tripped over a cot and fell to the floor. Laura halted her own flight to help the woman to her feet.

With his arm raised for a fatal blow, one of the painted savages grabbed Laura by the hair. Zach's shot caught him in mid-flight, and he fell to the floor just as another invader reached her.

"Laura, get down!" Zachary shouted. He leaped at the attacker and knocked him aside. Zach ducked the deadly swing of the man's machete and swung his rifle, knocking the weapon out of the assailant's hand. Zach felt a painful sting as the sharp weapon grazed his leg in its fall to the floor.

With rifles in hand, Bryce and Hoffman raced through the doorway and joined the battle. Rifle blasts, Indian war cries, and the screams of the terrified women intensified the chaos. While the two soldiers fought off the remaining attackers, Zach and his assailant remained locked in mortal combat on the floor.

The powerful Indian succeeded in clamping his hands around Zach's throat. Zach tried to break the man's hold and groped to reach the pistol at his hip. His fingers closed around the handle of the Colt and he yanked it from the holster, pressed the barrel against the savage's stomach, and pulled the trigger.

For an instant the Indian looked startled, then his eyes rolled upward and he slumped over on top of Zach. Shoving aside the dead man, Zach staggered to his feet. His hurried glance swept the room until he found the person he sought—Laura. She looked dazed, but unharmed.

When several shots sounded from the outside, he saw her eyes widen with renewed alarm. "Peter! Oh, dear God!"

She tried to bolt past him to the door, but Zach grabbed her. "You're not going out there."

"My son's in danger. I must get to him," she cried.

Zach clamped a firm arm around her waist. "Bryce, close that trap door and latch it," he ordered as Laura continued to struggle to free herself. "Hoffman, check those bodies. Make sure they're dead." The two men hustled to obey his orders.

"All six hostiles dead, sir, along with the two wounded men and . . . one of the nuns," Hoffman said with a

sad glance at the tiny circle of nuns gathered around a
fallen figure.

When shots sounded again from outside, Bryce and
Hoffman looked at him worriedly. Zach understood their
anxiety; their comrades-in-arms were out there.

"Laura, I haven't time to argue. You must stay here.
The rest of your family is with your husband, and he is
armed. I'm sure they're safe. Do you understand?" Tears
streaked Laura's cheeks as she nodded numbly.

"Take her, will you?" Zach told Teresa. The young
woman hurried over and put an arm around Laura's
shoulders. "Come, Laura, they need our help," she said
gently.

"Lieutenant?" Bryce asked impatiently, his glance
darting toward the door.

Zach pulled the red bandanna from his neck. "Sister Francesca, lock this door when we leave, and don't
open it unless it's someone you know," he ordered as he
wrapped the bandanna around the bloody wound on his
leg.

"I understand. But your leg, Lieutenant. Sit down and
I will treat it."

"I haven't time."

"That wound should be cleaned," the nun cautioned.

"Later." He snatched up his rifle.

"Be careful, Zach." Laura's whispered plea drew his
gaze. His eyes lingered on her stricken face as he nodded. Not knowing what to expect outside, he wondered
if this moment would truly be their final one.

He pulled his Colt from the holster. "Here, Laura, take
this. You know how to use it, if you have to." There was
no time for further talk. "Okay, let's go," he told the two
waiting soldiers who had already moved to the door.
"We'll take a position right outside and stay together."

"*Vaya con Dios, Teniente,*" the nun said softly.

"Thank you, Sister," Zach replied before slipping
through the doorway. The nun made a quick sign of
the cross and closed the heavy door behind him.

As Laura watched woodenly, the bolt sliding into place seemed like a knife being driven into her heart.

The yard was deserted, and sporadic firing sounded from above. After allowing time for their vision to adjust to the darkness, the three men cautiously began to cross the courtyard. Suddenly, several savages raced down the stairway. Zach knelt on one knee and took a steady aim. His shot brought down one of the attackers while Hoffman and Bryce's shots took care of the others.

The two soldiers immediately ran up the stairway, but Zach stopped to pound on the door of the priest's room. "Father, are you okay?"

"Yes," he replied. Father Montevideo unlocked the door and opened it.

"The courtyard is clear, Father. Get to the hospital." The priest nodded and hastened across the yard.

Zach dashed to the nuns' quarters on the opposite side of the courtyard. "Everybody out. Let's go," he shouted, pounding on the door. At the sound of the increased shooting from above, he shouted louder. "Hurry up, let's go."

The door of one of the rooms swung open and Luis Esposito appeared with rifle in hand. "What has happened, Lieutenant?"

"Later," Zach said. "Right now, I want everybody to get to the hospital. Hurry. Grab whatever weapons and ammunition you have."

Luis turned to those behind him. "¡Vámonos. Dése prisa! ¡Dése prisa!" Holding Peter and Ramon by the hand, Luis's native mistress emerged from the room and the huddled group ran to the hospital.

"Anyone else in these other rooms?" Zach asked.

"No. When the firing began, I came here to protect the boys," Luis said.

"Well, get to the hospital, Esposito. That's where we'll make our final stand. If anyone gets by us, it'll be up to you to defend the hospital."

"As you wish, Lieutenant." Luis hurried across the courtyard.

Zach raced up the stairway. O'Hara sat slumped against the front wall. Bryce and Hoffman were at the north wall fighting off more Indians. Johnson was alone at the south wall. There was no sign of Malloy.

Zach dashed over to help Johnson, who was swinging a machete at one of the savages who had almost reached the top of an improvised scaling ladder raised by the Indians. Zach's shot toppled him off, and his next one picked off another of the attackers. Johnson suceeded in shoving away the ladder, which crashed to the ground. The men below fled into the trees.

"Call out if they charge again," Zach said. He rushed back to the other wall and saw Bryce using his rifle stock to fight off an Indian who had reached the top of another ladder that had been raised against that wall.

Bryce knocked the savage away, but another aggressor immediately replaced him. Zach shot that attacker, and the next Indian scrambled back down to the ground before Bryce and Hoffman succeeded in shoving away the scaling ladder.

Suddenly everything quieted. The battle had ended. Hoffman was the first to break the silence. "We've won. They've all gone," he cried victoriously.

"They'll be back," Zach said. His grave frown reflected the grimness behind the message.

He knelt down at O'Hara's side. The sergeant sat clutching his stomach. Bryce and Hoffman had already stripped off O'Hara's uniform shirt and were making a makeshift stretcher with the shirt and their empty rifles.

"How are you doing, Sergeant?"

"My gut's on fire, sir."

"Blame it on that Irish whiskey you drink," Bryce joshed. The corporal's glance met Zach's, and Bryce shook his head in a gesture of hopelessness.

"Aye, and how I cud be usin' a sip of that mother's milk right now," the Irishman said.

"I've got a bottle in my pack, Mickey," Bryce said, with a pat to O'Hara's shoulder. They carried him down the stairway.

With a somber glance, Zach viewed the devastation. Dead bodies were strewn on the galleria. "Where's Malloy?" he asked.

Norm Johnson's reply barely carried to Zach's ears. "He's over here, sir."

Zach went over to where Johnson sat holding Malloy's hand. Tears streaked the cheeks of the veteran soldier. Sadly, Zach stared at the lifeless face of the young man who had wanted to learn more about life before becoming a minister. Zach reached out and lowered the lids over eyes the color of Texas bluebonnets.

"Report, Johnson," Zach said, drawing on his fortitude. He wanted to weep with Johnson, but he knew he had to remain in control.

Johnson swiped an arm across his eyes. Zach watched with pride and respect as the veteran soldier regained his composure, stood up, and came to attention.

"Dozen or more hostiles with scaling ladders, sir. Penetrated the defenses on the north wall."

"That's where Malloy was standing watch?"

"Yes, sir. They were suddenly swarming all over this damn roof. Don't know how they got past him without Malloy seeing or hearing them coming. He never even fired a shot. His throat's been cut."

"I'll help you carry him downstairs, Johnson. We'll bury him in the courtyard."

They picked up Malloy and carried him down the stairs. Then they returned to the galleria. Bryce and Hoffman soon joined them.

Zach's head began to ache and his leg throbbed. He reached down and felt the sticky, wet bandage. Looking around at the desolation, he felt as lifeless as the scattered bodies streaked with red and black warpaint.

Dead. All dead. How in hell could this one piece of land be worth the lives of the men who had already died for it?

"Can I be of service, Lieutenant?" Luis Esposito asked.

Zach glanced up. He nodded toward the dead Seminoles. "Let's get rid of these bodies. Dump them over the side of the building and let the Indians come and claim their dead."

The rest of the night remained quiet. Nearing sunrise, Father Montevideo climbed up the galleria steps. "What are you doing up here, Father?" Zach asked.

"I come up here every morning to say my breviary, my son."

"Father, it's dangerous up here."

"No more for me than for you, Lieutenant." The priest walked over and sat on a stool. With his head bowed in prayer, he went through his morning ritual, apparently unaffected by the events around him.

Bryce came over and hunched down next to Zach. "Lieutenant, you better go down and get your leg attended to. Now that it's daylight, we can handle the watch."

"I guess I will. I want to check on O'Hara anyway."

"He ain't gonna make it, Lieutenant?"

"I don't want to think about it, Corporal," Zach said, leaving the sad-faced scout.

Laura's relieved glance swung to him as soon as he entered the hospital. Zach nodded and limped over to where O'Hara lay. "How are you feeling, Sergeant?"

"Just fine, Lieutenant. The sisters have fixed me up real good. Should be able to return to duty any time now."

"Well, we can use you, Mickey. In the meantime, enjoy the rest." For a long moment the two men looked into each other's eyes. Both knew the truth, but neither could admit it.

Sister Francesca approached them carrying a tray.

"Here, Sergeant, I want you to take these." As he lifted O'Hara's shoulders to help him swallow the pills, a sudden thought crossed Zach's mind. "What are you giving him, Sister?"

"Just a sedative to relieve the pain and relax him. It's an ester of barbituric acid," Sister Francesca said.

"Did you give this same sedative to Private Malloy?"

"Is that the young soldier with the sprained ankle?"

"Yes," Zachary said.

The nun nodded. "Yes, I gave him two pills. I knew he would have pain with that severely sprained ankle, so I tried to make him as comfortable as possible. Did he sleep?"

"Yes, Sister. I'm afraid he did," Zach said bitterly. "He's going to sleep for a long time."

"What do you mean?" she asked.

"He's dead."

Recalling the face of the friendly young soldier, Laura wanted to weep. To keep from crying, she knelt down beside Zach and removed the bloody wrapping on his leg. "I think you'd better look at his leg, Sister."

The cut went almost to the bone. "I'm going to have to stitch that up, Lieutenant," Sister Francesca said.

Reluctantly, he sat down. As Sister Francesca closed the wound, Zach clamped his teeth together and glanced around him to take his mind off the pain. Teresa lay asleep on a cot. The other two nuns were stitching blankets around the dead bodies. *I don't even know their names*, he thought as he watched them proceed quietly at the unpleasant task. Whatever their grief over the loss of their sister, they suffered silently. To his relief, Sister Francesca finished stitching his leg. He shifted his glance back to Laura, who began to gently bind it. From the moment he sat down, he had been aware of her presence just a few feet away.

"Now I want you to take these pills and lie down and rest," Sister Francesca said, reaching for the bottle of tablets.

"No pills, Sister. I have to get back on duty. Pain helps to keep me awake."

"It is important that you stay off that leg, Lieutenant, or you'll break open the stitches."

"Sister, come nightfall, I don't think it's going to matter much." He limped away.

Shortly after returning to duty, Zach stood guard alone while the others gathered in the courtyard below to bury the dead. From his vantage point on the galleria, Zach watched the simple ceremony as the bodies of the nun and the two Indians were put to rest. When Father Montevideo finished, he went over to Bryce and Hoffman, who had begun digging a grave for Malloy.

"Was your comrade a Catholic, my son?"

"No, Father," Hoffman replied. "He was Presbyterian. Planned on becoming a minister himself some day."

"Then I'm afraid you can't bury him here. This is consecrated ground, young man."

Dumbfounded, Bryce looked at the priest in disbelief. For an instant, Zach thought he would have to intercede, but Bryce carefully chose his words.

"Yeah, that's right, Padre. And Malloy consecrated it with his blood." Bryce continued to dig the grave.

Shamefaced, the old priest explained. "Forgive me, my son, but it is the rule of the church. Only Catholics can be buried here."

Bryce lifted his head and leaned on the shovel. "Look, Padre, I don't care if you speak over him or not. Figure the Lord knows what was in Malloy's heart, and He don't need no one to remind Him. So, with your words or without 'em, we're burying him here."

When Hoffman glanced up at him for direction, Zach nodded. Their situation was desperate; they needed a miracle to survive. So many had died. And Malloy . . . consecrated ground. Shit! Once the sun went down and the Seminoles launched another attack, any dumb church rules would be as worthless as spit in the wind.

Below in the courtyard, the two soldiers tossed their shovels aside and lowered their comrade into the grave. While the others watched with uncertainty, the priest opened his Bible and offered the last rites to the fallen soldier.

Later, Zach sat alone in deep concentration. Bryce and Hoffman had exhausted all of their ammunition during the attack. O'Hara had a couple rounds remaining. He and Johnson each had a clip which they had divided with Bryce and Hoffman. So when the next attack came, they would not have the manpower or ammunition to drive the Indians away. He figured their only hope lay in getting out of the mission before the attack.

He formulated a strategy and sought out Father Montevideo in the chapel. "Father, do you have any rope in the mission?"

The priest nodded. "Of course, Lieutenant. We have several skeins we use for repairing the church bell. Why?"

"We have to abandon the mission, Father. Our ammunition's too low to fight off another attack. I figure the only way out of here is that back wall. As soon as it gets dark, we'll lower two of my men down the cliff. They can run some guide ropes from the rocks to shore. Then we'll lower the rest of you down. Those rocks below will be sharp and slippery, but we'll have a better chance there than staying here. Once out of the water, we'll have to make a run for the boat waiting five miles south of here."

"But that will all take time, Lieutenant," Father Montevideo said. "And what if we're discovered? We could never outrun them." With a perceptive stare, Father Montevideo regarded him. "But you have thought of that, haven't you? There is more to your plan than you have told me, isn't there, my son."

"I've thought of a diversion to keep them occupied in order to give you a good start. Once you're all down,

I intend to surrender myself to them as soon as you leave."

Aghast, the priest drew back in dismay. "No no, my son, you must not do that. You know they will torture and kill you."

"Father, if we remain here, I'll be killed anyway. My plan will give the rest of you a chance."

"There is always hope, Lieutenant. We must never abandon our belief in help from the Almighty."

"Sir, I'm a professional soldier. I have to look at things more realistically. *There is no hope.* There isn't the remotest possibility of a relief force arriving for at least another three days. We don't have ammunition or manpower to hold out that long. And since I am responsible for the welfare of the women and children, I see no other course of action."

Zach rose to his feet. "I have already made my decision, Father. Your full cooperation will make it easier to convince the others to leave. Particularly the nuns."

Saddened, the priest lowered his head. "You have my cooperation, Lieutenant."

"I will inform my men of my intentions, but I think it wiser that we do not say anything to the others."

"I understand," Father Montevideo said kindly.

"Thank you, Father." Zach started to leave, then hesitated and glanced back at the priest. "Father, after this is all over, will you tell Laura that . . . that . . . I've never . . ." He broke off what he intended to say. Nothing would be gained by his admission of love for her. "Oh, nothing. Just forget it, Father."

The priest nodded. "I understand, Lieutenant." His eyes glistened with moisture. "God bless you, my son."

After Zach's departure, Father Montevideo sat silently immersed in sad contemplation. His aged face, usually serene, reflected his troubled thoughts. Slowly, he rose and moved to the altar, where he knelt in prayer.

Chapter 14

Toward sunset, Zachary assembled all the civilians along with Bryce and Johnson in the hospital to relate the plan to them.

"Bryce, I want you and Hoffman to go first and string guidelines. Then, Johnson, you take Peter down with you. Mr. Esposito, you go next with Ramon, then the boys' mothers and the young girl. Father, the sisters and you can follow them. Then I'll lower O'Hara down in a sling. Do you all understand?"

He glanced around at the circle of faces: some showed trepidation, others hope. "And, Sister Francesca, bring only a few medical supplies. The important thing is to move fast and silently."

"Is this your wish, Father?" Sister Francesca asked.

Father Montevideo nodded. "That is my wish, Sister."

When the nuns left to obey the orders, Zach turned to Laura and Pilar. "Ladies, get your sons ready. Either gag them or tape their mouths shut so there's no chance of them crying out." The women nodded and hurried away with Father Montevideo.

"Lieutenant." Nearby, Sergeant O'Hara had lain quietly during one of his infrequent moments of consciousness. Zach had observed him listening. "What is it, Sergeant?"

"What's the diversion?" O'Hara asked.

"I . . . ah . . . intend to surrender."

"Whatta ya mean by surrender?" Bryce asked. Flint Bryce had remained unusually silent until now, but Zach had sensed the veteran corporal's displeasure.

"I'll go out under a white flag."

Bryce snorted in derision. "Lieutenant, you know them Seminoles ain't gonna honor no white flag. They still haven't forgotten what the army did to Osceola back in '37 when he came out under a flag of truce."

"That's a chance I'll have to take, Corporal," Zach said.

"You know if you surrender, they're gonna torture you before they kill you."

Zach knew the inevitable. He had already gone through this same argument with himself, as well as with Father Montevideo. There was no alternative if he hoped to save the others. "I'm an American officer. There's a good chance they'll ransom me."

"That's bullshit and you know it, Lieutenant," Bryce said angrily. "These savages don't want ransom, they want us all dead."

"Well, if you keep arguing with me, they'll get what they want, won't they, Corporal? You men have your orders," he said obdurately. "Now, carry O'Hara up to the galleria." He walked away.

"Goddammit!" Bryce said, frustrated.

"What should we do, Sergeant?" Johnson asked, as distressed as the other two.

"You heard the Lieutenant," O'Hara said. "Let's go." Painfully, he raised himself off the cot. "The two of you give me a hand here."

Laura brought sandwiches and coffee to the soldiers who had returned to guard duty. "Zach, I want to talk to you."

"I would advise you to spend these moments with your husband, Mrs. Esposito. I don't know how many more remain."

"Please, Zach. This isn't the time for sarcasm."

"No, I guess it isn't."

They moved to the rear of the galleria. Nearby, Father Montevideo sat alone on his bench, gazing at the sunset.

"Do you think your plan will work, Zach?" Laura asked.

"Considering the alternative, it's worth a try. It should be dark enough in about another half-hour." His gaze swept the expanse of blue water. "The Gulf of Mexico. Beautiful, isn't it? Seems hard to believe that Texas lies across that pond."

"Yes, it does, doesn't it? Remember how we used to talk about sailing across the Gulf one day?"

Zach shifted his glance to her face. Her delicate profile was bathed in the flush of the setting sun; her tempting mouth bore the faint curve of a wistful smile.

He yearned to reach out and grasp her hand—to stand together and watch the sun dip into that infinite stretch of blue water just as they had done so often back home.

She looked at him. He made no effort to turn away. Inundated with memories, they stared with raw hunger into each other's eyes. He yearned to take her in his arms and cover her mouth with his own, to savor that sweet taste of her for the last time.

The scent of mimosa seemed like a narcotic. He stepped closer and started to reach out. Then he dropped his hand. What in hell was he doing? Their love had been lost seven years ago.

Laura stepped back and returned her gaze to the blue water. "I know why I came to Dario, but why are you here, Zach?"

"I was ordered here," he said, amused.

"No, I mean . . . the army. When did you join the army?"

"After *The Windsong* disaster, Senator Long and I floated on a raft in the Gulf for almost two weeks.

By the time we were rescued, and I was well enough to return to Texas, I discovered there really wasn't any reason for me to remain there."

"I wished I had known of your rescue," she said.

"I can't believe it didn't make the *Galveston Daily News*, Mrs. Esposito. Senator Long was a notable dignitary."

She was visibly shaken by his accusation. "When I heard you were dead, I shut off any mention of the outside world, Zach."

"The senator got me an appointment to West Point. So here I am. Or should I say, here we are. Just like old times. The three of us reunited again: you, me, and the Gulf of Mexico," he said cynically.

Laura had made up her mind not to quarrel with him. It was possible that these would be their final hours, and she did not want them to end in bickering. "Wouldn't it be nice if we could just climb in a boat and sail across the Gulf back to Texas . . . to our beach?" she said with a sigh.

His hungry gaze lingered on her soft smile, and for another moment they both allowed their thoughts to again drift back to those bliss-filled days. Then the grim reality of where they were, and what had to be done, shattered the picture.

"I'm afraid we haven't got time for fantasies, Mrs. Esposito. You had better get back to your husband and son."

"Yes, I guess so." She stared for a lingering moment, her brown eyes warm with longing. Then she left him alone with his thoughts.

Within the next half-hour, the civilians came up to the galleria and remained huddled behind the walls. They did not want to attract the attention of any Indians at the far end of the village.

As soon as the sun set, Zach anchored the ends of two long ropes to the galleria. Then he tied one of the loose ends around Hoffman's waist and the other around

Bryce. The two men got into position to go over the back wall. Hoffman began to lower himself, and Bryce slung his rifle over his shoulder, prepared to follow. "Good luck, Corporal," Zach said.

"Lieutenant, are you sure—"

Zach cut him off. "I'm counting on you to get them through, Flint."

"I will. I promise you. For what it's worth, I want you to know you're the finest officer I've ever served under, sir."

"Thank you, Corporal."

Zach and Johnson guided the ropes as the two soldiers were lowered to the treacherous rocks jutting out of the ocean waters below. Zach watched anxiously as they struggled to keep their footing. They slipped into the water several times; only the ropes around their waists prevented a strong current from pulling them out to sea.

After receiving four sharp tugs on the ropes, Zach and Johnson released more slack so the two soldiers could maneuver below. Minutes later, the lines were pulled taut and Zach knew Bryce and Hoffman had reached the shore and tied the ropes to a tree. Several quick tugs on the lines confirmed it. The two parallel ropes were now strung like clotheslines, angling from the top of the mission to the shore below.

Strips from sheets had been tied around everyone's palms to prevent rope burns. Zach motioned to Johnson. "You're next with the Esposito boy."

Peter was already gagged and tied in a sling on the soldier's back. His frightened brown eyes looked as round as saucers. "You hold on tight, honey," Laura cautioned. "Your father will be right behind you with Ramon." She kissed his cheek and watched fretfully as Johnson grasped a rope in each hand and began to shimmy down.

Luis followed with Ramon. Pilar next, Teresa, then the nuns. Laura was the last woman to depart.

"Good-bye, Laura," Zach whispered as she prepared

to lower herself. He reached out and lightly grazed her cheek with his fingertips.

Laura looked at him in surprise. His touch. The parting remark. It all sounded so final. Then there wasn't time to think about anything except trying not to lose her grasp on the ropes.

"All right, Father, you're next," Zach said, after all the women were safely down. He turned, but there was no sign of the priest.

"Where in hell did he go?" Zach grumbled. He was running out of time and still had O'Hara to lower.

"I saw him go down the stairs," O'Hara said from the nearby sling which had been rigged for him from two knapsacks belted together.

"Goddammit," Zach cursed. "There's no time for a delay. I'll lower you."

"I ain't goin' anywhere, Lieutenant. I'd only slow you up. We both know I'm a goner." He raised his hands off his stomach to prove his point. His midsection was soaked with blood.

Sudden shouting from the village broke off their argument. "Oh, God no," Zach mumbled, gazing over the front wall of the mission. In the light cast by the campfire at the far end of the village, he saw Father Montevideo walk into the camp holding up a cross before him.

Zach rushed down the stairway. The gate was ajar. Sickened, he closed and locked it, then hurried back up the stairway.

O'Hara had crawled to the railing and the two men watched helplessly as the yelping Indians converged on the priest. Whooping and howling victoriously, they dragged him to a post.

"There's your diversion, Lieutenant. Get goin'."

"I'm not leaving you here alone, Mickey."

"Yes, you are." O'Hara picked up the pistol at his side. "Time's a wastin', Lieutenant. Don't let the good father die for nothin'."

Perspiration dotted his brow as O'Hara grimaced with pain. "If you don't go now, I'll shoot meself to get you to leave. Don't make me take me own life, Lieutenant, or I'll be denied the Kingdom of God." His voice had weakened to a bare whisper.

Zachary had served long enough with O'Hara to know the sergeant did not make idle threats. Once the strong-willed Irishman made up his mind, there was no changing it.

Reluctantly, Zach grasped the ropes. "You've put me in a hell of a spot, Sergeant."

In spite of his pain, O'Hara grinned. "I'll keep 'em off your back as long as I can. I'm countin' on you to get those holy sisters to safety," he said.

"I'll do my best, Mickey."

Suspended over the cliff, Zach began the slide down the ropes. Zach had not quite reached the shore when O'Hara cut the first rope and it dropped toward the ground.

For a long moment, Zach dangled above the rocks and water, struggling not to lose his grasp on the other rope. He grimaced with pain and almost lost his grip when the jagged edge of a rock scraped his wounded leg.

Finally, his groping left hand closed around the remaining line, and he managed to work himself down the rope until waiting hands grabbed him. His feet touched solid ground just as O'Hara finished sawing through the rope and it dropped free.

Father Montevideo's scream of pain rent the air as the savages impaled him. O'Hara crawled back to the front wall. "You bloody heathens." Tears streaked his face and he raised his hand and shook his fist in the air. "You goddamn bloody heathens," he shouted out with his last breath. Then the empty pistol slipped through his fingers as he pitched forward in death.

"Where's the padre?" Bryce asked when he reached Zach.

"He's not coming."

"And O'Hara?"

Zach shook his head. "I'll explain later. Let's get out of here."

Alarm showed on the faces of the nuns as they hurried up to him. "Where is Father Montevideo?" Sister Francesca asked.

"I'm sorry, Sister, he's not coming."

"Then we must return to the mission," Sister Francesca declared.

"Sister, he's not in the mission. It's too late to help him. And we don't have time to argue. Bryce, take the point." The corporal immediately started off on a trot. "Johnson and Hoffman, cover the rear. Ladies, you're going to have to run. We need as much of a head start as we can get. Esposito, carry one of the boys. I'll take the other."

Zach was surprised to see Luis pick up Ramon instead of Peter. Then without a backward glance for his wife's welfare, the Spaniard followed Bryce. Pilar hurried after him.

Sister Francesca folded her arms across her chest and refused to move. "I am not leaving."

"Sister, I've never hit a woman in my life, but there's a first time for everything. Get moving *now*." The determination in his eyes allowed for no argument. After a moment's hesitation, the nuns followed after the others.

Laura and Teresa had remained with Peter. Zach lifted the youngster into his arms. "Get moving, ladies. And fast. Let's go."

There was no path to follow. In darkness, they splashed through salty marshes and across muddy flats. Their progress was often slowed when Bryce had to hack an opening through the dense thicket. Limbs snagged their hair and scratched their faces; saw grass cut their skirts and trousers.

Laura tripped on the aerial root of a mangrove and went down on one knee. Zach stopped and quickly shifted Peter into one arm.

"Are you okay?" he asked, helping her to her feet. She nodded. Grasping her hand, he continued to run.

By the time they reached the rendezvous point, the women were on the verge of collapse. Bryce fired two shots in the air to signal the boat. Breathless, the exhausted party slumped down on the beach. Only then did they remove the gags from the young boys' mouths.

Ramon's dark eyes blazed with fury at his mother. He raged at her in Spanish, too rapid for Zach to follow. "Hush up that kid, lady, or we'll have to gag him again," Zach ordered.

Pilar tried to pacify the boy but to no avail. The ten-year-old stormed over to where Zach sat slouched against a mangrove.

"Why do you bind my mouth like a *crio*?" he raged. "Why do you have me carried like a *niño*? I am not six years old like Peter."

"How old are you, kid?" Zach asked.

"I am ten years old. I am almost a man," the boy declared with an arrogant toss of his head.

Zach thought of himself at that age and of the responsibility he had carried on his ten-year-old shoulders. "My apologies, Ramon. I'm sorry, I misjudged you."

Zach saw that his unexpected capitulation took the youngster off guard. "Then I no longer must be carried?"

"Not if you can swim," Zach said.

The boy walked over to Peter. "You see. Ramon is a man. The American lieutenant says that Ramon does not have to be carried."

"I can swim too, Ramon. Why must I be carried?" Peter asked.

"Because you are only six. I am ten," he said smugly. Smiling, Ramon walked back and sat down between Luis and Pilar.

Zach had listened to the whole conversation. When Laura began to console the forlorn youngster, Zach motioned for Peter to come over to him.

"You want to do me a favor, Peter?"

"What?" the youngster said dejectedly.

"When we wade out to the boat, would you mind carrying my rifle? I don't want to get it wet. It's pretty heavy, and I'd understand if you don't want to."

With a guarded look, Peter glanced at Zach. "No, I don't mind. I'll carry it."

"You know a soldier only lets his best buddy carry his rifle."

Peter's interest perked up considerably. "Gosh, you mean I'm your buddy?"

"I'd like to think so, 'cause I sure need one right now."

"You do?" Peter asked, flabbergasted.

"Well, you know, buddies don't keep secrets from each other. And I've got a big secret."

"Well . . . you can tell me. I'll be your buddy."

"Well, buddy. I'm scared."

"You are?" Peter said, amazed.

"Yep."

"If I tell you something, will you promise not to tell Mama or Papa? And 'specially not Ramon."

"That's what buddies are for," Zach assured him.

"I'm scared too," Peter confessed. "That's why I'm glad you're carrying me. 'Cause I feel safe when I'm with you. You're 'bout the bravest man I know."

As the two talked, Luis moved to Laura's side. Unable to hear the conversation, she had been watching Zach and Peter. Her heart ached at the sight of the two dark heads lowered together in whispered conversation.

"Peter appears to have become quite attached to Lieutenant Houston."

"Can you blame him?" she said. Not once on the desperate run had Luis shown any concern for Peter's welfare, much less her own. Laura glanced over to see Peter laughing up at Zach. "Even a child knows who he can depend on."

Suddenly, the sound of gunfire nearby jolted them all to their feet. "Run to your mother, Peter."

Johnson and Hoffman stumbled out of the brush.
An arrow was embedded in Hoffman's shoulder, and
Johnson had an arm around the waist of the wounded
man to keep him on his feet. Winded, Johnson gasped
out the message. "About two dozen of them headed this
way, Lieutenant."

"How close?"

"Right behind us," Johnson said. In the distance they
could hear the approach of the whooping Indians. "We
slowed them up until we ran out of ammunition."

"You women and children get into the water," Zach
ordered. "Start wading out to meet the boat. Johnson,
help Hoffman to the boat."

The small group dashed into the surf. Zach and Bryce
turned their backs toward the beach, their rifles pointed
toward the bushes. "Where in hell is that Esposito?"
Zach shouted. "We could use his firepower."

"The bastard's probably busy stickin' it into his girlfriend again," Bryce said.

"Get ready," Zach ordered. "They're going to come
charging out of those trees any minute."

Zach had no sooner said the words than the first
Seminole appeared. Bryce fired and the Indian went
down. Zach's shot got the next one. The Indians halted
and pulled back into the trees.

"They're probably going to try and flank us," Zach
warned.

"Lieutenant, the boat has arrived and the women have
just reached it," Bryce said after casting a glance behind
them.

Relieved, Zach looked back and saw that the survivors
were being helped out of the water by the two sailors.
"Okay, fall back," he ordered.

The two men backed up cautiously. Several arrows
came flying at them. Grunting in pain, Bryce stumbled
as one of the arrows plunged into his leg.

"Get to the boat. I'll cover you," Zach yelled. Zach
fired several shots into the trees, then his gun clicked

on an empty chamber. He dashed into the surf.

"Help them," Laura cried to Luis, seeing the plight of the men in the water.

Luis did not even raise his rifle. "I only have a few bullets left," he said. "We might need them."

One of the boatswains opened up from the boat with a rifle as several Indians began swimming toward the soldiers. Exasperated, Laura snatched the rifle from Luis and took aim at one of the half-naked savages gaining on Zach. The darkness made it difficult to distinguish one figure from another.

Bryce reached the boat and Luis pulled the wounded man out of the water. Johnson swam back to aid Zach, who was struggling with an Indian. The private shoved his knife into Zach's attacker as Laura and the boatswain drove back the others with rifle fire.

Meanwhile the nuns bent over the two wounded soldiers, Bryce and Hoffman. Sister Francesca glanced up to see a savage climbing up the bow of the ship. Rallying her courage, she picked up Hoffman's empty rifle and smacked the Indian with all her might. He fell back into the water.

"God forgive me," she mumbled and made a quick sign of the cross.

Grasping hands reached out to Zach and Johnson, and the two men were hauled on board. "Get moving," Zach shouted, but the boatswain already had the vessel in motion.

Fighting for breath, Zach slumped to the deck and rested his head on the rail. In the moonlight, the shoreline quickly dwindled to a shadowy grove of treetops swaying gently in the breeze.

It looked so peaceful.

Chapter 15

Although they had just eluded capture and certain death by torture, the survivors felt no jubilation; they were weary and humbled. Despite the few medical supplies on the boat, the nuns managed to remove the arrows from Bryce and Hoffman and rebandage Zach's leg wound, which had reopened during the escape.

Lulled to immobility by the motion of the water and by their own numbed faculties, most sat dazed and stunned, mourning the loss of those left behind. Occasionally, they dozed.

Luis Esposito did not suffer such torment. Once they were underway, he curled up in the stern of the boat and went to sleep.

As frightened as the youngsters had been during the escape, now with the danger past, Ramon slept next to Pilar, and Peter lay asleep with his head resting in his mother's lap. Teresa sat slumped next to Laura.

Laura lovingly stroked her son's forehead, but her thoughts and glances strayed to Zach seated opposite them. She could tell he was in pain.

Zach felt her stare and turned his head. Silently, their gazes locked. *Thank God Laura and her son were safe.* Relief flickered momentarily in his eyes, then pain suffused it.

"Is your leg bothering you?" she asked softly.

"It's okay," he said. His suffering stemmed from a deeper wound—one that could not be covered up with a bandage. Tormented by guilt, he closed his eyes. Seven men had followed him into that jungle hell, and he had brought out only three. *What could he have done differently to prevent their deaths, or the priest's martyrdom?*

"You can't blame yourself, Zach."

Startled, he opened his eyes. Empathy showed on her face. Once again, Laura had been able to read his thoughts and feel his emotion. He wanted to crawl across the deck and bury himself in the sanctuary of her arms, to allow the touch of her hand to soothe his fears as it did the youngster in her lap. He turned his head away from her compassionate brown gaze.

Damn you, Laura, will I ever be free of you?

As the wretched party neared the city of Miami, the Stars and Stripes snapped in the breeze above Fort Dallas, the army post that had been erected in 1836 at the time of the first Seminole War.

To Laura, who had lived for the past seven years on the outskirts of an isolated native village, Miami looked like the legendary city of Atlantis shimmering in the sun.

The post commander and his aide were waiting on the pier as one of the boatswains jumped out and tied the ship to a piling on the dock. They approached Zach as soon as he stepped off the deck.

"Glad to see you back, Lieutenant," the colonel said after returning Zach's salute.

"Thank you, sir." The colonel's glance shifted to the small party being assisted ashore. "Nine civilian survivors, sir: three nuns, three other women, two children, and one man."

"Father Montevideo?" the colonel asked.

"Presumed dead, sir." Zach's jaw hardened. "Two of my squad wounded, four dead—Sergeant O'Hara, and Privates Malloy, Ryan, and Zanowski."

"Sergeant O'Hara?" the colonel said grimly. "He was a good soldier."

"Yes, sir. They all were."

"And Gregorio?"

"Still at large, sir."

The two figures before him became obscure outlines as Zach's vision suddenly blurred. Weaving, he reached out.

Amidst the fever and frenzy of delirium, Zach's groping hand found the object it sought. Grasping the hand like a lifeline, his long fingers closed around it. Immediately, his thrashing body calmed and he lay in peaceful slumber.

Laura's worried gaze remained fixed on his tormented face. As she sat at his bedside, the strain of the past week showed on her own drawn features.

"Well, how is this young man doing tonight, Mrs. Esposito?"

Laura smiled at the tall, thin man who had just entered Zach's quarters carrying a black medical bag. The knee-long, white hospital jacket he wore added to his lean appearance.

"He seems about the same, Doctor Berg."

The doctor began the routine of checking Zach's vital signs. "Well, at least his temperature hasn't risen any higher," he commented after reading the thermometer. "Now let's take a look at his leg."

Laura waited with trepidation as the doctor removed the dressing and examined the wound. "I think we've got the infection under control."

Her eyes glowed with hope. "No gangrene, Doctor?"

"Barring any unforeseen complication, I'd say this young man will walk out of here on *two* legs."

"Thank God," Laura murmured, tears filling her eyes. In her relief, she squeezed the hand she was holding. Suddenly realizing she had been clutching Zach's hand throughout the examination, Laura blushed and slipped free of his grasp.

Zach began to thrash again.

"Hmmm, that's interesting," Doctor Berg said, his gaze shifting to her over the top of Zach's medical record. "Hold his hand again, Mrs. Esposito."

Laura took Zach's hand. His thrashing immediately subsided.

"Well, Mrs.—"

"Please call me Laura, Doctor."

"Well, Laura, I think we might be on to something. When was the last time you were here?"

"Last night, Doctor. I can only come at night when my son's asleep."

The doctor carefully studied the record. "And you've been here the last three nights?"

Laura nodded.

"Uh-huh! Seems to be a definite pattern," he said. "I notice Lieutenant Houston had been considerably calmer when you've been here . . . and when you held his hand just now, well, it appears that could explain the erratic fluctuations in his condition." He finished making his entries and laid the chart on the table.

"When do you think he'll return to consciousness, Doctor?"

"I have no way of knowing. The high fever is keeping him in a delirium right now, and unfortunately, the antipyretic is not as effective as we hoped. Continue with the cool sponge baths. They, at least, help to keep him comfortable. Since you seem to be the best medicine we can give him, I hope you can continue to remain with him."

"How are Corporal Bryce and Private Hoffman doing, Doctor Berg?"

"Their conditions have stabilized, and they're anxious to get out of bed. I'm releasing them tomorrow. However, this is the young man who concerns me. I wish I could spend more time with him, but unfortunately, you arrived during an outbreak of dysentery. The number of cases is putting excessive demands on our limited staff and hospital beds. I can't tell you how invaluable

your services have been, Laura. Thanks to you and Miss
Moreno nursing him here in his quarters, we've been
able to keep him isolated from the dysentery patients.
And the nuns' assistance at the hospital has been a god-
send."

"We're all glad to do it, Doctor Berg. Lieutenant
Houston and his squad saved our lives."

"Well, if there's any change in Lieutenant Houston's
condition, please notify me at once. I'll be at the hospital."

"I will, Doctor."

Long after the doctor's departure, Laura continued to
sit at Zach's bedside. The doctor's optimism had heart-
ened her considerably. Since their arrival, Zach had lain
near death, flushed with fever, infection ravaging his
body. He often alternated between wild, incoherent mut-
terings and sporadic attacks of uncontrollable shivering.
Having once accepted Zach's death in the past, Laura
knew she could never again bear that despair.

She studied his cherished face—the firm jaw darkened with a week's growth of beard, thickly lashed
lids hooding the dark eyes she found so unsettling. She
reached out and gently caressed his brow. "I love you,
my darling," she whispered.

Her frown deepened at the feel of his hot forehead.
Regardless of what the doctor said, she would not know
peace of mind until his fever broke. After putting a cool
compress on his brow, she moistened his lips with a
damp cloth and trickled a few drops of water down his
parched throat.

Laura lowered the sheet and began to bathe him. As
she ran the sponge down his arms, her gaze fell on the
scar on his shoulder. The poignant memory of a long-
ago day filled her thoughts as her loving caress skimmed
across the muscular brawn of his chest and followed the
tapering trail of dark hair to his lean stomach. She hesitated momentarily, not from any sense of modesty but
from the knowledge of his vulnerability; then, as she

had once done long ago, she cleansed his most intimate areas.

This time, as hard as she tried, she could not recapture the same impassiveness. For since that bygone day, she had been his lover. Her mind became inundated with memories of how often his lithe, muscular body had become aroused by her simplest touch.

For the sake of her own sanity, she shifted her efforts to his legs—the long, powerful legs of a horseman. And as she gently bathed the wounded limb, she recalled the many times she had watched him agilely swing his leg onto a saddle. Tears glistened in her eyes; one day, he would ride again. Finishing the bath, she leaned down and gently pressed a kiss to his lips.

Sometime in the hushed hours between midnight and dawn, Zachary regained consciousness. For a long moment, he lay in a stupor, but despite his disorientation, he felt serene. Then he sensed the reason; Laura was holding his hand.

He opened his eyes and saw her. Still sitting in the chair, she had fallen asleep with her arm curled under her head on the bed. He reached out and tenderly fingered several long strands of dark hair that had slipped from the bun on top of her head. They felt like silk. He smiled, filled with longing as he watched her sleeping face. The faint fragrance of mimosa drifted up to him. He closed his eyes and slept.

Laura awoke with a start. Realizing she had dozed off, she glanced around guiltily. Slowly slipping her hand free of Zach's, she stood up and stretched. The awkward position she had slept in had caused stiffness in her neck and shoulders. Closing her eyes, she twisted her head and neck to loosen the tight muscles. When she opened her eyes again, Zach was watching her.

"Hi."

"Zach! Oh, thank God you're awake."

"How long have I been out?"

"Three days and three nights."

"Three days and . . . ?" He glanced around the dimly lit room. "This looks like my quarters. Are we in Miami?"

"Yes, we are. Don't you remember arriving here?"

"Vaguely."

"You've been very ill, Zach." She stood for a moment, staring at him in relief. Suddenly galvanizing herself to action, she put a hand on his forehead. "It feels as if your fever's broken. I'll get the doctor."

When she turned to hurry away, he grabbed her arm. "No, wait, Laura." His hand slid down her arm and clasped her hand. "I would like to get my bearings for a few minutes before I have to answer a lot of questions."

He saw her smile of understanding. For an awkward moment they gazed at each other. *Oh, God! I love you, Laura.* Then he released her hand. He started to fumble at his leg and tried to sit up.

"Zach, if you don't lie still, I'll have to get the doctor now."

"My leg, is it . . . ?" He felt rising panic.

"It's going to be fine, Zach," she assured him. Relief gleamed in his eyes and he laid back. "Now don't you move until I return." She rose to leave.

"Laura." A tremor rippled along her spine. She had not heard the intimate huskiness of his voice for seven years. Her legs began to tremble and she turned to face him.

"Thanks for your help." Transfixed, she stared into his disturbing, dark-eyed gaze. Then, forcing herself to turn away, she hurried from the room.

Pilar had arisen early and was preparing cornmeal for breakfast when Laura entered the house and slumped down at the table. "The lieutenant, he is dead?" Pilar asked worriedly at the sight of Laura's listlessness.

"No, he has regained consciousness. Teresa is with him right now."

"I'm glad. The lieutenant, he is a good man." She took a seat at the table opposite Laura.

"Yes, he is," Laura said softly. "Are the boys still sleeping?"

Pilar smiled with fondness. "*Los niños* will sleep for hours yet."

Yawning, Laura leaned back in the chair. Despite Pilar's unusual role in the household, Laura felt no resentment toward the woman. Actually, she liked her. Pilar had a pleasant, even-natured personality and a heart overflowing with love toward everyone. Even Luis. Laura couldn't understand how the woman could love him, but there was no doubt that Pilar worshipped him. She had even converted to Catholicism to please him.

However, Laura was grateful for the love and kindness Pilar gave to Peter. She treated him like her own son. The poor woman had given birth to Ramon when she was only fifteen and due to the complication of that birth, she was unable to bear other children.

Strangely enough, Laura reflected, although of different ethnic heritages, they could have been mistaken for sisters. Not only were they identical in age, but both of them had long black hair and sloe-shaped brown eyes. Only her own lighter, tawnier complexion distinguished her from Pilar's deeper coloring.

Recalling the day she had arrived in Dario, Laura remembered her shock and embarrassment upon discovering Luis's mistress and bastard son living in her husband's home. But as her loathing for him intensified, she had grown to welcome Pilar's presence, a distraction that kept her husband away from her own bed, since she had refused to sleep with Luis from the time Peter was born.

With neither feeling threatened by the other, they had developed a fondness for each other, and since the time Peter could walk, their sons had been inseparable companions.

The only thing Laura now found bizarre about the whole relationship was Pilar's unusual connection to her tribe. Although only a few people knew it, she was the younger sister of the rebel leader Gregorio, and she adamantly insisted that her brother had not lead the raid on Dario.

Laura was unaware that Pilar was studying her just as intently. She observed the weariness on Laura's face. "Why don't you lie down and get some sleep? I will go and take care of the lieutenant when Teresa is through."

Laura raised a hand to stifle another yawn. "The doctor said that since Lieutenant Houston has regained consciousness, it's most likely he will no longer need bedside nursing. We'll probably only have to check on him hourly."

Pilar leaned over and patted her hand. "You care about the lieutenant, don't you?"

"Of course, I do, Pilar. I'm grateful to him. He saved the lives of our sons."

"No, I think you carry much love for him in your heart. I have seen how your eyes linger on him when you think others do not see. You have been lovers in the past."

Too weary for further denials, Laura lowered her head, unable to look at Pilar; Laura knew the truth would be evident on her face.

Pilar squeezed her hand. "You are a good woman, Laura. You have always been kind to me and Ramon. And you have never beaten any of my people. This, too, is a sign of your goodness. Your secret is safe with me. I wish for you and the lieutenant to have the love you deserve."

Laura looked up with a smile of gratitude. "Thank you, Pilar, but I'm afraid that day has long passed for the lieutenant and me. I am a married woman now . . . and . . . the lieutenant has grown to hate me."

Sorrowful, Pilar shook her head. "Then he is a fool. The lieutenant is a good man, but he is a fool." Her lovely face saddened. "But Pilar fears that love makes fools of us all."

* * *

Later in the afternoon, Doctor Berg thanked Laura and
Teresa for their efforts and told them that since Zach
had regained consciousness he would no longer need
nursing during the night.

Laura accepted the change with mixed emotions; the
doctor's assurance of Zach's recovery gave her peace of
mind, but staying away from Zach would be a living
hell.

Her only solace at the moment was not having to bear
the presence of Luis. Upon their arrival in Miami, they
had been given temporary housing in the quarters of an
officer who had recently been reassigned to Washington,
D.C. Luis had then sailed to St. Augustine to arrange
the transferral of his funds from the bank there to one
in Miami.

The close confinement in the mission and the startling
appearance of Zach in Dario had put a strain on Laura's
nerves, which had already been stretched to the limit by
the Seminole attack. Coping with Luis during the critical
nights of Zach's illness would have been an additional
complication and she welcomed her husband's absence.
Pilar appeared to be the only person in the household
who missed him.

However, in the days that followed Dr. Berg's announcement, Laura existed in a state of restlessness and
frustration—grateful that Zach was on the road to recovery, but wrestling with the despair of her futile love for
him.

"Be thankful that he has survived, Laura," Teresa said
kindly, trying to console Laura.

"I am, Teresa. And I know we must put the past behind
us. But God forgive me, I just can't stop loving him, no
matter what I tell myself."

Teresa squeezed her hand in understanding. "Of course
you can't, Laura. And you should not feel shame. Only
a very few are blessed to know the beauty of an eternal
love."

"What would I ever do without your friendship,

Teresa? If it weren't for you, I would have gone out of my mind a long time ago. You've been such a strength and counsel to me all these years."

After Laura left, Teresa sat in deep reflection. For a long time, she had realized that the day when she would have to leave Laura was drawing ever nearer. She was no longer comfortable in the household of Luis Esposito. His presence disturbed her. Too often, his eyes seemed to feast on her, and the suggestive gleam in his expression brought a blush to her cheeks. Although saddened by the thought of leaving Laura and Peter, Teresa felt the time had come for her to go, before a disaster occurred.

She had been reconsidering her earlier thoughts of becoming a nun. The incident at Dario had reinforced that idea. But how could she bear to tell this to her dear friend?

Chapter 16

Zach was almost finished shaving when a light tap sounded on the door. He knew who the caller would be. "Come on in," he shouted.

Peter Esposito burst through the door like a ray of morning sunshine. "Hi, Zach."

"Well, good morning, buddy. All set to go into town?"

"Yep." Peter sat down on the bed and watched Zach glide the razor across his chin. "When will I be big enough to shave, Zach?"

"Well . . . let's see. How old are you now?"

"Six years old," Peter piped up proudly.

"I'd reckon in about another year." Grinning, Zach wiped the remaining shaving soap off his face and tossed the towel at Peter.

Giggling, the youngster snatched it off his face and flung the towel aside. "Is your leg all better now?" he asked when he saw Zach trying to work the stiffness out.

"Getting there."

"Mama thinks we shouldn't go today. That you should rest your leg. She said I shouldn't bother you so much."

"Tell your mother I said you aren't bothering me. Women don't understand about buddies, pal." Zach put on his uniform shirt and pulled the suspenders of his pants up over his shoulders.

"You like wearing s'penders, Zach?"

"Nope," Zach tolerantly replied.

"Why do you wear 'em then?"

"To keep up my pants."

"Why don't you wear a belt like me? My belt keeps up my pants."

Zach tried not to grin. "Because your belt wouldn't fit me." Grabbing his hat from a wall peg, he pulled it low on his forehead. "Let's get going, buddy."

"Goody—e-e-e!" Peter exclaimed. He jumped off the bed. Suddenly attracted by an object on the nightstand, he ran over to the table. "You finished it!" he cried enthusiastically, picking up a carved wooden whistle.

"Yeah, last night. Now, do you remember what I taught you while I carved it?" Zach questioned.

"Sure," Peter declared with a grin.

"Well, let's just see," Zach said. "I had a wooden whistle . . ."

"But it wooden whistle," Peter immediately responded to the cue.

"I got a steel whistle . . ."

"But it steel wouldn't whistle," Peter came back, grinning broadly.

"So . . . I got a tin whistle . . ." Zach recited.

"Now I tin whistle," Peter shouted, throwing his hands in the air.

Laughing, Zach scooped up the youngster into his arms and carried him outside. He put him down when he saw Laura standing in a nearby doorway. "Did you tell your mother where we were going?"

"Yeah. Why don't we ask Mama to come with us, Zach? She's all alone today. Papa's not back yet, and Teresa went with Pilar and Ramon to visit a friend in the village."

Zach hesitated. Two weeks had passed since their return to Fort Dallas, but he and Laura had not spoken since the morning he had regained consciousness. He glanced down at Peter, waiting with wide-eyed innocence. "Well, maybe your mother might prefer a quiet day alone, Peter."

"Let's ask her." The youngster dashed ahead of him as Zach reluctantly followed.

Peter rendered the question with typical youthful rhetoric. "Mama, Zach wants to know if you want to come with us."

Meeting her surprised glance, his expression remained inscrutable. "Well . . ." she murmured, "I don't know—"

"Come with us, Mama," Peter begged, tugging at her hand.

"I'm tempted," Laura said. "The idea of seeing the city sounds more appealing than just staying around this fort." Nodding, she allowed Peter to pull her along with him.

Stepping outside the gates of the Spartan army post was like stepping into a tropical paradise to Laura. She found that the quaint community was rich in Spanish architecture. Colorful bushes of hibiscus and azaleas abounded along the streets and in patios. Leafy stalks of brilliant purple bougainvillea crept up the walls of buildings, and galleries were lined with terra cotta pots holding delicate camellias, bright red-leafed poinsettias, and golden begonias. White gardenias and yellow jasmine scented the air like a summer's garden.

They toured the city slowly. Wherever they roamed, her senses were courted by the sights and fragrances of the wonders surrounding them. Pink flamingos waded in the warm blue waters that lapped at the white sands of the beaches stretching from the city's shores.

They stopped in the city square to read a plaque that commemorated the founding of the city of Miami in 1870. "My goodness, the city isn't very old at all, is it?" Laura remarked.

"Well, actually the migration began much earlier," Zach said. "Fort Dallas was built in 1836 at the time of the First Seminole War. Many Floridians sought refuge at the fort then and during the next two Seminole wars that followed. Some remained here and opened businesses rather than return to the dan-

gers and hardships of the Everglades. Other than the
military, there's a civilian population of over two hundred. That's quite a sizable number, considering Miami's
distance from the more populated northern part of the
state."

"Well, I haven't seen northern Florida either," Laura
said.

"Not even St. Augustine?" Zach asked, surprised.

She shook her head. "Luis has gone there several times
in the past on business or a holiday, but he has never tak-
en me with him."

Zach didn't reply. If he were married to her, he would
never leave her for any length of time.

Bored with the conversation, Peter darted ahead, so
they began to move on. "Well, Miami has nowhere near
the sophistication of Galveston, but I love it," Laura
enthused.

"Have you been back to Texas since your marriage?"
Zach asked.

"No."

Peter came racing back to them. "Mama, Zach, come
and see the big crocodile." He grabbed Laura's hand and
started to tug her toward several tents.

"Must be some kind of a medicine show," Zach said.

The medicine show had only two acts: an Indian wrestling a crocodile and a dancing bear, and a barker, who
was selling an elixir promised to be the cure-all for everything from gout to the restoration of hair.

After listening to him hawk the medicine for several
minutes, Zach murmured aside to her, tongue-in-cheek,
"Maybe I should buy a bottle to see if it will help the
stiffness in my leg."

"I'm sure Dr. Berg will appreciate that," Laura scoffed
as they moved on.

Zach bought a bag of popcorn, then he and Laura
walked over to watch the dancing bear. The declawed
animal was chained around the neck and had a metal
vise on its jaws. The trainer kept prodding the creature
with a stick to make it stand on its hind legs. The bear

then lumbered about to a tune the trainer squeezed out of a concertina.

Laura turned away in disgust. "I hate to see animals treated so cruelly."

"You remind me of my dad," Zach commented as they walked over and joined Peter, who was engrossed in watching a man wrestling a crocodile whose jaws had been bound by rope.

He glanced up excitedly when Laura put her hand on his shoulder. "Boy, Mama, I bet that croc's almost as big as Old Slither," he exclaimed. "Can we come back here tomorrow and show Ramon?"

"We'll see, honey," Laura said. "Zach bought some popcorn. Do you want some?" she offered.

"Not now, Mama, I'm watching the wrestling."

Chuckling, Zach winked at Laura. "Can't expect a man to eat and watch at the same time."

After several minutes, Laura had seen all of the wrestling she cared to. She strolled over to a dapple gray mare tied to a hitching post. Apparently the horse was used to pull the wagon.

"Hi there, girl," she murmured, patting the animal's head.

"She looks like she's been rode hard and put away wet."

Laura turned at the unexpected sound of Zach's voice behind her. The comment was a favorite one of cowboys to describe a particularly run-down nag. "Now don't be nasty," she scolded lightly. "Look at the poor dear. There's no reason why she couldn't be kept in the shade instead of out here in the sun."

"Well, we can fix that easy enough," Zach said.

He grinned when he saw the impishness that gleamed in her eyes. "Do we dare?" she asked.

Laughing, he untied the reins. "All they can do is shoot us for being horse thieves."

Laura followed as he tethered the gray in the shade of a nearby oak. "There, girl, doesn't that feel better?" She drew a handful of popcorn out of the bag. The mare nibbled at the kernels on her outstretched hand.

"Zach, whatever happened to your sorrel?" Laura asked as she continued to feed the horse.

"Drowned, I reckon, along with the rest of the livestock when *The Windsong* went down."

He watched her face shift into sadness. "He was so beautiful." When the bag was empty, Laura brushed the crumbs off her hand. "Wish I had more, but that's all there is, girl. "

"You always were a lollipop when it came to strays, Laura," he said, unaware of the affection that softened his voice. "I remember the time you fed some mangy stray dog half of an apple pie you had just baked for me."

She glanced askance at him. "Well, you didn't like it anyway. You told me the pie was too tart."

Grinning, he leaned his hips on a nearby barrel, crossed his arms over his chest, and stretched out his long legs. "I liked it. I just wasn't going to give you the satisfaction of telling you so. And if you remember, that damned dog hung around for months." He shoved his hat to the back of his head. "Ugliest critter I've ever seen. Only thing uglier was the bitch he finally took off with into the brush."

"And they lived happily ever after," she declared. "Trouble with you, Zachary Houston, is that you have no romance in your soul." With a saucy toss of her head, she pivoted and walked back to Peter's side.

For a long moment Zach remained still. He watched her hair bounce on her shoulders and the subtle sway of her hips as she strode away. Then he followed.

A short time later, they stopped at an apothecary to give Zach an opportunity to sit down and rest his leg.

He winked at Laura when Peter's eyes rounded with delight at his first taste of a Hires rootbeer. "Mmm-m-m, this sure tastes good, Zach," Peter said, smacking his lips together.

Laura had passed up the rootbeer for a glass of lemonade. "What is it exactly?" she asked curiously.

Zach offered her his glass. "Here, taste mine. It's a soft drink a Philadelphia pharmacist concocted. I understand he originally intended for the drink to be used as an herbal tea."

"Oh, it is good!" she exclaimed after a few sips. She finished his rootbeer and he drank her lemonade.

Then he leaned back in his chair and stretched out his aching leg while Laura and Peter each proceeded to consume a dish of chocolate ice cream. He grinned broadly when she licked the spoon clean.

"What?" she asked sheepishly when she glanced up to discover herself the focus of his amusement.

"Would you like another one?"

"No, of course not." She put down the spoon and primly laced her hands together on the tabletop. After several seconds, she stole a glance at him. The grin hadn't left his face.

She shifted her eyes back down. A faint smile tugged at the corners of her mouth, causing the sudden appearance of two captivating dimples. "Well it *was* delicious," she said. He responded with a warm chuckle.

"Hurry up, Peter," Laura quickly added, in an attempt to divert attention from herself. "Pity Ramon isn't here to enjoy a dish of this ice cream."

"Is Pilar from this area?" Zach asked. "Peter mentioned she was visiting friends in the village."

"No, I don't think so. But I understand some of the friendly natives who escaped the attack on Dario either came here or took refuge in the Everglades."

"Boy, this ice cream was the bestest thing I ever ate," Peter declared solemnly as he shoved away his dish.

"You want another dish, buddy?" Zach asked him.

"Can I, Zach?" His brown eyes were bright with eagerness.

"Ask your mom, pal."

"Can I, Mama?"

Laura sat basking in the pleasure of watching the affection between the two. Helpless to resist Peter's plea, she smiled and nodded. "All right, sweetheart."

Zach motioned to the druggist to bring another bowl. As soon as it was put before him, Peter enthusiastically attacked the confection.

"Didn't he ever taste ice cream before?" Zach asked.

"No, this is his first opportunity."

"Don't tell me that rich husband of yours couldn't afford to buy his son a dish of ice cream?"

The sarcasm in his voice put her on the defensive. "Zach, Dario is a remote native village. What do you expect?" Somehow the previous feeling of companionship had suddenly slipped away from them.

Neither tried to recapture it on the walk back to the camp. The specter of Luis Esposito had risen between them.

As though the day hadn't taken enough of a turn for the worse, Luis Esposito was waiting when they arrived back.

At the sight of his father, Peter rushed up to Luis. "Papa, Papa, guess what? I had ice cream and rootbeer."

"That's nice, Peter." When he brushed aside the boy impatiently, Laura lifted Peter into her arms.

"Lieutenant Houston, do you have any idea when the army intends to return to Dario?" Luis asked.

"I'm not abreast of the army's plans, Mr. Esposito. I've been officially on sick call since we returned."

"Oh, that's right. You were injured. It slipped my mind, Lieutenant," Luis remarked indifferently.

"Lieutenant Houston almost lost his leg, Luis," Laura reminded him sharply.

"I apologize for my lapse of memory, Lieutenant. Of course, they say you can't keep a good man down," Luis said with a simper.

"So I've heard," Zach said. "I had better get back to my quarters." He nodded to Laura. "Mrs. Esposito . . . Peter."

"Good-bye, Lieutenant. And thank you for your kindness to Peter." She looked at her son. "Peter, don't you have something to say to Lieutenant Houston?"

"Bye, Zach. See you in the morning." When she looked askance at him, Peter added hastily, "Oh, and thank you for the ice cream and rootbeer."

"It was my pleasure, Peter."

As Zach walked away, Laura brushed past Luis and entered the house. He followed her inside. "Peter, go to your room and get ready for your nap. I want to talk to your mother alone for a few minutes," he said.

"Where are Pilar and Ramon?" Luis asked after Peter scampered off.

"They're visiting the village. Some of our field hands are there."

"That's good to know because I intend to return to Dario as soon as possible."

"Return? But it's not safe. Aren't you relieved we got out of there alive? Consider the families who perished. And Father Montevideo."

"The Indians have long since returned to the swamps. You know as well as I do that Gregorio doesn't remain long in any one spot."

"Pilar believes Gregorio wasn't among the Seminoles who attacked us."

"Nonsense, of course he was."

"She said he is not a murderer, and what's more, he would never endanger her life or Ramon's."

"Pilar is an idealistic dreamer," he scoffed.

"She would have to be, to love you," Laura lashed out.

"Tut, tut, Laura. Is that any way to speak to me, considering I was thoughtful enough to bring you a new gown?" He walked over to a stack of boxes on the floor, lifted the top of one and pulled out a ruby-colored gown of chiné silk.

"That's a ball gown, Luis. As badly as I need a change of clothing, of what use is a fancy ball gown to me?"

"I have transferred my funds. You can buy whatever clothing you need right here in Miami. But I wanted to make certain you have a proper ball gown to wear at the party I intend to host."

"A party? Good God, Luis, what is there to celebrate when so many have lost their lives? That exceeds even the limits of your normal bad taste. Don't expect me to be a part of it."

His eyes narrowed in contempt. "How you misjudge me, my dear. The party is not a celebration, but rather to thank the army for their services. And as my wife," his voice deepened to a threat, "I expect you to be at my side."

"You aren't fooling me for a moment. You're not thanking the army, you're just trying to bribe them for permission to go back to Dario."

His cold chuckle put a chill down her spine. "You're always so suspicious of my motives, my dear. It's no wonder our marriage took such a disastrous turn."

"Our marriage is disastrous because you're a sadistic, hedonistic bastard with no conscience."

Laughing, he shrugged off the accusation and walked to his bedroom. "When Pilar arrives, send her to me. The whores in St. Augustine were as inept in bed as you are. And tell her if she keeps me waiting too long, I might have to . . . ah . . . whip her." He stopped at the door and turned back, his face curled into a salacious smirk. "Unlike you, my dear wife," his tongue snaked out of his mouth to wet his lips, "she enjoys it."

Long after Laura went to bed that night, she lay thrashing restlessly, covering her ears to try to close out the sounds of lovemaking that filtered through the thin wall of the next room. Finally, unable to bear another moment of it, she rose from the bed and left the room. Not wanting to disturb Teresa or the two boys, Laura went outside.

She didn't know that one of the boys was not sleeping; Ramon lay with tears streaking his cheeks as he too listened to the sounds coming from the other room.

Crossing her arms over her breasts, Laura leaned against a post and gazed up hopelessly at the moon. *How much more of this can I bear? Oh, Zach, help me. Get me away from here. I love you. I need you so badly*, she cried out silently.

Nearby, a tall figure stood in the shadows of a doorway. Zach had seen her come outside. Mesmerized, he stared at her; his yearning gaze devoured her. Everything about her was so exquisitely lovely to him. Moonlight had transformed her skin into golden bronze and her disheveled black hair hung in a shimmering cloud past her shoulders. He could feel his need for her blaze up within him, licking at his loins like fingers of fire.

He loved her so much—wanted her so desperately—but he dared not tell her. He could only watch from shadows.

Yet all he would have to do was walk over, take her in his arms, and carry her back here to his bed—where she belonged. In his arms. Their bodies entwined. And he knew she would come willingly. Their minds were as one. Always had been.

Perspiration began to dot his brow. Why deny what both of them wanted so passionately? Honor be damned, he told himself. When he felt himself on the brink of losing his control, he cursed himself for being a goddamn fool, turned, and walked back to his room.

Two days later, Luis carried out his plans. Laura finished dressing for the ball, but she did not look forward to the evening ahead. Luis's insistence on this party was an embarrassment to her. While she had never owned such an elegant gown before, that fact did not generate any excitement for her. She glanced in the mirror for a final inspection.

The bodice of the ruby-colored gown of chiné silk was

draped in loose folds across her full breasts and ta-pered down to a fitted waist; ribboned garlands of pink and white silk oleanders formed narrow shoulder straps. Kilted, pink folds of the same material hugged her hips and were drawn into a small ruby and pink bustle at the rear.

To try and remain cool during the evening, she had swept her long hair into a loose bun on top of her head.

She was about to turn away when Teresa hurried in with a tiny garland of fresh oleander. "Why aren't you dressed?" Laura asked.

"Forgive me, but I prefer to remain here with the chil-dren. Parties do not appeal to me," Teresa said shyly as she pinned the garland of fresh flowers around the bun on Laura's head.

"I certainly feel the same way about this one," Laura bemoaned. She pulled on long pink gloves that covered her arms to above the elbows. "Well, how do I look?" She spun around in a circle for Teresa's inspection.

Teresa smiled as the ruby skirt swirled above the pink satin shoes Laura wore. She hugged Laura enthusiasti-cally. "You look so lovely. Everything is perfect."

Laura slipped her arm around Teresa's waist. "Thank you, dear, but I'm afraid I don't feel very lovely."

When she entered the kitchen, Laura found Luis already dressed and waiting. He looked elegant. His slim figure was sheathed in a short, waist-long jacket, black fitted trousers, and a white ruffled shirt.

When he saw Laura, Luis swept her with his dark gaze, gleaming with admiration. "You look exception-ally exquisite tonight, my dear."

Peter jumped to his feet excitedly and ran over to her. "Oh, Mama, you're so pretty." His hand stroked the red silk skirt. "This is the most beautifulest dress I've ever seen. Wait until Zach sees it. Bet he'll like it too."

"I'm sure he will," Luis replied with a sneer.

Laura was delivered from having to respond when

the bedroom door opened and Pilar entered. She wore a stunning white Chinese shantung gown, hand-painted with large orange, red, and blue flowers. The vivid pattern enhanced her native beauty. Her dark hair, brushed to a silken sheen, hung to her shoulders, and two large white ginger blossoms were tucked behind her ear.

"What are you dressed for?" Luis asked.

"The party, of course," Pilar answered with youthful enthusiasm.

Luis laughed. "Surely, you don't expect to accompany us, Pilar? We are going to a ball, not a bordello," he said in a voice rife with mockery.

Teresa covered her mouth to stifle a sob. Laura gasped with shock at the insensitive remark, and saw the eagerness drain from Pilar's face. Her chin quivered and her dark eyes welled with tears.

"But . . . the dress . . . I thought . . ."

Luis went over and slipped an arm around her shoulders. "Is for later, my little *chica*." He gave her a light swat on her rear. "When I get back, you and I will have our own little party."

Blinded by tears, Pilar dashed from the room. Teresa quickly followed to comfort her.

Shrugging his shoulders, Luis threw up his hands in mock innocence. "What can I do? I cannot offend polite society by bringing a wife *and* mistress to a ball."

"I would be delighted to remain behind," Laura said with contempt.

"But then you would disappoint your Lieutenant Houston," Luis replied sarcastically.

He offered her his arm. "Come, my dear, as host and hostess, we mustn't be late for our own party."

"You're such a bastard, Luis," Laura mumbled with loathing in a low voice. Ignoring his proffered arm, she brushed past him.

Forgotten were the two young boys who had sat silently witnessing the pitiful scene. Peter's eyes were moist with tears of compassion; Ramon's eyes were stark with hatred.

Welcoming the diversion from the mundane routine of army life, the full garrison of Fort Dallas turned out for Luis's party.

Luis carried off the role of gracious host with panache, exuding the continental manners that often deceived people who met him for the first time. He greeted each officer individually, kissed the hand of each wife, bowed, smiled, flattered, charmed.

Standing side-by-side with Laura, Luis knew that they made a handsome couple: he in the formal attire he had purchased in St. Augustine, and Laura looking ethereal and elegant in her new ball gown. Frequently, he slipped his hand around his wife's bare shoulders or slim waist as he introduced her to an approaching guest.

After the last guest arrived, Luis made a fervent speech thanking the army and extolling their valor and sacrifice in the rescue of the Dario refugees. He spoke of the terror of the attack, of the anxiety of a husband and father for the welfare of his wife and son, as well as that of his other household members. He agonized over the deaths of dear friends and their families, of the sacrifices of Father Montevideo, Sister Carlotta, the Christian natives. By the time he finished his speech, most of the women in the room were sniffling into lace-edged handkerchiefs.

Then the regimental orchestra struck up the strains of a Strauss waltz and Luis led his wife to the dance floor; to the applause of the spectators, he waltzed her around the floor.

From across the room, Zach leaned against the wall with his arms across his chest. His expression remained inscrutable. Standing beside Zach, Flint Bryce and Norman Johnson could not disguise their obvious disgust.

"Somebody ought to get up and tell the people the truth about that bastard," Bryce grumbled.

"If I know you, Bryce, you probably will after a couple more drinks," Johnson teased.

"Every time a shot was fired, he buried his head like a goddamned ostrich. The bastard's lucky he didn't get a bullet up his ass." Johnson started to laugh. "Well, it's true. Hey, did anybody here ever see him fire his rifle the whole goddamned time?"

"No, but his wife sure knows how to handle one," Johnson piped up. "You should have seen her, Lieutenant, when you were fighting off those Seminoles in the water. I think Esposito must have been peeing in his pants 'cause she grabbed that rifle out of his hands and started to pick off those bastards around you."

"Why do you suppose a great lady like her ever married a bastard like that Esposito, Lieutenant?"

"I wouldn't know, Corporal," Zach said, grim-faced.

"Bet it was for his money," Johnson said.

"Naw. She ain't the kind of woman to marry a guy for his money," Bryce protested.

"How the hell do you know what kind of woman she is?" Zach snarled, and moved away. The two soldiers exchanged puzzled glances, then shrugged and headed for the punch bowl.

When the time came for the regimental singers to perform, everyone sought seats or lined up against the wall. Relieved to finally sit down for the first time that evening, Laura sank thankfully into a chair. As she glanced around her, she noticed that Zach stood nearby. He looked so sullen, she wondered if his leg was bothering him. She had not had the opportunity to speak to him since Luis's return. As she studied him now, he appeared so handsome in his blue dress uniform that her heart ached just to look at him.

The regimental singers began their songs, and she put aside her thoughts to listen. But no matter how she tried, she could not keep from stealing glances at the tall figure standing so silently against the wall.

The men's voices blended in beautiful harmony in the

songs "In the Gloaming, Long, Long Ago," and "In The Evening By the Moonlight." Then they began to sing the favorite song of so many of these lonely men in uniform, the haunting ballad "I'll Take You Home Again, Kathleen."

Her eyes shifted to Zach and her gaze locked with his disturbing, dark stare. Each word of the song wrenched at her heartstrings.

Take me home, Zach. Take me home across the wide ocean the way the song says . . . to where I was your blushing bride, Zach. I could never be any man's wife but yours.

Her pleading eyes were tearing him apart inside. He wanted her so badly he felt tied up in knots. He had to get out of the room.

Breaking the current that arced between them, he hurried out the door that led to a small backyard surrounded by a low wall. He flattened his palms against the top of the brick wall and stretched, drawing much-needed oxygen into his lungs.

He sensed she was behind him even before she spoke. "Are you all right, Zach?"

"Yeah, I'm fine. Just needed some air." He drew another deep breath, then turned to face her. He felt angry. *Goddammit, why had she followed him!*

"Yes, it was getting stuffy in there." She offered a slight smile. "Listening to those beautiful songs made me stop and think that I've never asked you if you ever married." When he raised a brow in mockery, she changed the question. "Well then, did you ever fall in love again?"

"Once was enough. I learn from my mistakes."

Her lovely brow curved in amazement. "No other women in your life in seven years?"

"I didn't say that. Men have certain needs; women suffice them," he said.

She gasped in shock at his callousness. "Do you hate all women, or just me, Zach?"

"Well now, with such paragons as you and Lavitia

Randolph as examples, what do you think?" He had hoped his unpleasantness would drive her away, but he should have known that Laura didn't back down from any fight.

"I don't think the Zachary Houston I knew would allow bitterness to warp his life. The man I remember took his knocks on the chin, then brushed himself off, and went on."

"Well, maybe that man you remember finally took one or two punches that he couldn't brush off."

Suddenly, he clutched her shoulders in a painful grasp. "Now you can answer a couple questions for me. Why this inquisition, Mrs. Esposito? You just curious, or you figure there's still a couple pints of blood yet to suck out of me?"

She cringed beneath the fury of this sudden rage. "No, I only want . . ."

"Want what, Laura? Why did you follow me out here? Is this what you want?" His lips plunged down on hers.

The kiss was bruising. Damning. Without gentleness, or tenderness—only an attempt to inflict punishment. Whimpering under the assault, she struggled to free herself. He devoured her, pressing quick, moist kisses on her eyes, her face, her throat—every kiss a fiery ember that fueled the fervor that began to sweep through her.

Her lips parted as she labored for breath. He plunged his tongue into the vulnerable hollow and ravished the moist chamber. His passion feasted upon her, consuming all her resistance until his hunger aroused the same craving within her. Any capacity for reasoning was incinerated under an earthy and primitive urgency for the return of his familiar touch. Reeling under the intoxicating dizziness provoked by his kisses, she molded her trembling legs against the pressure of his in an effort to maintain her balance.

Her head lolled back languorously, giving him free access to her neck. He nibbled a trail of moist kisses down to the rounded swell of her breasts as his hands slid the narrow straps of her gown off her shoulders.

He raised his head only long enough for his smoldering dark gaze to sweep her exposed breasts. Dipping his head, he flicked his tongue over the stiff nipples. She whimpered in a sound that neither beseeched nor discouraged; then he closed his mouth around one of the thrusting peaks and began an exquisite, sensual sucking that replaced her ambiguous whimper with a rapturous groan. Erotic tremors swept her spine as she swirled in sexual ecstasy.

He raised his head, slipped a warm hand upon her slender neck, and tipped up her chin. Her eyelids felt heavy as she lifted her slumberous, brown eyes to his smoldering gaze.

Taking her hand in his, he pressed her palm against his arousal. "Feel my need for you, Laura. Is that what you wanted to know?"

Fueled by the feel of the heated, throbbing hardness of his male sex, her desire escalated. "You want it, don't you?" he rasped as the pressure of her hand increased. "Say it. I want to hear you say it."

"Yes. Please, Zach. Please," she pleaded mindlessly.

His shifted his hand in a sensuous slide to the junction of her legs. The delicate fabric of her gown was a flimsy barrier against the heated palm that now stroked the very core of her need with slow, erotic rotations.

"How bad, Laura? Tell me how bad you want it." He still held her chin in a clasp which prevented her from turning away from the dark eyes that impaled her.

"I'll do anything." Her breath came in ragged gasps. "Anything you want."

"Even cheat on your husband, Mrs. Esposito?" His hands slipped from her body.

Her indrawn breath froze in her throat. *Oh God! No! No! No! This can't be happening*, she screamed in silent anguish.

In the few seconds of her suspended heartbeat, she stared in shock at him, then her breath expelled like the whimper of a wounded animal. "Why . . . why, Zach?"

"It's called honor, Mrs. Esposito. I guess I can't sell out mine as easily as you can yours."

Her fumbling, trembling fingers adjusted the straps of her gown. "How much longer are we going to keep hurting each other before we die from the pain of it?" she asked numbly. Then she left him.

He knew the tortured look in her eyes would haunt him for the rest of his life.

Chapter 17

Luis's ploy worked.

A week after the party, Zachary was summoned to the office of Colonel Scott. "Lieutenant Houston, now that you are well enough to return to active duty, I'm putting you in command of a detachment to restore the mission at Dario for the purpose of reestablishing the civilian population in the vicinity." He shoved a paper across his desk. "I received this from the Catholic Archbishop of St. Augustine. A priest will be arriving soon in Miami to replace Father Montevideo."

Zach quickly perused the letter and glanced up at the colonel. "And who is this Romero family referred to in the letter?"

"Romero has a plantation at Dario. Esposito told me when the family failed to show up at the mission, they were presumed dead. But apparently Romero succeeded in getting himself and his family to safety. If the danger has passed, he is anxious to return."

"Sir, I don't wish to question your judgement, but do you think it's advisable to return civilians to Dario before we secure the area?"

"Mr. Esposito has lived in Florida his whole life. He feels confident the hostile Seminoles will have left the area by this time."

"I do not have that kind of confidence in Esposito's opinions. Frankly, sir, the man's a coward."

"Come now, Lieutenant, if Esposito were a coward, I

doubt he would put his life at risk by returning there."

"But why put the lives of women and children at risk? If Esposito and this Romero wish to return to Dario, let their families and the nuns remain here until we are certain they will be safe."

His brow knit in a frown and the colonel leaned back in his chair. "Lieutenant, I respect your opinion, but, unfortunately, I already told the Archbishop and Esposito that we would honor their request. The priest and Romero family are due to arrive any day. However, because of your recent injury, I am willing to relieve you of this assignment if you prefer."

"No, sir, that won't be necessary."

"Good. We'll await the arrival of the priest."

"Will that be all, sir?"

"For the time being, Lieutenant."

Zachary saluted and turned to depart. "And, Zach . . ." The colonel rose when Zach turned to look at him. " . . . I'm not sending you underarmed into that hellhole again. This time, you'll have a full battalion of four squads plus two additional squads of army engineers under your command."

"Thank you, sir."

"And one more thing. Bryce's extra stripe has been approved. He's been promoted to sergeant."

Zach grinned. "Thank you, sir, he'll be glad to hear that."

"Well, since you recommended him for the promotion, I thought you would like to be the one to tell him the good news."

"It will be my pleasure, sir."

As soon as Zach left the colonel's office, he immediately sought out Flint Bryce. "I have some good news . . ." The smile left Zach's face when he saw Luis Esposito just preparing to drive away from the sutler's store. "Esposito, hold up there," Zach called out.

Luis pulled up on the reins of the wagon. "Lieutenant."

"Colonel Scott has just informed me of your intention

to return to Dario. I recommend you do not have your family accompany you."

"And why not?"

"You know as well as I do that it's too dangerous."

"That's why the army will accompany us."

"You're a bigger fool than I thought, Esposito."

"Not so much a fool that I haven't guessed the real reason why you want my wife to remain here with you, Lieutenant."

"Esposito, I will be accompanying you. I'm only thinking of her welfare, as well as Peter's."

"I will be sure to inform her of your concern tonight in bed, Lieutenant . . . just before I make love to her. The mention of your name always . . . arouses . . . her passion." Luis's thin lips narrowed into an infuriating, self-satisfied expression.

Zachary's hands balled into fists. Only the unexpected restraint of Bryce's hand on his arm kept him from yanking Luis off the wagon seat.

"The bastard's not worth a court-martial, Lieutenant," Bryce cautioned as Luis flicked the reins of his horse.

Bryce released him. A muscle twitched nervously in Zachary's jaw as he watched the wagon roll across the parade ground to the barracks. He drew a deep breath and turned to Bryce.

"Thank you, Sergeant Bryce."

"Hey, Lieutenant, you're letting that bastard get to ya. You forgettin' who you're talkin' to?" Bryce joked good-naturedly. "I'm only wearin' two stripes."

"Not for long, *Sergeant* Bryce." The anger that had gripped Zach only moments before subsided.

Bryce's usual laconic expression showed signs of disbelief. "You sayin'—"

"Your third stripe's been approved." Zach grabbed the scout's hand and shook it. "Congratulations, Sergeant Bryce."

"Goddamn!" Bryce exclaimed, shaking his head. "This is worth celebratin'. If it wasn't against regulations for an officer to fraternize with an enlisted man, I'd ask you to join me for a drink in my quarters, Lieutenant."

"To hell with regulations." Zach slapped him on the shoulder. "Let's go, Flint."

No longer able to lie awake in the stifling, overcrowded bedroom, Laura stepped outside in the hope of catching a breeze. Her troubled thoughts were on the trip to Dario in the morning. She had not welcomed Luis's announcement that they would be returning to the village. The horrifying events of their escape were still vivid memories, not easily set aside. She feared for the safety of them all.

If there was any positive aspect of their return to Dario, it would have been getting away from Zach, not catching glances of him as he moved about on the post, not listening to Peter relate his daily visits with him. But Luis had added to her misgivings by revealing that Zach would be in command of the soldiers accompanying them. She couldn't even escape from the torment of having him near her.

They had not spoken since the party. She could not forget the humiliation she had felt any more than she could forget the feel of his kiss, his mouth, his hands. Her heart ached with the knowledge that he now detested her.

A light breeze carried the pleasant fragrance of gardenia to her senses. She strolled over to some nearby potted plants and picked one of the delicate blossoms. Closing her eyes, she buried her nose in the white petals and inhaled their sweet aroma.

Laura suddenly stiffened as she sensed his presence. At this moment of awareness, her heart began pounding wildly.

A whispered "Zach" slipped from her lips and she turned slowly. He stepped out of the darkness, his face still veiled in shadows. His uniform shirt was open. She glimpsed his muscular chest covered with dark hair that narrowed to a slim trail and disappeared beneath the waistband of his trousers.

As he stepped nearer, his handsome bronzed face materialized in the moonlight—the compelling blue eyes, the dark moustache over wide sensual lips, the rugged jaw made even more manly by a day's growth of beard. His seductive masculinity mesmerized her and she trembled like some snared quarry.

He broke the silence with a husky whisper. "Laura, there's something I have to say to you."

She could feel the quickened beat of her heart. "What is it, Zach?" she whispered past the sob lodged in her throat. He seemed to struggle for words, and finally spoke in a low voice.

"I'm sorry, Laura. I didn't mean what I said——"

"No . . . no, you were right in what you said, Zach. I deserved it," she managed to murmur hastily before her voice wavered.

"No, you didn't, Laura. I had no right to do what I did. Or to say what I did. I was angry. With myself more than you."

"I understand, Zach. Thank you for telling me."

When he spoke again, the tenderness in his voice threatened to shatter her waning control. "And I'm sorry for what we lost, Laura. I wish there could have been more time for us. It was so short. There was so much I wanted to say to you and never did. And now it's too late . . ." He faltered momentarily.

"All because of your honor," she said. "I understand, Zach. Honor is the strength in you that makes you the man you are. Nothing is more priceless than honor."

"No, Laura. Nothing is more precious than love." He reached out a hand and his long fingers gently caressed her cheek. "But I lost the only thing that mattered to me—honor is all that I have left."

He slipped back into the shadows as silently as he had appeared.

"I'll always love you, Zach," she whispered into the darkness.

*　　*　　*

The small flotilla of boats approached the shoreline of the serene beach near Dario. Having heard the stirring speech Luis Esposito made at the party, the more curious soldiers crowded to the rails of the boats.

But there was no curiosity on the somber faces of the four soldiers who stood at the rail of one of the vessels—only grimness from never-to-be-forgotten memories. And these same memories bound Zach, Bryce, Johnson, and Hoffman into an inviolable phalange.

Unlike the last time, when eight men had waded to shore with only survival rations and the weapons they could carry, now four seven-man squads plus fourteen army engineers landed on the beach. They met no resistance.

After setting up perimeters, complete with two gattling guns, Zach sat down next to Bryce. "What's your gut feeling, Sergeant?"

"Seems peaceful enough to me."

"Well, I've got a bad job for you, Bryce."

"You want me to scout the village."

"Yeah. Take your squad and approach it with caution. If the Seminoles are still there, do not engage them. Assess their ranks, then hightail it back here."

"You can be sure of that, sir," Bryce said. After a quick briefing with his squad, the seven men moved out.

On an offshore boat, Laura stood with her arm around Peter's shoulders and somberly watched the activity. She knew Zach was among the figures moving about on shore, but she didn't try to distinguish him from the rest. Her hand tightened on Peter's shoulder.

"When are we getting off the boat, Mama?" he asked restlessly.

"As soon as Lieutenant Houston feels it is safe for us to come ashore."

"I'm tired of being on this old boat," he grumbled.

"We all are, honey, but Lieutenant Houston wants to make sure there's no danger."

When he glanced up at her, his face was puckered in a frown. "If there's danger, why did we come back?"

Out of the mouths of babes, Laura reflected as she cast a disgruntled look at Luis. "Watch the soldiers over there in the water, Peter," she said, pointing to the engineers who had begun to link pontoon barges together. "They're starting to build a bridge to the shore."

"How come, Mama? Why can't they just walk to shore like the other soldiers did?"

"They need a bridge to get all this equipment off the boats, honey."

"Can we walk on the bridge when they're through?" he asked.

"I'm sure we can," she said. She hugged him to her side, her gaze shifting back to the shore.

An hour after they left on patrol, Johnson and Hoffman returned to the beach. "Village is deserted, sir. Sergeant Bryce has taken a position in the mission. Said for you to come on in," Johnson reported.

Zach expelled a sigh of relief. "Well, *that's* good news, Private. Guess Esposito was right. Gregorio has left the area."

With a relentless sun beating down on them, the sweltering contingent began the arduous task of unloading construction tools and equipment, household provisions, clothing, and medical supplies for the mission. There were also two heavy wagons for hauling, cartons of food, cases holding dynamite and ammunition, and tents for the soldiers. The sounds of harsh braying and shrill neighs rose above the curses and shouts of the soldiers who tugged and prodded the two dozen balking pack mules and skittish horses onto the pitching, undulating pontoon.

By the time the final carton was unloaded, the last animal fettered on shore, and the remaining civilians had disembarked, the soldiers' uniforms were soaked with perspiration. After loading up the pack mules, the column was ready to begin the five-mile trek to Dario.

The civilians were offered army mounts to ride. Mrs. Romero declined and sat with her children in one of the wagons. Teresa chose to remain with the nuns in the back of another and Father Naverro chose the seat next to the wagon driver. Luis and Romero each rode a horse. Pilar also mounted a horse, and Ramon climbed on behind his mother. Laura rode a chestnut mare.

Zach picked up Peter. "Now you sit still, buddy, or I'm going to have to put you in the back of the wagon," he said softly.

He handed the youngster up to Laura. Zach and Laura made brief eye contact before Peter's body blocked their view of each other. She settled a beaming Peter on the saddle in front of her.

Zach's head was just inches from her hand. He silently adjusted the length of the stirrup straps. She was acutely conscious of his nearness—so near that the male essence of him stirred her senses. The sleeves of his uniform were rolled up to his elbows, and a smattering of dark hair covered his muscular forearms. His hand gripped her ankle, and she felt the strength in his long, tapered fingers when he anchored her foot in the stirrup. She couldn't help but recall how often he had done the same thing for her in Texas, laughing up at her with devilment in his dark eyes as he fondled her leg or tugged at her bare toe.

Now, with his head lowered, she had no idea what he might be thinking, but she wondered if those same poignant thoughts were going through his mind.

When he glanced up, his expression was inscrutable. "Feel okay?" he asked.

Laura nodded. "They feel fine. Thank you."

She watched Zach stride over to his own mount, and with the familiar, fluent motion she remembered so well, he swung himself into the saddle.

Unlike the route they had taken on the night of their desperate flight through the swamp, the procession followed the rough-shodden path the squad had traversed on their first arrival. This time, however, no stops were made to check out the two houses they passed. Zach's goal was to get the contingent settled in and around the mission before nightfall.

As soon as they arrived in Dario, the soldiers began to unload supplies and pitch tents. Zach rode to the end of the village. The area appeared to have been swept clean of everything except several empty huts. Even the post on which Father Montevideo had been bound was gone.

Zach came upon a huge, gaping hole made from a dynamite blast, the only evidence of the violence that had prevailed. For a long moment, he stared solemnly at the massive crater, then he turned his mount and trotted slowly to the middle of the village where the Stars and Stripes flapped from a hastily erected flagpole.

Zach dismounted when Bryce approached him. "You bothered to hoist the flag, Sergeant? Didn't think you were that patriotic, Bryce."

"Well, seems there's always a flag flying over every military cemetery, Lieutenant. We lost four good men here, sir. Johnson, Hoffman, and me were hopin' you wouldn't mind if we gave 'em a proper military burial."

"Of course not, Sergeant." Zach's somber gaze swept the area. "You and your squad clean up here before we arrived?"

"No, sir, we found it this way. The mission too. Kind of spooky, ain't it? Sure don't make sense to me why them Seminoles would clean up this place before they pulled out."

"Nothing about this goddamn place makes sense, Sergeant," Zach said. He led his horse back to the billet area.

Toward sundown, after helping the nuns set up the hospital, Laura climbed up the stairway to the galleria. To her surprise, she found Sister Francesca there sitting on the stone bench staring out over the Gulf. Laura walked over to her and slipped an arm around her shoulders.

"He loved this spot so much," Sister Francesca said

sadly. "He would come up here every morning at sunrise and every evening at sunset."

Laura had no words of comfort to offer her. The older woman turned away and with head bowed in prayer, she walked slowly down the stairs.

When a slight breeze rustled the skirt of her gown, Laura pulled off the scarf holding back her hair. She shook out the long black strands and lifted her face to catch the breeze. Then she moved to the front of the galleria to watch the activities below.

Assembled in the center of the village, the men of the battalion flanked three sides of the flagpole. Zachary stood before it, Bryce, Johnson, and Hoffman behind him.

As the ranking officer, it was Zachary's task to conduct the honorary burial. The sound of his husky voice carried up to the galleria. After reading the words of the Twenty-third Psalm, he closed the Bible.

"Lord, we commend to your keep the souls of our fallen comrades: Sergeant Michael Patrick O'Hara, Private David Richard Malloy, Private Francis Sean Ryan, and Private Stanley Joseph Zanowski." He paused briefly, then quoted softly, "'Thou wert my guide, philosopher, and friend.'"

He stepped back and snapped to attention in a salute. The three men behind him raised their rifles heavenward and each man in turn fired four shots.

Tears misted Laura's eyes when the sentimental strain of taps from a battered bugle sounded a plaintive funeral dirge. And in the quiet dusk, the battalion stood stiffly at attention in a military salute as the Stars and Stripes slowly descended on the staff.

When the men broke ranks, Zachary glanced up and saw the lone figure on the galleria. The wind whipped at her hair, and the long strands streamed behind her like a black scarf.

At the sight of her slim figure, silhouetted in the setting sun, a newer pain gnawed at his heart.

Chapter 18

❧ ❧ ❧

The next morning, under a military escort, the Esposito household returned to their plantation. Deserted since the day of the attack, the house bore the ravages of the raiders.

Most of the windows were broken and the interior of the house was in a shambles. Draperies had been yanked from the windows and ripped apart, pieces of art and crucifixes torn off the walls. The fine china and crystal had been dumped from cabinets and lay smashed on the floor.

The stunned family walked among the rubble. Nothing appeared to have been missed: furniture hacked to pieces, books pulled off the library shelves and chopped to bits.

Neither had the bedrooms been spared. The mattresses and pillows were all slashed, lamps broken, armoires tipped over and their contents strewn among the shards and feathers.

Despite her loathing for Luis, Laura couldn't help but feel a pang of sympathy at the destruction of keepsakes that had been in his family for generations.

The three women exchanged woeful glances. "I guess we better get busy," Laura said with a sigh. Pilar hurried after Peter and Ramon when they ran off to their bedrooms to see if any of their playthings had been spared. Teresa went to begin cleaning up her own bedroom, and Luis remained downstairs to check out his

papers in the library. Zach and Laura found themselves
alone.

"Quite a clutter," he said awkwardly.

She nodded, looking around helplessly at the devastation. "I don't know where to begin."

"I'll have the engineers start boarding up the broken
windows." Side by side, they started to walk down the
stairway. "Laura, how did it happen you escaped the
attack?"

"Just by chance. Ramon and Peter had snuck out of the
house at dawn that morning. They were in the swamp
and saw the band of Seminoles. When they told me about
it, I suspected the worst. We all got to the mission just in
time."

"Well, the folks in those houses we checked when we
arrived weren't as lucky," he said grimly.

Unexpectedly, she tripped over a broken piece of balustrade lying on the steps. Zach quickly reached out and
snagged her around the waist, pulling her against him.
Startled from the shock of almost pitching head first
down the stairway, she gasped with alarm and found
herself looking up into his blue eyes, their mouths only
inches apart. His hungry gaze shifted down to her parted lips, then he dropped his arm and released her. "You
okay?"

"Yes, I'm fine. Thank you," she said, continuing down
the stairs. Her voice carried an edge of shakiness—an
edge not caused from her near fall.

When they went outside, they found the engineers had
already dug a large hole and had begun to dump the
remains of the slaughtered livestock into it. The handle
of the pump had been broken off, and two of the men
were working to repair it.

Laura returned to the house to begin the cleanup
operation inside. Despite the lack of water, she and Pilar
decided to start at the top and work down, attacking one
room at a time.

The air soon rang with the pounding of hammers and

the hum of saws as windows were boarded up and doors replaced on their hinges.

"The engineers are accustomed to building roads, not cabinets, but I think they'll be able to make some of this furniture usable until you can replace it," Zach said as a crew began to shovel debris out of a bedroom.

Soon Laura's room was swept clean. The armoire, beyond repair, had been fed to the bonfire, but after replacing a table leg, and the footboard and legs on the bed, at least two items were serviceable. Laura even discovered several pieces of clothing which she knew the skillful plying of a needle and thread would salvage.

Having seen the destruction in the other homes, Zach had anticipated the need for the replacement of common household articles such as lamps, mattresses, pillows, and blankets. Cartons of such items had been brought along. So by the time the crew had finished and moved on to the next room, Laura's bedroom had been restored, if not elegantly, at least functionally.

All activity suddenly came to a halt when a patrol under Bryce came racing back to the house. "Lieutenant, we sighted six Seminoles heading this way," he reported breathlessly.

"Were they scouts?"

"Didn't hang around to find out," Bryce said. "Thought we better hightail it back here to warn you."

"Take cover," Zach ordered. The men dropped their tools and grabbed their rifles. "All civilians inside the house. Bryce, set up your squad along that front wall. Sergeant Donovan," he said to another squad leader, "you and your squad cover the downstairs windows."

Inside Laura grabbed Peter and held him in her arms. Teresa and Pilar waited beside her with Ramon. While the men stood with cocked weapons, tension hung as heavily as the humidity.

Suddenly a white flag appeared dangling at the end of a stick. All rifles swung toward the edge of the swamp.

After several seconds, a man stepped out of the dense growth waving the flag. "*¿No dispare usted?* No shoot. No shoot. *Señor* Esposito, *está* Diego," he called out frantically.

"It's Diego," Luis said. "He's one of the natives who worked for me."

"Hold your fire," Zach told the men at the windows. He stepped outside on the porch. "Bryce, hold your fire, these natives may be friendly," he called out.

The native advanced with trepidation and Luis came out of the house to meet him. After a hurried conversation in Spanish, Diego waved and other natives emerged from the bushes, followed by several women with babes in arms.

"What's going on here, Esposito?" Zach asked, annoyed.

"Diego said they have been scared and hiding in the swamps since the attack." Clearly irritated, Luis launched a string of expletives. In his fury, he snatched up a discarded chair leg and began to strike the man repeatedly across the head and shoulders.

Zach shoved Luis away from the cowering servant, yanking the cudgel from Luis's hand. He tossed it aside. "What the hell are you trying to do, Esposito, start another Indian uprising?"

"He must have known about the attack and he didn't warn us," Luis snarled. His eyes bulged with fury.

"No, *señor*, Diego not know. Diego swear he not know." The frightened native continued to babble a denial.

Laura hastened out of the house and put her arm around the terrified man. After several words of comfort, the native smiled at her with gratitude. "*Gracious, señora. Gracious,*" he murmured, clasping her hand between his own and kissing it.

Laura smiled and said several more words to him in Spanish, then the man and his companions hurried off toward their native huts.

"Well, I see you're coddling these natives as usual, Laura. Haven't you learned your lesson yet?" Luis snapped.

"I think you're the one who hasn't learned from your mistakes, Luis." She walked back inside.

Zach's expression revealed his contempt for the man. "I don't understand you, Esposito. What kind of man puts his family in this kind of danger? This goddamned land isn't worth the life of your wife and child."

"Lieutenant, my family has owned this land for almost a century."

"The Seminoles owned it before that. No sugar plantation is worth dying over, Esposito. There's plenty of land elsewhere."

"A strange sentiment from a professional soldier, Lieutenant," Esposito scoffed. "And an American too. What of the Alamo? Or your own Civil War?"

"Causes, Mr. Esposito. A just cause can be worth a man's death. The Seminoles are dying for a cause—you're dying for a sugar plantation."

"And what are you dying for, Lieutenant?"

"For damn fools like you. There will always be a need for men like me to go in and clean up your messes. If I see or hear of you mistreating any of these natives again, I'll have you arrested."

"You have no authority to tell me how to handle my servants or run my plantation."

"Think again, Esposito. Your theatrical performance in Miami was more effective than you thought. Didn't Colonel Scott inform you that this area has been declared under martial law? *That* puts the military in charge here, Esposito. And as ranking officer, *that* is me."

Luis looked stunned. Pivoting, he stormed away in a huff. The soldiers relaxed and returned to their previous tasks.

"Come on, Ramon, let's go back and play," Peter said, dashing into the house. For a long moment, Ramon stood motionless. His eyes glowed with hatred at his father's retreating figure, then he turned and followed Peter.

The work continued throughout the morning. The three women squealed with pleasure whenever they discovered an unbroken cup or piece of china among the rubble. Even the recovery of a tiny crocheted doily became a source of satisfaction. Peter hopped around in excitement after retrieving all the scattered pieces of his toy train set.

Shortly before midday, repairs on the pump were completed and soon several pots of coffee bubbled on the hearth next to kettles containing pork and beans topped with thick strips of smoked venison.

By the time the army pulled out later that day, the Esposito household had become livable again. The next day the Romero family would be able to move from the mission to their home as well.

Slowly the natives straggled back to the village. By the end of the week, the Mission of Our Mother of Perpetual Help had returned to treating the bruises, snakebites, cuts, and various miseries of the suffering who sought her benevolence.

On Sunday morning, the Esposito family prepared to ride into Dario to attend mass. Teresa had an upset stomach and chose to remain home.

"Oh my, you do feel feverish, dear," Laura exclaimed, putting a hand on the young woman's brow. "Perhaps, I should stay home with you."

"No, you go to mass, Laura," Teresa insisted. "I will try to sleep while you are gone."

"Well, I'll ask Sister Francesca for some medicine to settle your stomach. But I don't feel right about leaving you when you're ill."

"Come, Laura, or we will be late," Luis grumbled impatiently.

Against her better judgement, Laura climbed onto the wagon with Pilar and the boys. Luis mounted his stallion.

Seeing Laura's evident concern, Pilar offered to remain with the ailing girl. "Teresa is not a child. She can fend for herself for a few hours," Luis declared. "*Vámonos,*" he ordered in a sharp command.

After they rode off, Teresa managed to fall back to sleep. Upon awakening, she put on a robe and slippers and went down to the kitchen to brew a cup of tea.

The hot tea soothed her stomach, and as she sat at the kitchen table, she reflected deeply on becoming a nun. Since the siege at the mission, when she had had the chance to work closely with the sisters, her desire to become one of them had grown. She had even discussed the matter with Sister Francesca, who had advised her that she must be totally committed to dedicating her life to God and service.

Teresa knew in her heart that she still had reservations, but once Laura was resettled and no longer needed her help, she would follow her dream.

Teresa decided to reveal her intention as soon as Laura returned from mass.

Resolved, Teresa got up from the table to go back to her room to dress. She drew up sharply on discovering Luis standing in the drawing room. She had not heard the wagon return.

"Where is Laura?"she asked uneasily. She never felt comfortable alone with him.

"My family remained at the mission to get you medicine. They will be along shortly, my little Teresa. But it is well we have this chance to be alone." He started toward her.

Frightened, Teresa moved away until her back pressed against the wall. "Why do you fear me, little rabbit? Have I not protected you and given you food and shelter these many years?" He smiled salaciously. "It is a most opportune time for you to show me your gratitude."

Paralyzed with fear, she stood helplessly as he opened her robe. His lewd gaze swept her body. At the sight of her breasts poking through the thin gown, he reached out with both hands and rubbed them. "No, please leave me alone," she pleaded.

His tongue flicked over his lips. "Come little one, we will go to your room." He took her hand and led her to the stairway.

She grabbed the balustrade and clung to it. "If you touch me, I will tell Laura."

Chuckling at the absurdity of her threat, he peeled her fingers off the railing and grabbed her wrist. "I think not. I think you will enjoy our secret, little rabbit." The fright in her round, brown eyes increased his passion. "I think you and I will have many more secrets to come."

She tried to pull free, but he quickly grabbed her, hauling her to his side. His arm clamped around her waist. Teresa's legs trembled as he pulled her up the stairway.

As they neared the top, she stumbled and fell to her knees. He hissed a vile expletive and tried to yank her to her feet. The movement threw him off balance and he lost his grip on her arm.

With a shout of fright and flailing arms, Luis tumbled backward down the stairway. Horrified, she stared at him lying below. She rushed down the stairs, and as she tried to climb past him, he sat up and grabbed her leg.

Fury had replaced his passion. "You will pay for this, you wretched bitch."

She kicked free and raced toward the door. Luis stumbled to his feet, grabbed his riding whip from the table, and chased after her.

Once outside, Teresa looked around helplessly. There was nowhere to run except into the swamp. The danger ahead seemed less threatening to her than the devil behind.

She raced into the thick vegetation. In a blind fury, Luis followed. He soon caught up with her and knocked her to the ground. As she tried to crawl away, the robe fell away from her shoulders. Luis grabbed the collar and yanked her back. The thin material rent apart.

"You little *puta*," he snarled. Raising the riding whip, he began to beat her naked back and shoulders. She cried out with agony as he continued to strike her mercilessly.

Out of control, Luis kicked Teresa over and straddled her. With his clenched fist he began to strike her. Sobbing, she tried to cover her face to ward off the blows.

She felt her strength waning and began to slip into unconsciousness. As her arms dropped listlessly to her sides, she felt his hands ripping at her gown.

"You make the sport even more exciting, my little rabbit," he snarled.

Semiconscious, she heard his grunt and waited defenselessly for the violation to follow. After several terrifying seconds, she rallied the strength to raise her eyelids. The shallow countenance of Luis Esposito no longer loomed above her. Instead, the bronzed figure of the Everglades' most notorious renegade loomed above her. As Gregorio bent closer, she lost consciousness.

The heat of the day was at its height when the family returned from Dario. Laura climbed down from the wagon, and the boys accompanied Pilar to the barn to unhitch the horses.

Carefully carrying the bottle of tonic Sister Francesca had sent along for Teresa, Laura entered the house and went to the kitchen for a spoon.

Luis sat at the table holding his head in his hands. She glanced askance at him. "What's wrong with you? Are you coming down with the fever too?"

"She tried to kill me," he said.

"Kill you? What—"

"See for yourself." He raised his head and Laura saw the bruise on his temple.

"Who tried to kill you? What happened?" She wet a cloth and handed it to him. "Here, put this on the bruise to soothe it and tell me what happened."

"Your precious Teresa tried to kill me," he snarled. "She pushed me down the stairway."

Laura doubted his statement at once. "Teresa wouldn't hurt anyone. What did you try to do to her?" Laura accused.

"When I came home, she was in the kitchen having a cup of tea. She was so weak, she could barely climb the stairs, so I tried to assist her. Maybe she was crazed with fever," he added.

Laura never suspected for a moment that the gentle woman would intentionally commit a violent act, but she knew Teresa had been suffering with fever. "I'm sure this tonic will help."

"She's not in her room," Luis said when Laura hurried to the stairway.

"Where is she?"

"After she shoved me down the stairs, she ran out the door. By the time I recovered and followed, she had disappeared into the swamp. I tell you, the girl has gone mad, Laura."

"Oh, dear God! You mean she's alone out there? Didn't you follow her?"

"Of course I did! I couldn't see any sign of her." Laura had already run out the door. Luis got to his feet and shouted after her. "You're as mad as she is, if you're going to chase through that swamp to try and find her."

For the next hour, Laura and Pilar searched the nearby swamp, shouting Teresa's name. The field hands returned from Dario and joined in the search. Darkness had descended by the time they abandoned the effort for the night. They lit a string of torches along the edge of the swamp as a beacon for her.

Laura paced the floor for the rest of the evening. All she could think about was how frightened and endangered the young woman must be.

Finally, toward midnight, Pilar convinced her to go to her room and rest. "You are so agitated now, *señora*, you are unable to think clearly. Lie down and calm your nerves. At daybreak, the men will resume the search."

"I should send for Zach. The army will help us find her."

"Yes, that is true. We will find our little Teresa in the morning," Pilar assured her.

Laura glanced fretfully at her. "Alive, Pilar?"

Pilar put her arm around Laura's shoulders. "Our Precious Lord looks after His lambs, *señora*." Reluctantly, the two women climbed the stairs.

Chapter 19

Laura awoke with a start. She looked at the clock and saw that it was two o'clock in the morning. Hearing voices coming from below, she suddenly felt fearful. The news would have to be about Teresa. She slipped on her robe and sped downstairs. A light shone from under the closed door of the library. As she hurried over to it, she heard Luis's voice raised in anger and Pilar attempting to pacify him. A third voice, a man's, which she did not recognize, entered the conversation. She tried to place it, but to no avail. Most certainly, the discussion involved Teresa, so Laura opened the library door.

Pilar and Ramon were both in the room. Luis held his pistol pointed toward someone in the corner. "What's wrong?" Laura asked, alarmed.

"Oh, do join us, my dear," Luis said. She had heard that self-satisfied tone of his enough times to know he was up to no good.

"We seem to have the honor of a visit from an uninvited guest . . . as distinguished as he may be," Luis added with a snicker. Laura tried to identify the caller, but the corner of the room was in darkness.

"Has there been news of Teresa?" she asked, concerned and impatient with Luis's games.

"Actually, our distinguished guest comes not to visit us, but rather to speak to my dear Pilar. You can imagine my surprise when I discovered them here in my library."

241

"What are you talking about, Luis? If you're implying this is a tryst, you are insane. Pilar would not betray you," Laura scoffed.

"Betrayal? Who spoke of betrayal? But deceit . . . yes, indeed."

Laura looked quizzically at Pilar. The young woman's frightened expression was of no help.

"I did not deceive you, Luis. I love you."

Luis glared at his mistress with contempt. "I take you into my home, I buy you lovely clothes, and you show your thanks by deceiving me with lies."

"Luis, don't you think it would be wiser to conduct this conversation once Ramon has returned to bed?" Laura suggested.

"I wish to stay," Ramon said stoutly. "My uncle is telling the truth."

"Your uncle?" Laura asked, more confused than ever.

"Yes, my dear. Pilar has opened our home to our unexpected night-caller who is none other than the infamous Gregorio himself."

"Gregorio!" The name struck a chord of terror in Laura's breast. In panic, her glance swung again toward the corner and Gregorio stepped out of the shadows.

Laura gasped—from shock, not alarm, at the spectacular beauty of the man; his commanding presence as a warrior eclipsed all others in the room.

A tempered blend of strength and energy, his muscular body moved with lithe suppleness. The corded muscles of his bare shoulders and firm biceps sloped into the smooth, bronzed brawn of his powerful chest. He wore a leather loincloth, and the sleeveless red shirt that hung to his thighs was belted with a yellow sash. The Indian's long, muscular legs and feet were bare.

But the splendor of his body paled in comparison to the glory of his face; his flawless features and bronzed perfection conveyed a powerful spiritual serenity.

Long lashes surrounded obsidian eyes, rounded and evenly set above a straight nose. A strong jaw flowed into the high cheekbones that gave youthful agelessness to the face of the thirty-five-year-old warrior.

Rather than a turban, the popular headdress of his tribesmen, a red band encircled Gregorio's forehead, and a white eagle feather dangled at the side of his face amid several braided strands of long, jet-black hair that flowed to his shoulders.

Laura stared in awe. *He was beautiful.*

If her sudden appearance gave him any concern, his thoughts remained concealed behind a calm expression.

"Gregorio entered your house with no weapon, for he wishes only to speak to his sister or the *señora*," the tall warrior said in a gentle timbre that belied his size. "He brings word of the woman you seek."

"You have word of Teresa?" Laura said anxiously.

"Gregorio has taken her to the mission hospital."

"Oh, dear God, is she seriously injured?" Laura asked.

The Indian's gaze turned to Luis. "The woman carries many blows. Gregorio goes now."

"After the murdering carnage you caused in this region, surely you don't think I'll allow you to leave," Luis mocked. Laura felt uneasy at the obvious pleasure Luis was deriving from the situation.

If Luis hoped the warrior would plead, he did not get the satisfaction. Gregorio explained, "The raids were done without my knowledge. Gregorio arrived too late to prevent them . . . or the death of the priest." Laura could not help but admire the warrior's noble stature as he faced his armed accuser.

"You're lying, Gregorio," Luis scoffed. "You're just trying to keep me from killing you."

"My brother does not lie," Pilar said. "Please, Luis, you must believe him. What my brother says is true. Even my people all say he did not lead the raid."

Laura managed to find her voice. "If that is true, Gregorio, then talk to Lieutenant Houston. Tell him the truth, or you'll be hunted down like a criminal. Lieutenant Houston is a fair man and will listen to you."

"That is true, my brother," Pilar said. "The lieutenant will not harm you if he believes you are innocent."

"My people have learned that one soldier does not speak for all your people. We have been betrayed too often by your leader. No, Gregorio leaves here and will not return. Come with me, Pilar. This is not a good house. The woman you call Teresa will tell you as much."

"Tell us what, Gregorio?" Laura asked hastily. "You know more than you're telling us. What is it?"

Luis broke out in nervous laughter. "You people amuse me. Talking among yourselves as if the choice is yours to make. I am the one with the gun. And you are not leaving this room alive, Gregorio."

"Don't talk nonsense, Luis. There's been enough killing already," Laura declared. "Arrest him, if you must. But let the army handle this."

"Do you think I'm as gullible as the rest of you fools? I have no intention of turning him over to the army," Luis snarled in contempt.

Gregorio ignored the threat and walked boldly toward the door. "I have no qualms about shooting you in the back, Gregorio," Luis said coldly. "I expect the United States will pin a medal on me for killing you."

Gregorio turned and faced him calmly. "Gregorio does not fear the Spaniard's bullets. He has faced men like you before. Hiding their fear behind guns and whips." He reached to open the door.

Without further hesitation, Luis took aim, his intention clear.

"No, don't kill him," Pilar cried out. She threw herself in front of Gregorio a second before Luis heedlessly pulled the trigger several times.

Laura screamed as a splotch of crimson blossomed on the front of Pilar's gown. Pilar opened her mouth as if to cry out, then clutching her chest, she slumped to the floor.

"Mama! Mama!" Ramon shouted. Ramon and Laura,

her heart pounding, ran over and knelt at her side while Luis gaped in astonishment.

"*Mi pequeño*," Pilar said lovingly. Reaching out to Ramon, she smiled; then her hand dropped away, and her eyes closed.

"She is dead!" Gregorio shouted in disbelief. He looked at Luis and his beautiful face turned ugly, twisted with hatred. "She is dead. You have killed my sister!" he raged as he leaped at Luis.

In panic, Luis fired the pistol again, but the shot went wild and the gun flew out of his hand. Grappling, the two men fell to the floor and rolled in a violent struggle.

Terror burned in Luis's eyes and he began to whimper as Gregorio's hands clamped around his throat. He groped to break the strong fingers on his neck, but the pressure only increased.

Then Luis's mouth opened in a soundless scream, his eyes rolled to the top of the sockets, and his hands fell from the bronzed hands at his throat.

Gregorio rose to his feet. For a long moment he stared at the lifeless man, then he moved to kneel at his sister's side. His gentle gaze rested on Pilar's lovely face, and he reached out to caress her cheek. Finally he stood up and strode out the door.

Stunned by the incredible violence, and loss of life, Laura sat on the floor rocking Ramon in her arms. Only his muffled sobs broke the silence of death.

Laura was pacing nervously in the drawing room when Zach arrived later that morning to question her about the deaths of Luis and Pilar. Removing his hat, he stood stiffly in the doorway. Frightened and confused, she yearned to run into his arms and draw strength from him.

If only for a few moments Zach would forget that the dead man was her husband, take her in his arms, and convince her that everything would soon be all right. That they would be together again. Damn your sense of honor, Zach. Can't you see I love you and I need you? I'm so weary, so tired of fighting this life of hopelessness. Please, Zach.

"Would you like a cup of coffee, Zach?" she asked listlessly.

"This is not a social call, Laura. I've come on army business. Your husband is dead, Pilar is dead, and Teresa is lying badly beaten in the hospital. I'm afraid I need some answers."

"I understand," she responded in a vacant tone.

"Laura, I regret that I have to ask these questions so soon after your husband's death, but I'm required to report this incident to my headquarters. Just what happened here last night?"

She cleared her throat and sat down. "Yesterday morning Teresa was feverish and did not accompany us to church. When we returned home, Luis had already arrived. He had come back ahead of us because we had gone to the infirmary to get some medicine for Teresa's fever. Teresa was gone. Luis told me that after trying to kill him, Teresa ran into the swamp. We couldn't find her, and I planned to ask for the army's help this morning. Then . . . ah . . . I woke up about two o'clock in the morning and I heard voices, so I went downstairs. Luis, Pilar, and Ramon were in the library. Luis was holding Gregorio at gunpoint."

"Gregorio?" Zach asked, astonished.

Laura nodded and began to pace the floor again. "He had come to tell us where we could find Teresa. How is she, Zach?" Laura asked anxiously.

"She's badly bruised, but the nuns say she'll recover. However, she refuses to come back here."

"Why?" Laura asked, stunned.

"I think she should tell you that herself. So Teresa's condition had nothing to do with Luis's death. Then how did he and Pilar die?"

"Gregorio tried to persuade Pilar to leave here and go away with him."

"You mean he was in love with her?"

Laura stopped and, frowning, glanced at him in surprise. "Gregorio is Pilar's brother. I thought you knew that."

Frustrated, Zach slapped his hat against his leg. "How the hell would I know that? Goddammit, Laura! Why didn't you tell me this sooner? I had no idea they were brother and sister. I would have considered putting Pilar under military confinement to try and draw out Gregorio. Are you saying you've met this savage before?"

"No. Through the years, he often slipped back to Dario and met secretly with Pilar and Ramon, but I actually met him for the first time last night."

"You're lucky it wasn't a couple weeks ago, lady, or you wouldn't be around to talk about it."

"Zach, Gregorio did not lead the raid on Dario."

"Oh? And how would you know that?"

"Last night he denied he had any part in it."

"And you believe him?"

"Yes, I do. I think you would too, if you could talk to him."

Grimacing, Zach crossed his arms and leaned against the wall. "Well, go on. Finish what you were saying."

"Luis tried to shoot Gregorio in cold blood."

"In cold blood? You mean this poor savage who hacked apart three-fourths of this community?" Zach's light, derisive laugh rankled her.

"I told you Gregorio denied taking part in the raid on Dario," she declared. "Zach, he took Teresa to the hospital. He came in here unarmed. Does that sound like a crazed savage to you?"

"Laura . . . just finish the story."

She sat down again. Closing her eyes, she leaned her head in her hand. "Pilar jumped in front of Gregorio when Luis fired. The two men grappled over the gun and Gregorio strangled him." She looked up at him. "Then Gregorio ran off."

"Where is Ramon now?"

"He's upstairs. I think he finally cried himself to sleep."

Zach's tone softened. "How's Peter taking all this?"

She drew a shuddering sigh. "How do you think? He's confused . . . brokenhearted. I don't think he has fully grasped what's happened. He's so young . . . They both are."

"I'll have to ask Ramon a few questions," Zach said.

She looked up in anguish. "Oh, God, Zach. The child saw his mother . . . and father . . . killed before his eyes. What do you expect of him?"

"Laura, please give me credit for having a little compassion. I know what a difficult time this is for you and the two boys. I'm just trying to do my job. I have to speak to all of the witnesses."

"Isn't my word enough?" she cried out.

"Your word? I'm the wrong one to ask, Laura."

He pivoted and left the room. She heard his boots climbing the stairway.

Later that day, Father Naverro's voice sounded a faint drone to her ears as Laura stared listlessly at Luis's casket. Throughout the funeral ceremony, she stood holding Peter and Ramon by the hands. She glanced around at the assembled people and wondered how many of those present actually mourned Luis's passing.

God forgive her, but she wasn't one of them. Luis had been an evil man; his wickedness could not be nullified by the act of dying.

She felt Peter tighten his grasp, and she glanced down at the top of his head. Ramon had remained as unflinching throughout the ceremony as she, but Peter's little body shook with sobs. She wished she could ease his heartache. The innocence of his tears lent an undeserving purity to Luis's death.

She lifted her head and met Zach's gaze. Despite his loathing for Luis, she knew he had come for Peter's sake. The compassion Zach felt because of Peter's grief showed in the warmth of his eyes; that familiar warmth that she had glimpsed so rarely since his arrival in Dario.

She knew the time was drawing ever nearer to tell Zach the truth about his son . . . but it was still too soon. Peter needed a time for healing.

Feeling neither joy nor sorrow, she watched the casket bearing Luis's body being carried into the stone crypt set in the center of the small graveyard. The walls of the mausoleum had been splashed with paint the day of the attack, but fortunately the locked door . . . and their own superstition . . . had kept the Seminoles from breaking into the tomb to desecrate the caskets.

Her ears were deafened to whatever followed as Luis was put to rest among the other Espositos who had lived and died there. Suddenly, she found herself accepting the condolences of the departing Romero family, Father Naverro, and the nuns from the mission.

Then hand-in-hand with Ramon and Peter, she walked down a worn path leading to the natives' huts. Lagging back at an unobtrusive distance, Zach followed them. The trio stopped and joined the natives gathered around a hastily erected wooden bier in a clearing.

The primitive four-day funeral rite of the Seminoles was only practiced deep in the swamps of the Everglades away from the eyes of an advancing civilization; their ancient ritual of leaving the corpse to rot in a palmetto log box or hollowed tree stump was now forbidden by law.

The Indians were too superstitious to place a body in the ground, and since their traditional burial rites were illegal, the corpse was now cremated on a high scaffold where the Indians believed the spirit of the deceased could fly up to heaven.

Pilar's body had been prepared for disposal in this manner. She was dressed in the floral gown that Luis had bought for her on his last trip to St. Augustine, and her long, dark hair had been brushed to a silken sheen and lay in sharp contrast against the white gown.

Tears glistened in Laura's eyes as Ramon stood stoically beside her, trying not to weep. Recalling her own grief on the day of her father and mother's funeral, she ached for the young boy. She slipped her arm around his shoulders and hugged him to her side. She momentarily released her hold on Peter's hand when Ramon grasped her waist with both arms and clung to her.

Peter dashed back to Zach and clutched his legs, burying his head against them. Zach knelt down on one knee, slipped an arm around Peter's waist, and held him. The two of them watched sorrowfully as a torch was put to the pyre.

Flames consumed the wooden bier, creeping ever nearer to the beautiful woman who lay in peace. Laura could not watch any more. She turned away in tears.

Laura and Ramon began to walk slowly back to the house. She stopped at Zach's side and reached out a hand to Peter. The boy's sobs had subsided, and he grasped his mother's hand.

When Zach stood up, Laura offered a smile of gratitude. "Thank you for being here for him," she said softly, then continued on to the house.

Toward evening, she fed them soup and after a short while the boys went to bed. She went down to the library, lit the lamp, and sat down at the desk . . . to wait.

She knew he would come.

The shadows lengthened. Not a noise or creak sounded in the house. Toward midnight, she looked up. He stood in the doorway, his beautiful face serene. She felt no fright, yet he was the most feared warrior in the Everglades.

"You've come for Ramon, haven't you?" she said with calm resignation.

Gregorio nodded. "He belongs with his people now."

"You know I love him, Gregorio. I want to raise him as a son."

"Ramon is a son of the Seminole, *señora*. Gregorio will raise his sister's son as his own."

"Is this what Ramon wants too?" she asked.

"Yes. We have spoken of it together. If this wish were not in his heart, Gregorio would not take him."

"And what will become of Ramon if something happens to you?" she challenged fretfully.

"Gregorio is the *Micco* of his people . . . their chief. One day Ramon will take my place as their leader."

She looked at him with eyes that pleaded for understanding. "He's so young. No matter what he says, he's still a scared little boy, Gregorio. At least let him stay with me for a few more years."

The warrior's face softened into gentleness, appearing even more handsome in the dim light. "What my people say about you is true. You are a good woman, *señora*."

"Then why take him from me?" she pleaded.

"Your husband was a bad man, *señora*. Cruel to my people. But you have always been good to the Seminole. Gregorio has been told this by many. And you have been good to my sister; this Pilar has told her brother. Gregorio has eyes that see your love for his sister's son, so there is trust in my heart for you. Gregorio does not wish to cause you this hurt. But Ramon is of the Seminole and must join his people."

"Were you telling the truth last night when you said you are not responsible for the raid on Dario?"

"Gregorio spoke the truth, *señora*. The raid was led by one who is not of my village." She saw his dark eyes deepen with sorrow. "He was named Ishmetee. His foolish actions have caused the death of many of our warriors too."

"Then turn this Ishmetee over to the army," Laura said.

"Ishmetee has met his death. He has paid for his actions. His acts were not the wish of Gregorio and his people. We have not made war on the white man for twenty-five summers. We do not wish to be taken to the Indian Territory in the West like our brothers long ago."

"Then you must clear your name with the government,

Gregorio. And the wisest way to do that is to give yourself up."

Laura had not heard Ramon's approach, but without turning around, Gregorio suddenly said, "You are ready, nephew?"

Laura drew a shuddering breath when Ramon's little figure stepped into the room. "Yes, Uncle."

"Oh, Ramon," Laura said helplessly. The young boy rushed into her open arms. She hugged and kissed him. "We'll miss you, dear. Teresa will be devastated to have missed the chance to say good-bye and poor Peter will be brokenhearted." She smiled through her tears. "Did you say good-bye to him?"

"No. We have made the oath in blood, so we will always be brothers. I will think of my little brother often. I hope he will come to no harm without me to take care of him. But I have left him my good luck amulet with the feather of the eagle. Maybe it will bring him the good luck . . . from me."

"Oh, Ramon, I can't bear to see you go." Laura hugged and kissed him again. "I won't be able to stop worrying about you."

"My uncle will see that I come to no harm," he said proudly. "Good-bye, *señora*. You will always be in my heart."

"Good-bye, Ramon," she said in a half-whisper.

Then the two slipped away as quietly as they had appeared.

Wearily, she climbed the stairs. She opened the door and peeked into Peter's room. The youngster sat up in bed, rubbing his eyes. "Where is Ramon?"

She sat down on the bed and gathered him into her arms. "Ramon has gone away with his uncle, sweetheart."

"Is Ramon mad at me? Is that why he went away?" His lip began to quiver.

"Of course not, sweetheart. It has nothing to do with you. His uncle asked Ramon to go with him. Now that his mother and father are gone, Ramon wants to be with someone he knows will love him."

"But we love him, Mama."

Laura felt the rise of tears. "Of course we do, honey. And we always will." She kissed the top of his head. "But when you lose someone you love dearly, you have to make a choice. And Ramon wanted to be with his uncle more than anyone else."

"Will he be coming back, Mama?"

"Maybe . . . someday," she said sadly.

"Will Papa and Pilar come back some day?"

She pressed her cheek to the top of his little head. "No, sweetheart."

"Will Teresa?"

She hugged him tighter. "Teresa will be back soon. Tomorrow we'll go to the village to visit her."

"Will you go away too, Mama?" he asked in a tiny voice that tugged at her heart. She cupped his chin in her hand and searched his frightened eyes. "Oh no, Peter. I'll never go away. There's no one I'd rather be with than you. But let's play pretend, honey. Let's pretend Mama *had* to go away, even if she didn't want to. Who would you want to be with?"

"I'd want to be with Zach," he said without hesitation. "But we're playing pretend, aren't we, Mama? You aren't really going away."

Tears glistened in her eyes as she hugged him to her breast. "Yes, sweetheart, we're only playing pretend. Mama's not going away."

She held him in her arms until they both slipped into slumber.

Chapter 20

Early the following morning, Zach returned to the plantation. He found Laura at the kitchen table with her dark head bent over Luis's ledger books.

"I'm trying to determine my financial situation," she said. "Luis never confided in me, and he was a very poor ledger keeper. I guess I'll have to contact his bankers to get the whole picture."

"Laura, I've saved a little of my army pay. You're more than welcome to it."

"Thank you, Zach, but I don't think that's necessary." She closed the book and leaned back in the hard, wooden chair. The stress of the past few days had begun to take a toll: her shoulders were slumped in weariness, and fatigue had forged dark shadows under her eyes.

"The plantation appeared to have prospered every year; we didn't lose any of the sugar cane crops," she said. "The question is, how much debt did Luis have against the land? I'd like to sell it, and leave here."

Her announcement came as a surprise to him. "Where would you go?" he asked guardedly.

"I don't know. Maybe when Teresa is well enough to travel, I'll go back to Texas. But certainly not to the Lazy R," she added quickly. "I only know I don't want to remain here, Zach. It seems a waste of money to replace

254

all the drapery and furniture that was destroyed in the raid. Besides, I hate this plantation. It would always be a grim reminder to me of my life with Luis."

"I think this is a matter that affects both of us. We'll talk about it when all this mess is behind you. You've got enough on your mind right now." There was an undertone of anger that belied his attempt at casualness. "Well, I promised Peter I'd stop in and see him this morning."

"Thanks, Zach. He looks forward to being with you. Peter's having a very hard time trying to understand all that's happened. He's afraid now that I'm going to go away like Luis . . . and—"

As if propelled, he suddenly leaned across the desk. His deep blue eyes impaled her. "You're not going anywhere, Laura. Not without him . . . or me," he said in a voice firm with conviction.

She drew back in surprise, her eyes wide and her mouth agape. But he had already strode from the room.

When Zach entered the bedroom, he found Peter on the floor playing with the contents of the silver box he always kept in his pocket. The youngster looked up with a sorrowful smile. "Hi, Zach."

"What have you got there, Peter?" Zach asked, sitting down on a nearby chair.

"Just my silver box. Mama says I'm the man of the house now." He sighed deeply. "So I guess I'm getting too big to carry my box around anymore."

"That doesn't mean you still can't keep it," Zach said gently. "Think of it as a friend who has moved away. Just because you don't play together anymore doesn't mean the friendship has ended."

"You mean like me and Ramon?"

"That's right, Peter. Your mother just told me that he left last night with his uncle. I'm sorry."

"Will Ramon always be my friend, Zach, even though we won't be playing together anymore?"

"I'm sure he will." Zach tousled the dark head bent over the cherished items.

"Does that mean Ramon won't try to kill me, like his uncle killed my papa?"

"I hope so, Peter," Zach said solemnly.

"I'm gonna miss Ramon . . . and my Papa."

"I know you will, but someone will eventually come along to take their places, Peter."

The child glanced up quickly. "Will you take my Papa's place, Zach?"

"Well . . . ah . . . I'd like to, Peter, but I'm in the army . . . and—"

"I understand," Peter said forlornly.

Seeing the boy's desolation, Zach quickly added, "But that doesn't mean we can't still be buddies."

Zach felt empathy for the youngster. Loneliness and heartache were feelings he understood . . . he had lived with them for much of his life. "It's not that I don't want to, Peter, but you see, it's pretty hard to take the place of someone's father."

"Can't you even try?" Peter asked, his young voice rife with desperation. "Mama says a person don't know what they can do 'til they really try."

"Your mother's right, Peter." The boy's pathetic little smile wrenched at Zach's heart. "I'll try if you want me to."

Peter's eyes brightened with pleasure. "You will? And since you and me are buddies, you could take Ramon's place too, couldn't you, Zach?"

"Makes sense to me, buddy," Zach said with a warm chuckle. He was learning fast about the quick thinking of a six-year-old.

"I'm gonna go and tell Mama that you're gonna take Papa's place." Peter started to race across the floor.

"Hey, hold up there, little man. I think you better let me tell your mother. It might take some explaining."

Peter grinned and two dimples cleaved his cheeks. "Yeah, maybe you better be the one. Sometimes Mama don't think much of my ideas. She says I've got a over-acted magic nation."

Zach had to stop a moment to interpret the statement. "Sure she didn't say overactive imagination?"

Peter's eyes brightened in recollection. "Yeah, that's it." He picked up the silver box and carried it over to Zach. "You wanna see what I've got in here? I'll let you 'cause you're my best friend."

Zach knew the keepsakes were Peter's most treasured possessions and understood the seriousness of the offer. "I'd love to see what you've got."

Zach started to rifle through the box with his fore-finger, brushing aside a shark's tooth, a heron feather, and several colored stones. Peter grinned broadly when Zach picked up the whistle he had carved. Zach winked and returned to his rummaging.

Picking out a seashell, Peter held it up to Zach's ear. "See? If you listen, Zach, you can hear the ocean."

After several seconds, Zach nodded in agreement. "You're right, Peter."

"And isn't this the most beautifulest stone you ever seen?" the youngster said with reverence, fondling a chip of sparkling pink coral.

"Don't remember seeing one more beautiful," Zach agreed, grinning.

Suddenly, the smile left Zach's face. Torn between shock and astonishment, he picked up the last object in the box, a familiar-looking gold band and chain Laura had worn around her neck. Peter's round-eyed gaze remained locked on Zach's face.

"Where did you get this, Peter?"

"My mama gave it to me."

Zachary held up the ring to the light and saw the dou-ble H inscribed on the inside. His hand clenched into a fist around the plain gold band as memories surged through his mind: the image of his father's face . . . the Double H . . . Laura . . . the night of her birthday when he gave her the ring . . . the first time they made love.

"Can you keep a secret, Zach?" Deep in sentimental reverie, Zachary did not respond. Peter repeated his question.

"I'm sorry, what did you say?" Zach asked, trying to withdraw from his meditation.

With his little face contorted into an intense frown, Peter leaned toward Zachary. "If I tell you a secret, will you promise not to tell?"

The poignant memories were not easily shaken off. Still preoccupied, Zach offered an absentminded response. "I'm the best secret-keeper in the world, little buddy."

"Cross your heart you won't tell anybody else? Mama made me promise not to tell anyone . . . not even Ramon. And I never told him either, 'cause sometimes Ramon acted so smart . . . like he knew everything. But this time, I was smarter than him, 'cause I had a secret he didn't know about."

"Well . . . maybe you shouldn't tell me either, Peter," Zach cautioned.

"But I want to 'cause you're my best buddy." Zachary wanted to hug him when Peter looked up, solemnly shaking his little head. "And best buddies don't *ever* keep secrets from each other. That's what you told me, remember?"

Peter groped to open Zachary's clenched fist. Relaxing his hand, Zach extended his fingers. The ring lay in the center of his palm. Solemnly, Peter picked up the gold band. His lips puckered as he brought a finger to his mouth. "This is my father's ring," he said in a conspiratorial half-whisper. "But Mama told me it's gotta be hers and my secret. But now I'm telling you, too. Mama said if anything ever happens to her, I should always keep the ring."

Zachary thought he had misunderstood the boy. "You mean your mother said this was *her* ring."

Inflated with the importance of the secret, Peter widened his brown eyes as he shook his head. "Oh, no. Mama said this was my *father's* ring."

As the significance of the words sunk in, Zach felt his chest constrict. He could hardly breathe. "Your . . . father's . . ." Still doubtful that he had correctly understood the youngster's words, Zach clutched Peter's shoulders and pulled him closer. "Peter, look at me."

Zach stared intently into Peter's startled eyes. Seeking a clue, he found none. They were Laura's eyes, no doubt about that. He cupped Peter's face between his hands. His dark gaze roamed over every contour of the youngster's face, his thumbs every groove. Then he stopped abruptly as his fingers traced the child's jaw.

The truth was evident; had been right before his eyes the whole time. Zach realized if he hadn't been so blind with bitterness, he would have seen it sooner. Peter had the sculpted, square jawline of a Houston.

Slightly annoyed by this close inspection, the very owner of the chin jutted it out at a pugnacious angle which emphasized the resemblance all the more.

"Oh, God, Peter. Oh, sweet God!" Zach mumbled. He pulled Peter into his arms and hugged him to his chest. Moisture glistened in Zach's eyes as he rested his cheek atop of his son's dark head.

"Are you sad about my Papa, Zach?" Peter asked in confusion when Zachary finally released him.

Zach grinned and tapped Peter lightly on the chin with a fist. "No, I just think you're a brave little man. And I'm proud of you . . . son. So proud that I just had to hug you."

Peter looked perplexed. "Proud? What does that mean, Zach?"

"Well . . . it means that I'm pleased with you."

"You mean it's like saying you like me."

"Well . . . more than just like. Didn't your . . . papa . . . ever tell you he was proud of you?"

Peter shook his head. "No, Papa never told me that." He returned the ring to the silver box and snapped it shut, then he carefully placed the box on a shelf. When he turned around, his little face had sobered. "I don't think Papa was very proud of me 'cause he . . . he never . . . hugged me either."

Zachary felt a rising outrage. Outraged that for the past six years, his son had been denied the love of a father, that he had been denied his son. For seven years Zach had not cared whether he lived or died when a purpose for living had existed all the time.

Zach began to tremble with anger. How could Laura have done this to him? She could have told him the truth anytime in the past weeks—*should* have told him the truth. He might have been killed during the goddamn campaign. He would have died never knowing he had a son. There was no excuse for what she had done.

Angrily, Zach rose to his feet. "I have to go now, Peter."

"Don't forget to ask Mama if you can take my papa's place," Peter reminded him.

"I've changed my mind, Peter."

Devastated, the little boy looked up. His lower lip quivered as he tried not to cry. "Aren't you gonna ask Mama if you can be my papa, Zach?"

Zachary pulled him into his arms and hugged him. "No, I'm not going to ask her, I'm going to tell her. And I'm not going to be your papa, Peter. I'm going to be your dad. You call me 'Dad' or 'Daddy.' But I don't ever want you to call me 'Papa.'" Zach would not tolerate a word that conjured up the image of Luis Esposito in his son's mind.

He cupped the child's face in his hands. "Do you understand, Peter?" Zach covered the boy's face with kisses. "Do you understand? From now on you call me Dad or Daddy. And from now on, a day won't pass without me telling you how proud I am of you."

Tears of happiness streaked the little boy's face as he threw his arms around Zach's neck. "I will, I promise. I love you, Daddy. I love you."

"And I love you, son." Their tears mingled as they hugged each other.

* * *

After leaving Peter, Zach charged down the stairway, rage and resentment rising with every step he took. Laura jumped to her feet in alarm when Zach stormed into the library and slammed the door shut behind him.

The black fury in his eyes was frightening. She backed away. "What . . . what's wrong?"

"I ought to kill you." She tried to bolt, but he was already on her, his fingers biting into the flesh of her shoulder. "I should strangle you right here on the spot."

"Stop it!" she cried out. "You're hurting me, Zach. Let me go!"

He loosened his grip, but didn't release her. "Of all the scheming, money-grasping little—"

"I don't understand—" she said, wide-eyed and confused.

"Did you ever intend to tell me that Peter is my son?" he shouted furiously.

Laura closed her eyes and all resistance slipped away. "So you know," she said softly.

Zach released her. "Yes, *I know*."

Laura opened her eyes and met the full force of the wrath in his dark eyes. "I swear, Zach, I was going to tell you when the time was right."

"When the time was right!" He snorted in contempt. "And when would that be, *Mrs. Esposito*? A last-minute confession on your deathbed?"

Her legs were trembling so violently, Laura could no longer stand. She sank into a nearby chair. "Well, I'm glad the truth is finally out. The secret has weighed heavily on my conscience."

"*Your* conscience?" He threw back his head in scornful laughter. " 'I'll wait for you forever, Zach,' " he mocked. "Yeah, until a better prospect came along. What happened, Laura? You wake up one morning and decide that marrying a rich man was a lot more appealing than marrying a poor one?"

"No. I woke up one morning to discover I was pregnant . . . with your child." She hurled the words back at him. "I thought you were dead."

"Oh, please, Laura, spare me the repetition. You've already acted out that scene for me. I wrote you at least a dozen letters. You never answered a *single one*. Senator Long even wired you when we were rescued."

He began to pace the floor, reliving the pain of that long-ago memory. "By the time I was finally well enough to get back to Texas, you had already sailed off in the sunset with your husband. I nearly went out of my mind when Lavitia told me you were married. I don't know how I got through it. I can't even remember. Thanks to Senator Long, my appointment to West Point finally gave me some sense of a purpose."

She reached out imploringly. "I never received any wire . . . or letters."

Zach stopped his pacing and shouted in disgust, "Oh, Christ, Laura. When do the lies stop?"

His continual insults to her integrity finally wore thin. She leapt to her feet in anger. "Do you think you're the only one who suffered? When I heard you were dead, I wanted to die."

"Goddammit! Quit saying I was dead. I wasn't dead. If you had stayed around long enough, you would have found that out for yourself."

"I don't think so, Zach. It might have been too late. Luis's proposal kept me from killing myself."

"What are you trying to convince me of now . . . that Esposito's love saved you from destroying yourself? Dramatics again, Laura?"

In the force of her anger, she shouted out the one secret that she had kept locked in her conscience since the day it happened. "No, it's true. I did try. I stopped when I realized that if I killed myself, I would be destroying our child, too. I stayed alive to keep our child alive. And I vowed then that I would do whatever I had to in order to protect him. So I married Luis Esposito. He didn't marry me for love; Aunt Lavitia bought him. From the beginning, the marriage was a nightmare. Luis loathed me because I carried another man's child. He enjoyed inflicting pain: verbal and physical. He debased me physically in the marriage bed and he taunted me with verbal abuse out of it. When we reached Florida, he flaunted his mistress in my face by having her and his bastard son live with us."

Still skeptical, Zach challenged her. "Then why didn't you leave him after Peter was born?"

"Because I had no money . . . and no place to go. Aunt Lavitia paid him to take me off her hands, remember? After Peter was born, I told Luis I would kill him if he ever touched me again. So he left me alone. We never shared a bed again. I suppose I can thank Pilar for that. She kept him . . . occupied. In truth, Pilar and I were very fond of each other. Tragically enough, the poor woman actually loved him."

Laura regained her composure. Drawing a shuddering breath, she sat down. "You're not the victim and neither am I, Zach. Our son is. When you suddenly showed up here, I couldn't tell you the truth. I would have had to tell Peter the truth about his father, too. I didn't want to disrupt his life more than it already had been."

"You didn't think raising him in this hellhole was disruptive? Having him almost get killed?"

"The Indians were always peaceful until recently."

"So I noticed," he scoffed.

"It's true."

"True? When your friend Gregorio has been terrorizing this area for years?"

"Terrorizing, yes, but not murdering. He only tried to drive away the Europeans. He never harmed anyone other than to steal some livestock or burn some crops. Gregorio is a rebel, Zach . . . a Robin Hood . . . a Joaquin Murieta. These kind of men become legends. Their people sing ballads and write stories about them. Every country in the world has dissidents and outlaws.

We had them in Texas, too. Had I believed Peter was in danger, I never would have remained."

Zach suffered a righteous anger that could not easily be appeased. He walked to the door and paused with his hand on the knob. "Right now, I can't separate truth from fiction. There are just too many unanswered questions . . . and too much pain." He turned around with a glare as hard and black as marble. "But I'm telling you this, Laura. Either you tell Peter the truth, or I will." His face twisted with bitterness and he left.

Laura wanted to rush after him. To plead with him— beg him if she had to—to convince him to trust her enough to tell Peter when she felt the time was right. Now it was just too soon after Luis's death. *Would Zach carry out his threat and tell Peter the truth himself?* He was so full of bitterness, she feared he would. She crossed her arms and paced the floor nervously. Perhaps it had been a mistake to allow Peter to believe Luis was his father. The man never showed the child a sign of affection. And although Luis had never physically abused Peter, he had often ridiculed the boy before others.

The thought that Peter might have been killed during the attack brought a lump to her throat. Her resolve to protect her child had almost led to his destruction instead.

"Mama." The tiny voice came from the doorway.

She quickly wiped away her tears and turned to him with a smile. "Hi, sweetheart." She hunched down and opened her arms. Peter ran into them. He slipped his arms around her neck and kissed her cheek.

"I thought you were going to take a nap," she said. She stood up and walked over to sit down. Her legs were still trembling.

Peter followed and climbed up on her lap. "You're getting so big, pretty soon you won't fit on my lap anymore." She hugged him tighter, trying not to think of how painful that day would be for her.

"Are you mad at me, Mama?" he asked shyly.

"Mad at you?" Her smile was tender. "I wouldn't get mad at you just because you didn't take a nap, sweetheart."

"I mean, are you mad at me 'cause I broke our promise and told Daddy about the ring?"

"Daddy?" In her shock, she stumbled over the word. *Damn you, Zach! You already told him. You had no right.*

"Zach told me to call him that." His brown eyes looked up adorably at her. "I love him, Mama. And he loves me. He told me so. And he promised to take Papa's place."

Laura was at a loss for words. She wondered what else the two had exchanged. If Zach hadn't told Peter the truth, he certainly had come near to telling him. She had to have time to think about the situation. It was just too delicate to blurt out the truth.

But how long before his anger cools? she wondered. She had never seen him this angry before. Whatever cruel twist of fate had separated them, they now had the chance to redeem the paradise they had lost. But would it be lost again? Would Zach find this latest truth too insurmountable to forgive her?

Oh, Zach, can't we put the mistakes of the past behind us once and for all? she cried silently.

Throughout the seven years of domination and humiliation as Luis's wife, her love for Zach had remained steadfast. His love for her may have faltered, but it had never died. *Yes, once his anger cools . . . we'll forgive again . . . will love again,* she told herself.

Laura didn't see any sign of Zach when she and Peter rode into Dario that afternoon. Laura was shocked at the sight of Teresa's injuries, but Sister Francesca assured her that the bruises were superficial and Teresa should be able to return to the plantation the next day.

"Sister, will you take Peter for a few minutes? I want to talk to Teresa alone." When the nun left with Peter in hand, Laura sat down at Teresa's bedside. "What happened with Luis, Teresa?"

Teresa's brown eyes welled with tears. "I'm so sorry, Laura. When Luis came back to the house, he tried to . . . to . . ." She broke off with a sob.

Laura took her hand. "Oh, dear God, Teresa. Did he—"

"No," Teresa quickly replied, shaking her head. "Gregorio stopped him. The next thing I knew, I woke up here in the mission."

"Oh, thank God." Laura sighed. Seeing Teresa's eyes begin to droop with drowsiness, Laura stood up. "We'll come back tomorrow to see you, dear. I've brought you fresh clothing, and if you're well enough to leave tomorrow, we'll take you home."

Laura still hadn't seen any sign of Zach by the time they left.

Chapter 21

The next day dawned with a sky of dark, threatening clouds. Overhead, thousands of squawking birds flew in from the sea, seeking refuge in the swamps. The barometer dropped drastically, indicating the approach of a major storm.

Recognizing the first signs of a hurricane, the three native families who lived on the plantation had hurried to safety within the walls of the mission church at Dario, which left Laura and Peter alone in the house.

Laura wrestled with the thought of going to Dario to visit Teresa and take refuge in the mission. She envisioned how hot and crowded the mission would become, and knew that the plantation's stucco walls could withstand the force of a hurricane. So she closed and secured all the shutters, and decided to remain.

By late afternoon, strong winds trumpeted the storm's approach; huge waves battered the coastline. The army personnel had spent the morning preparing for the impending storm. Horses and mules had been hauled to protective cover, tether lines on tents had been reinforced, and everything loose had been secured.

Zach leaned against one of the unfinished barracks under construction, his gaze fixed on the front of the mission. Throughout the morning, he had watched natives passing through the gate, but had seen no sign of Laura and Peter. Thinking that he might have missed their arrival, Zach decided to check.

As soon as he entered the mission again, Sister Francesca approached with a tolerant smile. "No, Lieutenant, they are not here."

"Thank you, Sister." Zach left, his dark brows drawn together in a worried frown.

Despite the threatening clouds overhead, Teresa decided she would return to the plantation. Luis and Pilar had been put to their final rest, and Laura most certainly would need her help. Teresa thought of how strange it would be now, with Luis, Pilar . . . and even Ramon gone.

Her eyes darkened with sorrow at the thought of poor Pilar. Then her face twisted with loathing when the image of Luis Esposito entered her mind. How she had detested him . . . even in Texas. She rejoiced that the evil man was dead. Recalling what he had done to her, and the abuses he had inflicted on Laura, the servants and field hands, and even Pilar, Teresa shuddered. She had lived in fear of him for seven years. At least that was now over.

Despite what Sister Francesca had told her, Teresa could not bring herself to pray for Luis's soul. Without mercy in her heart, Teresa knew she was not worthy to enter the sisterhood. She would have to pray harder for guidance.

For no matter how much she tried, Teresa could not put aside the memory of the nightmarish ordeal in the swamp. The horror . . . Luis's brutality . . . her pain . . . and then a pair of dark eyes that had haunted her these past days.

After saying good-bye to the nuns, she left the mission.

When Teresa was halfway to her destination, the wind increased and began to lash the trees lining the road. Soon huge, fan-shaped palm leaves thrashed through the air like huge whips. Despite her attempt to avoid them, she often felt the sting of the broad fronds. She began to run, hoping to reach the plantation before the wind grew more powerful.

Racing down the road, she passed a rotted water oak just as one of the heavy limbs cracked and toppled. She scrambled to dodge the falling branch, but its end struck her shoulders and drove her to the ground. Struggling, she lay pinned beneath the unwieldy bough just as a hard rain began to pelt her face.

Soon the ground softened into mud and the ruts in the road became filled with water. The fierce wind continued to hurl branches and tumbling leaves until she was all but entombed. As she lay helplessly, she suddenly became aware that she was not alone; paralyzed, she watched with horror as she saw a snake slither toward her along a branch. Fearful that the reptile would strike, she held her breath as long as she could—then she panicked. Screaming, she closed her eyes and started to struggle.

Teresa felt the sharp fangs sink into her leg. Sobbing, she waited for the next painful bite. But before the deadly fangs could inject more venom into her, the powerful swipe of a machete decapitated the reptile.

She opened her eyes to the same apparition from her earlier torment—the same pair of haunting dark eyes.

Then, as before, Teresa slipped into oblivion.

From the concealment of trees at the far end of the village, Gregorio had watched the American officer pacing nervously back and forth in front of the mission. Despite the risk of being caught, he had purposely come to observe this army lieutenant for himself. The *señora* said that he was a fair man, and Pilar had believed it too. Throughout the previous night, he had weighed the wisdom of their words. Dare he trust his fate to this army officer?

When Zachary had disappeared into a tent, Gregorio had decided to leave. He would think on the matter more and return after the storm.

About to slip back into the trees, he had seen Teresa come out of the mission. His gaze had followed her as she left the village and continued down the road. He wondered where the girl was going with such a severe storm approaching. Curious, he had followed, but reached her too late to prevent her misfortune.

Gregorio knew he had to act quickly before the poison spread through her body. Thankful that the woman remained unconscious, he drew his knife, cut a vertical slash across the puncture in her leg, and crossed it with a horizontal cut. Then he lowered his head and sucked at the wound, drawing out the venom. He spit out the mixture of blood and poison, then repeated the process several more times. He left the wound unbound to allow the bleeding to drain the poison from her body.

The fury of the wind and rain increased drastically and Gregorio knew there was no longer time to take her back to the mission. The powerful muscles of his shoulders and arms stretched tautly as he hoisted the heavy tree limb and lifted it off her. Then he picked up the unconscious woman and carried her a short distance into the swamp to a snug cove in the sanctuary of an oak stand. The large tree trunks formed a protective refuge against the force of the wind, and their leafy boughs a canopy to ward off the rain. Now, temporarily sheltered from the fury that pressed around them, he placed her on the ground and cut a strip of her gown to bind the wound.

"Am I going to die?" Teresa murmured.

Gregorio glanced at her. She lay tranquil, her solemn, brown eyes watching every move he made.

"Death will take us all one day." He glanced skyward as the wind whistled around them; the faintest of smiles curved his lips. "Perhaps today is the day."

"You are the same one who saved me in the swamp," she said softly.

He nodded and sat down beside her, crossing his legs. "The wind blows too hard to make a fire to dry your clothes."

At the moment, wet clothing was the farthest thought

from Teresa's mind as she studied the handsomest man she had even seen. Despite his awesome size and the storm that raged around them, Teresa had never felt such a sense of serenity.

"Laura said you were the one who took me to the mission."

"It would not have been wise to leave you with the one who sought to harm you."

"Thank you." Teresa hesitated, then trying to keep the quaver out of her voice, said, "She told me you are Gregorio."

"Does the knowledge bring trouble to your heart?"

"It would have once. But now, I'm not afraid of you."

Again a faint smile hovered at the corners of his mouth. "Your heart holds no fear for the fiercest warrior in the Everglades?"

Teresa felt the blackness begin to overcome her, but before she succumbed, she smiled sweetly. "I'm sure it will . . . if I ever . . . meet him."

He gazed with affection at her. Through the years he had watched her from afar and had seen her change from a little girl to a woman. She had a grace and gentleness about her that touched his heart.

At the sight of the ugly bruises on her face, Gregorio's own features hardened in grimness as he recalled the day Luis had tried to ravage her. He should have killed Luis that day. Then Pilar would still be alive.

Teresa moaned softly. Gregorio's expression was grave as he studied her; he knew her body would soon feel the effects of the snakebite. Both the mission and the plantation were too far to reach in the raging storm. She needed shelter, but he had nothing with which to cover her except leaves. As soon as the full force of the storm passed, he would carry her to a nearby Seminole *hutis* where he had taken Ramon. There he could find dry clothing and a fire to warm her.

As he had expected, Teresa soon began to shake.

Gregorio piled more leaves on her, but the wind swept them off, and her body continued to be racked with tremors.

"I'm so cold, Gregorio," she whispered.

He lay down beside her and gathered her into his arms, pulling her against the heat of his own body. And as the full might of the tempest raged around them, she lay in the haven of his arms with the powerful flesh and muscled strength of his body enveloping her like a blanket.

He held her as the day passed into darkness.

After finishing their evening meal, Laura made a game out of having Peter help her tote a keg of fresh water, candles, and extra matches to his room. She also made certain she had her pistol. Then tucking him in bed, she sat down at his bedside and began to read to him from a book that Zachary had given him.

Within hours the hurricane struck with full force. Tree limbs slapped at the roof and sides of the house. Rotted mangrove and palmettoes were wrenched from the ground and tossed through the air as lightly as pieces of straw. In the force of the wind, the younger, flexible saplings bowed in half, their boughs sweeping the ground like lacy brooms.

Inside, Laura feared that at any second one of the huge trunks would crash through the wall. Peter became too frightened to listen to her read. He covered his ears to try to shut off the screech of the wind and the deafening drum of the rain which pounded at the roof like a host of hammering woodpeckers. Laura jumped to her feet at the sudden sound of shattering glass.

"What was that, Mama?" Peter cried out.

"Just a lamp, honey," she soothed, trying to calm him. "One of the shutters must have torn loose downstairs." In the past, Luis or one of the servants would have rushed to fasten it, but Laura had no intention of leaving Peter alone. Soon the sound of the flapping shutter became an added assault on her already tattered nerves.

"Just lay back, honey, and go to sleep," she said. "I'll fix it in the morning."

Her heart swelled with love as his round, trusting eyes looked up at her. "When I wake up, will the storm be all gone, Mama?"

She slipped her arms under him and hugged his trembling little body. "Yes, sweetheart. Go to sleep," she murmured.

"Will you stay with me?" he asked, lying back.

"Of course."

"Don't you be afraid, Mama. We'll be okay."

Laura leaned over and kissed him. "I'm so proud of my brave little man."

Peter closed his eyes. A smile graced his tiny face as his voice trailed off into slumber. "Daddy told me he's proud of me, too."

Outside, the wind and rain continued their rampage; but inside, with Peter asleep and no one to talk to, Laura felt the loneliness of the empty house intensify. She glanced around the darkened room, its corners in murky shadows. The only source of light came from a flickering lamp on the table next to the bed.

Why hadn't she taken Peter to the safety of the mission? Why had she remained alone in the house? What if the hostile Seminoles returned? What if something happened to her and Peter was left on his own? The storms always drove snakes and wild animals out of the swamps. He would be defenseless against them. Her hand slid to her pocket and her grip tightened around the pistol. She took it out and sat down on the floor beside the bed.

She had no idea how long she sat immersed in her fears. Finally, the full fury of the hurricane passed over and headed across the Gulf to ravage the Texas coastline. But the steady drum of the rain and the thud of flapping shutters did not abate.

Her eyes drooped and she laid her head on the bed. The pistol slipped from her hand.

* * *

Laura's eyes popped open. She jerked up her head and glanced at Peter. He was sleeping peacefully. What had awakened her? Her hand instinctively groped for the pistol laying on the counterpane. She listened intently, her senses alerted to every sound. Rain still beat on the roof, but the wind had died. Suddenly, the stairs creaked, and she swung her head toward the door. Holding her breath, she waited . . . listened. The sound came again. Someone, or something, was climbing the stairway. Her breath began to come in quick gasps as she heard the pad of approaching footsteps. Grasping the gun in both hands, she pointed the weapon at the door. Transfixed, she watched the knob slowly turn and the door swing open.

Zach's rain-drenched figure appeared in the doorway.

"Zach." She sobbed his name in relief. The courage she had maintained throughout the evening gave way to an attack of violent trembling. Unchecked, tears ran down her cheeks, and her arms fell to her sides. The pistol slipped from her fingers and dropped to the floor.

In a single glance, Zach took in the sleeping boy and Laura kneeling at his bedside. Her fear-stricken face told him all he needed to know.

His emotions erupted as tumultuously as hers. Casting off his dripping poncho as he rushed to her, he was beside her at once—kneeling and pulling her into his arms. "It's okay, love. Don't cry, you're safe now. I won't let anything happen to you or Peter."

His hat fell off as she wrapped her arms around his neck and clung to him. "Zach. Oh, Zach," she sobbed endlessly as he rained quick kisses on her cheeks, her closed eyes, her hair.

"You're okay, love, you're safe now, love," he muttered as he continued to press repeated kisses to her tear-streaked cheeks and eyes.

Then his mouth found hers.

The touch was too sweet to break. Her lips parted and

fitted to his. Tenderly cupping her face in his hands, he kissed her.

The kiss grew hungrier. The pressure increased. Passion overpowered compassion. He slipped his tongue between her teeth and laved the moist chamber in hot, erotic sweeps. Her sobs became responsive moans and she shifted restlessly in his arms.

Lest he remove his mouth from hers, she slid the fingers of one hand into his dampened hair, the other hand to the base of his neck. The cords of his strong neck felt taut under her fingertips and she curved her palm around it to increase the exquisite pressure of his lips against her own.

Breath became too precious to waste on words; seconds too short to dally. He slipped his hand under her knees and lifted her into his arms. Rising to his feet, he carried her into the next room.

His hands worked the buttons of her gown as her fingers fumbled to release his pants. Boots and clothing were hurriedly discarded until they were naked, their bodies entwined on the bed.

The game of denial had been played too long. Driven by mutual hunger, each body feasted on the other. And each shared kiss became the nourishment that their fasting lips had craved.

Time was their enemy—as it had been for the past seven years. There was no time for foreplay . . . for exploration. No time for reacquaintance.

There was only time for him to carry her to the bed. To feel her touch on his fevered body . . . to enter her . . . and to sink deeper and deeper into the woman he loved—his mind and body drowning in a sublime sea of remembered bliss called Laura.

PART III

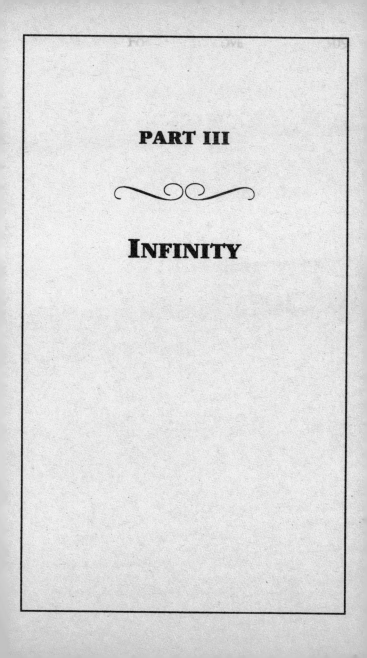

INFINITY

Chapter 22

〜◦◦◦〜

As soon as the sun rose, Gregorio built a small fire. He checked the stream and found several large shells. Filling one with water, he added some willow bark and set the shell in the fire. While he waited for the willow bark to boil, he searched for aloe to make a poultice for the wound.

Teresa thrashed in fever as Gregorio mashed up the plant and formed a paste. He spread it on the snakebite and bound the wound with another torn strip from her skirt. By that time, the liquid had boiled, then cooled enough to drink. He lifted her head and forced the tonic down her throat.

In her delirium, Teresa tried to shove him away, but Gregorio nursed her patiently. He put cool compresses on her forehead, and when that didn't soothe her, he undressed her. Holding her in his arms, he waded into the stream and allowed the cool water to bring down her fever.

For several hours, he repeated the process, feeding her the willow tonic, bathing her in the stream, and changing the poultice on her leg.

His dark eyes glowed with compassion at the sight of the welts and bruises that still covered her body from Luis's beating and her misfortune with the oak tree. Tenderly, he sponged her face and body with a cool strip of cloth.

Throughout it all, Teresa fell in and out of consciousness, her awareness vacillating between the demons of her delirium and the comfort of the arms holding her.

Relaxed, his long body stretched to its full length, Zach lay facedown on the bed and was completely content for the first time in seven years. Deep in slumber, Laura lay snuggled against him. He gazed somnolently at the dust motes swirling around like tiny bubbles amidst the shafts of morning sunlight that filtered through the narrow cracks of the shutters.

His thoughts were on Laura and their recurring lovemaking throughout the night—sleeping . . . only to awaken and pull Laura to him . . . caressing her . . . dropping back into slumber, then awakening once again to the sublime awareness of her hands upon him. Loving, or being loved—neither one could get enough of the feel, the taste, the smell, or the touch of the other.

As if seeking reassurance, he slipped his leg over hers. And in slumber, she responded by reaching out and resting her hand on his hip.

Suddenly a dark outline obliterated the dust motes and sunlight.

"Hi."

Zach raised a brow and found himself staring into a pair of round, brown eyes. "Hi."

"Why are you in my mama's bed?"

Yawning, Zachary propped up an elbow and rested his drowsy head in his hand. "What time is it, Peter?"

"I don't know. I can't tell time. Why are you in my mama's bed?" Peter pursued.

"You asked me to take your papa's place, didn't you?"

"Papa didn't sleep in Mama's bed. He slept in the other room with Pilar."

"Well . . . ah . . ." Zach struggled for an alibi, " . . . ah . . . your mother was afraid of the storm." Zach smiled, pleased with himself for coming up with a logical explanation. The smile dissipated into a grimace as Laura kicked him under the sheet.

Peter's face curled up with satisfaction. "I was afraid of the storm too. But I sleeped by myself."

"That's because you're a very brave little man," Zach assured him, but his eyes widened with shock as Laura slipped her hand down to his buttocks.

"How come you didn't hang up your clothes? They're all wet."

As Laura's fingers played havoc with his lower spine, Zach cleared his throat and tried to concentrate. "I was too tired."

"You should have asked my mama to hang them up. She hangs up my clothes."

"Well . . . she seemed very anxious to get to bed." Groping under the covers, he managed to snatch Laura's hand, pull it between his legs, and press it against his throbbing sex. "But tell you what, Peter, I'll remember to ask her the next time. Maybe you could do me a favor right now."

"Sure," Peter said agreeably.

"Will you pick up my uniform, take it downstairs, and spread it out on the table to dry?"

Peter ran over and picked up Zach's trousers and shirt. "And while you're doing that, I'll try and find something to put on in the meantime," Zach said.

As soon as he heard the boy going down the stairs, Zach got out of bed and closed the door. Then he turned back to Laura.

She was sitting up in bed. Her eyes glowed with mirth and her long, disheveled hair hung past the rounded curve of her bare breasts.

"You handled that admirably, Lieutenant Houston," she said, bringing her hand up in a snappy salute. She slid a slim leg out of bed. "I'll find something of Luis's for you to wear."

Zach reached behind him and turned the key in the lock. "Right now, you're not going anywhere. In case you haven't noticed, lady, you've got some unfinished business to attend to."

He returned to the bed and reached for her. Laura put up a hand to ward him off. "Zach, we've got so much to talk about . . . and Peter . . ." She faltered as he drew her nipple into his mouth. Sweet sensation surged through her. "Oh, God, Zach, you're not being fair," she murmured. Then the demanding pressure of his mouth on hers stifled any further protest, and she yielded to the music and rhythm of his mouth, his touch, his body.

A short while later, a cavalry patrol rode up to the house as Zach was repairing the broken shutter he had crawled through the previous night to enter the house. Flint Bryce detached himself from the troopers and came over to him. "I figured this is where we'd track you down," Bryce declared. "Goddammit, Lieutenant, you scared the hell out of us when we couldn't find you."

"I rode out here . . . early this morning . . . to make sure Mrs. Esposito and Peter were not injured during the hurricane, Sergeant." Then he quickly changed the subject. "How much damage is there in the village?"

"Lost a couple of tents is about all. Figured you would have seen that yourself . . . before you rode out . . . *this morning.*" Amusement gleamed in his eyes.

Zach suppressed his grin. "Don't choke on that dust you're blowing, Sergeant. As long as you and your squad are here, hitch up ropes to those fallen trees and get rid of them."

"Yes, sir," Bryce said with a sharp salute. Bryce wheeled his horse to leave.

In a guarded voice for their ears only, Zach called out to him. "I appreciate your concern, Flint." Bryce grinned at him and rode back to the mounted squad.

Zach resumed repairing the shutter. When he finished, he put aside the hammer and sat down on the floor.

His casual gaze swept the barren room, then came to rest on Laura, who stood in the entrance.

"You know, Laura, I think you're right about this place. It would be very costly to refurnish the whole house.

Especially since you're not happy here anyway."

"I'm happy here right now," she said as she walked over and sat down beside him.

Zach grabbed her and leaned her back in his arms. "Well, you've sure changed your tune, lady," he said lightly.

She laced her fingers through the rich texture of his dark hair. "I'm happy as long as I'm with you."

He nibbled a moist trail along her neck, then kissed her deeply.

She felt the tantalizing swirl of passion, pulled away, and sat up quickly. "That's enough. It's getting very warm in here, don't you think? And Peter's liable to come in any minute."

"He's occupied," Zach assured her. "Take a look for yourself." He pointed down toward the road.

They watched with parental pride as Peter, trailing after Flint Bryce, tried to match the sergeant's long strides. Even from a distance, they could see that Peter's mouth was moving incessantly. Bryce appeared to grunt an occasional reply.

The sound of Zach's warm chuckle brought a smile to Laura's lips. "I think Sergeant Bryce has a new junior officer."

She settled back contentedly in his arms. "Zach, what are we going to do about Peter?"

"We could try putting a muzzle on him."

"I'm serious, Zach. We've got so much to decide."

"Honey, I don't know what to tell you. I think you're right about keeping the truth from him right now. We'll give him a little bit more time to heal."

He tilted her chin and his troubled eyes gazed into hers. "We all need a time to heal, Laura. Can you ever forgive me for the way I've treated you . . . the things I've said?"

She put a finger to his lips to hush him. "Zach, both of us have been lost for these past seven years, but now we've found each other again. That's all that matters."

"I've never stopped loving you, Laura. And Lord knows, I tried hard enough."

"And a day never passed without my thinking of you." She smiled through the tears that had begun to fill her eyes.

His arms tightened around her and he leaned his cheek on her head. "Don't cry, honey. We're together now. Nothing's ever going to separate us again."

"I'm not crying, Zach. Just brimming over with love." She closed her eyes to savor the sensation as his warm lips pressed a kiss behind her ear. When his hand slid to her breast, she covered it with her own. "Zach, what if one of the soldiers comes in here looking for you?"

He turned her and eased her to the floor, cradling her head on his arm. "Sweetheart, if you're going to be my wife, you've got a lot to learn about the army. No enlisted man ever comes *looking* for an officer. They prefer to leave well enough alone."

Laughter glowed in her eyes as she slipped her arms around his neck. "Do you like the army, Zach?"

"Hell, no!"

"Then let's go back to Texas and start a spread near Brownsville the way we talked about," she said excitedly.

He shook his head and laughed lightly. "It's not that simple, honey. I can't just shed my army uniform and head back to the range. My enlistment's not up for another two months."

"As handsome as you are in your uniform, my love, I can't wait to see you astride a horse again . . . in a blue shirt . . . with a red bandanna around your neck." She sat up and clasped her hands together enthusiastically. "Oh, you were so handsome! My girlish heart used to flop over in my breast every time I saw you."

Clearly intrigued, he lifted his head. Devilment gleamed in his eyes. "Is that right? I want to hear more of this."

She drew a deep breath. Gazing into space, her eyes

were round and dreamy as she conjured up her cherished image of him. "You had such strength and energy about you." She sighed in a voice rife with emotion. "You looked so . . . so . . . powerful . . . and magnificent. Bronzed . . . and muscular . . . and . . ."

"Dusty and sweaty," he intoned drolly.

She expelled a deep sigh as the vision vanished. "How did I appear to you, Zach?" she asked breathlessly.

She sat entranced by his handsome profile as he reflected on her words. "Well, kind of bony . . . flatchested . . . long, wobbly legs like a newborn colt. And a skinny little bottom that couldn't sit a saddle to save her soul."

"Oh, you're lying." She groaned and she shoved him away. "I'm not going to listen to you."

Laughing, he fell back, pulling her down across him. He grasped her head, weaving his fingers through her thick hair. "Yeah, I'm lying. You weren't any of those things." His sapphire eyes deepened with the intensity of his emotions. "You were Laura."

By that afternoon, other than some water-filled potholes and several sections of flooded fields, the plantation showed little evidence of the hurricane. As much as Zach would liked to have remained with Laura, he bowed to the responsibility of his duties and prepared to depart with the patrol.

He drew her into his arms. "I'll come back tonight," he said and kissed her.

Peter came running over to them and Zach released her to pick him up. "You take care of your mother while I'm gone."

"Where are you going?"

"I have to go back to the village."

"Why?"

"I'm on duty."

"What's duty?"

Zach shook his head, then he kissed Peter on the cheek

and handed him over to Laura. "What did I say to get him started?"

"You'll know better next time, won't you?" Laura said, laughing. Zach pressed a quick kiss on her lips and mounted his horse. "I'll see you tonight."

Holding Peter in her arms, she smiled up at Zach. "Tonight."

When he thought she was well enough to be moved, Gregorio lifted Teresa into his arms and carried her deeper into the swamp. After several miles, he reached a *hutis* set in the center of an island of red cypress. The tiny village consisted of three huts.

Ramon ran up to Gregorio as soon as he saw him. The boy was surprised to see Teresa in his uncle's arms. "What has happened to her?" he asked.

"She was bitten by a serpent." Gregorio carried her into one of the *chickees*. The open-sided house was nothing more than a ten-foot-long platform built on stilts about three feet high; four upright pine posts supported a thatched roof made of palm leaves. He laid Teresa on a mat of woven grass in the corner.

Gregorio spoke to one of the women and she hurried away, returning shortly with a cup of sassafras tea containing the willow potion. Holding up Teresa's head, Gregorio managed to get more of the medicine down her.

Teresa regained full consciousness that night. Awakening, she looked around, disoriented. Moonlight cast the trees around the small clearing in shadows, and she could not recognize her surroundings. She lay stiffly, listening, and thought she heard the sound of breathing from somewhere near her. She saw no sign of Gregorio. She wanted to call out for him, but stifled her cry of panic.

Finally quieting her mind, she became aware of a sweet aroma. Turning her head, she discovered a single white camellia lying beside her. She knew he had placed the flower there.

Once again, Teresa felt a deep peace when she thought of Gregorio. Picking up the delicate bloom, she brought the flower to her nose and inhaled its fragrance. Her thoughts drifted into fantasy as she tenderly held the blossom. Then a fever-induced lassitude came over her once again and she slipped back into slumber.

Chapter 23

An hour before dawn the following morning, Laura sat with her legs crossed in the center of the bed. Transfixed, she watched the ripple of muscles across Zach's broad shoulders as he dipped the razor in and out of the water. Her gaze strayed to the trail of dark hair that tapered from his chest to disappear beneath the waist of his cavalry trousers.

Unable to ignore the temptation a moment longer, she got out of bed and padded barefoot over to him. She slipped her arms around his waist and leaned her cheek against his back. Within seconds, his exciting masculine scent, the combination of bay and shaving soap, began to tantalize her. She pressed a kiss to the center of his back, then peeked around him and her eyes met his in the reflection of the mirror. She smiled with approval.

"I love your moustache. You look so handsome in it."

He only grinned. "Behave yourself, Laura. I can't be late for reveille. I missed it yesterday morning as it is."

She began to caress her chest. "And I love the feel of it brushing my body when—"

He put down the razor. "That's enough, temptress." He pried away her hands and turned to face her. "I'm already late." He grabbed a towel and wiped off the remaining shaving soap. Then, grasping her by the shoulders, he kissed her lightly.

At her disappointed sigh and the appealing pout which accompanied it, he pulled her back into his arms for a long, passionate kiss.

"Think about that kiss all day, you seductive little minx, because I sure as hell will be," he murmured huskily. Then he moved away and grabbed his shirt.

With a resigned sigh, she pulled on her robe and went down to the kitchen. After setting a pot of coffee to brew, she glanced despondently out the window at the very moment when a tall figure stepped from the trees.

She gasped as she recognized Gregorio, then cast a fretful glance toward the stairs. She heard the murmur of voices and realized Zach had gone into Peter's room to say good-bye.

Laura opened the door and hurried outside. When Gregorio saw her approach, he stepped into the shadows to wait.

She spoke frantically when she reached him. "Gregorio, Lieutenant Houston is inside. It's dangerous for you to be here."

"Gregorio has come to tell you that the woman called Teresa is safe in Gregorio's camp."

"Teresa? What are you talking about? Isn't Teresa at the mission hospital?"

"No. The woman left to come back on the day of the storm. Gregorio found her injured."

"How badly?" Laura asked, concerned.

"She was bitten by a snake." When Laura's eyes rounded with distress, he quickly added, "Gregorio has taken the venom out of her. When she is well, he will return her to you."

"Oh, dear God! She must be so frightened. I must go to her."

His glance shifted to the house at the sound of a slamming door. "Laura!" Zach called out.

"The woman is safe. Gregorio goes now," the Indian said, and slipped away into the shadows.

"Laura, where are you?" Zach shouted. She hurried back to the house.

Zach immediately saw her agitation. Concerned, he grasped her shoulders. "Honey, what is it? What were you doing outside barefoot?"

Laura could not lie to him. "I was talking to Gregorio."

"Gregorio!" Instinctively, his hands dropped from her shoulders and he reached for the Colt at his hip.

"He's gone, Zach."

"What was he doing here?"

"He came to give me a message about Teresa. The poor girl has been bitten by a snake and he's been taking care of her."

"What in hell's going on around here, Laura?" Zach said angrily. "That Indian is a murdering renegade wanted by the United States government. By protecting him you're consorting with the enemy and could be arrested and thrown into a federal prison."

"Zach, the man is not a murderer. I wish you would believe me."

A nerve jumped in Zach's jaw as he tried to control his temper. "Laura, there's too much at stake here. If you had walked into those houses and seen what we did when we arrived at Dario, you wouldn't be so damn trusting."

He strode away in anger, but she chased after him. "What are you going to do?"

"I'm putting this house under military protection."

"Zach, that's not necessary. If Gregorio wanted to harm us, he could have done so long before now."

He ignored her as he saddled his mount. Swinging into the saddle, he glanced down at her. "I'll be back, but not alone."

Long curls of morning mist still hung over the camp as Teresa watched a squaw at work in the next *chickee*. Unlike Teresa's hut, the other *chickee* was used exclusively for cooking. She saw that it had no platform for a floor. Cooking fires were set on logs in the center of the hut.

Teresa saw the woman pound dampened kernels of corn into powder and then sift the powder through a crude strainer made from woven fibers of palmetto. Then the squaw poured the sifted powder into a kettle of boiling water.

"What is she making, Ramon?"

Obeying his uncle's stringent orders, the ten-year-old sat next to Teresa, keeping a close eye on her.

"*Sofkee*," he replied. "It is a favorite food of my people. You will like it."

Gregorio's return to camp disrupted the early morning activities. After a perfunctory greeting to the others in camp, he came over to Teresa. His glance shifted to the camellia she had tucked into her hair. "The fever has left you?" he asked.

"Yes, I am feeling much better, Gregorio." Seeing him again, she felt shy. "Thank you for saving my life."

"Gregorio has told the *señora* of your injury."

"Oh my, she'll be so worried. I know she will," Teresa said, alarmed.

"Gregorio told the *señora* he will return you when you are well."

When it came time to eat, Gregorio carried her out and sat her down in the ring with the dozen or more Indians in the village. After the pot of *sofkee* had been placed in the center of the circle, Gregorio was handed a large wooden spoon. He dipped the spoon into the porridge and ate, then passed it to Ramon. Ramon followed suit and passed the spoon to the person beside him. The spoon had made a full circle by the time it reached Teresa.

She did not relish eating from the same utensil as all the others, but fearing they would be offended if she refused, she smiled weakly and dipped the spoon into the porridge. After several tiny swallows, she passed the spoon to Gregorio.

Later, as Gregorio sat down to talk with the other men in the village, Teresa and Ramon returned to the *chickee*.

"Do your people always eat from the same utensil?" Teresa asked Ramon.

"Eating from the *sufkee* spoon is a custom of the Seminole," he said.

"I see," she said desolately. Teresa did not look forward to the prospect of sharing future meals with them.

Ramon eyed her with what appeared to be newfound interest. "What's wrong?" Teresa asked self-consciously.

"You have become the squaw of Gregorio?"

Shocked, Teresa's hand fluttered to her chest. "Of course not, Ramon. I was bit by a snake. Gregorio found me and nursed me back to health. He has promised to take me back to the plantation."

"It is good you have not become his squaw, for soon we leave this place. You would not like the hard life of a Seminole."

Teresa resented the remark. "What makes you think you will like it any more than I would? You've been raised in a different environment too."

"But I am a Seminole like my uncle," Ramon boasted.

"Well, I imagine I could learn to accept this life if I had to," she added hastily. Her glance swung back to linger on Gregorio in the square. "Tell me about your uncle, Ramon."

"My uncle would not be pleased. His life has been filled with much sorrow," the boy declared with a compassion that far exceeded his years.

"You love him very much, don't you?" she said kindly.

"As a father."

"Was he ever married?"

"My mother told me his squaw died twelve summers ago from the swamp fever."

"And what of his parents?" she asked.

"They died summers ago. Gregorio had reached his eleventh summer when the last war ended between the Seminole and the Americans—"

"If I remember correctly, that was around 1858," Teresa quickly calculated.

"My grandfather was a chief and he had agreed to let the Americans move him and his people to the Indian Territory in Oklahoma. Over four thousand of our people had already been moved there along with our Creek brothers to the North. Gregorio told me that when the ship reached your great village of New Orleans, a tragedy befell his family. The American government gave permission to slave owners to claim any of the black runaways who were accompanying the Indians. My grandmother had been a slave."

"Oh! . . . You mean she was forced back into slavery?" Teresa asked sadly.

"Gregorio told me his father would not allow them to take his wife, even though she was a black runaway. His father told the soldiers that the American government had promised, if the Seminole surrendered, his people would not be put in slavery. But the soldiers gave no heed to his father's pleas, and even though my grandfather was shackled, he attacked the slave owner leading away his wife. Many shots were fired as soldiers and other of my people joined the fight. And when it ended, both of my grandparents were dead."

"How tragic." Teresa glanced again across the small clearing to where Gregorio sat talking earnestly. She thought it a coincidence that both of them had been orphaned early in their lives. Both knew the loneliness of such a loss. "And when did Gregorio escape from the reservation?"

"Not until three years later when my mother had her fourth summer," Ramon continued. "Gregorio took her with him. It took them a year to cross the plains to get back to our homeland. Then another tragedy happened to them." Ramon hesitated.

"Go on, Ramon, what kind of tragedy?" Teresa urged.

"Maybe Ramon should not tell Teresa. My mother told me of this, not my uncle. It is not good to be speaking of it with you."

"Oh, please do, Ramon," Teresa pleaded. "I won't tell anyone else. I want to know everything about him."

For a long moment, the boy seemed to struggle with his conscience, then he continued. "Upon reaching Florida, Gregorio and my mother were taken into captivity by the Espositos and suffered slavery on their plantation. My mother said that even though Gregorio had only fourteen summers, he was tall and powerful. His body was as beautiful to behold as his face. So he was kept chained alone in a cabin."

"But why?" Teresa asked. "He wasn't violent, was he?"

Teresa saw Ramon's blush. "No. But the way of some men is not that of the Seminole. Because of his beauty, my uncle was used for the . . . pleasure . . . of the Espositos' overseer."

"Pleasure? What do you mean?" Teresa asked.

Ramon's eyes hardened with bitterness as he remembered the relationship between his mother and Luis Esposito—and the sounds of their lovemaking that had carried to those in the house. He knew Teresa must have heard them too.

"In the manner Esposito used my mother."

Despite her awareness of Esposito's perversions, Teresa could not fathom that a man would prefer another man as a sexual partner. But she did not interrupt Ramon to express her confusion.

"After two years of this indignity, Gregorio succeeded in strangling his tormenter and fled into the swamp."

Her tender glance turned back to Gregorio. "Now I understand. He has bitter cause to hate the United States, and his enmity for the Spanish is equally justified."

"My uncle summons me now," Ramon said. He got up and joined Gregorio.

Feeling exhausted from the earlier activity, Teresa laid down to nap. Hot and sweaty, she awoke several hours later in the heat of the afternoon. Once again, she found a white camellia beside her. Smiling with pleasure, she brought it to her lips.

She glanced up with pleasure when she saw Gregorio approaching from across the clearing. "Teresa is feeling stronger?" he asked.

"Yes, but very warm. I would love a swim in a cool pond right now."

"Teresa is not strong enough to swim. But Gregorio will help."

"What are you doing?" she asked when he lifted her into his arms.

"Gregorio will take you to where you can cool yourself."

He carried her almost a mile through the swamp until they came to a small, secluded cove. Teresa thought she had found Eden. A subterranean spring of clear water glistened amidst the fragrance of flowering white oleander and large crimson-colored hibiscus shrubs.

Gregorio put her down and quickly shed his shirt. Only a loincloth covered his nakedness. The heat of her blush seemed more severe than the heat of the day. "Come, Teresa, cool yourself."

The many times he had held her naked slimness in his arms did little to ease her discomfort when she felt his dark gaze on her. Shyly she shed her bodice and skirt, then her petticoat. But her modesty prevented her from removing her camisole and drawers.

His tall figure moved to her. She could feel the power in the hands that effortlessly lifted her into his arms. As Teresa slipped her arm around his neck, she felt his hard muscles beneath her fingertips. Trying to will her foolish heart still, she lay docilely in his embrace. With an easy grace, he waded into the water. Clearer and cooler than the stream in the swamp, the spring water quickly soothed her from the torment of the external heat; but the fervor flaring within her, stirred by his nearness and the excitement of being held in his arms, could not be so easily tempered.

She closed her eyes. He began to glide her through the water. Giggling, she turned in his arms and slipped her other arm around his neck. He slid his hands down to her waist, lowering their bodies into the water.

When she opened her eyes, for a long moment his dark gaze rested on her face. Then he raised his hand to brush several strands of wet hair off her face.

He carried her out of the water and put her down next to her clothes. Then he lowered his powerful body to her; she felt dwarfed beside him. "It is so beautiful here, Gregorio. What a pity all of the Everglades can't be like this."

"Everything in the Everglades serves a purpose."

"But accompanied by so much danger and death."

"One creature's death can mean life to another."

"But that death can be someone you love," she said softly. "I'm sorry about Pilar. We were friends. And Ramon told me about the death of your wife. You must have been a young man. I think, despite what you say, that you draw little comfort from death."

"I have lived with its sting often."

"Have you ever thought about getting married again, Gregorio?" He shook his head. "Do the Seminole have churches and marriage ceremonies?"

"Is not the earth and the sky a temple? Only a white man must have a house of stone to worship within."

"I have seen drawings in books that show lavish temples built by Aztec and Inca Indians," she said.

"I do not know those tribes."

Teresa smiled. "They are from a different country." Changing the subject she asked, "But what of your marriage ceremonies?"

"If a man and woman lie together and he wishes her to be his squaw, he will go to live with her people. When they no longer wish the marriage, he leaves and goes back to his own *chickee*."

"That's all there is to it?" she said, astounded. "Well, what if he or she . . . lusts . . . for another?"

"This is not allowed among my people. For such an

act, the ear is cut off." Teresa paled at the thought of such a severe punishment.

"Gregorio can see that Teresa tires. We will return to camp. After the rise of tomorrow's sun, Gregorio will take you back to the plantation."

Teresa felt cause for alarm when they returned to the camp and she saw some natives had arrived to spend the night in the village. The sight of the fearsome warriors recalled the terror she had felt at Dario and she couldn't help but wonder if these new arrivals had been among them.

"You have no need to fear these men," Gregorio said, upon seeing her fright. "One is the brother of one of the villagers. They are peaceful fishermen and we will feast well tonight for they have brought us fresh fish from the sea."

However, that night to ease her fears, Gregorio lay next to her. The knowledge of his nearness was a great comfort. She slept peacefully.

The next morning, after they shared another *sofkee* spoon meal with the people in the village, their departure was delayed while Gregorio talked with the visiting warriors. The sun was a carmine glow in the western sky by the time Teresa and Gregorio left the camp and headed for the Esposito plantation.

Teresa's heart ached with every step she took; after today, she might never see him again. She knew she had fallen in love with the gentle man whose reputation had been so maliciously maligned. *If only others could know him, as I have come to know him in these past few days*, she lamented to herself.

Moonlight guided their path by the time they neared the spring they had visited the previous day. "Can we go swimming again?" she asked hopefully.

"If Teresa wishes," he said.

He spread a blanket and after shedding his shirt, entered the water. This time she did not hesitate. She stripped off her clothing, removing her drawers and camisole, and waded into the spring.

The waters of the cool spring lapped at her breasts, turning the nipples into stiff peaks. She gasped from the chill and glanced at him. His gaze was fixed on her breasts. She felt herself swell under the steady stare of his dark eyes.

Hastening out of the water, she sat down and wrapped herself in the blanket.

When he finished swimming, Gregorio climbed out of the water. Teresa stared to marvel at his beauty: wide, sinewy shoulders, slim hips, long muscular legs. Garbed only in a loincloth, the bronzed perfection of his body glistened with moisture. Shaking out his long, dark hair, he brushed it off his face, then turned and looked at her.

Their gazes locked. The raw hunger in his eyes matched her own blatant desire. Slowly, he walked toward her. The pounding in her breast carried to her ears and temples.

She stared up at him in open invitation as the scent of their desire hung on the air. Passion arced between them like lightning—vibrant and arousing. The difference of cultures had no relevance—this man was her destiny. She had known it from the first moment she looked into his eyes. And only one need prevailed—for him to make love to her. To kiss her. To hold her in his powerful arms with passion, as he had once held her with tenderness.

He knelt before her. The weight of his body propelled her back and his head hovered above her. Her senses responded to every facet of the man; the long damp hair, his sensual mouth, the beauty of his face. But it was the dark eyes glittering with lust that most excited her.

"You know what Gregorio desires," he said.

"Yes, I see it in your eyes."

"And does the sight of his lust frighten you, little flower?"

"No . . . no," she said breathlessly. His mouth was so close, she could feel the warmth of his breath.

Her expectation continued to soar when he slipped his hand under the blanket and palmed her breast. "Have you been with a man before?" he asked in a husky murmur.

"Only that day in the swamp . . . with Luis Esposito." She felt exquisite sensation as his thumb toyed at her nipple.

He raised his head and his dark gaze held hers as he parted the blanket. Gleaming against the dark coverlet, her body glowed with the luster of a pearl.

She felt on fire, flushed with an escalating excitement that far exceeded her maidenly modesty. He lowered his head and drew a stiffened nipple into his mouth. She had never known such a feeling. She closed her eyes with a sigh of pleasure.

Then he covered her mouth with his own. The pressure of his lips seduced her with a sensation that kept spiraling and spiraling, swirling pleasure throughout her body. She shivered from pure carnal thrill until the last breath was drawn from her.

As she struggled to restore her breathing, his mouth returned to her breasts. He caressed her slimness with his hand, drawing her tighter against him. The feel of his latent strength became an added aphrodisiac. Her head spun from this awakened sensuality, each kiss, each caress increasing the glorious thrill.

The feeling within her was building toward a promised release until she feared she could die. Yet she urged him on with every tremor, every responsive twitch and shift of her body.

His suckling at her breast intensified as his own passion escalated. He slid his hand into the mound above the throbbing core of her desire. Writhing beneath him in hedonistic bliss, she had no idea of his needs—only her own.

"Open, little flower. Open for me," he murmured.

He parted her legs and pleasure replaced shock when she felt his fingers probe the tender opening. She cried out when he found the sensitive nub of that chamber. He stroked it until her cries were as incessant as the paroxysms which shook her body.

When her shudders ceased, she opened her eyes. He loomed tall and menacing, straddling her hips as he stood above her. When he released his loincloth, she gasped at the size of his extended sex.

Instinctively she separated her legs. She gloried in the thought of that mighty staff within her. Blushing with embarrassment over her lascivious fantasy, she feared he would read her thoughts.

Her lack of inhibition increased his passion. He lowered himself and lifted her legs to ride his hips, then he inched himself into the moist chamber. She thrilled to the feel of him—the hard, throbbing heat of him. When he reached the virgin barrier, he pressed deeper.

Gasping with pain, she sucked in her breath, but tightened the hold of her legs around him. He broke through and slid the rest of the way into the velvet recess.

Glowing with fulfillment, in her naiveté, she lay sated and content, thrilling to the knowledge that their bodies were linked as one.

When he slowly began to stroke her from within with his hardened sex, she felt her pleasure heighten. The rhythm of his thrusts increased and their breathing rose into gasps.

His mouth swooped down and his tongue plundered her mouth as their bodies convulsed in spasms of shared bliss.

Chapter 24

Rising above the water's edge like a host of spectral sentinels in the night, a chain of white mangroves stood amidst the labyrinth of the narrow river winding through the swamp. Moonlight filtered through the delicate filigree of Spanish moss, strung from limb to limb on the spreading branches, and cast a silvery glow on the yellow flowers and glossy leaves that bedecked the trees.

Absorbed in his troubled thoughts, Gregorio sat huddled in an undergrowth of spiny stalks of saw palmetto. His warrior's heart was burdened with doubts about the future decisions he must face.

He turned his head to glance tenderly at Teresa asleep at his side. He had not felt love for a woman since his wife had died of the swamp fever twelve years before. But now this gentle girl had found a place in his heart; he loved her with his soul as he had his body.

But Gregorio was plagued with doubts. Had he done the right thing? If Teresa remained with him, she would be a hunted fugitive like himself, without the peace and safety she would have had with *Señora* Esposito.

The nagging doubts in the back of his mind continued to plague him. The army blamed him for the recent attack on Dario, as they did for every misdeed, and they would continue to hunt him and other innocent Seminoles.

Teresa stirred and opened her eyes. She became instantly awake and studied the princely profile silhouetted in the moonlight. The nobility of kings was finely etched on his handsome features. She picked up the fragrant blossom lying beside her, his message of love to her. "Why always a camellia, Gregorio?" she asked softly.

He turned his head and smiled tenderly at her; his dark eyes glowed with the warmth of passion. "You are like the blossom, my little flower. Beautiful for the eyes to behold, with a sweet fragrance that lingers in the memory. And yet so delicate that its white petals are easily destroyed by those who would bruise them."

She smiled and shook her head. "I'm not that delicate, Gregorio. I may look fragile, but I've a tough hide." Then seeing his troubled frown, she felt the smile leave her face. She sat up and put her hand on his shoulder. "What is troubling you, Gregorio?"

"My thoughts are on the summers to come. Maybe the *señora* was right. Maybe Gregorio should try to speak to the army leader. To tell him the truth. Ishmetee was to blame for the raid on Dario."

"Who is this Ishmetee?" she asked.

"A chief of one of the villages. Ishmetee sought vengeance for the ravishment of his youngest daughter by Juan DeVarga. Ishmetee killed this man who violated the young daughters of the Seminoles for many years. Then his followers went on a rampage."

"Couldn't you have stopped the massacres?" Teresa asked.

"Gregorio arrived too late." His eyes grew sad. "And Gregorio was driven to fight Ishmetee to the death."

She gasped with shock. "You killed him?"

"Ishmetee had turned wild like beasts of the swamp. He vowed to drive out all white men from the Everglades. In the house of Juan DeVarga, Ishmetee and his warriors found many bottles of the white man's firewater. This drink is not like the Black Drink of the Seminole. It drove them to madness. And at each house, they found more bottles of the white man's spirits. They not only killed many white men, but caused many Seminoles to die too."

"Well, then they should be tried for their crimes, Gregorio."

"They have been. Ishmetee is dead, and the drunken warriors who followed him have been punished by the rest of the tribe. But Gregorio fears that more deaths will follow. Even now the army builds their fortress in Dario, and soon they will seek vengeance for the massacre. The Seminole will again be hunted down like criminals."

"Then you must tell the army the truth, just as Laura says."

"The army will not believe Gregorio."

"If only Ishmetee had not killed others," Teresa said, troubled. "Juan DeVarga deserved to die. He was not a good man. I remember when I was just a child, he put his hands on my breast. I did not tell Laura because I was too ashamed."

Her nearness and soft scent were creating a subtle distraction from the problems that plagued him. Gregorio slid his hands down to cup her breasts. "And does it shame you to have Gregorio touch you?"

She slipped her arms around his neck and drew him down as she lay back. "It shames me because Gregorio's touch pleasures me so much," she confessed.

"But not as much as it pleasures Gregorio," he murmured before his lips covered hers.

After making love again, they slept. Later, she awoke with a start and sat up. She gazed tenderly at his sleeping face, serene in slumber. Teresa knew she could never bear to leave him. According to his customs, she was his wife now that they had made love. Tomorrow she would tell Laura good-bye.

As if sensing her gaze, he awoke. For a long moment, they looked with love into each other's eyes.

"I dreamt you went away from me," she finally said.

He pulled her down into his arms. "My people believe that the body has two souls. One leaves at night when we dream, but it always returns before we awake."

"And the other?" she asked.

"That soul leaves the body only with death."

"But when I dreamt you had left me, I felt as if I were dying," she murmured. "Gregorio, now that we have lain together, does that mean I have become your squaw?"

"Why do you ask, little flower?"

"Because I never want to leave you."

"Would you find happiness among my people?"

"As long as I'm with you."

He pulled her back into his arms and lay silently with his troubled thoughts. The path he trod had narrowed even more.

Sunday morning, Laura hitched up the team to drive to Dario. A mounted army escort immediately fell in behind the wagon.

When Flint Bryce rode up beside her, she glanced in disgruntlement at the sergeant. "Now, Mrs. Esposito, is that any way to treat a friend?" he joshed. "We're just doing our duty."

"Sergeant Bryce, I wish you would tell your commander that I have had just about enough of the United States Cavalry. I hate to sound crude, Sergeant, but I can't even visit the . . . *privy* . . . without having one of you troopers accompany me."

"Lieutenant Houston's orders, ma'am."

"Well, you can tell Lieutenant Houston for me that he can—"

"Reckon you can tell him yourself, ma'am. Here he comes now." Bryce wheeled his horse and rode back to the front of the column.

Zach rode up and hopped from his horse onto the wagon. "Wow!" Peter exclaimed in awe.

Laughing, Zach crawled into the seat next to Laura, leaned over, and kissed her on the cheek. "Hi, honey." He took the reins from her.

"Zach, when are you calling off these bloodhounds?"

"As soon as you return to Miami with me," he said.

"Who said I'm returning to Miami with you?" she demanded, feeling irritated enough to offer an argument.

"Well, if we get married, you don't intend to stay here, do you?"

"Zachary Houston, are you proposing to me?"

"I did that years ago, remember? I thought that after mass this morning, we could ask Father Naverro to marry us."

She tucked her arm through his. "I'll marry you, if you promise to call off your troopers. I need some privacy, Zach."

"All right, I'll call them off, but only on the nights I'm there with you."

As soon as mass was over, they sought out the young priest and told him of their wish to wed. Father Naverro dashed their plans by insisting they wait the customary local period of six months of mourning.

Zach was incensed and vented his anger as he returned with Laura to the plantation. "I'm in the army, Laura. I can't stay in Dario until my enlistment's up. And I'm not going to leave you here alone."

"Well, I'll go back to Fort Dallas with you," she said.

"The army won't allow an unmarried woman to live on the post."

"Well, we can live in Miami."

"A bachelor officer is not permitted to live off the post."

"So it would appear the church and the U.S. Army are conspiring to keep us apart," she said with forced lightness.

"First it was a husband keeping us apart . . . now it's the damn army and church. These are our lives, Laura. Don't we have any control over them?"

She put her hand on his arm. "I'll do whatever you say, Zach. I want us to be together as much as you do."

"Well, we'll work out something because when I leave

Dario, you and Peter are going with me," he said obdurately.

Peter, having finished a one-sided conversation with Zach's horse, which was tied to the back of the wagon, crawled over the seat and sat down between them.

"Daddy, what is the name of your horse?"

"He doesn't have a name that I know of, Peter. Cavalrymen usually don't name the horse they ride."

"How come?"

"Because a trooper often rides different horses. He's not like a cowboy who always rides the same animal."

"How come a cowboy always rides the same animal?"

Zach realized he had fallen into Peter's question and answer trap. "Uhmm, you see, Peter, a lot of time and training goes into the making of a good cow pony. It must be taught to know every movement of the reins and rider's knees."

Zach's side glance revealed Peter mesmerized by every word and Laura trying to stifle her amusement.

"So a cowboy spends a lot of time with his horse. It kind of becomes his best friend. That's why he'll call it by a name. And when he's out riding the range alone, his horse is the only one he has to talk to most of the time."

"And does the horse talk back to him?" Peter asked, wide-eyed.

"Does sometimes," Zach said, tongue-in-cheek.

"Wow!" Peter exclaimed.

At the sight of Laura's disapproving frown, Zach chuckled warmly. "But usually only after the cowboy's had too much sun," he added with a wink at Laura.

"Were you a cowboy before you were a soldier, Daddy?"

"Yep."

"Did you like it?"

"It's a lot of hard work, pal." Zach paused in reflection. "But, yeah, I liked it."

"Better than being a soldier?" Peter pursued.

"Much better than being a soldier," Zach responded more fervently.

"Then why'd you become a soldier?"

"Ran out of cows to punch, pal."

"You punched cows!" Peter frowned with concentration. "Wow! I bet that hurt your hand."

Zach and Laura broke into laughter. Joining their levity, the youngster's eyes gleamed with adoration as he glanced up at his hero. "I think I'm gonna be a cowboy when I grow up."

Zach turned his head and smiled into Peter's upturned face. "I think you are too, son."

Peter flashed a dimpled smile. "And I sure like riding a horse."

"Do you ride often, Peter?" Zach asked.

"No. Just that one time with Mama. You know, when we came back here with the soldiers. But I sure liked it."

"You mean you were never on a horse until that day?" Visibly surprised, Zach turned to Laura to seek confirmation.

"Luis always claimed he didn't have time to teach the boys," she said upon seeing his bafflement.

"Laura, you handle a horse as well as any man. Why didn't you teach him?"

"Luis wouldn't permit me to. He said it was unrefined for a woman to straddle a horse, and he reminded me that as the wife of a Spanish don, I was expected to leave my 'philistinism' in Texas where it belonged." She turned her head away from him. "I missed riding."

"I missed riding *with you*," he said gently. Her glance swung back to him and her smile returned the love she saw in his eyes.

"Will you take me riding, Daddy?" Peter asked as soon as they arrived at the house.

"Sure will." He swung Peter down from the wagon.

"And Mama too?"

Zach reached up and grasped Laura under the arms. His dark eyes gleamed with deviltry as their gazes locked. "Your mama and I will ride together later."

Laura blushed under the outrageous innuendo, and rather than swing her to the ground, he slid her sensuously along his body until her feet touched the ground.

"Zachary Houston, you have become perverted," she whispered hastily, but the sparkle in her eyes and the rosy blush on her cheeks belied the sting of the chastisement.

With a flirtatious backward glance, she took Peter by the hand and led him inside to change his clothes.

Zach drove the wagon to the barn. His thoughts were on Laura, and he grinned as he unhitched the horse. He was unprepared when a figure stepped out of the shadows. Zach dropped the reins and started to draw the Colt at his hip.

Gregorio raised his hand in a gesture of peace. Zach checked his draw upon seeing that the Indian was not wearing the red and black paint of the Seminole sign of war. When Teresa appeared at his side, Zach relaxed and dropped his hand.

"Hello, Teresa."

"Hello, Lieutenant Houston. Gregorio wishes to speak to you."

"Does he speak English, Teresa, or are you the interpreter?" Zach wanted to kick himself for letting Laura talk him into calling off that patrol.

The tall figure beside her responded to the question. "Gregorio can speak the tongue of Houston."

For a long moment, the two military commanders assessed one another. In his western campaigns among the Apaches, Zach had encountered several of their chiefs, but none appeared more formidable than the man he now faced.

Gregorio broke the silence. "Gregorio has been told Houston has an ear for the truth."

"And Houston has been told that Gregorio has a tongue for speaking it," Zach replied. Zach saw the remark appeared to please the warrior. "What is it the leader of the Seminoles has to say?"

"Gregorio has been falsely accused of leading the raid on Dario."

"I regret to tell you that my orders are to arrest you, Gregorio."

"For a crime Gregorio did not commit? He has already made certain that those who were guilty were punished for their actions."

"Then return to Fort Dallas with me to clear your name so you no longer will be hunted for the crime. If you voluntarily give yourself up, Gregorio, the army will be more willing to believe you."

"If not, they will still lock Gregorio in their prison."

"Not if you convince them of your innocence." Zach had already reached his own conclusion. The man was not lying. The essence of integrity about the Seminole leader could not be denied.

"Gregorio will never wear chains again."

"Again? You've been arrested before, Gregorio?"

"As a youth."

"I can only speak in your behalf to my commander, Gregorio, but I cannot disobey my orders. Because of the Dario massacre, the army will continue its search for you."

A glint of anger flared in the warrior's eyes. "Then more of your number will fall."

"And more of your people will perish along with them. Our numbers are greater than yours, Gregorio. You know that from the past. The best way to prove your innocence and prevent further bloodshed to your people is to voluntarily surrender to me."

Zach felt uneasy that the conversation had turned to sword rattling. He was relieved when Gregorio went to the barn door.

"Gregorio has thought on the words of Houston. By the rise of tomorrow's sun, he will return and do as Houston wishes."

Zach watched the two figures walk away. Unconsciously, his hand slid to the holster on his hip as he thought of how easy it would be to draw his pistol and just capture the unarmed man. Perhaps the dishonorable act might prevent further bloodshed. But lasting peace could be achieved only between men of honor . . . not dishonor, Zach reflected. His hand slipped from the holster.

When he returned to the house and told her of the meeting, Laura was beside herself to hear that Teresa had been with Gregorio. "You mean she didn't even stay to speak to me?"

"Gregorio said they would return in the morning. I hope that doesn't mean we'll wake up with our scalps missing," he joked.

"But why would she leave with him?" Laura wondered.

"Honey, I saw those two together. I think they mean something special to each other."

Laura looked aghast. "Zachary, you definitely are perverted. My goodness, they just met."

"We've loved each other since the moment we met. Maybe the same thing happened to them." He took her in his arms and kissed her.

Peter came dashing into the room and stopped when he saw them in an embrace. "Daddy, how come you're always kissing my mama?"

Zach broke the embrace and stared with a long-suffering look into Laura's gleaming eyes. "Yeah, Daddy, how come you're always kissing Peter's mama?" she teased.

"Let's go, pal, it's time for the riding lessons I promised . . ." He turned to Laura with a meaningful glance. " . . . the both of you."

Later that night in bed, Zach abandoned the problems of six-year-olds and men in war for the more sensual diversion of having Laura in his arms.

He drew the thick braid from her back and placed

it between her breasts. "I used to torment myself by fantasizing moments like this." His voice was a husky murmur.

Slowly, he pulled at the tie until the ribbon released and the ends of her hair spilled into his hand. He unraveled the heavy woven plait, and the loose waves dropped around her shoulders. Zach brought several strands to his nose and breathed deeply of the perfumed silkiness.

He curled his fingers into the silky mass. Silently, but deliberately, he drew her to him and lowered his head. Her lips parted beneath his own.

Raising his head, he looked at her face. She closed her eyes and her long dark lashes lay thick against her cheek. He pressed a kiss to each closed lid.

"You're so beautiful, Laura."

She rolled her head languorously, giving him free access to her slender neck. Unable to ignore the seductive temptation, his mouth and hands explored the soft curves of her throat, her breasts, her stomach.

Her eyes were wide and luminous. "Oh, Zach, I love you." She repeated the words in a sensuous purr as he lowered his mouth to her quivering breasts.

He toyed with each hardened nipple, then took one into his mouth in a rapturous sucking.

"Please! Please, Zach," she whimpered in ragged gasps.

He felt her nerves jump beneath the slide of his lips as he trailed kisses down her stomach. Parting her legs, he slid his hands beneath her buttocks and raised her slightly.

"Oh, Zach. I can't—"

"This is my fantasy, remember?" Then he closed his mouth over the apex of her sex.

Her body convulsed in ecstatic shudders and her head reeled with dizziness. She trembled beneath him; throaty groans escaped from the depth of her throat. She felt driven by a primitive urgency to be enveloped by him, consumed by him. Her hunger for more of his touch, his scent, his overwhelming strength was insatiable.

His mouth crushed her lips in a bruising kiss. She flung her arms around his neck, caressing the corded column. Sliding her arms down to his waist, she hugged his firm body against her curves.

She buried her face against his chest and licked it passionately, erotically; the taste of his salty skin became an added aphrodisiac. His hardened arousal pressed against her, and she curled her hand around it. She stroked him and parted her legs to ride his hips.

He groaned with pleasure when she rubbed him against her heated sex. He thrust into her.

"Zach." She repeated his name with each thrust until he smothered her blissful cry of love with his mouth.

He spilled into her and lost himself in the sensual marvel that was Laura: the satin gloss of skin, a seductive scent of mimosa, the tantalizing tangle of silken hair, and the sweet, sweet ecstasy of her lips, her arms, and her body.

Chapter 25

F our days later, an army patrol accompanied by several civilians attracted little attention when it arrived in Miami. A few on the dock glanced with curiosity at the Seminole warrior who wore a bright yellow turban like a crown as he walked majestically in the center of the entourage.

Laura, Teresa, and the two boys remained with Bryce's patrol while Zachary and Gregorio entered the colonel's office. Within minutes, the raised voices of the men carried through the open window to the ears of those outside.

"Sir, I gave Gregorio my word that if he came in peaceably, he would not be incarcerated."

"I'm afraid you overstepped your authority, Lieutenant Houston," Scott declared. "This man is responsible for the death of a dozen civilians, a mission priest and nun among them. I should order a firing squad, not treat him like visiting royalty as you would indicate." Gregorio remained silent as the debate between the two officers intensified.

"Gregorio is not responsible for the massacre at Dario," Zach said, continuing to press his argument.

"Do you have evidence to substantiate that claim, Lieutenant?"

"Gregorio's word, sir."

Scott's face curled into a smirk. "The word of a murdering savage!" He shook his head. "I'm afraid not, Lieutenant. No doubt he'll end up before the firing squad! At the very least, this Indian will be interned until he can be transferred for deportation to the Indian Territory. That will be all, Lieutenant Houston." He turned to his orderly. "Sergeant Adams, remove this prisoner to the stockade and see that he is shackled."

"Colonel Scott, I assured Gregorio we would not put him in irons," Zachary protested.

"Again you overstepped your bounds, Lieutenant."

"My bounds?" Zachary's patience expired. "Sir, the army is expected to secure and maintain the peace and safety of the citizens of this area. Yet, you now claim that the word of your officers in the field trying to negotiate that peace is not to be honored."

For a brief moment, the piercing dark gaze of the Indian swung to Zachary, the silent message rife with reproachment. He spoke for the first time since entering the room. "Did Gregorio not tell Houston the white man does not honor a promise made to a Seminole?" He shrugged off the restraining hand of the sergeant and, with head held high, turned to leave.

Colonel Scott jumped to his feet. "Damn you, Gregorio, I pride myself on my honor and principles. And despite Lieutenant Houston's belief, I do respect his judgement and integrity." The hardened veteran officer eyed the warrior grimly. "So I'll give you your day in court. Tomorrow, you can defend the charges against you before a military tribunal of my senior officers." He hurriedly wrote the orders on a sheet of paper, then handed them to his aide. "Sergeant Adams, after the prisoner has been incarcerated, see that these orders are distributed to Major Pfeiffer, Major Donaldson, and Captains Raasch, Banner, Allen, and Frank." Frustrated, Zachary watched as the orderly led Gregorio away.

"A job well done, Lieutenant," Scott said.

"Sir, I have a request. I ask permission for Mrs. Esposito and her son to live on post for the next two months."

"Doesn't the Esposito family have a plantation at Dario?"

"They do, sir, but Mr. Esposito is dead."

The colonel glanced up in surprise. "Esposito dead? Good Lord, how, Lieutenant?"

"He was killed in an attempt to murder Gregorio." At Scott's skeptical look, Zachary quickly added, "I've investigated the incident, sir; it was witnessed by Esposito's wife and his son."

Zachary knew he had not clearly defined the truth, but he did not want to heap further suspicion on Gregorio. Zach suspected Scott did not know Luis had an illegitimate son who was half Seminole, and that the colonel would assume Peter had been one of the witnesses to the killings. The young boy's innocence was beyond reproach.

"The Esposito family has returned to Miami with me."

"I regret their plight, but I am sure they will be able to find residence in the city, Lieutenant."

"Well, sir, there is one other thing. Mrs. Esposito and I intend to wed as soon as the church will permit it."

Scott raised an eyebrow in surprise. "My congratulations, Lieutenant. Mrs. Esposito is a fine lady besides being a very lovely one. You're a fortunate young man."

"Thank you, sir, I think so too. And under the circumstances, I would feel more comfortable if she and her son were housed here on the post."

"Lieutenant Houston, you know the regulations. Unmarried women are not permitted to reside on the post unless they are family members of a man stationed here."

"I understand, but she will be as soon as we can marry, sir."

"I'm sorry, Lieutenant Houston. If I stretched the regulations for one person, I would be expected to do so for others. You do understand my position. The family may remain on the post for three days, then they will have to leave."

"I understand, sir." Zach stood rigidly at attention and spoke again. "Request permission to live off the post, Colonel Scott."

Scott drew a deep sigh and picked up a sheet of paper on his desk. "You know the regulations, Lieutenant Houston. Permission denied." He started to read the paper.

"Sir, request permission to leave the post to help find housing for the Esposito family." Zach's expression and stance had not altered.

"Permission granted, Lieutenant." Scott hastily scratched out a twenty-four-hour pass, then glanced up with a look of suffering indulgence and handed the pass to Zach. "Will that be all, Lieutenant?"

"Yes, sir. Thank you, sir." Zachary saluted. Scott returned the salute and resumed reading the letter on his desk.

Laura and Teresa awaited Zach outside. The gloomy look on his face told them what to expect. "Bad news?" Laura asked.

Zach nodded and slipped his arm around her shoulders as they began to walk slowly across the parade grounds.

"We saw them take Gregorio away. Ramon and Peter went with him," Laura said sorrowfully. "Sergeant Bryce said he'd bring the boys back to us."

"Colonel Scott has ordered his senior officers to convene in a military tribunal tomorrow to determine Gregorio's guilt or innocence."

"What will happen to Gregorio if he can't convince them of his innocence?" Teresa asked.

"I don't know. At the very least, they'll ship him to Oklahoma."

"But I thought the government stopped doing that years ago," Laura protested.

"They did stop . . . but if they feel Gregorio's a problem, they won't hesitate to send him away."

"I'm sure he'll convince them of his innocence," Laura said to bolster Teresa's spirits.

Teresa continued on to their housing as Zach and Laura paused under the shade of a large oak near the barracks. She glanced at Zach's solemn profile. "What else is bothering you, Zach?"

"Colonel Scott has denied permission for you and Peter to live on the post."

"And for you to live off it," she added. "Just as you thought he would."

Zach nodded.

"You can remain here for three days. All we can do is try to find you a decent and safe place to live until my enlistment's up. Then we'll get married and get out of here."

"You mean you'll be leaving the army?" she asked, surprised.

"Not soon enough," he said, with an added squeeze to her shoulders. "Especially now that it's standing between us and our happiness. Colonel Scott has given me a twenty-four-hour leave, so let's not stand here wasting time. We'll round up the boys and start looking."

Ramon and Teresa chose to remain with Gregorio in his cell and did not accompany them. Several hours later, after thoroughly canvasing the city, Laura and Zach returned to the post. Their search had been futile. The only available living quarters was a bug-infested room above a waterfront dive. Zach would not even consider the wretched place.

Later, after they ate dinner, Teresa and Ramon left to visit Gregorio. Laura sighed desolately as she looked at Zach's long face. "I guess we'll have to go back to Dario and just wait until you're discharged."

His eyes mirrored his anxiety. "I'll never have a restful moment worrying about you and Peter alone in that isolated house."

"We won't have to be there alone. I'll hire some servants to live with us."

Unable to finish his meal, he got up from the table. "Goddammit! A two-month separation."

She followed him and put her hand on his shoulder. "Zach," she said softly, "I don't like the idea of our being apart any more than you do, but what else can we do?"

He turned back to her. His hands cupped her cheeks, his dark eyes pleading. "Honey, we've already lost seven years of our lives together. I can't think of us ever being apart again."

She grasped his hands and kissed each palm. "Whether we like it or not, I'm afraid we haven't any choice."

Peter had watched the two with wide-eyed apprehension. "Are we going away from you, Daddy?"

Zach and Laura sat down again at the table. "Only for a short while, son. As soon as I get discharged, your mama and I will get married, then we'll all go to Texas."

"Texas? Where's Texas?" he asked, enthused.

"Right across the Gulf of Mexico. That's where your mama and I were born."

"Will I like Texas?"

Zach tousled his hair. "You'll love Texas, pal."

Peter grinned, then asked another crucial question. "Do they have chock . . . late ice cream in Texas?"

"They've got all the chocolate ice cream you can eat," he said. Zach grinned at Laura, but the smile didn't carry to his eyes.

That night, after making love to Laura, Zach lay back and drew her to his side. She lay in sated contentment with her cheek resting on his chest.

"What will happen if they find out you're not in your quarters?" she asked.

"I'm on a pass, remember? I'm not due back until noon tomorrow."

"Will the day ever come when we won't have to think about parting in the morning?"

He drew her tighter against him. "In two months." A

note of hopelessness had returned to his voice.

"Zach, I've been thinking about Dario. If Gregorio is cleared of the charges, maybe we could persuade him to remain at the plantation for two months. I'm sure we'd be safe with him there."

Zach recognized the wisdom of what she said. There would be no doubt Laura and Peter would be safe under Gregorio's protection. That would solve one of the problems preying on his mind, but the problem of their forced separation had no solution. "Two months is a lifetime."

"But then we'll be together forever."

The more he reflected on Laura's suggestion, the more Zach hoped it could come to pass. He teased lightly, "Of course, I wouldn't be too happy at the thought of you spending a couple months with that handsome Indian."

She reared up her head in indignation. "Handsome! Why he's beautiful! His face . . . his body . . . his nobility. But you have nothing to worry about. Teresa told me that according to Seminole laws, she and Gregorio are already married."

Zach rolled over, trapping her beneath him. "That's certainly comforting to hear. Don't suppose I can convince you that I have a few merits too?"

"Well . . . I suppose you could try," she said in mock consideration.

Zach raised his head. He laced his fingers through hers and pinned her hands above her head. Levity was forgotten as he gazed at her: the curve of her slender arms framed the dark hair fanned in silken dishevelment against the pillow, her brown eyes appeared slumberous with afterglow, and her lips, swollen from his kisses, were parted in invitation.

"God, Laura, I love you," he said huskily. He dipped his head and circled her swollen lips with his tongue.

Then he trailed kisses up the inside of her arm. When he repeated the same on her other arm, she shifted sensuously beneath him, but his grip on her hands held. With tiny nibbles, he retraced the path up one arm and down the other as exquisite sensation coiled around the core of her sex.

His moist tongue painted a sensory path down her neck until he reached her breasts, then he laved the turgid peaks until she moaned with ragged pleas. Still his grip held.

As she writhed helplessly beneath him, his warm, moist mouth suckled at her breasts.

"Oh yes, Zach . . . yes," she murmured as rapturous sensation spiraled through her. "Never . . . never stop trying to convince me."

The next morning, Gregorio stood unbowed and defiant before the seven men who presumed to judge his fate. He thought they looked hot and foolish in the tight blue jackets buttoned up to their necks, with their legs covered in long trousers, and their feet in heavy boots and stockings. How much wiser was the dress of the Seminole with only a short shirt and a codpiece to protect his manhood. Even moccasins were forsaken to allow the heat of his body to escape through his bare feet.

He thought of how the white man had learned none of the ways of the Seminole; the invaders did not even have the common sense to build a *chickee* with open sides so they could feel the breath of the wind god, while the roof of palm leaves warded off the kiss of the sun and the frequent rains. For on such a day as this, with the rays of the sun drying up the mud of the Everglades, even reptiles sought the coolness of the waters and bobcats hid in the dark corners of glades. But the white man . . . his gaze swept the small, airless room . . . the white man remained behind the wooden walls of their hot houses.

His enigmatic gaze studied each of the men seated behind the table. These warriors of the white man's army had listened in silence as he spoke of Ishmetee's rage, of how the leader had paid for that foolish act with his life. And he told them of his fear that the army would heap revenge on his people for the misdeeds of Ishmetee and his followers.

Now he waited as Houston told the court that Gregorio had surrendered willingly. Gregorio heard the words and knew the Lieutenant spoke eloquently of his belief in the truth of Gregorio's words. Houston was, as Gregorio had been led to believe, a man of fairness. Gregorio had seen few of his kind among the white man.

When Zach finished speaking, a moment of silence followed as the men reflected on his words. Then Colonel Scott posed a question. "Tell me, Gregorio, would you and some of your people be willing to move to the Indian Territory?"

This was the question Gregorio feared, for he knew his answer would not please the army colonel. "When the white man came to our land, the Seminole tried to live in peace with his white brother. He dressed in the clothes of the white man and learned his tongue. He farmed his land, raised cattle, and built his house of wood in the manner of his white brother."

Gregorio's dark eyes flared with bitterness. "But soon the white man desired the land of the Seminole, so my people were driven from their *hutis*, shackled, and herded like cattle to the Indian Territory far to the west. Those among them who resisted were killed."

He held up three fingers to emphasize his point. "Three times more of our number perished than survived the journey. The trail became paved with the tears and blood of our dying. Would it not have been nobler for the Seminole to fall beneath the bullets of his enemy than to be struck down by the white man's diseases and the hardships of the journey?"

The deep resonance of his voice never faltered. "We have killed the one among our people who broke your law. We have punished those who followed him. This brought much heartache to my people. Much weeping in the *chickees*. But we have done justice as the white man would wish. Gregorio came here in honor to tell of this truth and the white man now speaks of taking his people to the West."

Conviction showed on his face as he crossed his arms across his chest. "Gregorio will not trod that trail again."

A lengthy silence followed the declaration. Scott finally cleared his throat. "We will return you to your cell, Gregorio, and inform you of our decision tomorrow. You are dismissed also, Lieutenant Houston."

Throughout the hearing, Teresa and Ramon had waited for him outside. As soon as Zach appeared, Ramon ran up and questioned him. "Will my uncle be released now?"

"We'll know in the morning, Ramon." Zach put a hand on his shoulder as they all walked back to Laura's house.

"How did it go?" she asked as soon as they came through the door of her lodging.

"It's hard to say. I think they all believed him, but I know that Allen and Frank hate Indians in general. The other officers are usually fair. Scott brought up the question of shipping him west. Gregorio was pretty outspoken on that issue."

Teresa listened with a heavy heart, then hurried to her room to keep from crying.

Later, as Zach prepared to leave, he kissed Laura good night. "I'll let you know as soon as I hear anything," he assured her and returned to his quarters.

Several hours later, Teresa approached Fred Hoffman, who was on duty guarding Gregorio. "May I go in to be with him, Private Hoffman?"

"Sure, ma'am," he said with understanding. As he unlocked the door, he never saw the blow coming that knocked him unconscious. And the guard on the palisades never saw the two figures that slipped through the shadows.

*   *   *

Zach awoke to a loud pounding on his door. "Lieutenant Houston." He recognized the voice of the colonel's orderly.

As he sat up in bed, Zach glanced at the clock. Two A.M. "What is it?"

"Lieutenant Houston, you're ordered to report to Colonel Scott's office at once," Sergeant Adams called.

Five minutes later, Zach arrived at the colonel's office as several other officers, tucking their shirts into their trousers, hurried from their quarters. Colonel Scott sat behind his desk. Within minutes, all of the senior and junior officers had assembled.

The men exchanged shrugs and questioning looks among one another as Scott lit a cigar. After several drags, the tip glowed with a red ash. He clamped the stogie between his teeth and leaned back in his chair. "Gentlemen, our prisoner has escaped." His actions were unhurried, his voice calm.

An undertone of murmurs circled the room. "Yes, you heard right, gentlemen, Gregorio has escaped."

Suddenly he leaned forward and slammed his hand down on the desk. "Goddammit! One prisoner in the whole goddamn stockade and he escaped!"

"Was anyone injured, sir?" Zach asked, concerned. He knew that if Gregorio had seriously harmed anyone, his fate would be sealed.

"Private Hoffman's sprouting a lump on his head." Scott snatched the cigar out of his mouth and tossed it into a brass cuspidor. "Tomorrow, gentlemen, I want every trooper under your command drilled until he drops. I expect every man in this goddamn unit to be prepared for the unexpected at all times." He jumped to his feet. "Eighty-seven men on this post and one goddamned Indian. *And . . . he . . . escaped.*" Scott sat back down. "You're dismissed, gentlemen. Lieutenant Houston, please remain."

As soon as all the other officers were gone, Scott glared

at Zach. "Well, your honorable savage appears to have run out on us. Do you have any theories this time, Lieutenant?"

"Well, sir, I think he was afraid you intended to ship him west."

"Pity. He should have given us the benefit of the doubt. We voted to release him."

"Then, sir, since that was your intention and no one has been seriously harmed, why don't you just consider Gregorio's departure as a . . . premature release?"

"I'm glad you find humor in this situation, Lieutenant Houston."

"Not humor, sir, just relief."

"Well, son, I'm afraid you'll find little humor or relief in your next assignment. I want you to find Gregorio and get his word he will cease any further action against the army or the citizens of Florida. And you tell that young buck for me that I advise him to find himself a dry hammock somewhere in the middle of the Everglades, settle down and raise a family, some chickens, and a couple of cows." His eyes hardened. "Because if he pulls any more of his shenanigans in my jurisdiction, he's going to find himself on the wrong side of a firing squad."

A rap sounded and Scott's orderly poked his head into the room. "What is it, Sergeant?" Scott said impatiently.

"Colonel, the Creek scouts have returned."

"Send them in."

Two Creek Indians entered the room. After a hurried conversation, they departed. "Well, at least the scouts think they know where Gregorio entered the swamps. Take one squad only."

"If you don't mind, sir, I prefer just one man, Sergeant Bryce. If I go in with Creek scouts and a full squad, Gregorio will believe I've come to arrest him."

"Without scouts, how do you expect to find him?"

Zach grinned wryly. "I think he'll find me, sir."

"As you wish, Lieutenant."

"Colonel Scott, may I ask that Mrs. Esposito be allowed to remain on the post until I return?"

Scott nodded and stood up. He reached out and shook Zachary's hand. "Good luck, Zach," he said in an unusual display of informality.

After consulting with Fred Hoffman and Flint Bryce, Zach went to tell Laura what had transpired. "Where is Teresa?"

"In her room."

"I don't think so. You better check."

Laura hurried to the room and found it empty. "I'm afraid you're right," she said.

"I just spoke to Hoffman. He was on guard duty at the time. He said that Teresa helped Gregorio to escape."

"You mean he didn't report that to Colonel Scott?"

"No, Hoffman said that he figured he owed Teresa that much for all that went on in Dario."

"Oh dear." Laura sighed, sinking down into a chair. "What will happen to her if Colonel Scott hears about her role in the escape?"

"He'll arrest her."

Laura buried her head in her hands. "Oh, God, Zach, I thought all this warfare was behind us. Now Teresa's gone. You're going back into the swamp. What if you run into hostile Indians?"

"Well, hopefully, we'll find Gregorio and Teresa before that happens."

He kissed her good-bye and she bade him a tearful farewell, then watched in desolation as he returned to his quarters.

Back in her room, she lay in bed unable to sleep, knowing that Zach and Bryce would begin their search at sunrise.

Chapter 26

Ramon awoke when Zach came to the door. He lay in his bed and listened to Zach telling Laura of Gregorio's escape. As soon as Zach departed, he arose and dressed.

His movements awoke Peter. "What are you doing?"

"I am leaving," he said, cautioning Peter to silence.

"Where are you going?" Peter climbed out of bed and padded barefoot over to Ramon, who was shoving his meager belongings into a knapsack.

"I wish to join my uncle."

"You mean in the prison?" Peter asked, perplexed.

"The army prison could not hold my uncle," the boy boasted. "I shall follow the lieutenant and find him," he said after relating to Peter all that he had overheard. "I must go now. Good-bye, my brother."

"Aren't you gonna say good-bye to Mama and Teresa? They're gonna be very sad."

"No. Teresa is with my uncle. And the *señora* would try to stop me. You must tell her that Ramon said he has much love in his heart for her." He grabbed his knapsack and disappeared through the door.

Peter hastily pulled on his own clothes and ran after Ramon. He found Ramon huddled in the bushes outside, awaiting Zach's departure. Peter hunched down beside him. "Ramon, don't go. You could get hurt. Maybe even killed."

"I am not afraid."

"Then I will come with you like I did when you went to kill Old Slither."

"But I will not be returning," Ramon warned.

"I'll come back with Daddy," Peter declared with self-assurance.

"Why do you call the lieutenant by such a name?" Ramon asked.

"Because he told me to."

"That is the name the Americans call their fathers," Ramon informed him.

Peter's chest swelled with pride. "Daddy said he would take the place of my papa."

"Gregorio has said that he will raise me as a son," the older boy declared, returning the boast.

Upon hearing this announcement, the six-year-old sat frowning. "Why do you pinch up your face like an old man?" Ramon finally asked.

"I was just wondering 'bout something," Peter replied. "If the lieutenant's gonna be my father, and Gregorio's gonna be your father, are we still gonna be brothers?"

Ramon put his arm around Peter's shoulder. "We will always be brothers, my little brother."

At the sound of approaching voices, Ramon put a finger to his lip. "Shhhh," he cautioned.

The boys remained concealed in the bushes as Zach and Bryce passed them. Crouched low in the grass, Ramon and Peter waited for a moment, then followed behind at a safe distance.

The sun had just risen when Laura awoke. She lay for a few moments thinking about Zach. There were so many dangers in the swamps besides the Indians. And he had said Sergeant Bryce was the only man going with him.

She finally gave up the effort to return to sleep and got out of bed. After dressing, she went into the kitchen. As she was about to light the stove to put on a kettle of water, Laura glanced out the window. At the sight of Ramon and Peter sneaking across the compound, she drew up in surprise. *What were they doing up at this early hour and where were they going?*

Something about the stealth of their movements alarmed her further. She ran to the door to call out to them, but stopped when she realized she would disturb others at this early hour. Laura closed the door and hurried after the boys.

Peter turned around and saw his mother approaching. "Ramon, Mama's coming."

Ramon glanced behind him, then took off at a run. Torn between obedience to his mother and loyalty to his brother, Peter hesitated for a moment, then chased after Ramon. Laura broke into a run after them.

"Peter! Ramon! Get back here this minute," she called out. Neither boy replied. She followed them into the swamp.

The ground felt mushy underfoot as she hurried to catch up with them. She could hear them ahead, splashing through stretches of watery marsh, and again she called out, but there was no answer. Every step took her deeper into the swamp. She feared she would not reach them before they got so far into the maze, they would all be lost.

For what seemed like an eternity, she continued her pursuit. The bottom of her gown became sodden and splattered with mud from the murky morass. She shuddered as a black snake slithered across the path.

Breathless, she rested for a moment on a hammock of mangrove. Aerial roots from the tree had stretched out in the stilt to develop new stems. Now twisted and curved, the branches of roots formed a grotesque, misshapen matrix along the ground.

"Peter, Ramon," she shouted loudly. With shrill squawks and flapping wings, a flock of cranes in a nearby pond took flight.

A ray of hope gleamed in her eyes as she heard a plaintive shout. "Mama."

"Peter!" She jumped up and trudged forward toward the cry. "Peter, where are you?"

"Here, Mama. Here." His shouts grew louder. She wanted to sob with relief when she saw the boys on a raised scrub of yellow pine. They ran into her outstretched arms.

"We was scared, Mama. We got losted," Peter said. Hugging both of them, she sank to her knees.

"What was that?" Zach asked when a cry sounded from somewhere behind them. The two men stopped to listen. The cry sounded again.

"Must be a wailing wildcat," Bryce said.

"It sounded human to me." Zach turned his head sharply when another cry sounded. "That's Laura!" He took off on a run. Bryce followed as Zach raced back down the trail they had just covered.

When they reached the pine scrub they stopped abruptly. Uncertain he could believe his eyes, Zach stared in shock at the three people seated on the ground. "What are you doing here?" He knelt down next to them. "Are you okay?"

"We're fine. We've been following you," Laura said. "That is to say, I've been following the boys . . . who have been following you, as I've just been told. Ramon wishes to join his uncle."

"Ramon, this was foolhardy of you." Zach turned his anger on Peter. "And you, young man, what is the idea of coming along with him?" Peter's lower lip quivered and he hung his head.

"Ah . . . Lieutenant," Bryce said softly.

Zach glanced up at him. "What?"

"I think we've got company."

Zach stood up slowly. "What do you mean?"

"Listen."

Zach stood motionless. The swamp had an unnatural silence; not even the tweet of a bird sounded. Sensing the danger, Laura felt her heart hammer in her chest, then she gasped when more than a dozen figures stepped suddenly out of the trees. Alarmed, she swung her glance to Zach. He was looking around at a circle of inscrutable faces . . . and pointed rifles.

The two soldiers lowered their weapons. Wordlessly, the Seminoles collected them. "You come," one of the warriors ordered.

Zach reached out a hand to Laura and helped her to her feet. Her legs trembled and she could barely walk. Concern for the safety of her son had driven her into the swamp. Now, with Zach's strength to lean on, her fortitude had waned. As they were hustled along, only Zach's hand on her elbow kept her from falling.

After an hour's walk in silence, they reached a small village. It came as no surprise to Zach when Gregorio stepped out of one of the *chickees*, Teresa behind him. At the sight of Laura and the two boys, she let out a cry of surprise and ran over to them. The two women hugged and kissed.

"Why does Houston follow Gregorio?" the warrior asked.

"I come in peace, Gregorio," Zach replied.

"You carry weapons."

"Not to be used against you. The weapons are to protect ourselves against the dangers of the swamp. If I had come in war, Gregorio, I would have brought soldiers with me."

Laura's eyes opened in amazement when Gregorio grinned. Until this moment, she had never seen an expression of pleasure on his face. "That is why you still live, Houston."

Laura closed her eyes and said a silent prayer of thanks. The two men understood each other perfectly, but she would never understand men in war.

"You have been watched since you entered the swamp." His gaze swung to her. "As have the others."

"You mean we were being followed all the time?" Laura asked in disbelief. "Why didn't you stop the boys? They might have been injured."

"They were never in danger."

Laura thought of how frightened she had been for the two boys in her dash through the swamp. Now he casually dismissed that danger. Her trembling resumed. She slumped to the ground and sat staring, dumbfounded.

"The white squaw frightens easy," one of the female Seminoles scoffed.

Gregorio glanced with displeasure at the squaw who had spoken. "Quiet, old woman. The *señora* is a brave woman. I have seen this for myself." Then Gregorio returned his attention to Zach. "We will smoke a pipe and speak further of this matter," he said.

Laura and the boys were designated to sit on the side of the fire with Teresa and the other women and children; Zach and Bryce sat opposite with Gregorio and the men of the village as they smoked a peace pipe.

Gregorio drank from a vessel and then offered the container to Zach. "You must drink the Black Drink with us."

Zach took a swallow. "It is made from black currants," Gregorio went on to explain. "My people call it *cassina*."

"It's very good, Gregorio," Zach said, and passed the vessel on to Bryce.

As the men talked in low tones, Laura had ample time to study the women. Most wore shirts with low necklines and long full skirts made of bright calico tied at their waists with plain cords. Although they were barefoot, they wore numerous strands of beads piled around their necks. The children, however, roamed naked, and Laura could not help but smile at the sight of these same brightly colored beads wrapped around the necks of the female infants.

Later, as they ate pieces of red snapper roasted on sticks of sweet bay for flavor, Zach and Laura spoke to

Gregorio and Teresa of their plans to wed. They asked him to return to Dario.

"I do not want the plantation. Zach and I intend to return to Texas in two months," Laura said.

"And what of the son of Esposito?" Gregorio's glance fell on Peter, who lay sleeping on the ground next to Laura.

Zach and Laura exchanged a private look, then Zach spoke up. "Luis Esposito was not Peter's father, Gregorio. I am. I fathered Peter when Laura and I were together in Texas. Ramon is Esposito's true son. And since Laura does not wish to remain here, she feels Ramon should inherit the plantation."

If this stunning news came as a surprise to him, Gregorio disguised it behind an impassive stare. Picking up the argument, Laura went on to explain, "You have been cleared of the accusations against you, Gregorio. If you would agree to remain at Dario with Ramon, I would sign the plantation over to him. But Ramon's so young, he needs a guardian."

"Gregorio must think on this," the warrior said. "For such a life sounds much like the way of a white man. Gregorio has trod the path of the black bear, swam the water of the turtle of the sea. He is not certain a white man's life would be to his liking."

"But I'd be there with you, Gregorio," Teresa said. Laura could tell that the thought of living at the plantation held considerably more appeal to Teresa. But she knew Teresa would go wherever Gregorio wished.

"The Everglades would still be right outside your door, my friend," Zach added. "There will always be deer to hunt . . . fish in the streams to spear."

"Gregorio knows that the time of the Seminole has passed . . . that the way of the white man has come to our land to remain," he said solemnly. "When the *señora* returns to Dario, Gregorio and Teresa will be there. Gregorio sees much wisdom in the *señora's* offer."

"And we must think of getting back to the fort, or the colonel will have the whole garrison searching for Laura and the boys," Zach said. He stood up and reached out a hand to her. Then Gregorio flashed his remarkable grin and added, "Gregorio can see humor in a Seminole owning a white man's land." His eyes were warm with humor. "And it is the way of my people for a warrior to live in the *chickee* of his squaw."

Laura and Teresa hugged each other joyously. "I'm so happy," Teresa said. Then she whispered aside to Laura. "I did not look forward to spending the rest of my life sharing a *sofkee* spoon."

A small party of Seminoles escorted them safely back to the fringe of the swamp.

Zach immediately reported the news to Colonel Scott. "I'm relieved to see your safe return, Lieutenant. I'm also pleased to hear that Gregorio might consider settling down to the life of a planter."

Chomping on a cigar, Scott said philosophically, "Well, if that buck's gonna settle down to becoming a gentleman farmer, I guess the day has finally come when we no longer have to fear a Seminole war."

"That may be true, Colonel Scott," Zach replied with a measure of caution. "But if you remember your history, sir, the Seminoles never started the wars to begin with."

At the less-than-subtle reminder, Colonel Scott glanced with brows furrowed in displeasure. "Congratulations on a job well done, Lieutenant."

"Ah . . . Colonel, sir, I don't suppose you would reconsider allowing Mrs. Esposito to remain on post?"

"Regulations are made to be followed. That will be all, Lieutenant Houston."

"Yes, sir." Zach saluted and departed hastily.

Laura had just finished dressing after bathing away the swamp dirt when a knock sounded at the door. The young soldier at the door held an envelope. "Ma'am, this letter has been received for forwarding to you."

"A letter?" Glancing at the envelope, she discovered it was from Lavitia Randolph. In the seven years Laura had lived in Florida, she had never received a letter from her aunt, not even in response to the letter she had sent informing Lavitia of Peter's birth.

After thanking the soldier, Laura sat down at the table and stared at her aunt's script. She felt a sense of foreboding as she held it; each neatly lettered word was like a voice from the past. With trepidation, Laura opened the envelope.

A quarter of an hour later, she still sat staring at the letter when Zach tapped on the door and entered. "Hi, honey." He bent down and kissed her. "Ummm, you smell good."

She remained unresponsive. Surprised, he straightened up. "What's wrong?" he asked, concerned.

She looked up and met his worried frown. "I just received a letter from Aunt Lavitia."

"And?" he asked uneasily.

She got to her feet and walked over to the window. Crossing her arms, she stood staring outside. "She's dying, Zach. She has asked me to come home. She says she has something to tell me before she dies."

"You mean it's time to confess all, so she can die with a clear conscience. And what do you plan on doing about it?"

She turned to face him. "I'm trying to decide."

"You don't owe her anything, Laura."

"That's not true. She took me in when I had nowhere else to go. I owe her the courtesy of honoring her dying request."

He grasped her by the shoulders and stared at her in disbelief. "You don't owe Lavitia Randolph anything. You paid her back with seven years of our lives . . . six years of Peter's. Have you forgotten?"

"Of course not. How could I? But whatever role she played in my marrying Luis, she had nothing to do with my getting pregnant. And no matter what she has said or done, if I hadn't been pregnant . . . I wouldn't have married Luis . . . I would have been there when you came back . . . and we wouldn't have lost those seven years. Why place the complete guilt on her?" She shrugged out of his arms and began to pace the floor.

"If she hadn't contrived to get her greedy hands on the Double H, I never would have left Texas."

"Zach, you can't change fate."

"Fate, hell! It's up to you. We don't need to lose any more years."

She glanced at him with exasperation. "Zach, it would only be two months at the most. If I'm not back by then, you could join me there." Unable to bear the sight of the betrayal in his eyes, she stepped away from him and returned to staring blindly out of the window.

"*Only two months.* Is that how you see it?" he asked incredulously.

She pivoted to confront him. "Well, it might be a solution. I can't stay here, so we were going to be separated anyway."

"Your being in Dario, where we could see each other occasionally, is a far cry from your being in Texas."

She waged the same tempting argument with herself. Defensively, she struck out against her own feelings as much as his. "Is that all that matters to you, Zach? An occasional weekend tumble in bed?"

She might just as well have slapped his face. "Laura," he said simply and shook his head.

She tried to soften the blow of her unjust remark. "Oh Zach, I know how much you'll miss Peter and me. And you should know we'll miss you just as much. But I think right now your bitterness toward Lavitia is clouding your sense of fair play."

"Fair play? Lavitia Randolph doesn't even know the meaning of fair play."

Laura felt a beginning of hopelessness with the argument. "Zach, yesterday even my staying at Dario was unacceptable to you. Now, my remaining there has become a satisfactory answer. That doesn't make sense."

The faintest sign of a crack appeared in his armor. "I never said it was *satisfactory*. I only meant it was a solution for now, since Gregorio has agreed to be your protector. I still would have preferred our being together."

"If I could stay here as your wife, I wouldn't hesitate to do so. But since that's impossible, I don't see what difference it makes if I wait for you at the Lazy R or in Dario."

"The difference is Lavitia Randolph," he lashed out in a naked revelation of his underlying fear. "The woman is evil. A witch. She's trying to destroy our love. She has haunted me my whole life with her wickedness. And she's still doing it."

"Zach, she's a dying old woman. She can't hurt us anymore." She wanted to hug him and chase away his fears as she did for Peter whenever he was frightened. Instead, her words sounded patronizing. "Besides, sweetheart, don't you see we're destined to be together? Didn't we find each other again after seven years?"

But she was dealing with a realistic man—not an idealistic boy. "And you want to put it to the test again. It's for damn sure I don't."

"Oh, Zach, we're not going to be separated for another seven years, for goodness sake. This is a moral obligation I must honor."

Previously, he had argued out of a feeling of desperation; now his argument was driven by anger. "And you have no obligation to me?"

"That's right, Zach, I don't. Nor do you to me, because I don't think of our love as an *obligation*."

He walked to the door and paused. "Looks like you've made up your mind."

Laura saw the wounded look in his eyes and heard the accusation in his voice when he said quietly, "I would never have done this to you, Laura." Then he was gone.

* * *

After a tearful, sleepless night, Laura began the next day by checking on a boat schedule. Taciturn and brooding, Zach accompanied her. She was able to book passage on a steamer scheduled to sail to Galveston the following day.

Then they went to the office of the attorney who handled Luis's affairs. Although he expressed several objections to Laura's decision, he had to honor her wishes. With Zach as a witness, the lawyer legalized the transfer of the plantation deed to Ramon's name, with Gregorio authorized as the boy's guardian until Ramon became twenty-one years old.

Because of her impending departure from Florida, and in order to avoid delay in the execution of the transfer, Laura signed a document giving Zach power of attorney to answer any further questions that might arise regarding the matter.

That evening as they shared their last meal together, it was difficult for Laura and Zach to keep up their spirits for Peter's sake. Laura dreaded the separation as much as Zach did, but she felt he doubted that fact.

"Daddy, why don't you come to Texas with us?" Peter asked guilelessly.

"I'm in the army, Peter. I can't leave."

"Well, just tell 'em you don't wanta be in the army anymore. 'Sides, you told me you didn't like the army anyway."

Zach grinned. "I wish it was that easy, son. I have to remain here."

Leaning an elbow on the table, Peter cradled his head in his hand and toyed with his food. "Then I wanta stay here too."

"Daddy will join us in two months, honey. That time will go fast. You'll see," Laura interjected quickly.

She glanced at Zach and their gazes locked. His expression was one of silent misery. She closed her eyes and choked back her tears.

* * *

The same heaviness of heart carried over to the next morning when they went down to the dock to board the ship. Sergeant Bryce accompanied them.

Teresa and Gregorio stepped out of a warehouse shadow. Looking sorrowful, Ramon lagged behind them. The sight of them almost broke Laura's control.

The two women embraced. "You are leaving," Teresa said.

"How did you know?" Laura asked.

"Gregorio awoke in the night and he knew. That is why we came."

"I explained everything in a letter and gave it to Zach to give to you," Laura told her. She took Teresa's hand. "Teresa, are you certain you do not wish to come back to Texas with me?"

Teresa smiled. "No, Laura. I'll miss you and Peter, but my life is with my husband now."

Laura suddenly had the horrifying fear that she would never see her again. Forcing back her tears, she grabbed Teresa and hugged her. "Why is life filled with nothing but good-byes to the living or the dead?"

Turning to Gregorio, she felt some of her misery ease as she looked into his deep, wise eyes. "You'll take care of them, Gregorio?"

He nodded. "Gregorio will not leave them."

Laura smiled through her welling tears. "I'll always be grateful to you."

She knelt down and opened her arms. Ramon stepped into her embrace. "I'll miss you, dear. But I know I'm leaving you in good hands."

"My heart will always hold love for you, señora. And for my little brother."

As the boys said good-bye, Gregorio spoke to Zach. "Houston is grieving in his heart."

"I don't want them to leave, Gregorio. We were separated for seven years, and now, we'll be separated again."

"Then why does Houston not tell his squaw to stay?"

"She feels she must leave to honor an obligation."

Gregorio pondered the remark for several seconds. "Honor is a heavy burden and often must be shouldered alone. We will leave you to your farewells."

"I'll come to Dario as soon as all the papers are in proper order, Gregorio."

"What the *señora* and you do for the adopted son of Gregorio gives much hope to the hearts of the Seminole. My people will farm and make a home on land they can call their own."

"Then perhaps the men who died for that land have died for a worthwhile cause, Gregorio," Zach said solemnly.

The eyes of the two men met in understanding. Each weary combatant carried the scars of war within him. Both men knew that the sacrifice of a man's life in battle could never be diminished—only the hope that some good would follow to give a purpose to that sacrifice.

They reached out and shook hands.

When the time came to say good-bye to Peter, Zach knelt down and hugged him. "You take care of your mother until I see you again," Zach said, releasing him reluctantly.

Bryce tipped his hat. "Good-bye, ma'am. Have a good journey." He grabbed Peter's hand. "Let's go check out your quarters, trooper."

As Bryce led Peter up the gangplank, Zach took Laura in his arms. The parting moment had arrived, and her heartache was so intense, she feared she would die from the pain of it.

Her eyes brimmed with tears as she reached up and caressed his face. Pressing a kiss to her palm, he drew her hand against his cheek. For a long moment they gazed deeply into each other's eyes, memorizing every detail of the other's face—details already engraved on their minds.

Zach reached into his tunic and pulled out a chain. His father's ring dangled from the gold links. He slipped the chain over her head and, for several seconds, tenderly fingered the ring.

"First thing we'll have to buy when we set up house-keeping is an ice cream churn." Despite his despair, a faint smile tugged at the corners of his mouth. "To get the ring back, I bribed Peter with a promise of a never-ending supply of chock . . . late ice cream."

Every word he spoke wrenched at her heart. Throwing her arms around his neck, she told him, "I love you, Zach. We'll be back if you don't come and get us."

His eyes deepened with renewed pain. "I'll be coming to get you in two months, Laura." Although spoken softly, the message was adamant.

A blast sounded from the ship's horn. Pulling her into his arms, he covered her mouth in a long, lingering kiss— bruising in its bitterness, poignant in its sweetness.

She clung to him until breathlessness forced them apart. After stealing one last look at his beloved face, she sped up the gangplank before she could change her mind.

"I'll be with the horses, Lieutenant," Bryce said, returning to the dock.

Zach stood alone on the wharf, waving to Laura and Peter at the ship's rail. Slowly the steamer moved out of the harbor. He remained motionless, his gaze fastened on the shrinking vessel until the mast became nothing more than a white glimmer between an azure sea and sky.

Chapter 27

Laura's return to Galveston touched her deeply. From the moment she stepped off the ship, she was inundated with memories of the day she and Zach had spent together exploring the city.

She already missed Zach beyond reason; two months would be an eternity. The memory of his wounded blue eyes when she left him was painted on the canvas of her mind. How would she ever make amends for this decision, which he saw as a betrayal? Regardless of her reason, she had hurt him again—this time knowingly.

Observing Peter's awe at the sights and sounds of the bustling seaport warmed her heart, momentarily enabling her to push her feeling of guilt to the back of her mind.

Wherever she glanced, there were signs of the city's growth: the waterfront was busier, there were more shops, more houses—more people. But the same ferry still ran between the island and the Texas coast.

Laura fell under a greater spell of nostalgia when she reached Bay Town. The town appeared to have transcended the passage of time. Stevens's General Store, the Bay Town Bank, the Lone Star Saloon, Slocum's Livery Stable, all seemed to have remained unaffected by the passing decade.

Slocum's youngest son drove Laura and Peter out to the Lazy R. Astounded, she stared in shock. The ranch was in worse condition than the Esposito plantation had been after the Seminole attack on Dario.

With mouth agape, she climbed from the wagon, then lifted Peter down. After the driver put the baggage on the porch, Laura paid him and thanked him for his help.

She stood on the porch and looked around her. The house and outbuildings needed a coat of whitewash, several windows were broken, doors hung ajar on cracked hinges, parts of the corral fence had split or cracked. A weathervane with a missing cock's head lay twisted on the roof of the chicken coop. The herd of horses no longer grazed in the corral, and the grama grass had grown tall and shaggy.

"Is this where we're gonna live, Mama?" Peter asked, glancing about him. "Where's the horses?"

"I don't know, honey." She knocked on the door, but there was no answer. Laura turned the knob and pushed the door open.

The house was stuffy with a faint smell of mustiness, and the closed shutters on the windows cast the rooms in semi-darkness. Stirred by the breeze from the open door, dust motes purled the air like feathers in flight.

"Hello," she called out. "Anybody home?"

"Who's that?" Footsteps shuffled across the wooden floor leading from the kitchen, and Whiskers Merten appeared in the doorway of the drawing room.

"Whiskers!" Laura exclaimed with pleasure. "It's Laura."

"Miz Laura? Well, tarnation!" the old man exclaimed. "Didn't hear ya comin'." The sight of the beloved old cowpoke warmed her heart. She saw that he favored his left leg as he limped over to her.

Laura threw her arms around him. "It's so good to see you, Whiskers."

As he stepped back to admire her, his weathered face broke into a grin. "If you ain't the prettiest sight these old eyes have seen in years, missy."

"How have you been, Whiskers?"

"Hearin' ain't what it used to be. And I busted up my leg few years back. Aside from that, I'm about the same."

"You look the same," she said with affection.

His blue-eyed stare fell on Peter. "And who's this young'un?"

"This is my son, Peter."

"Well, how do, sonny. Name's Whiskers Merten."

"How do you do, Mr. Merten," Peter replied politely, much to his mother's pride and pleasure.

The suspicion of a tear glistened in the old man's eye. "Joey's grandson. Never thought I'd live to see the day." He snorted into a bandanna, then tucked it back into his pocket.

"How's Aunt Lavitia, Whiskers?"

He shook his head. "Not too well, missy."

"What's wrong with her?"

"Her heart. Doc's got a fancy name for it. Lavitia got herself soakin' wet 'bout a year back roundin' up some strays. Got so sick, she took to her bed. Doc said the fluid from her lungs backed up into her heart and that's what caused the heart attack."

"I'll go up and see her now. Will you take care of Peter while I do? He's probably thirsty."

"Sure will. Come on, sonny, let's go to the kitchen and see what we can find."

"You got any Hires rootbeer, Mr. Merten?"

"Nope."

"You got any chock . . . late ice cream?"

"Can't say I do. How 'bout some beef jerky?"

"What's beef jerky, Mr. Merten?"

"How 'bout you calling me 'Whiskers' same as everybody else?"

"How come everybody calls you 'Whiskers'? 'Cause you got long whiskers?"

"Reckon so."

"How come you've got long whiskers?" Peter asked, slipping his hand in the cowpoke's.

"You always ask all these questions, sonny?" Whiskers grumbled as he led Peter away.

"What questions?" Peter asked.

Smiling in amusement, Laura stood listening to their
fading voices and receding footsteps. Then she turned
and glanced upstairs. Her smile vanished, replaced with
a look of despondency, and she climbed the stairs.

Lavitia Randolph looked skeletal lying in the center of
the oversized bed that had once belonged to her father.
Her flesh had shrunk almost to the bone and the skin
lay in loose wrinkles. Now pale and drawn, her usually tanned face showed the ravages of her illness: her
nose appeared more dominant, her eyes sunken shells,
and her chin was eclipsed by the deep lines grooved on
the corners of her mouth.

Lavitia's white hair, which she had always worn cut to
her ears, now hung to her shoulders in straggly hanks.

"Aunt Lavitia," Laura said softly.

Lavitia opened her eyes.

"So, you've come back to watch me die," Lavitia said
in greeting.

"I came back because you asked me to, Aunt Lavitia.
I'm sorry to hear you've been sick."

"Sick, hell! I'm dying," Lavitia announced. "And I'm
glad too, seeing what's happened to the Lazy R. I
bet my Daddy's turning over in his grave." The pale
blue eyes had an unnatural glint that Laura had never seen before. Lavitia's eyes had always seemed cold
and compassionless. Laura found herself distracted by
the look.

A splotch of red appeared on each of Lavitia's cheeks.
"Don't excite yourself, Aunt Lavitia."

"Did your handsome husband come with you?" Lavitia
asked.

"Luis is dead, Aunt Lavitia."

"Dead? How'd he die?" she asked indifferently.

"He was killed by a man in self-defense."

"Humph," Lavitia mumbled. She closed her eyes.

Laura waited for a long moment to see if Lavitia had
any more to say—perhaps to welcome her back, or to
offer a word of sympathy over Luis's death. But soon

the even rise and fall of Lavitia's chest indicated that her aunt was asleep. For a long moment, Laura stared at the sleeping woman and tried to feel sympathy for her. But she could not.

God forbid! Am I as coldhearted as that woman in the bed that I can't even feel sympathy for her dying? Laura left the room.

She entered her old bedroom. The room was bare of all adornment, just as it had been when she arrived at the Lazy R years before.

She sank down on the edge of the bed, and images from that long-ago day whirled about in her head: Zach's solemn eyes . . . Whiskers's friendly grin, Teresa's compassion . . . Lavitia's insensitivity, her first glimpse of the sun-kissed Lazy R . . . the sinister countenance of Whitey Wright.

Faces . . . places . . . the ghostly specters all closed in on her, bombarding her senses.

She felt as if she couldn't breathe. Jumping to her feet, she hurried to the window. For several minutes she struggled to open the window, but the sash maintained its tenacious grip on the frame.

In her frustration, she pounded on the glass. "Damn you! Damn you! Damn you!" she cursed, unleashing the futility that had begun to suffocate her from the moment she entered the house.

Why had she allowed herself to be lured back to this hellish place? To the presence of this bitter woman? Everything Zach had said was true. Lavitia was evil; her wickedness seemed to permeate the house. Why hadn't she followed her father's instinct and ridden away, never to look back?

"Zach. Oh, Zach," she sobbed, throwing herself on the bed. "Why didn't I listen to you? I was a fool to hurt you again. Forgive me . . . please forgive me."

She shed tears of contrition.

When she finally composed herself, Laura went downstairs. There was no sign of Peter or Whiskers. She went outside and found them in the barn, feeding a chestnut-colored stallion.

"Where's my mare, Whiskers?"

"Sold her a couple years back," he said. He glanced askance at her. "You talk to Lavitia?"

"For a short time. She fell asleep."

Laura left the barn. With a sense of hopelessness, she glanced around at the signs of neglect. Whiskers followed her out.

"What happened here, Whiskers? Where's all the crew?"

"Oh, they've moved on. Five years ago, we lost the bull and most of the herd to anthrax disease. Lavitia put a lot of money into replacing it. Next year there was a drought. Then the bottom dropped out of beef prices, so she lost more money when she sold the herd. Then she got sick. We ain't run a cow on the Lazy R for over two years now, missy."

"It's hard to believe how quickly she got wiped out."

"Lavitia tell you she put the ranch up for sale?" Whiskers asked.

"No. We hardly spoke." She looked around in disgust. "But as long as we're living here, we can at least fix up this place. I think a hammer and nails, plus a few buckets of whitewash, will make a big difference."

"We've got a hammer, but we ain't got no nails or paint," Whiskers told her.

"We do have soap and water. We'll begin inside the house. Come on, Peter," she called as she returned to the gloomy interior.

Laura opened all the shutters and windows. Whiskers put kettles of water on the stove to heat and a few hours later, Laura had the bedrooms cleaned and sheets and pillows on the beds.

"What's going on here?" Lavitia snarled when Laura carried a tray into her room later that day.

"I've been cleaning the bedrooms. And tomorrow, Aunt Lavitia, I intend to clean this room."

"Humph," her aunt barely murmured.

As Lavitia ate, Laura opened the window to air the room, then carried out the slop pot to empty it. When she returned, her aunt had finished eating.

"Is there anything else you would like?"

"No."

"No, thank you," Laura said reflexively.

"I see you haven't lost your sassy tongue," Lavitia grumbled.

"I'm sorry, it just slipped out. I'm used to correcting Peter." She picked up the tray. "Would you like to meet my son, Aunt Lavitia?"

"No. I'd be happy if that Houston bastard wasn't even in this house."

Laura's eyes flashed angrily. "Don't you ever refer to Peter in those terms again. You're a spiteful old woman, Aunt Lavitia. You're to be pitied."

"I didn't ask you to come back here for pity, girl."

"Why did you ask me to come back?"

"There's a couple things I wanted to tell you before I go. Sit down."

Laura was in no mood for any more of Lavitia's unpleasantness, but curiosity overcame caution. She pulled a chair to the bedside and sat down.

"I'm selling the Lazy R."

"Whiskers told me, Aunt Lavitia."

"I could sell just part of it and pay off my debts, but there's no Randolph to leave the ranch to anyway." Her face took on the pinched look Laura recalled so well. "If I'd leave it to you, I know it would end up someday in your ba . . . kid's hands. He's got Houston blood, and no Houston's gonna end up with the Lazy R."

"You're carrying your bitterness right to the grave, aren't you, Aunt Lavitia? Is this what you called me home to tell me? You could have said as much in a letter."

"Oh no, my beloved niece, I have more." The maniacal gleam in Lavitia's eyes returned. "But you may go now. I'm tired. I want to sleep." Lavitia closed her eyes in dismissal.

Before going to bed, Laura took time to pen Zach a letter to let him know of their safe arrival. Then she dropped into bed, exhausted.

The next morning while the others were still asleep, Laura went down to the study. The ledger books were in the drawers where Lavitia had always kept them.

She studied the entries until Peter woke up. After making breakfast and tending to Lavitia, Laura left Peter in Whiskers's care and rode into town.

She posted the letter to Zach, bought some nails and paint, then headed to the bank. She needed answers to several questions.

Laura was unprepared for the man who rose to his feet when she asked to see Mr. Davis. The distinguished-looking man had light hair and appeared to be in his late fifties.

"How do you do. I'm Laura Esposito, Lavitia Randolph's niece."

"A pleasure to finally meet you, Mrs. Esposito. I'm Burton Davis. I was living in Boston when you last were here in Bay Town, but my father has spoken of you."

I'm sure he has, Laura thought caustically, recalling the pretentious, gray-haired man whom Lavitia Randolph had led around like a puppet on a string.

"I expect my business is with your father, Mr. Davis."

"He died several years ago. I've taken over the business. Please sit down, Mrs. Esposito."

"Thank you, sir." Laura took the proffered chair before the desk. "I understand that my aunt has put the Lazy R up for sale. Have you had any offers on the ranch?"

"Not as yet."

"This is a very awkward situation for me, Mr. Davis. I hope you understand I'm not trying to pry. I have been going over the books at the ranch, but there have been no entries made since my aunt's illness. At that time, though, it would appear she was practically insolvent.

And now, the ranch is in need of some major repairs. I would be interested in knowing her financial situation."

Davis cleared his throat. "Well, I, too, am in a rather awkward situation, Mrs. Esposito. Your aunt—"

"Sir, my aunt has already informed me that I am not her heir. The news does not distress me, so you don't have to feel embarrassed. However, she has asked me to remain at the Lazy R until she . . . until her demise."

"How is Miss Randolph's health?"

"I can't say for certain. I'm not a doctor, Mr. Davis. I'm sure you're aware that she is totally bedridden and needs constant care."

"Yes, I was under the impression Mr. Merten was looking after her."

"He has been, but his money is exhausted. I have a meager fund which I am willing to contribute toward her upkeep, but I think I am entitled to know how my aunt stands financially."

"I think you are too, Mrs. Esposito. Therefore, I am going to take a professional liberty and explain the situation to you in its entirety."

He unlocked a file and removed a thick portfolio. "To be frank with you, your aunt is dead broke, as they say. Her only asset is the ranch. But, even so, there are liens against it. If she doesn't find a buyer soon, the ranch will have to be auctioned to pay off the debts."

"I can't believe it!" Laura exclaimed.

"Everything is legally documented right here in the record, Mrs. Esposito."

"I'm not questioning your integrity, Mr. Davis. I'm just so astounded. The ranch was flourishing when I left seven years ago."

"Unfortunately, Miss Randolph made some injudicious investments which were followed by several unfortunate setbacks on the ranch. Here is my file relating to the Lazy R, including your aunt's will, as well as the will of your grandfather, William Randolph. Recently, while accumulating the deeds and titles of the ranch in preparation for selling it, I read William Randolph's will and discovered something which deeply distressed me."

"What is that, Mr. Davis?"

"Your grandfather legally bequeathed the ranch to his daughter Lavitia and provided for a permanent home at the Lazy R for Mr. Merten; there is no question about that. Mr. Randolph did not make any provision for his son Joseph. But there was a codicil attached to the document which I never saw, or heard of, until I read this official copy."

"What does it say, sir?"

Burton Davis picked up the document which had begun to yellow with age and flipped it over to the last sheet. "Read this. According to the date, William Randolph executed the codicil three months before he died."

Laura started to read the paper. Surprised, she glanced up at the man sitting silently behind the desk, then reread the paragraph to make certain she had understood it.

Frowning, she met his steady gaze. "He left my father ten thousand dollars?"

"I assume your father was never informed of the bequest."

"Why, no. He always told me that he had been completely disinherited. He certainly didn't have any wealth when he died."

"Well, there's more. Read on, Mrs. Esposito."

Her eyes widened with disbelief. When she finished reading, the will slipped out of her hand as she stared numbly into space. "Zach never really had to leave the Double H."

"William Randolph never forgot that Wes Houston had saved the life of his son Joseph. In gratitude, your grandfather cancelled any debt owed to him by the Houstons and declared in the will that the Double H would remain in their hands."

She looked up at him in bewilderment. "So all those years of hard work that Zach and his father spent struggling to pay back the note were not necessary?" She shook her head in disbelief. "The Double H belonged to them all the time. Lavitia not only cheated her own brother out of ten thousand dollars, but she stole the Double H from the Houstons as well."

"She couldn't have done it without my father's help," Burton Davis said sadly. "My father knew that codicil existed, but he became a willing pawn to Lavitia Randolph."

He clasped her hand. Her fingers felt cold. "Your story has become a romantic legend to the whole town," he said gently. "It especially touched me, Laura; I knew your father and Wes. We were all schoolmates. When I discovered how my father had been a party to Lavitia's deceit, I experienced much of the same shock that you're suffering now."

Laura was too devastated to discuss any further business. Lavitia was everything Zach accused her of being . . . and more. She stood up. "If you'll excuse me, Mr. Davis, we'll have to finish this conversation later. Right now, I just can't think clearly."

"I understand perfectly." He took her arm and walked her to the door. "Forgive me for my informality, Laura."

"I appreciate your telling me what you have, Mr. Davis," Laura said gratefully. She held out her hand. "Thank you for all your help."

He offered a sheepish grin. "Ethically I shouldn't have violated the confidentiality of my client, but I feel I owe Joey and Wes that much for old time's sake."

As soon as she returned to the ranch, Laura hurried up to Lavitia's room. When she appeared in the doorway, Lavitia snarled an order to her. "Tell Whiskers not to send that kid of yours up here with any more trays."

"His name is Peter," Laura said, matching Lavitia's hostile tone. "Tell me, Aunt Lavitia, how can you extend your spitefulness even to an innocent child?"

"Because he's one of those damned Houstons."

"Don't flatter the worth of your curses, Aunt Lavitia. The only person I've ever heard *damn* a Houston is you. What could they have done to make you cheat and steal from them, the way you did from your own brother?"

Lavitia's mouth narrowed to a slit. "He betrayed me."

"Who? Who betrayed you?" Laura cried out.

"Wes Houston."

"How?" Laura asked, aghast.

"He loved me. I know he did," Lavitia snarled. "And he made a fool of me in my father's eyes. But he paid heavily for that betrayal. Just like my brother did, who supported what he said. And just as my father did because he didn't believe me. They all betrayed me, and they all suffered for it." Her eyes glistened with excitement. Stunned, Laura saw the madness beneath the excitement.

"And you betrayed me too, didn't you, Laura? And you suffered just like they did." Lavitia's face looked hideous in a smug smile of satisfaction. "I burned all the letters he wrote you, you know."

"What letters are you talking about?"

"The letters that your lover wrote you when you thought he was dead. Oh, what a laugh they gave me. First he pleaded . . . then he begged for you to write to him."

"You knew that Zach was alive and you let me go on believing he was dead?" Zach's words of warning were pounding in Laura's ears. Lavitia had almost destroyed their love.

Laughing softly, Lavitia closed her eyes and mumbled, "You betrayed me and had to suffer too. Just like the others did. I burned his letters to you, Laura. All those letters he wrote to you." Lavitia's voice trailed off and she drifted into sleep.

Laura stared speechless at the woman in the bed. *Was her aunt in league with the devil?* Horrified, she fled from the room.

Laura found Peter outside with Whiskers. "Honey, Mama has to talk to Uncle Whiskers. Why don't you go to that clover patch and try to find one with four leaves? It's good luck if you do."

"Will you come and help me?" he asked, skipping away.

"In a minute, honey. As soon as I finish talking to Whiskers."

"What's botherin' you, missy?"

"Whiskers, I think Lavitia has gone mad."

"Reckon so."

"You coming, Mama?" Peter yelled out, kneeling in the clover patch.

"Couple minutes," Laura yelled.

"The boy told me he can't wait 'til his daddy comes."

"Neither can I." Laura sighed.

Whiskers stuck his tongue in his check. "Thought your husband was killed, missy." He paused for a moment, then said purposely, "When are ya gonna tell him who his real daddy is?"

"Who do you think Peter's real daddy is, Whiskers?"

"My hearin's failin', missy, not my eyes," he said. "Boy's a Houston if I ever saw one."

"That's part of what I want to talk to you about. I have to know why Lavitia hates the Houstons so much. And I think you know the reason better than anyone."

"Maybe so," he said.

"I think her bitterness has driven her mad. I found out today she cheated my father out of ten thousand dollars and the Houstons out of their ranch."

"Gal's always been kinda peculiar. Even when she was younger, she was always scheming to get her own way."

"What do you mean?" Laura asked.

Whiskers sat down on an upturned barrel. "Don't like to tell tales out of school, missy."

"Whiskers, I've got to know the whole story," she said desperately.

She sensed the old man's struggle with his conscience. Finally, he nodded. "Wes Houston was about sixteen when it began. He was a good-lookin' young'un just like Zach. Well, Lavitia took a hankerin' to Wes. Lord knows he never gave her any cause. Wes was one of those happy-go-lucky kind of guys who liked everybody and everybody liked him. 'Specially the gals. Used to swarm around him like bees to a honeycomb." Whiskers grinned widely. "Drove your pa crazy. Never could figure out what Wes had that he didn't."

"I met Mr. Houston a few times, and I think I understand what you mean," Laura agreed. "He had an irresistible charm. I adored him in the short time that I knew him. And when he died, I felt as if I'd lost my best friend."

"Well, Lavitia rode roughshod over her brother Joey. She nagged and complained about whatever he did. Joey hated it. I think your pa really disliked Lavitia. Gotta say, most people did. She didn't even have a girlfriend."

Whiskers grimaced in sadness. "Lavitia was a cold kind of person. She really didn't like people. Everyone 'ceptin' Wes. But your grandpa always put stock into what she said. And whenever it'd suit her purpose, she'd blame Joey for somethin' he hadn't done."

"You mean she deliberately lied?" Laura asked.

"Without even blinkin' an eye," he remarked. "Well, Wes was the kind of guy who tried to see good in everyone. There could be a mad dog, and he'd try to talk people out of shootin' it. So being the way he was, he felt sorry for Lavitia and come to her defense more than once."

Whiskers stopped talking when Peter came running back to Laura. "Mama, Mama, I found a cattapilla," he said.

"Go and find a jar in the barn to put it in, honey," she told him. Peter hurried off.

"Go on, Whiskers," she said.

"Lavitia took Wes's carin' ways as meanin' he loved her. She started spreadin' tales that Wes had asked her to marry him. Course there weren't no truth to it, but

Lavitia told the story enough times to begin believin' it herself."

"Didn't Mr. Houston deny the rumors?"

"He just laughed them off instead of makin' her face him with them. Then Carrie came to town, and Wes fell head-over-heels in love with her. When he said that he and Carrie were gonna get married, Lavitia went kind of wild. She told your grandpa that Wes had ... ah ... taken advantage of her."

The old man blushed. "I think that's what caused the final break between Joey and Lavitia. Joey knew it weren't true. The two of 'em had a big row over it." He scoffed lightly. "Reckon the whole town knew it weren't true too. Even your grandpa guessed that Lavitia was lying this time. He always had a soft spot in his heart for Wes anyway, ever since the boy saved Joey's life. So your grandpa told Lavitia to admit the truth or get off the ranch.

"Well, you know how much Lavitia loves the Lazy R, so she went to the weddin' and admitted to Carrie that she had lied.

"Everything finally settled back to normal, but things were never the same between Joey and Lavitia. Your pa left the Lazy R shortly after the wedding, and Lavitia never spoke to Wes again."

"And after my grandfather died, she began to wield her power and wealth to get even with the Houstons."

"Yep," Whiskers Merten said sadly.

Peter came running back, carrying a jar holding the caterpillar. Laura helped him find some pine leaves to put in the jar, then she saddled the horse.

"Where are we going, Mama?" he asked as they rode away from the house.

"We're going to visit your grandfather, honey," she told him. "I've got something to tell you."

In an exercise of emotional fortitude, Laura rode with Peter to the Double H. The cabin was still there, but Laura did not enter it.

She dismounted at the gravesite of Wesley and Carissa Houston. She laid a sprig of flowering primrose on each grave. "Come over here, Peter."

Laura knelt down on her knees and slipped an arm around his waist. "These are the graves of your Grandma and Grandpa Houston."

"You mean my grandma and grandpa are dead?" he said, disappointed. "Like Papa and Pilar?"

"Yes, they died a long time ago." She sat down and pulled him onto her lap. "These are the graves of Daddy's mama and daddy."

His brow creased in a frown as he tried to put all the pieces together. "Then they're not really my grandma and grandpa. They're just taking the place of them, like Daddy's taking Papa's place."

"No, honey, these are really your grandparents. Papa was not your real father . . . Daddy is."

Laura could see the youngster was confused. She hugged him tighter. "Daddy used to live right over there in that house. He and Mama were in love."

His smile warmed her heart. "Like you are now."

She brushed the dark hair off his forehead and smiled tenderly. "Daddy and Mama loved each other from the moment we met. And we . . . had a baby from that love."

"Was that me, Mama?"

Tears misted her eyes, and she hugged him tighter. "That's right, sweetheart. That was you. Well, Daddy had to go away. The ship he was on was lost at sea, and I thought he was dead. So I married Papa and left here." Peter's trusting eyes looked up at her as she continued. "But you see, honey, Daddy was your real father."

Peter reflected on her words for a long moment. Then he grinned. "I'm glad, 'cause Daddy loves me. I can tell. And I love him too. Papa never loved me. He never hugged me like Daddy does. Was Papa Ramon's real father?"

"Yes, honey. Why do you ask?"

" 'Cause he never hugged Ramon either." His little face

sobered. "Too bad Daddy can't be Ramon's father too," he said sadly.

"Ramon has Gregorio now. He'll love Ramon like Daddy loves you."

Laura knew the young child still did not understand it all, but some day he would. More important, until that day, Peter would be nurtured by Zach's love and guidance.

Peter sighed deeply. "I sure miss Daddy. I wish he was here with us."

"I do too, sweetheart. I do too."

Peter scampered out of her arms and came back carrying a Texas bluebonnet in each hand. Imitating what he had seen his mother do, he put a flower on each grave.

"I know you miss Daddy like Mama and I do, but we'll come back and visit with you again, Grandma and Grandpa."

And as the days passed into weeks, Laura and Peter returned often to keep that promise.

The mail packet had brought him two letters. Zach opened the one from Laura first. Hungrily he devoured every word on the page. He smiled at a picture of a misshapen horse that Peter had drawn in pencil. For a long moment, he held their letter, feeling their love.

Then he put it aside and opened the other envelope from a law firm in New Orleans. As if his spirits weren't low enough, he read the sad news informing him of the death of Senator Long.

Zach mourned the loss of the man who had been a mentor and source of strength to him throughout the ship disaster and the nightmare of the loss of Laura. Sadly, he returned the letter to the envelope.

Seeking solace, he reached again for Laura's letter.

Chapter 28

ᑐᗕᑐᖕ

Sitting on the steps in front of Stevens's General Store, Peter licked a peppermint stick as he waited for his mother to finish shopping. He ran his tongue up one side of the stick of candy, then down the other. He had reasoned if he ate it that way, the candy stick would last longer.

At the sound of the ferry whistle, he glanced toward the wharf. He wanted to run down and watch the ferry dock, but his mother had given him strict orders to wait for her right there on the steps.

He wasn't going to disobey her. Ever since they left Florida two months ago, his mother had not been herself. She scolded him more often and even yelled at Whiskers sometimes. Peter wished they would go back to Florida. His mother had been happier there.

He didn't like that Aunt Lavitia either. She scared him. He wished the mean old woman would hurry up and die like she was supposed to. But she wasn't ever going to die. Whiskers had told him she was too mean to die. They'd never get back to Florida.

Wishing he could go down and pitch stones into the water, Peter glanced back at the dock. Two men were just getting off the ferry.

The candy stick fell from his hand as he jumped to his feet. Forgotten, it lay in the dust as, with outstretched hands, he dashed toward the dock.

"Daddy," he called out joyously. "Daddy!"

*   *   *

Laura stood in the back of the store contemplating whether or not to purchase the kettle she held. As much as they needed a new one at the ranch, her funds had dwindled down to almost nothing, and she had made up her mind she would not write to Zach for money to help support Lavitia Randolph.

If only they could sell the ranch. Burton Davis told her that after the debts were paid, she could legally collect what was due her father. And Laura had every intention of doing so. Her aunt's insane schemes would not all be successful: Zach would have the Double H back, and she would have the money that had been rightfully due her father.

Her eyes narrowed in bitterness. But that wouldn't bring back her parents. If Lavitia hadn't cheated him, her father might have become a rancher instead of a lawman, and her parents might be alive today. Lavitia had destroyed all of them.

She shook her head to force aside the grim thoughts. She mustn't allow bitterness to consume her, the way it had devoured her aunt.

The bell tinkled above the door and Howard Burns, the town wastrel and primary source of gossip, rushed in excitedly. "Hey, Harry, guess who's back in town?"

Absorbed in the task of totalling up Laura's purchases, the shopkeeper mumbled indifferently, "Who might that be, Howie?"

"Zach Houston," Burns said importantly. "Just arrived on the ferry."

The kettle crashed to the floor and Laura dashed out of the store.

Zach saw her as soon as she came through the door. In a single sweep, his gaze brushed the silken sheen of dark hair that hung in a single braid to the middle of her back, the white bodice hugging the rounded swell of her breasts, and the dark skirt that buttoned at her waist and flowed to her ankles; then his blue eyes sought her cherished face. Carrying Peter in one arm, he came toward her.

Mesmerized, Laura watched as his smooth, supple strides brought him ever nearer. His long, muscular legs were still encased in cavalry pants, the uniform blouse replaced by a buckskin shirt that conformed to his broad shoulders and hard chest in a sensuous symmetry. The hat, low on his forehead, shrouded his eyes from her sight, but she could feel the magnetism of his dark-eyed gaze and her heartbeat raced in response.

And when he reached her, unmindful of the dozens of pairs of eyes that watched, he reached out and gently caressed her cheek as their locked gazes spoke a message of love and longing. Then he lowered his head and kissed her.

Some of the spectators snickered nervously. Others smiled tenderly. A few even dabbed at a tear in the corner of an eye—but all watched unabashedly. And their hearts swelled with jubilation.

For Romeo had come home to claim his Juliet.

And in this small, dirtwater town in eastern Texas, those in observance knew that a new ending to that tragic tale had come to pass.

Flint Bryce approached the couple as they drew apart. "Howdy, ma'am," he said. "Pleasure to see you again."

"Sergeant Bryce!" Laura exclaimed.

The ex-scout grinned. "Not anymore, ma'am. Took me twenty years to make sergeant, and twenty minutes for Zach to convince me to give it up for ranchin'."

Other well-wishers closed in on the couple to welcome Zach home. He bore their greetings politely, but after several moments he whispered in a desperate tone, "Let's get away from here, Laura." She nodded.

Reaching for Peter, Flint said, "I'll take care of the boy for a couple hours." He slapped Zach on the shoulder. "Get goin'."

Zach and Laura hurried to the wagon. He lifted her

up on the seat then climbed up beside her and took
the reins. "Where are they going, Sergeant Bryce?" Peter
asked when Bryce put him down.

"Reckon they've got a thing or two to get settled."

A dimple flashed in Peter's cheek. "Are they gonna
start doing all that kissing like they did before?"

"They might have a little bit of that in mind," Bryce
said.

Peter's eyes rounded in contradiction. "No! They do a
lot of kissing. Why do you think they like kissing each
other so much, Sergeant Bryce?"

"Wouldn't want to venture a guess, trooper," Flint
remarked with a laconic grin.

"Do you like kissing, Sergeant Bryce?"

"Ain't done enough to take exception to it." He started
to walk toward the cafe.

"Do you think I'll like kissing when I grow up?" Peter
quickened his steps to keep up with the scout.

Flint could see it was going to be a long two hours.
"Not if you'd have to keep your mouth shut long enough
to find out."

"What do you mean, Sergeant Bryce?"

"I'm not a sergeant anymore, trooper. I quit the army,"
he said, skirting the question.

"How come you quit the army?"

Bryce cast his eyes heavenward for guidance. "Come
on, pal, let's try and find us a glass of rootbeer." He
swung Peter up on his shoulders. "And if I fall into luck,
there'll be some chocolate ice cream too."

They made it no farther than the copse of oak where
one tree still bore their carved initials.

Messages of eternal love, of the pain of yesterday's
separations, the promises of endless tomorrows were
intertwined with sighs, kisses, stroking, caressing. Boots,
bodice, shirt, skirt, trousers, petticoat were cast aside in
quick succession, until no barrier remained between their
heated flesh.

Naked and entwined, they sank to the ground and their bodies spoke the messages their words could no longer express, each kiss . . . each caress . . . each whispered word of love dearer than the one before it.

Together they soared to the dizzying, swirling heights known only to lovers, and for several seconds tottered on the brink of ecstasy where the grasp on life seemed held by a delicate thread of sublimation—then, together, they plummeted over the edge into the depths of the promised rapture.

Two hours later, with only Peter and Flint Bryce in attendance, Zach and Laura stood before the church altar. Father Jacoby dispensed with the lengthy wait of reading the banns to pronounce them man and wife. The couple grasped hands and stood smiling into each other's eyes. They had waited almost a decade for this moment. Zach lowered his head and placed a tender kiss on his wife's lips.

And then he lifted their son onto his shoulders, slipped an arm around his wife, and they left the church.

Once outside, Laura's mind whirled with a dozen matters that needed attention. "Oh my goodness!" she lamented. "I ran off and left a stack of supplies setting on the counter of the general store. I better get back to it."

"Well, while you do that, I've some banking business to take care of," Zach said.

"I'll go with you and help you load your wagon, ma'am," Flint Bryce offered.

"Sergeant Bryce, are you going to keep calling me ma'am? My name is Laura." Her eyes lit with merriment and a dimple danced in each cheek. "Laura Houston." Groaning at the sight of the temptation, Zach pulled her into his arms and kissed her.

Peter tugged at Flint's shirt sleeve. Rolling his eyes, Peter scrunched up his face in chagrin. "Didn't I tell you 'bout all that kissing?"

"Let's go help your ma, trooper," Flint said, grinning.

Zach watched the three walk away: Laura, Peter, and the laconic scout who had become his best friend. With Laura at his side and Flint helping to work the spread, Zach felt confident he couldn't fail at building one of the largest spreads Texas would ever see. And one day, his son would ride beside him.

Laura looked back and waved. Zach smiled and waved back to her. He had never known such contentment.

When Zach entered the bank, Burton Davis hurried out of his office to congratulate him. "News travels fast in this town," Davis said with a laugh.

"I have to transfer my bank account from the east. And the sooner the better. I'd appreciate your help, Mr. Davis."

"Well, I'm glad to see you, because it saves me the trouble of contacting you," Davis said. "Can you step into my office for a few minutes?"

Zach glanced out of the window. "Laura will be ready to leave soon, but I've got a little time," he said.

Once they were seated, Davis pulled out the Lazy R portfolio and let Zach read the codicil to the will. "I've already explained this to Mrs. Espo . . . ah . . . your wife, Mr. Houston."

Upon learning the truth, Zach felt the same indignation as Laura, except he reacted more violently. Outraged, he tossed the will on the desk. "That bitch! That evil, unconscionable bitch!"

"I can't tell you how much I regret my father's role in this deception," Davis said.

Zach paced the floor as Davis went on to explain Lavitia Randolph's plans for selling the Lazy R.

"When I think of how she almost destroyed our lives. And my father!" Zach suddenly exclaimed. "He worked himself to death to pay back that loan."

Zach realized his hands were trembling with anger. "I'm sorry, Davis. I have to get out of here. I'll come back in a couple of days and we'll settle this."

"Again, my apologies, Mr. Houston. And I hope this information doesn't put a blight on your wedding day. I see now how indelicate it was to have even broached the subject at this time. I simply assumed your wife had already informed you of some of these details." The two men shook hands and Zach left.

One look at the anger in his eyes and Laura guessed the reason. "You talked to Burton Davis." He nodded, but held his tongue until they could be alone.

The men rented horses and Laura drove the wagon. Zach reined up when Laura turned into the road leading to the Lazy R. "Where are you going?"

"Why, to the house, of course."

Zach lifted Peter out of the seat and handed him to Flint. "Flint, Laura and I have something to discuss. Just head straight south, and you'll come to a stream. Cross it and after you top the rise, you'll come to a ranch house."

"That's where Grandma and Grandpa are," Peter spoke up.

"That's right, Peter." He looked back at Flint. "You think you can find it?"

"I claim to be a scout, don't I? Besides, I've got this little trooper here to help me."

Zach climbed off his horse and then swung Laura off the wagon seat to the ground. She followed him over to the shade of a sycamore.

"Zach, I can't go to the Double H. Lavitia is too ill. I thought you all would come back to the house with me," she said.

He looked at her aghast. "I'd never stay under the same roof as Lavitia Randolph."

"It will only be for a short time, Zach. The doctor was here yesterday, and he told me he doesn't expect her to last more than a couple of days."

"Well, if I ever saw the evil bitch, it wouldn't be that long. I'd kill her myself."

She understood his anger, and put a hand on his arm. "I know how you're feeling, Zach. I went through the same thing. After awhile, the anger wears off." Trying to sound reassuring, she added, "And at least the Double H belongs to you again."

Too late to take back the words, Laura realized it was the worst thing she could have said. He looked at her in disbelief. "The Double H? Good God, Laura, she didn't just rob us of a ranch or money. She stole seven years of our lives."

His anger shifted to disdain. "Of course, since you want to weigh this using a dollar sign for a scale, I'll come out a winner. Once the Lazy R is sold, you'll get the ten thousand dollars you've got coming to you. I'll have a rich wife."

He sounded so pompous, she rolled her eyes in exasperation as Zach continued. "And by the time you and the debts are paid off, she won't have anything left from the sale."

As if to press home his point, he added, "Don't you see the irony of it? Davis told me the Lazy R is mortgaged to the limit. If they can't get a buyer, they have to sell the ranch at an auction. Your aunt's big scheme to disinherit you has all been for nothing. How can she disinherit you when she's got nothing to do it with? Zero from zero is . . . *nothing*." His chuckle of amusement bordered on scorn.

"Zach, you're scaring me. You're beginning to sound as crazy as she is," Laura said, disgusted with his smugness. "Lavitia can't hurt anyone anymore. She's on her deathbed."

"Good riddance."

"Zach, I was as angry as you, and then I realized I was only hurting myself. I was allowing the bitterness and hatred she breeds to spread to me. That's when I made up my mind I wouldn't let her do it. Zach, I feel for the sake of our own souls, we have to try to find some forgiveness in our hearts for her."

"Yeah, you do that, Laura," he said angrily. "You've got enough for the both of us."

"Oh, God! You're as bitter as Lavitia," she lashed out.

His eyes blazed with anger. "Maybe I am, Laura. Maybe I am. But *forgive* me if I don't understand how dying whitewashes her evils."

"I'm not saying it does. I'd just hate to think that we'd let ourselves become as embittered as she is. Look how she's destroyed her life."

"Her life . . . and a few others. My father. Your parents, and God knows how many others. I ought to use physical force to keep you from going back into that house."

"Don't try to stop me, Zach. I wish I could convince you that I feel the same as you do. My aunt is as evil and wicked as you believe. But she's dying. I can't turn my back on her now."

"You do what you think you have to do, but I won't let you take Peter back into that witch's lair. He's staying with me."

Her heart seemed to twist with pain. "Please don't do this to me, Zach."

"What in hell do you think you're doing to me?" The accusation cracked the air like a whip lash. Then he drew a shuddering breath, and softened his tone. "Honey, I'm not trying to hurt you. I want him safe and out of there. It's no place for him."

He climbed back on his horse. "Whenever you're through playing nursemaid, Laura, we'll be at the Double H."

Laura spent her wedding night crying in her room.

Chapter 29

⟨◦◦◦◦⟩

When she took her aunt a breakfast tray the next morning, Lavitia refused any offer of food. She was so weak, she could barely speak. Her voice was a breathless rasp. "You can't wait until I die, can you?"

"Aunt Lavitia, let's not argue. Just relax and save your strength. You'll live longer."

"Oh, I'm gonna live 'til this ranch is sold," the old woman vowed. "No Houston will ever own the Lazy R."

"No Houston wants to, Aunt Lavitia," Laura said wearily, turning away.

Later that day, Laura left Lavitia in the care of Whiskers and rode to the Double H. Zach and Flint were busy putting in a new wall of the barn. Zach glanced up casually when she rode up, then he returned to his labor.

Peter dashed up to her. "Mama! Mama!" He threw himself into her arms. "Guess what? I slept in the loft last night."

After hugging and kissing her, he continued to babble excitedly. "Thank you, Mama, for letting me stay here with Daddy and Flint. I hated that old house with that mean old Aunt 'Vitia."

"Well, it sounds like you're having a real good time."

"Oh yes, Mama. Daddy took me riding on his horse this morning. He said as soon as him and Flint are through fixing the barn and coral —"

"Corral, sweetheart," she corrected.

"He's gonna get some cattle and horses." He cupped her cheeks between his hands and stared wide-eyed into hers. "And guess what?"

"I can't imagine," she said, smiling.

"Daddy's gonna buy me a pony all my own. And he's gonna teach me how to ride it."

"Oh my, I sure wouldn't want to miss that," she exclaimed.

"Howdy, Laura," Flint commented, strolling over to them.

Laura stood up. "Hi, Flint, how are you?"

"That husband of yours has got me workin' harder than in the army." He grinned. "'Pears he's got some energy to work off." Glancing at Peter, Flint added, "Hey, trooper, how about you and me going down to the spring and filling the canteens."

"Thank you, Flint," Laura said with a grateful smile.

"My pleasure, Laura. I watched that man hurtin' for the past few years. Sure hate to see him like that. He's a good man, Laura."

"I know that, Flint."

Laura walked over to the barn. Zach had shed his shirt, and his shoulders and arms glistened with perspiration. As he labored to wedge a board into place, she watched his muscles contract and then ripple across his shoulders and down his arms. Lust licked at the core of her.

"Hi," she said softly.

He didn't turn around. "Hi."

"Still mad?"

"Not at you. I understand it's your duty, but that doesn't mean I like it."

"I love you, Zach," she said simply.

"I know you do. And I love you," he replied.

She hoped he would turn around, take her in his arms, and reassure her with kisses. She hoped. But he didn't.

"Zach, this is foolish. Why are you acting this way?"

He turned. "Let's just say I don't like the living arrangements and leave it at that." His eyes were filled with so much pain and anger, she could hardly bear looking into them. He walked away.

"Don't you walk away from me, Zachary Houston," she declared. "I rode all the way over here just to see you."

He turned around. Irritation flashed in his eyes and his cold laugh raked at her nerves. "Oh, forgive me, Mrs. Houston. You making a social call? Sorry, I didn't know, or I'd have prepared tea."

He strode into the house and she followed. For a moment, she glanced around at the cabin. It felt so right to be there again. Her anger melted. "Tomorrow I'll bring back your mother's dishes."

"I won't be here tomorrow. We're going to Houston for a couple of days. We've got to start stocking the ranch."

"Oh . . . I see. I'll . . . ah . . . take Peter back with me."

"I thought I'd take him to Houston with me," he said. "I figured he'd enjoy seeing the city."

"Oh . . . yes . . . I guess he would enjoy that," she said. She felt so desolate, she wanted to cry.

"Honey, come with us?" he asked suddenly. "We could turn it into a little honeymoon trip." His voice was deep with huskiness. She saw the supplication in his eyes.

Her own eyes pleaded for understanding. "I wish I could, Zach. But my aunt . . ." Her voice trailed away.

A nerve jumped in his cheek as his mood shifted. "I'll see you when we get back."

"Zach," she cried when he started to leave. "Aren't you going to kiss me good-bye?"

His hands lightly rode her shoulders as he drew her into his arms. His lips felt warm and firm on hers as the lingering intimacy of the kiss sent currents of desire through her.

Then he left her standing there helplessly, watching him walk away.

*   *   *

The following day, Laura brought Zach's trunk back to the house. Lavitia Randolph had never known Laura had stored it in the attic seven years earlier. With loving care, Laura unpacked each dish and linen. She placed each item in its proper place. After putting one of the sheets on Zach's bed, she returned to the Lazy R.

She came back the next day and washed the soiled laundry. The following day when she rode over, she still saw no sign of their return. Once again, she returned to the Lazy R, this time in despair.

Each hour passed like a year. Her anxiety prevented her from concentrating on her work around the ranch. Misgivings began to play havoc with her imagination. Soon she tried to convince herself that Zach had spirited her son away and she would never see either of them again.

Then she chastised herself for harboring such a thought. Zach loved her. The one, irrefutable certainty in her life was that Zach loved her.

But by the end of the week, Laura's face was drawn with misery and deep indentions lined her eyes. She began to think she was becoming as mad as the old woman who lay in the bedroom next to hers.

A week had passed since the last time she had seen Zach and Peter. As she crested the rise next to the ranch house, she suddenly heard the peal of Peter's laughter. Spurring her horse forward, she thundered into the clearing.

Peter was sitting astride a black pony that Zach led in a circle. Laura leaped from her horse and snatched Peter from the saddle.

"Oh, sweetheart," she sobbed, hugging and kissing him.

"Hi, Mama. Did you see me riding all by myself?"

When she finally composed herself, she put him down. "Peter," she said in a dulcet, controlled voice, "I'd like to talk to your father for a few moments in private." Then she turned to Zach. "May I see you in the barn please," she snapped through gritted teeth and stomped into the barn.

Zach followed. "What's the problem?"

"How dare you do this to me, Zachary Houston?" Her chin quivered from the intensity of her emotion. "Do you have any idea the hell I've gone through? I've been worried to death. I didn't know where you were, or if something happened to you."

"We went to Houston to buy stock for the ranch. I told you that."

"Zach, you told me you were going away for a couple of days. You never said a week!" she accused. Her eyes were tremulous and her voice quivered. "This is the first time Peter and I have ever been separated." She turned away to control her trembling.

Zach came up behind her. Clasping her by the shoulders, he drew her back against him. "Honey, I'm sorry. I didn't intentionally mean to alarm you."

She closed her eyes and leaned back, reveling in the comfort of his arms and the strength she drew from their embrace. He turned her to face him, and laced his fingers through her hair on either side of her face. "I wish you had been there with us."

Her eyes brimmed with longing. "I wish I had been too."

He kissed away the tears in the corners of her eyes, then gently covered her lips in a tender kiss. Then with a sigh, he increased the pressure of his lips and his kiss grew hungrier. She slipped her arms around his neck and he molded her body to his own.

Lifting her feet from the ground, he shifted their clinging bodies into a nearby haystack. His hands massaged and fondled her with repeated sweeps.

Sweet ecstasy filled her. "Zach, we've got to stop," she moaned as his lips trailed down her neck.

"No, sweetheart, no," he groaned. "Help me. I need you, love. Help me."

"I can't, Zach. Peter's right outside," she whispered breathlessly.

As if in response to her gasped warning, Peter suddenly called out, "Mama. Daddy. Come and see me ride my pony."

Zach groaned and collapsed on her. For a long moment, he lay motionless; then he sat up, and rolled off her.

Laura stood up and quickly tucked in her bodice and brushed the hay off her clothes and hair. "I'm sorry, Zach. Are you coming?"

He sat motionless, his head propped in his hands. "I can't right now. I'll be out in a couple minutes."

A few minutes later Zach had his body and emotions under control. As he walked out of the barn, Whiskers Merten rode up to the ranch house.

"What is it, Whiskers? Has Aunt Lavitia's condition gotten worse?" Laura asked.

"No, missy. That banker fella from town is waiting for you at the house. 'Pears like the Lazy R's been sold. He said he needs you there."

"I'm coming, Whiskers." With a last-minute glance at Zach, she mounted her horse and followed the buckboard.

As soon as they returned to the Lazy R, Burton Davis summoned Laura and Whiskers to Lavitia's room. They added their signatures on the document to witness Lavitia Randolph's shaky scrawl accepting the terms of sale of the ranch.

After Davis's departure, Laura returned to Lavitia's room. "Would you like to try to eat something, Aunt Lavitia?"

"Now I can die content." There was a smugness to the old woman's tone despite the fact that she hovered at death's door.

"I would have thought you would be sad at the thought of losing the ranch, Aunt Lavitia."

Lavitia's weak laugh reflected her draining strength. "No, dear niece, the Lazy R came near to losing me," she said, cackling. "But I've won."

"Won? Won what, Aunt Lavitia?"

"I know why you came back here. You haven't fooled me for a moment. You thought I would weaken and leave the ranch to you and your bastard son. Didn't work, did it? Ranch is sold now, and the church'll get what's left."

"Whatever made you think I wanted this ranch?"

"Oh, I know you and your lover schemed to get the Lazy R. You betrayed me just like all the others, but it didn't work, did it? And now your great lover is gone and you're saddled with his bastard."

Crossing her arms, Laura leaned back smiling against the door. "I'm afraid you miscalculated again, Aunt Lavitia."

"What do you mean?"

"Zachary Houston's returned to the Double H. You didn't succeed in cheating him out of his ranch after all. And he and I were married over a week ago."

"You're lying," she rasped.

"Good night, Aunt Lavitia."

A weight had been lifted from Laura's shoulders. Tomorrow, in all good conscience, she could leave this house and go back to the man she loved. She no longer owed Lavitia Randolph anything.

For the first time in over two months, Laura went to bed contented, knowing that the next day, her new life would begin.

Lavitia Randolph died that night in her sleep.

Laura and Whiskers brought her body to Bay Town in the buckboard. After making arrangements with the mortician, Laura went to the bank. Burton Davis invited her into his office.

"Well, Laura, I have to say events in your life have certainly moved swiftly in these last weeks. Your marriage, the sale of the ranch, Miss Randolph's death."

"I'm just relieved the ranch was sold before she died. It certainly makes disposing of her belongings easier for me. The furniture can stay with the house. I'll have to make arrangements for Whiskers, but I'm sure Zach will let him live at the Double H."

"Oh yes, Mr. Houston assured me when he bought the . . ."

Davis suddenly stopped and looked flustered. Laura eyed him suspiciously. "When he bought what, Mr. Davis?"

Davis cleared his throat. "I'm really not in a position to say, Mrs. Houston."

She had to express her rising suspicion. "Did my husband buy the Lazy R?" By the look in the banker's eyes, Laura knew she had guessed the truth. "But how could he? Where would he ever get the money? Certainly not on his army pay."

"I would feel more comfortable if you'd ask him yourself, Mrs. Houston."

Laura got to her feet. "I'll do just that, Mr. Davis. Thank you for your time."

She strode outside and bumped into Flint and Peter. "Well, if it's not my prodigal son," she teased, hugging and kissing him.

"Mama, I miss you. When are you coming to live with me and Daddy?"

"Right away, honey."

"And are you gonna stay with us this time?"

"Sweetheart, wild horses couldn't keep me away."

"Well, it's about time," Flint remarked. "Ah . . ."

"What is it?"

"If I were you, I'd ride out there right away. Zach's fixin' to go away again for awhile."

"Go away again? But where?"

"Reckon you should ask him that yourself, Laura."

"I certainly will. Can I borrow your horse, Flint? And will you find Whiskers Merten? I'm sure he's in the saloon. Bring him back to the ranch with you. The buckboard's in front of the mortuary."

"Yes, ma'am," Flint said, grinning.

"Oh, and Flint, take your time getting back." She

winked at him. Then after saying good-bye to Peter, Laura headed for the Double H.

When she rode up to the house, Zach's saddled chestnut was tied to the hitching post. Laura dismounted. Upon entering the cabin, she found Zach shoving some clothes into his saddlebags.

"Where are you going?"

"Thought I'd go into Galveston and drink myself senseless for about a week."

"You can save the trip. I think you're senseless already. You're the one who bought it, aren't you?"

"Don't know what you're talking about." He continued packing.

"Oh, yes, you do!" she declared. She strode over to him. "You traitor ... you idiot ... you ... you ..." She stamped her foot. "Zachary Houston, look at me!"

He turned back to her, his expression guarded. "All right. So I bought the Lazy R."

"But how? Where did you get the money?"

"Senator Long named me in his will."

"His will?" She paused for a moment to let the startling news sink into her already muddled mind. "Oh, Zach, I'm sorry. I know how much you cared for him. But why buy the Lazy R of all places?" she asked.

"Thought you didn't want to lose your home, Laura."

"My home! *This* is my home, Zach. This is where I became your wife the first time you made love to me. Not the Lazy R ... I hate the Lazy R. It holds nothing but painful memories for me. That house will always be Lavitia's. A reminder of how the woman's madness almost destroyed our love."

"Maybe that's why I bought it. The Lazy R matters to her more than people do."

"She's dead, Zach. She died in her sleep."

"Sounds like the devil will finally meet his match."

"I came here to talk about us, not Lavitia."

"Well, too bad she didn't live long enough to find out

that a Houston beat her in the end," he said.

"So you really did buy the Lazy R out of revenge. And if revenge was your motive, Zach, maybe Lavitia won after all."

"She didn't win. I'd have been content never to see the Lazy R again. I only came back to Bay Town because you were here."

"Well, I didn't want the ranch any more than you did. And if you'd asked me, I would have told you how much I hate Lavitia's house. And another thing, Zachary Houston! I'm tired of making explanations or excuses for the past. And I'm tired of your brooding. We can't change the past, and we're wasting the present. Both of us have been miserable these last weeks."

Zach barely listened to her. He'd been lost from the moment she walked into the room with her brown eyes blazing and her chin thrust out with determination. He never could resist her when she went on the offensive. Laura's fire . . . her conviction . . . all enhanced her beauty. Excited him.

Sitting down on the edge of the bed, he challenged her in a lighter tone. "Well, so just where do you intend to live?"

"Wherever you do. If it's at the Lazy R . . . well, then . . . so be it. But you can unpack those clothes because you're not running out on me again."

Zach shoved his hat off his forehead. "Running out on you?" He couldn't help but laugh as he grabbed her hand and pulled her over to him. "When in hell did I ever run out on you? You're the one who disappears as soon as I turn my back."

"Then I'll rephrase the question. When are we going to start living like a husband and wife are supposed to live? . . . You know, under the same roof? 'Whither thou goest,' as the Bible says." She sat down on his lap and slipped her arms around his neck. "Frankly, I'm content to stay right where I'm at."

"You mean it, don't you?" He hooked a finger under

her chin and stared intently into her eyes. "You'd be happy to raise our son right here in this cabin."

"Of course I would, if that's what you want. You were raised here, weren't you?" she said lovingly.

"And you agree, no more long separations?" he asked warily.

She nodded in agreement. "No more thoughts of trips to Houston or Galveston without me," she said.

He mimicked her head shake. "No more manipulating aunts," he stated.

With a show of dimples, she laughed. "Not unless you have one or two."

He grinned. "Not an aunt in sight."

"Now that that's all settled, just where *are* we going to live, Zachary Houston? Here or the Lazy R?" He was rewarded with another display of dimples. "You tell me where we're going to end up."

"At the moment? Right here in this bed." He started to unbutton her blouse.

She grabbed his hands and brought them to her lips. "Zach, wait, just for a short while." Standing up, she pulled him to his feet. "I want you to come with me." With his hand in hers, he followed docilely.

"Where are we going?" he asked when they mounted their horses.

"You'll see."

As soon as he saw the direction they were headed, he figured it out for himself. However, he couldn't pass up the opportunity to tease her. "Honey, about a quarter of an hour ago, you assured me you'd go wherever I decided. So here I am, trailing you when I don't have the faintest idea where we're going."

They reached the well-traveled trail and dismounted on the bluff overlooking the beach. "Now, if only you had asked me, Zachary Houston, I would have told you that this is where I really want to live." She glanced down at the beach below. "Overlooking the very spot where we've shared such happiness."

"If that's what you want, sweetheart, we will. We'll combine the two ranches, tear down the house on the Lazy R, and build our own home right here. And we can call our spread the Triple H." Hand- in-hand they walked down the dune to the beach below.

They undressed each other leisurely, then, laying her on the sand, he took her in his arms and kissed her. His gaze worshiped her as she slipped her arms around his neck.

"You've given me so much, Laura. Your love. Our son. I could never put into words how I felt when you were out of my life. And I've said and done so many damn fool things that have hurt you."

He cupped her cheek in his hand. "I could never stop loving you, Laura. I'm not whole without you. Could never be again. You're as necessary to me as the air around me."

With seagulls gliding in tandem overhead and gentle waves lapping at the sandy shore, he loved her with his body as he did his soul.

Then he carried her into the surf where they loved again. And later, as they lazed in the water, Zach glanced up to the ridge above.

"Yep, honey. I like the idea of our house right up there looking over our beach." Grinning, he glanced down at her. "The Triple H. It's got a nice ring to it."

Her eyes sparkled with devilishness. "Don't get too used to the ring of it, Zach, because in less than seven months I suspect you'll have to squeeze in another H."

His mouth gaped open in surprise. "You mean you're . . . ?" He slipped his hands to her stomach. "A baby?"

Laughing, she nodded and slid her arms around his neck. "I think so. I've been waiting for the right time to tell you."

"A baby!" he said with awe. His hands cupped her buttocks and drew her against him. "And this time, I'll be here for you when our child is born," he murmured in her ear before he kissed her.

Zach gathered Laura into his arms and carried her out of the water. They dressed, and climbed back up the dune to their horses.

Zach paused at the top and picked up a stick. He loped an arm around the waist of the woman he loved and pulled her to his side. Then he drew a circle and scratched an H in the center.

"The Circle H will be our brand, sweetheart. And that should take care of any additional Houstons—forever."

Almost a decade had passed since the first day they had stood together on the same spot. As Laura remembered the long-ago day, her eyes filled with tears and she smiled up into the eyes of her beloved husband.

"Forever, my love."

Avon Romances—
the best in exceptional authors and unforgettable novels!

MONTANA ANGEL   **Kathleen Harrington**
                                       77059-8/ $4.50 US/ $5.50 Can

EMBRACE THE WILD DAWN   **Selina MacPherson**
                                       77251-5/ $4.50 US/ $5.50 Can

MIDNIGHT RAIN   **Elizabeth Turner**
                                       77371-6/ $4.50 US/ $5.50 Can

SWEET SPANISH BRIDE   **Donna Whitfield**
                                       77626-X/ $4.50 US/ $5.50 Can

THE SAVAGE   **Nicole Jordan**
                                       77280-9/ $4.50 US/ $5.50 Can

NIGHT SONG   **Beverly Jenkins**
                                       77658-8/ $4.50 US/ $5.50 Can

MY LADY PIRATE   **Danelle Harmon**
                                       77228-0/ $4.50 US/ $5.50 Can

THE HEART AND THE HEATHER **Nancy Richards-Akers**
                                       77519-0/ $4.50 US/ $5.50 Can

DEVIL'S ANGEL   **Marlene Suson**
                                       77613-8/ $4.50 US/ $5.50 Can

WILD FLOWER   **Donna Stephens**
                                       77577-8/ $4.50 US/ $5.50 Can